the edge of the sky

Books by Drusilla Campbell

Wildwood
The Edge of the Sky
Blood Orange

the edge of the sky

Drusilla Campbell

KENSINGTON BOOKS
http://www.kensingtonbooks.com

KENSINGTON BOOKS are published by

Kensington Publishing Corp.
119 W. 40th Street
New York, NY 10018

All Kensington titles, imprints and distributed lines are available at special quantity discounts for bulk purchases for sales promotion, premiums, fund-raising, educational or institutional use.

Special book excerpts or customized printings can also be created to fit specific needs. For details, write or phone the office of the Kensington Special Sales Manager: Kensington Publishing Corp., 119 W. 40th Street, New York, NY 10018. Attn. Special Sales Department. Phone: 1-800-221-2647.

Kensington and the K logo Reg. U.S. Pat. & TM Off.

ISBN-13: 978-0-7582-0535-3
ISBN-10: 0-7582-0535-X

First Kensington Trade Paperback Printing: February 2004
10 9 8 7 6 5 4 3

Printed in the United States of America

For Rocky and Matt

1998

Chapter One

She was late. She was always late. If she left work immediately and if the chrome-and-steel troops on the freeway parted and let her speed right up the middle like a general to the head of his army, and if all the lights on Washington Street saluted her with green, Lana Porter would still be late.

If life was not a battle, why did she so often think of it in military terms?

She slammed her desk drawer shut with her hip, grabbed her purse off the credenza, stopped, turned, and looked for her umbrella. She could not help noticing the contrast between her desk and Jack's. Battlefield confusion—spreadsheets, order forms, and ledgers spread across hers while his was the Peaceable Kingdom: carefully stacked plant catalogs, design books, the fountain pens he loved and spent too much money on, sketches for the nursery's expansion (which they could not afford) neatly pinned up on a strip of cork.

And nowhere a red umbrella. She'd have to risk getting wet. And tomorrow she would have to do some serious filing or be buried in bumf. She smiled and thanked her daughters' English teacher, Ms. Hoffman, for a great new addition to her vocabulary.

As quickly as she stepped from her office at Urban Greenery, she forgot the mess; what had appalled her a moment before became immaterial. The loamy smell of the nursery, the plants' respiration (which on warm, still nights she felt like breath upon her skin), the comforting predictability of the place, all reminded her to pause and breathe and take her time. Life did not require a battle plan.

Jack said the garden kept her sane—just the kind of thing he would say, sweet but soft around the edges—and if he hadn't rescued her from the world of credits and debits and two packs a day, she'd be a withered hag by now. And what about him? If it weren't for her, Jack Porter would still be running a gardening business out of an apartment in Ocean Beach and owing money to half the planet.

But if she asked him where her umbrella was, he'd probably be able to say exactly. And he was never late.

To the west of San Diego the sky over the Pacific was full of clouds, a mountain range on the move; and every wind chime in the nursery sang, announcing that weather was on its way. Twenty meters across an expanse of flats and pony packs of fall seedlings, Jack was talking to Carmino, the nursery manager. Jack had his broad back to her. He was six-feet-five, two hundred and thirty pounds, almost twice the size of Carmino; but, sensitive to the way his height could intimidate shorter men, he leaned against a table of seedlings so he and his manager stood almost eye to eye. Jack's gunmetal-gray hair grew down over his collar, too long. The shaggy look was part of his appeal, part of what made him still, after almost twenty years, the sexiest man she knew.

Carmino saw her, said something to Jack, and he turned.

And smiled. The wide, embrace-the-world smile that had been the first thing she noticed about him when he was a gardener and she a chain-smoking cocktail waitress keeping the bar books for extra cash.

"I'm off," she called across the tables of stock and pansy and snapdragon seedlings which resembled the palette of a giant artist, pinks blending to violets and reds, whites into yellows into greens. "See you at home."

"I put your umbrella in the car."

He blew her a kiss. She blew one back. Then she was crossing the showroom floor, out the door, and thinking, holy shit, at this rate I'll be lucky to make it by halftime. It was a Tuesday in October and Beth had a basketball game.

The rain began as Lana turned off I-5 at the Washington Street exit, first spatters and then big, heavy drops that exploded on the oily road. Suddenly there were red-eyed brake lights everywhere and the sound of squealing tires coming and going. On a rainy day in Southern California everyone forgot how to drive. Except natives like Lana who knew what rain did to asphalt that hadn't tasted rain in six months. The transplanted Easterners, the Windy City expatriates and North Dakota snowbirds were lethal. At Arcadia School she parked in a ten-minute spot in front of the administration offices. For what she and Jack paid in tuition, she dared Grace Mamoulian to tell her to move.

Lana closed her eyes and sat for a moment, listening to the water drum down on the car. The southwestern corner of the continent had been without rain for half a year and the need for it was a hunger her body felt in its pores. She wanted to run in it, tilt her head back and drink it up. Instead she was going to sit in a smelly gymnasium and watch a basketball game. A practice game, at that.

It was not that she did not love Micki and Beth—she was mad about them and crazy about family life. But Jack was the better parent and they both knew it. He could sit through any number of basketball games without wanting to be somewhere else. She knew the games were important . . . and the student art shows and parent-teacher nights and student fund-raisers and field traps. Trips. But it never stopped, this parenting business. How did anyone ever manage it alone?

She had barely closed the car door and Grace Mamoulian, the director of Arcadia School, was on her. Despite the rain, she was groomed as carefully as a cat for show; not a dark brown wisp of hair had the nerve to escape from its chignon.

"Lana, so glad you're here." A predatory smile.

"I'm late for the game."

"I'll walk with you."

For a moment the only sound was the Minnie Mouse click-clack of Grace's high heels on the cement walkway and the rain on the roof that covered it.

"I only need a moment, Lana—"

"It's Micki, right?" It was always Micki.

Maybe the concern on Grace's flushed face was genuine. She ran a good school and just because Lana did not personally like her . . . Cut her some slack, Lana thought. Jack said Lana had a cynical streak because she suspected people's motives. But then, he hadn't grown up with Stella and Stan, the San Diego Steak House Man.

Grace was breathlessly describing an event that had happened that afternoon between fifth and sixth period. "I came in late, Lana. I don't know exactly what transpired and, of course, most witnesses disappeared into their lockers the moment they saw me. But apparently Micki was on one of her tears, mad about something. I never did find out what it was but in the process she threw a pencil at one of the girls. Hit her in the back of the head."

They dashed across a stretch of open lawn for the covered porch outside the gym.

"The girl was walking away but if she'd turned . . ." Instead of finishing her sentence, Grace raised her elegantly curved eyebrows, a small, regretful smile . . . Did she practice these expressions in front of a mirror at night? Lana leaned against the gym wall and felt the reverberation of pounding feet through her shoulders. If Jack were here he would be diplomatic and cooperative but Lana could barely be bothered. It was only a pencil and the back of the head is hard. The girl might have turned around, but she hadn't; she had not been blinded or scarred for life.

Besides, kids ganged up on Micki. "Somebody must have said or done something to her. You and I both know Micki doesn't attack people without provocation." Sunlight broke through the clouds and flashed in the rows of windows in the two-story classroom wing across the grass. "It's not fair, Grace. It's like these kids have a gun they bring out and whack her with whenever they want. I think you should be able to stop this. Have you ever heard the things they say to her?"

Now the look was prim and pained. "I've been told."

"Well, if I were Micki, I'd throw something, too. She's an adopted child—where's the big deal? There must be other adopted girls at Arcadia."

"If other girls flew off the handle the way Micki does, they'd be teased, too."

Micki's reputation as a wild wire—one of those sparking, crackling lines dropped by the wind, trailing near the ground, daring thrill seekers to grab hold—had trailed her from public school when she entered Arcadia in the sixth grade.

"It's not teasing, Grace. It's vicious abuse."

Lana heard the beat of the basketball, the pounding of feet, and it occurred to her that sometimes life was going up and down the court, back and forth between the goals, scoring or not; the same moves repeated with endless variations but still, essentially, the same.

When Micki started at Arcadia, she could not sit still in class and on the playground her voice had always been the loudest; jumping

up and down, waving her arms, she moved with a frantic eagerness to be included that dismayed Lana. In a game of keep-away
she so much wanted the ball thrown to her that kids perversely did
not. She could hit a softball out of the field, but team captains never
chose her first. She had walked and talked early, run before she was
a year old, and bossed the dog around in full sentences before she
was two. She was smart and learned quickly but she wore her emotions right out where anyone could see them. Wind Micki Porter up
and she'll cry. Plug her in and she'll have a tantrum.

Grace Mamoulian had switched the subject and was now talking about how proud she was of Beth for winning the eighth grade
"I Speak for America" prize.

"Uh-huh," Lana said.

Trashcan baby, Re-ject, the kids had teased Micki. Passed on from
year to year, the grotesque dissing had lost none of its power with
repetition.

"So what did you do, Grace, about Micki?"

"Didn't you hear me? She's in detention."

Home away from home.

"Jack'll talk to her," Lana said.

He could stay calm and steady under any assault . . . and for
sure there would be an assault. Hurt, Micki struck out at the only
targets she trusted not to retaliate in kind.

Lana started into the gym and then stopped. "Grace, I know she
can't throw things at people. And we both know if she didn't react
they wouldn't torment her. But even so, you can't let those girls off
the hook. You need to talk to them. Give *them* a taste of detention.
That's your job, Grace, and you're not doing it."

Eat that.

Grace cringed as if she read Lana's thoughts, and laid her
smooth, carefully manicured hand on Lana's forearm. "This will
pass, Lana."

"That makes it okay?"

"So long as she doesn't control herself, Micki will continue to
have social problems. She has to change, Lana. You can't protect
her from the real world."

The big Arcadia gym had been a gift from some rich parent
many years earlier and had begun to show the wear of constant
use. The smells of sweat and socks and adolescent girls had perme-

ated the shining hardwood floor and walls colored a shade Beth called turtle-urine green. Lana found a place on the bleachers a little separate from the other parents. She waved and smiled at several she knew, but she was in no mood to be chatty. Certainly not with Elly Segal, whose daughter had probably led the vulture attack on Micki that day.

Beth played well. At twelve she was the tallest girl on the team. Probably in the whole seventh grade. When Lana was growing up she would have cut off her feet to avoid being five-feet-ten, but Beth strode the world as if it belonged to her. She was so much her father's daughter, with his wide smile and easygoing, loving nature and what Lana always thought of as a confident core. You could shake Jack but he would not fall. He, too, had been a high school athlete but, unlike Beth, not much of a student. Instead of college he went to Vietnam, and got there just in time to help evacuate Saigon.

At Point Loma High School Lana's only sport had been running and she had done that on her own, out her front door. She would start out the door of the house on Sunset Cliffs wanting to scream, her intestines twisted around themselves like a bucket of night crawlers. A mile to the beach community of Ocean Beach, then up and over the hill to where she had a view of San Diego Bay and the city and on clear days saw the sunlight flash off the windows of houses and shacks in the Tijuana hills. By the time she got home, the worms had settled down. Lana had been offered a scholarship to American University in Washington, D.C., and she wanted to go because it was the farthest away she could get from her mother and stepfather. But instead she turned it down and attended San Diego State, living at home so she could be there for her little sister.

Jack said the reason Lana found parenting so difficult was that she'd been taking care of Kathryn all her life. She loved him for his insight but it could also make her crazy.

He also said she was a good mother, which she always amended to "good enough." And he told her not to feel guilty, which mostly she didn't despite leaving most of the challenges to Jack. He delivered the lectures, set the standards, taught the heavy lessons, and though he griped occasionally she thought in his heart he liked the power it gave him. Face it—she was no good at those jobs. She had used her entire arsenal defending Kathryn, helping her grow up safely in a house torn by the wars between Stella and Stan and between Stella, Stan, and Mars, her older sister. She had learned a long time ago not to wonder too much what kind of person she might have become if she had gone to AU and left Kathryn to fight her own battles. Or what might have happened to Kathryn.

Thinking about American University reminded Lana that Beth had already begun to talk about a basketball scholarship. From this the logical mental leap was to money and hence to the fact that she had to stop at an ATM on the way home. She took a notebook from her big leather bag and flipped it open to the endless list she kept running. She jotted down "ATM" and ran a thick line through *Beth's Basketball*. Without a list, she would lose the war against time and bumf. She half believed her list held all their lives together. No wonder Jack could be his daughters' favorite parent. No wonder he could take the time to make a friend of everyone he met. Lana worked most of every day at the nursery, took care of the house and bills, and made sure they had a social life. She visited her mother, held her little sister's hand, and listened to her big sister grouse about university politics and the general shortage of attractive heterosexual men.

The next time Jack got after Lana for being late, she was going to throw a Micki-fit. It drove Jack mad, the way she couldn't be ready or arrive on time. Sometimes she made herself late on purpose for the pure pleasure of cracking his irritatingly happy composure.

She and the girls drove home through brief, hard squalls, sunlight alternating with downpour; traffic on Washington was still slow and messy. Lana had driven beyond the last ATM before home when she remembered that she had nothing but moths in her wallet. She turned around, and sped through the empty back streets, half listening to the girls bicker about what had happened at school.

"You are so embarrassing," Beth said, turning around in the shotgun seat so she could fix all her outrage on her sister. Her cheeks were bright and shiny as poppies and the hard, sweaty game had brought up a little curl in her straight hair. "Why do you act like such a jerk?"

In the rearview mirror Lana saw Micki roll her eyes.

"What?"

"You tossed a complete fit, right there in the main hall where everyone in the whole world could see you. Couldn't you at least wait—"

"Why don't you just shut up?"

"They do it to piss you off. Don't you get it? Are you so stupid—"

"Don't use the 's' word," Lana said.

Beth turned on her. "You mean it isn't stupid the way she lets them get to her that way?"

Though a few months younger than her sister, Beth seemed older because she had her father's steadiness. Lana looked at Micki huddled in a corner of the back seat. Her birth parents must have been wildcats.

"Buckle up," Lana said.

"Why should I?" Micki threw herself down on the back seat and wailed, "So what if I die in a flaming wreck? Who cares?"

"Do. It. Now."

Beth implored Lana, "Why can't she go to public school? She's always saying she wants to, so why not let her?"

"Yeah, you'd love that, wouldn't you?" Micki kicked the back of the passenger seat. "Then you could just pretend I don't even exist. You and your snotty friends . . . Why don't you ever stick up for me?"

I can answer that question, Lana thought as she parked the car in the empty bank lot and ran through the rain to the money machine. Micki on a bombing run: it was her against the world and she didn't want help and she resented all offers. She was a porcupine crossed with a wildcat, with a whole lot of six-week-old puppy thrown in.

Lana slipped her card into the ATM slot and keyed in her code number, a combination of her daughters' birth dates. While she waited for her money, she distracted herself from thoughts of Micki by pressing the balls of her feet hard against the ground. This worked to focus her attention down and away from Micki, and generally, the trick worked; but sometimes she pushed so hard her toes curled and her foot cramped. That really got her mind off her troubles.

As she listened to the busy clicks and hums of the ATM making money, she remembered a line from an old musical. *"Plant a radish, get a radish, not a brussels sprout, That's why I love vegetables, you know what you're about."*

Vegetables, flowers, weed and pest control, columns of numbers, order forms, and tax documents. These she could handle.

She had been a cocktail waitress with a mediocre degree in accounting when Jack introduced her to the nursery business; back then she did not know a stamen from a staple. But she took to plant work immediately which surprised her until she realized she loved the *logic* of plants and garden, the calm predictability that was not too different from the fact that two and two would always add up to four. She put a cosmos seed in the ground, watered and fed it, and up popped a flower. Not a rose, not a cyclamen, but a daisy-faced cosmos.

Jack had wanted children; Lana would have been happy to do without, but she never regretted giving him what he wanted. When the girls were small and uncomplicated, caring for them had been a joy. By opening her heart to Micki and Beth, Lana had discovered new regions of herself, continents of love she had not known existed. And their home was nothing like the one she grew up in. The Porters—Jack, Lana, Micki, and Beth—were a happy family in their house on Triesta Way.

The house had been the first Jack and Lana looked at, and they fell in love with it instantly as the Realtor must have known they would. The wide-open, echoey, and light-filled rooms—so much space after living with two babies in the cottage on the nursery grounds! Lana was light-headed from the possibilities.

Lana knew they could not afford this house, the only derelict building in an excellent neighborhood. A flat-roofed, two story, southern California stucco, unpainted for decades, with windows the size of double beds, it sat like a plaster block in the middle of a vast, neglected garden. A sagging front veranda ran the width of the house; across the back was a long, dangerously bouncy, and termite-ridden balcony with a broken railing; the roof of the garage had fallen in.

Lana and Jack had not needed the Realtor's spiel to convince them this was the house they were meant to live in until they were old and feeble. The girls had been barely crawling and toddling then. All these years later, Lana felt a thrill of gratitude mixed with disbelief when she turned into the driveway beside her home. Her dreams had come true in this house. They were a happy family.

* * *

"It's Dad's and my night out," Beth said, dropping her book bag on the round oak table in the middle of the kitchen. She knelt to smooch Gala, the Irish setter.

"Where you going?" Lana asked.

"Big Bad Cat."

Micki sneered. "You guys are so boring. Dad and me are going to ride the roller coaster next week."

"Your father hates roller coasters." Actually it was Lana who refused to set foot in one.

"He promised," Micki said.

And Jack always kept his promises.

Lana looked at the coats and homework and book bags and raincoats and umbrellas that marked the trail her daughters had taken through the back door, into the kitchen, and up the stairs. She called to them, "Don't leave all your stuff down here. The housekeeper came this morning—let's try to make it last, okay?"

"*You* leave stuff around," Micki said, vaulting the banister.

"I'm the grownup." Lana dug in the cupboard for a dog biscuit and tossed it to Gala.

Damn. She had forgotten to stop at the market, and it had been right there on her list to pick up chicken for dinner. She dropped her purse on the floor and took a pizza from the freezer and set it on the counter. In the crisper there was an unopened bag of lettuce. She checked the pull date and tossed it in the direction of the compost pail.

Micki looked at the pizza box. "Pepperoni's greasy. I'll get pimples."

"No, you won't. Italians have beautiful skin."

"Am I Italian?"

Lana turned at the catch in Micki's voice and realized she had been holding back tears ever since the fight in the school hall.

"Oh, my honey, not with those eyes and that hair." Lana made her voice light as she wrapped her arms around Micki. "You know why the girls say those things to you. It's like when someone teases a dog, poking it and poking it so finally it bites. Can't you just shine it on? Let it roll off your back?"

Micki pulled away, a look of indignation on her face. "Why should I? I'm not the one who's doing anything wrong." She grabbed a fistful of hair and tugged so hard, Lana winced. "It's not fair what they say. How would you like it?" She made a growling sound and tugged again and again.

"Honey, you'll hurt—"

"I hate them! Why can't I go to Balboa High? What's wrong with public—"

"There's nothing wrong with Balboa. Micki, we've had this conversation a dozen times. You can't run away every time something you don't like happens or makes you unhappy. These things, these . . . challenges, they're part of growing—" Why should Micki be convinced by the tired words when Lana wasn't? But she did not know how else to respond to her daughter's pain. Certainly not with the truth that when Micki hurt, Lana hurt right along with her. She might as well be a little girl herself for all the help she was.

The doorbell rang.

Thank god. Saved by Jehovah's Witnesses.

Without pausing to look through the peephole, she opened the door. At first she did not know what they were—just a pair of young people—a man and woman in identical, full-length gray raincoats. Behind them Lana saw a clearing sky and across the street old Mr. Anderson in his dressing gown, sweeping away the leaves that blocked the gutter.

"Yes?"

"Mrs. Porter? Mrs. Jack Porter?"

"I'm Lana Porter."

She waited for them to say something. Instead they looked at each other and they were too young and new at their jobs to hide their discomfort. A fist clenched in Lana's insides.

"No," she said, speaking only to herself. She shook her head and started to close the door and then didn't. Gala whimpered and shoved her head under Lana's hand.

"You're not Lana Porter?"

"Who is it, Ma?" Beth yelled from the top of the stairs.

Lana heard herself say, "My husband?"

The young woman looked at her partner and her expression drooped with regret. "I'm so sorry. . . ."

2000

Chapter Two

Jack died and a part of Lana died with him. Just because it was a cliché didn't mean it wasn't true. Lana was a refugee afoot in a cratered world. Death and sudden invasion had bombed her homeland out of existence.

She did not forget her daughters but she lost interest in them.

Between the day of the accident in October and Thanksgiving, Lana survived by sleeping her way from one ruined hour to the next, comatose with shock, half blind without the light of Jack's smile, that beam of light that strangers basked in and the chilly required. And now the widow wept for it and awoke with gummy eyes. All slept out—it had to happen eventually—she lay in bed with her eyes closed, inhabiting a borderless, fogged-in world. She kept the blinds drawn and let the laundry pyramid; dishes of uneaten food piled up on the floor beside her bed.

When she could, her sister Kathryn came by to vacuum and dust; Mars lived in for the first week, paid the bills, fed Gala, and made sure there was toilet paper. The house stank of pepperoni and sausage. The women in Lana's run-and-read group brought food—salads and vegetable casseroles to balance out the pizza. Joan Lang sent her cleaning lady every Tuesday. Lana's best friend, Wendy, checked with Carmino daily to make sure Urban Greenery functioned normally; she supervised Beth and Micki's homework, took them to the movies and to spend the night at her house. Lana presumed Wendy also comforted the girls. She hoped someone did; it was beyond her.

She thought about getting up—knew she should, but didn't. Micki and Beth fixed their own breakfasts, and must have moved through the house like ghosts. She was able to forget about them for hours at a time. Even Gala stopped barking and larking around the house in her silly setter way, got the message that something had gone very wrong, and from then on slept on Lana's bed, occupying the foot on Jack's side. On Thanksgiving Day, Lana stayed home and the girls went to Wendy and Michael's. The next day, Wendy came upstairs to see Lana, who had wrapped herself in a comforter and moved from her bed to the chaise on the back balcony from where she could see the garden. What a mess it was, all overgrown and weedy after six weeks of neglect. She didn't want to think about what it would take to put it—and the business— back in order.

"What did you do today?" Wendy leaned against the balcony railing and her bright persimmon-colored hair caught the light of the midday sun.

"You look like a pumpkin," Lana said.

Wendy was breathless and spiky with energy. And mad at me, Lana thought. She had that wound-up look she always got just before she said something she thought was important.

Here comes the lecture.

"Did you eat that casserole Susan left you?"

"I forgot about it," Lana said, and then, "I know, I know, this can't go on."

"You're right about that."

"I just need more time." There would never be sufficient time; her heart would never heal. But this was the kind of thing grieving widows said. So she said it.

"Have you looked at your girls lately?"

Of course she hadn't. She could not bear to. For weeks she hadn't looked at anything; that was the point of lying in bed with her eyes closed—or didn't Wendy get how things were now? Did she have to spell it all out, every vowel and consonant?

Jack had not come home directly that October day. With a pile of packages on the truck seat beside him, he told Carmino he was going to the main post office. He had turned the truck into the intersection at Morena and Tecolote as he had countless times; and at the same moment, a man who happened to be mad at his wife and his boss and the bartender who had just kicked him out of the Harbor Bar skidded his panel truck across two slick lanes of traffic and slammed into the Urban Greenery logo on the driver's side of Jack's truck. Before the police got to the scene, Jack was dead.

"Micki and Beth are just as miserable as you," Wendy said. "Except for them, with you up here sleeping all day, it's like both their parents died."

I know, I know, Lana thought. But I can't help it.

"I want you to get out of bed and start being a mother again. Your girls need you, Lana. Get up because of them."

"This sounds like a bad movie. The one where someone tells the poor widow to live for the sake of her children. And she does and everybody lives happily ever after."

"This isn't a movie, Lana. It's your life. And theirs." Wendy's mouth looked stitched together, a seam. "I know you feel like you're dying, but the girls need you to live. So get up and pretend. For them."

"It's too hard."

"Then let them up here, let them cry with you, for God's sake. Grieve together, that's what families do. It'd be good for all of you."

It would not be good. Lana pulled the comforter up over her head. If she let the girls into her sea of grief they would all drown.

Wendy tugged the comforter down. "I'm taking them home with me. I'm moving them into the spare bedroom because they are in danger." She said the last four words as if they were written in six-foot orange neon matching her hair. "You can't do this to them. They're not eating right. They look like street kids. They're children, Lana. They need their mother."

In the almost twenty years they had been friends, Lana had never seen Wendy so angry. She pushed away from the balcony, coming to stand only a foot from Lana, her hands spread flat against her thighs. "Goddamn it, Lana, stop being so fucking selfish." Her face was bright red as if they'd been running a marathon together. "You have a family. Do the right thing."

"There is no family. Three people live in this house. And a dog. But that's not a family. It's a refugee camp."

Wendy snarled and left, taking the girls home with her for the rest of the weekend. Lana swallowed a sleeping pill and awoke in the middle of the night disoriented, headachy, and restless. She pulled on her old blue cashmere dressing gown, thin and soft as baby hair, and went downstairs barefoot. The silent house blazed with light so she moved through all the rooms, turning off switches until she stood in the dark with Gala pressed hard against her legs. She stood in the dark with nothing to do and then went back to bed.

The Monday after Thanksgiving, Beth stood at Lana's bedroom door in her school uniform, a tartan skirt and navy blue blazer, and peered into the gloom. Lana saw the frightened wariness in her expression as she said, in her smallest and least-likely-to-offend voice, that there wasn't any cereal and the bread had grown whiskers.

"Go to my purse," Lana said. "Take some money and stop at Jack in the Box." She turned her face into her pillow that smelled of bad breath and dirty hair.

The next time Lana awoke she felt sticky. Downstairs a warm winter Santa Ana blew between the slats of blinds that rattled like bones. In her bedroom the sheers billowed like ball gowns. She got up, took a shower, and washed her hair. She stripped the bed and ran a load of wash—not because she wanted to but because her underwear drawer was empty. She put on a jog bra and a long skirt and nothing else. The waist of the skirt dipped below her navel and between it and the band of the bra she saw her ribs for the first time in more than a decade. She went downstairs and forced down a spoonful of peanut butter and a glass of water. The milk was sour. Again or still, she didn't know which.

The rest of the day she concentrated on putting one foot in front of the other: dried and folded the wash, ran the dishwasher and emptied it, opened all the windows and let the Santa Ana rush through the miserable house. In the middle of the afternoon she dressed in Levi's and a tee shirt and drove to Von's and spent more than three hundred dollars on groceries, buying whatever took her fancy, from stuffed grape leaves to Asiago cheese bread. Back at home she put everything away and made a gigantic chopped salad with grilled chicken, baked a frozen pie, and took Gala for a walk down to the end of the block.

She did not dare go upstairs. If she saw her bed she would lie down and never get up again. She lay on the couch in the grownups' living room and cried.

On either side of the entry, there were spacious living rooms, one designated for adults and the other for children. The grownups' living room had been Jack's favorite place, with its round-shouldered, overstuffed couch and chairs upholstered in craftsman fabrics, the built-in bookshelves on either side of the wood-burning fireplace. While the kids watched television in their own living room across the entry, Lana and Jack had retreated to their adult haven to read and talk and listen to music. Talk.

That's what Lana missed—the sound of his calm, clear voice and the gift he had for telling funny stories, for making trivialities sound special, the way he wondered out loud and the way he listened—as if what she said was more important than anything he had heard all day. The way he saw the light and dark of her and loved it all.

She would never see him again. Not touch him, not hear his voice. He was dead.

"Dead."

The word banged against the windows and sucked the air out of the house. Dead. Forever dead. Lana wanted to die herself.

The girls dragged through the back door a little after four, and their faces lighted with relief and hope when she turned to greet them as she stood at the sink cutting back the stems of roses, filling a ceramic vase with big, overblown blossoms. She held out her arms to them and they came to her like they were starving.

"We'll be fine," she said and hoped she sounded convincing. "We'll get on with life—that's what Daddy'd want." Inside she was broken beyond mending, but the girls did not need to hear that any more than she needed to dwell on it. Wendy said pretend, so pretend she would—that life was like a spreadsheet: a little Wite-Out, a bit of rearranging, and all the numbers would tally just fine.

The relief of Lana's family and friends was embarrassingly obvious. Everyone praised her and promised that with time it would get easier. And to Lana's great surprise, as she staggered through Christmas and groped her way out of 1998 and into 1999, she discovered they were right. The days resumed their old length and shape. She returned to Urban Greenery. Never mind what she knew—that if she stopped pretending she would be sucked down the drain at the end of the world.

No one ever said that this was a dishonest way to live.

Get out of bed and brush your teeth. Smile at yourself in the mirror. Wash your hair and your clothes and your face and your hands. Act as if food and hygiene matter. Laugh at the girls' jokes, help Micki memorize theorems and vocabulary words, speak

Spanish to Beth. She brought men in and got the garden cleaned up, planted a sunflower smile on her face, and everyone praised her. Even her mother, Stella, said she was glad Lana had "come through the worst of it."

Act as if you have a life, Lana thought. And people will believe you do.

And one day in November, a little more than a year after Jack's accident, she began to believe it, too. Under flawlessly clear skies, temperatures dipped below freezing three nights in a row; diamond stars punctured the black bowl of night, and Urban Greenery went into its disaster drill. Snuff pots were set out among the perennials; the seedlings had to be covered by sunset, the tenderest specimens sheltered inside. For hours every day, Lana fielded panicky gardening questions about spineless frangipani, wilting plumeria, drooping jacaranda and what to do with the blackened bracts of prized bougainvilleas.

In the freeze Lana saw and heard and smelled more acutely than she had for months. Along Triesta Way, the leaves on the liquid ambars turned scarlet and yellow overnight and shone like Halloween lights. For the first time in thirteen months, she believed she had a future worth living.

She decided to give a New Year's party to celebrate the turn of the century with family and good friends, the kind of party she and Jack had often given together, with plenty to eat and drink. At midnight they would all walk down the hill to Presidio Park where crowds of people always gathered to watch the fireworks from Sea World.

She assumed there would be fireworks.

Chapter Three

Midafternoon on New Year's Eve and Lana was in Von's doing last-minute shopping. Maybe the carts held more champagne than was typical of a Friday night, maybe kids ran around more sugar-hyped than normal, but afterwards what would stay with Lana was the everydayness of the scene. She stood in the produce section, checking her list, looking down at the fresh salad greens and wondering which would be cheaper, the supermarket mix or prepackaged.

"Lana?" A familiar female voice and a hand on her shoulder. "Are you okay?"

Heaven save me, Lana thought.

It was Grace Mamoulian, dressed in her signature brown ensemble and sounding sympathetic. Lana wondered when people would stop taking this tone with her.

"Holidays are hard, aren't they? Thank goodness this Millennium thing'll be over by tomorrow. Unless the world ends, in which case it really will be over and it won't make any difference." Grace smiled to make sure Lana knew this was a joke.

Lana did not have time for conversation with someone she did not like. A crowd would descend on Triesta Way in a few hours. She opened her mouth to wish Grace a polite happy New Year and good-bye but she did not get a chance.

"I've been meaning to call."

Micki.

Lana lifted the plastic top covering the designer greens, and using the tongs provided, began to scoop the leaves into a plastic bag.

"It's probably nothing but it's been nagging my mind. I wonder if you know someone who drives a blue-green Jaguar sedan. New, I think. A beautiful car, I have to say."

Lana twisted a tie around the plastic bag and reached for another.

"Last week, before vacation, I saw Micki talking to someone in a blue Jaguar."

Lana stopped scooping and looked at Grace.

"After school. I saw it parked in front of the Unitarian Church and I assumed it was someone from the congregation." Grace shook her head. "Actually, I saw her talking to him twice."

"A man?"

"I suppose it could have been a woman but I got the impression it was a man."

They moved away from the lettuce to make room for a pregnant woman with a small, sticky-faced boy in the cart's kid-carry seat. Over the loudspeaker Frank Sinatra told Lana to have a merry little Christmas. Lana tested an avocado for ripeness.

Grace said, "I would have called you about this, only the end of the semester is always hectic. It's probably nothing, but you learn to be suspicious in my business. Hypervigilant, I guess you'd call it."

Grace had seen the car from her office window across the expanse of lawn and playground surrounding Arcadia School, through the branches of several eucalyptus trees, and between the bars of an old-fashioned, spear-point iron fence. Wendy drove a new blue-green Lexus. At such a distance it could easily be mistaken for a Jaguar.

"I think I know who it was," Lana said.

Grace smiled. "Then I'm not going to think about it anymore." Her teeth were so white and even Lana wondered if they were her own. "Micki's come through the last year better than I think any one of us would have expected. She's grown up a bit and that's good, but . . ." She let the qualification hang in the air.

Lana felt the absence of Jack like a ghost limb.

"God, the last thing I want to do is add to your worries." Grace touched Lana's shoulder lightly, as if she expected to be scorched. "And this Millennium thing, Y2K." She rolled her eyes and while they stood in the crowded checkout line, they talked about their plans for that evening. Grace and her husband were meeting friends at La Costa and spending the night.

Lana told her about the party.

"Well, enjoy yourselves—you deserve it. And don't worry about the Jag thing. I'm sure it's nothing."

It was to be an old-fashioned party with kids and adults, games and movies and music. Jack had loved these and said they made him feel like he lived in Minnesota. There would be food sufficient to feed a small nation and afterwards care packages for everyone to take home. Lana had roasted a shamefully expensive rib roast and a pork loin the day before. Kathryn had promised her sausage lasagna and a case of champagne—she and Dom could afford it; Mars was responsible for gourmet bread and cheeses and patés and a case of Killian's Irish Red. Wendy and Michael were bringing tequila and margarita mix and a cooked Virginia ham. The whole run-and-read club was coming, all her favorite people.

As she scrubbed Idahos the size of shoes, Lana watched Mars walk around the garden, following the gravel paths lined with basket-ball-sized granite rocks a million years old. Lana had sent her out to cut flowers for the centerpiece. Mars had an artist's touch and would arrange them with more style and elegance than Lana could come up with on her best day.

And this was not one of those. She had tried to dismiss Grace's mysterious car and driver, but they hung around the fringe of Lana's mind, a niggling worry. Much closer in was Jack. She kept thinking that in a backward way she was giving this party for him, not herself, not her friends.

In the garden, Mars was singing. Lana could not hear her but she knew that Connie Francis body language: *"Where the boys are . . ."* A perfect song for Mars. She sat on a wooden bench and lit a cigarette although Lana had told her plenty of times that nicotine was a poison to plants as well as humans. Around her at the end of long, drooping branches, red and yellow roses still bloomed gallantly because Lana had not found the will to prune them. The pink and yellow buddleia bushes along the garage wall were tall enough to sway like willows, and dust-colored bracts, crinkly and light as tissue paper, covered the bougainvillea that grew at the corner of the shade house.

The garden was still untidy. She should go out and work. But it had lost its ability to soothe. She left the hands-on work to Carmino and his crew. Lana felt more at home in her office than anywhere else in the world.

Squinting, with the cigarette pinched between her lips and the sun flashing in her autumn-colored hair, Mars removed the bone combs at her temples, bent forward, and ran her hands up through the thick curls, tossing them back as if to ease the weight, and dug the combs in again.

According to the family mythology, which their mother did nothing to discourage, Mars's father had been a Hollywood heavy-hitter along the lines of Irving Thalberg, Darryl F. Zanuck, or Louis B. Mayer. Certainly in personality and appearance, she was nothing like her fair and milky-skinned sisters.

Through the window, Lana watched Mars crush her cigarette on the gravel path, step away and then back. She picked up the butt and slipped it in her shirt pocket.

Bless you, dear girl.

Lana loved both her sisters, but especially Mars.

If she had seen her sister in a crowd she would have known instantly that she was a personage. Just standing still deciding which flowers to cut, she looked like the most important person to whom the roses had ever bent their stems. Lana could not remember a time when she had not felt pallid and forgettable beside her vivid sister. She was clean-cut and preppy plain with what Jack called the High Wasp look: even features, smooth, fair hair with a slight wave on the ends, blue eyes that were neither soulful nor startling, just the clear blue of the plumbago flower. Her nose was neither a pug nor a hook, just straight and excellent for breathing. Her chin was strong and her high cheekbones held her skin in place without calling attention to themselves.

Wendy said she looked like she should sail yachts and ride horses, but Mars belonged in a chariot riding off to war or leading her people to freedom. Of the three of them, Kathryn most resembled Stella. She was the starlet.

Lana wrapped the potatoes in aluminum foil and put them on the oven rack. As she crossed through *potatoes* on her list, Gala barked once, came out from under the round oak kitchen table, and hurried to the back door, tail swishing. Micki and Beth rushed in, out of breath and rosy-cheeked as milkmaids.

"We brought the ice," Beth said in a tone naturally several notes lower than her sister's. "Can you pay me back?"

"Ice costs more than a dollar and a half and it's just frozen water," Micki said. "What a rook."

"We're paying for the cost of the energy it takes to freeze it," Beth said, always a little bit the pedant.

"So? It's still a rook." Micki dumped her icy armload into the big cooler Lana had placed just outside the kitchen on the back porch which served as a mudroom, laundry room, and general junk collection area. She came back to Lana and draped her arms around her neck. "Hi, Gorgeous."

"Gorgeous yourself," Lana said and kissed her cheek. "Beth, you put your ice in the washing machine. We'll do beer and wine in there and soft drinks in the cooler, like always."

Because of their coloring, Micki and Beth were always assumed to be biological sisters. Beth's eyes were the same clear blue as Lana's; Micki's were also blue but very dark, the pupils ringed with a band of black that gave her the deep-eyed look of a wild animal. Both were streaky, fawn-and-gold, southern California blondes—their hair hung long and straight to just below their shoulder blades. Recently Micki had dyed a magenta streak in hers. Lana wished she hadn't done it, but she let it be.

Micki sat at the kitchen table. She bent her head forward and pulled several strands of magenta hair forward, peering at them critically.

"You think I should do my whole head?"

"Not if you want to live past fifteen," Lana said.

"That's child abuse, Ma. I could get you hauled up on charges."

"Speaking of which, you still have my MasterCard."

"There's this girl at school? She has half her head green and half blue. It looks extremely hot."

"My card, Micki."

Micki pulled the plastic charge card from the pocket of her carefully torn Levi's and tossed it on the lazy Susan.

"Ma," Beth said from behind the refrigerator door, "how come we're having a party and there's nothing to eat? Didn't you buy any chips or nuts?"

"She hides 'em. Like always."

"Wendy's bringing most of that stuff."

"Meanwhile, I'm starving," Beth said.

"Make yourself a sandwich," Lana said as she prepared to slice the pork loin. "You can have some of this and there's plenty of clean lettuce."

She watched her daughters make sandwiches, and listened to the noise of their bickering—"Gimme that . . . you took . . . I want." She hated the universe for denying Jack the sights and sounds of his beautiful daughters. She would have given anything right then for the freedom, the permission, to raise her fist and scream at God, but after more than a year she had become skilled at pretending life was back to fine on Triesta Way. Sometimes she convinced herself.

Lana said, "I met Grace Mamoulian at Von's today."

Micki groaned. "What have I done now?"

"You oughta see what she wears to work," Beth said.

"Everything she owns is turd brown."

Lana had also wondered about Grace Mamoulian's penchant for brown clothing. "She saw you talking to Wendy."

"Who?" Micki asked. "Me? When?"

"In front of the Unitarian Church."

Micki made a face. "Grace Mamoulian's crazy."

Lana wished she were not so busy, wished she could stop and pursue the matter of the Lexus or Jaguar or whatever it was, because at the back of her party-harried mind, a flag of caution had gone up. She was fairly certain Micki was not telling the whole truth. But Micki was a skilled liar and Lana had to pay attention, concentrate, to catch her bending the bow of truth as it suited her. She made a mental note to get back to the matter later.

Jack would not have procrastinated.

Chapter Four

Stella arrived just as Lana was heading upstairs for a fifteen-minute soak in the tub before the hordes arrived.

"Am I early?" She looked miffed. As if she had not been told that the party began at eight. As if she had been purposely misled, and it was Lana's fault there was no one there to admire her in black chiffon and the diamond earrings Stan had given her for their first anniversary. Tall and thin as a runway model.

No way I'll look that good at seventy-two, Lana thought.

"Hi, Ma. You look great." She bent forward and kissed Stella's pink and carefully powdered cheek, engulfed in the fragrance of Shalimar, a scent Lana recalled from her childhood when she had sneaked into her mother's bedroom in the cottage next to the Hollywood Cafe and sprayed herself. Such a heavy, clingy scent. Stella could always smell it on her afterwards. "That stuff doesn't come out of a tap," she would say. "I don't pay good money so you can take a bath in it."

Stella followed Lana upstairs and sat on the bed watching her undress. She crossed her legs and swung her narrow, patent-leathered foot back and forth with barely concealed impatience while a pleased little smile tilted up the corners of her mouth.

Lana asked, "Out with it, Ma. What's up?"

"Have you talked to your sister today?"

"Mars?"

Stella rolled her eyes.

"If you mean Kathryn," Lana said, "Tinera called a bit ago to say they'd be late." Lana fixed her mother with a stare. "Ma?"

Stella waggled her plucked and waxed eyebrows.

"No! I don't believe it. She swore she wouldn't have any more after Colette. That's eight years ago."

"There have been miscarriages."

Lana sat beside Stella on the bed. "I didn't know that. She never told me."

"Well, what do you expect?" Stella fluffed up the curls of her champagne-colored hair. "She knows your attitude."

Dom Firenzi was in his mid-fifties, almost twenty years older than Kathryn, whom he had claimed to have fallen in love with the first time he saw her behind the costume jewelry counter at Nordstrom. Lana believed him. Her sister was beautiful, fine-featured and delicate as a porcelain figure in a shop window. It was harder to understand why Kathryn loved a man old enough to be her father, short and stocky and rigid as an Old Country patriarch. He had grown up hard in Providence, in the city's Italian ghetto, but when he came to California a combination of brains, will, and ruthlessness had made him a successful contractor and businessman. The tough little Sicilian kid was still present, however, like a shadow image on a television screen and just as irritating. Lana and Mars had analyzed the chemistry between Kathryn and Dom and concluded that it was his domineering, the rigidity they found so unattractive, that attracted Kathryn. Dom took care of her; he made sure she never had to think for herself.

Dom wanted sons more than anything in the world but he doted on the eldest of his three daughters, a quiet girl named for Dom's mother, Tinera. She still wore her hair in braids but had been aptly described by Beth as "over the hill at eleven." Nichole, nine, and Colette, eight, were almost unnaturally quiet and well-behaved. None of them resembled their mother. If someone had set them down in a Sicilian village circa 1900, their dark hair and eyes would have looked perfectly in place.

Lana asked Stella, "How far along is she? Has she been to the doctor?"

"You are behind the times, Lana." Stella floated her large, graceful hands dismissively. "These days you just take a home pregnancy test and wait until the end of the first trimester to see the doctor."

While her mother talked about how motherhood suited Kathryn and what a good provider and devoted father Dom was, Lana went into the bathroom and turned on the shower. She stripped and stepped into the stream of hot water. For thirty seconds she let it pour against her face. Better a good scalding than say what she wanted to, that Dom was a troglodyte bully with his head up his butt.

Stella was convinced her youngest daughter had made a stunningly successful marriage, and no amount of debate was going to change her mind. As Mars said, Stella had always been a sucker for a rich, testosterone-heavy, A-type male. Particularly if he had a lot of chest hair.

Casa Firenzi was a dictatorship. A benevolent one, Lana supposed. Mostly. But Dom's wife and daughters barely took an independent breath or dared a creative thought without his interference.

Why did this matter so much to Lana? Mars said she should let Kathryn live her own life, fall out of her own trees. But Lana had begun watching out for her little sister when Stan's boozing and Stella's narcissism and Mars's demand for independence collided, creating firestorms that scorched them all. If Kathryn was sheltered and indulged, Lana knew it was partly her fault for having begun it years ago. She still protected her—how could she stop after almost thirty-four years?

She stepped out of the shower and grabbed a towel in time to hear the doorbell and, a moment later, Micki yelling up the stairs that Wendy and Michael had arrived and when did she want Michael to start making margaritas?

"Immediately," Lana yelled.

"You're running late as usual," Stella said. "Good Lord, what are you going to do with that hair?"

Lana wondered how many people were murdered on New Year's Eve.

That night drink flowed freely, the food was superbly extravagant, and the spacious old house held everyone comfortably: kids upstairs and in their own living room playing music and videos, adults in the kitchen and smoking on the front porch, someone in the backyard smoking pot—Lana caught a deserty whiff every now and then but she couldn't see who was smoking, although she suspected Mars and her current boy lover, a postdoc in the chemistry department at UCSD. For part of the evening, Stella huddled with Dom in the corner of the adult living room. Lana caught sight of them from behind: his thick, salt-and-pepper head, his muscular back and shoulders straining his dark blue sport coat, Stella glamorous and flirty. Hatching something.

Near midnight, as the guests were getting ready to walk down to Presidio Park to see the fireworks, Lana cornered Kathryn in the upstairs hall.

"You've been avoiding me," she said.

Kathryn opened her blue eyes wide.

"Ma says you're pregnant."

"God, that woman. We ought to duct tape her mouth." Kathryn's voice was high and sweet, modulated to offend no one. "Anyway, I was going to tell you. Tonight."

"You have three."

"Dom says you're jealous."

Lana smiled and pressed the soles of her feet against the floor. "You told me you wanted to go back to school. You had those catalogs. You said you were tired of being an appendage."

Kathryn laughed and floated her hands, exactly mirroring Stella's gesture. "Don't nag me, Lana. He wants a son so much, you have to understand. I just want to make him happy."

"Yes, but what about you?"

Kathryn laughed, a high, light sound of ripples and trills as musical as the song of a mockingbird.

New Year's Eve, 1999: if the date was portentous, if half the world waited for some great event to mark the Millenium ("The faux Millenium," as Mars called it), the weather in San Diego was unaware of the hype. The night was clear and mild, more like spring than midwinter, and as Lana and her crowd of family and friends walked through the silent streets down to Presidio Park, the span of the Milky Way was faintly visible in the moonless, midnight sky. Lana could pick out Orion and, faintly, Cassiopeia. Jack had been in the Air Force before they met and called this constellation The Flying Bra for the fun of making his daughters giggle.

"You sure about these fireworks, Lana?" someone asked.

"Of course," she said. "Haven't you been watching the television? The whole world is having fireworks."

But the streets of Mission Hills were empty and most of the houses dark except for the occasional blue glow of a television flickering through a window or screen door. From one house Lana heard Latin music and laughter; but with that exception, the neighborhood seemed to have decided not to celebrate Y2K and gone to bed early. Lana wondered if they were all just bloody relieved to see the old century go. She knew she was.

"Don't you think it's a little peculiar?" Kathryn said. "Where is everyone?"

Mars laughed. "What do you expect? It's San Diego."

Malcolm, the current boy-toy, walked ahead with the teenagers. Where he feels most comfortable, Lana thought and bit her lower lip. Was this what living on the edge of a crater had done to her, turned her bitter? She didn't want to be bitter. She wanted to be as Jack was, warm and reassuring. Maybe Malcolm was only being thoughtful, as Mars said he was, giving the sisters a chance to be together. They walked with their arms draped over each other's shoulders like winners after a soccer match. Three sisters, Lana thought—one mother but three different fathers.

She could hardly remember her own, Norman Coates, but he must have been bland. Between Kathryn and Mars, Lana felt beige and plain. Generic wheat bread between a croissant and a loaf of Russian rye.

Dom called to Kathryn from the other side of the street and she left them.

Mars muttered, "Why doesn't she just wear a choke chain?"

A moment later, Kathryn returned. "Dom wants to know if you're *sure* there'll be fireworks, Lana. He doesn't want to walk down there for nothing."

"Well, of course there will. During the summer, Sea World has them every night. You can set your clock by them. You know they'll do it up big for this kind of occasion." There had to be fireworks for the turn of the century. The faux Millennium.

Looking west from the top of the hill, Lana saw a band of light at the horizon, iridescent as radium, marking the point where the sky touched the edge of the sea. She thought of all the places in the world where the fireworks had already happened, and partygoers were just waking up on the first morning of a new century; she wished she were in one of those cities starting her life again. In the new century she would travel through space and time untouched by Jack. In the twenty-first century that Jack would never know, she might stop hurting and no longer need to pretend.

The party ambled down the hill and into the tree-dark silence of Presidio Park. On the Fourth of July this prime lookout was crammed with people and illegally parked cars, but tonight they had it to themselves. A drift of cold air rustled the needles of the pine trees and Lana shivered; a sense of uneasiness that she realized had been building in her since she stepped from the house into the unusually quiet neighborhood brought up the flesh at the back of her neck.

How could there *not* be fireworks on this night of worldwide celebration?

Around her, Lana heard people asking each other what time it was. Dom fussed to Kathryn about how he didn't like to sleep away from home. It wasn't yet midnight but Lana heard Micki, Beth, and their friends saying it was stupid to hang around the park when no one else was there. Obviously there would not be fireworks. They began to wander back up the hill in the direction of home, grousing.

"You could have called the Visitors' Bureau, Lana—they would have told you." Dom sounded sulky. "Nobody's here, nothing's going to happen."

From down on the freeway, Lana heard blaring horns and rising up from somewhere in Old Town, the strains of "Auld Lang Syne" and a pop like a firecracker or a champagne cork. Mars went looking for Malcolm, and around Lana, people began to hug and kiss each other.

"Happy New Year, Lana." Wendy hugged her hard. "Let's have a good year, okay?"

Beth broke away from her friends and ran back to Lana and threw her arms around her. "I love you, Mommy," she said, squeezing tight.

"Oh, me, too, Bethy. Me, too." Lana brushed aside Beth's fringe of bangs to kiss her forehead. Under the manufactured fragrance of shampoo and rinse and sweet soap, a breath of something sun-touched and creamy, a smell that reminded Lana of Jack, filled her eyes and stopped her voice. She had to clear her throat to speak. "We're going to have a good year, Beth. I promise you a good year."

"Me, too, Ma."

"Where's your sister?"

Beth shrugged.

Micki's particular friend, Tiff, was already at the top of the hill. Lana thought Micki must be with her.

From the corner of her eye, Lana saw Tinera stand on tiptoe and whisper in Kathryn's ear.

Kathryn looked at Lana, frowning. "Did Micki come with us?"

"She didn't, Aunt Lana," Tinera said in an excited and important voice. "She said she'd seen enough fireworks to last forever. She said they were boring."

Lana scanned the backs moving away from her, aware of a sudden crowding in her mind and the cinch across her chest. She saw Micki's best friend, Tiff, at the edge of the park where the streetlights began and called to her, telling her to wait a minute.

"I thought Micki was with you," Lana said when she reached her. "Where is she?"

Tiff stared at her feet in their glittery, backless, stack-heeled sandals; her toenail polish looked black.

"Tiff?"

At Lana's side Tinera announced in a singsong, tattletale voice, "She's at the house talking to a man."

"A man? What man?"

"He knew her name. He was in a Jaguar convertible. Micki said it was to die for."

Grace Mamoulian's image flashed across her mind, and as it did, Lana remembered seeing the beautiful car with its stunning starburst hubcaps early in the evening, parked in front of the Andersons' across the street. She had assumed it belonged to someone visiting them.

As Lana hurried up the hill and out of the park, Mars called after her, "Hey, it's a neighbor. . . . Someone has a new car. . . ."

But what did Mars know about the way disaster strikes, the suddenness with which it rips love out of your arms and scatters its bleeding parts across an intersection?

Lana began to run, aware of the others coming after her. She ran up the middle of the street, past the laughing, ambling teens and the silent houses. She was out of breath when she turned the corner onto Triesta Way in time to see a set of taillights the color of blood disappear around the curve onto Presidio Drive.

Without thinking, she cried after it, "Micki!"

"I'm here, Ma." She sat on the front steps, resting her elbows on her knees, tugging a handful of magenta hair. "Don't have a cow."

Air rushed out of Lana. She rested her fists against her hipbones and bent over, the breath burning her throat and lungs.

"How were the fireworks?"

Behind Lana, Tinera said, "San Diego's the only city in the entire world that didn't have fireworks."

"Who was that?" Lana asked when she could breathe.

"Who?"

"You know perfectly well." Lana heard echoes of her mother in that phrase. She looked at the house and saw Stella behind the screen door watching the scene with Gala beside her.

"In the Jaguar. Who was he?"

"Oh. Him." Micki acted calm and bored now. "Jesus, all he asked was directions." She stood up. "You are, like, so predictable. I knew you'd make a big deal of it." She glared at her cousin Tinera. "And you are such a snitch."

"That car was parked in front of the Andersons' half the night," Lana said, forcing down fear and rage and impotence.

Damn you, Jack. For not being here.

She knew what Micki was trying to do, consciously or not. Make her feel paranoid. Antiquated. She bore down on the balls of her feet to keep from screaming. "And this guy chooses midnight to ask for directions? Who was he?"

"He knew your name," Tinera said in a prissy voice that made Lana want to tie her to the railroad tracks. "I heard him ask if your name was Michelle. Don't say he didn't."

"So?"

"Is that true?"

"Ma, what's the big deal? Look around you."

Lana saw how safe the street was with its attractive homes and well-tended yards, no litter, no derelicts. Next door, the Tillmans' Newfoundland watched the scene through their side gate.

"He's been hanging around school, too," Beth said. "I saw him there last week and—"

"Fuck you, Beth."

Lana heard Dom mutter somewhere behind her.

She said, "Go inside, Mick. We'll talk about it later."

"But I didn't do anything," she wailed.

You don't have to do anything, Lana wanted to say. You just have to be your own pretty, innocent self. She wanted to rip into her daughter with the truth, to remind her of every monstrous tabloid story of kidnapped girls, raped and disfigured and ruined girls. She wanted to scream at Micki that she must run from a stranger who knows her name, who sits in his car and watches her school and her house.

"Get real, Ma." Micki stood up, looking down at Lana from the third step. "I talk to strangers all the time. How am I supposed to avoid them? Wear a gag?"

When Micki was little, four or five, she could not jump from the third stair. She would stand on it, bending her skinny knees and swinging her arms, trying to summon courage and never quite managing to do it. What a day it had been when she called Lana outside to show her that she wasn't afraid anymore. Now she stood on the third stair, formidable in her outrage, afraid of nothing.

"What am I supposed to do?" The more she talked, the more muscle and punch was in her voice. "You want me to take, like, a vow of silence. Be like a nun?"

"You know what I mean."

"I'm fifteen years old." She was on a roll now as her voice climbed the scale toward a shriek, a sound Lana could not endure for long. Where had Micki learned this? How had she become so good at fighting? "I don't need you to tell me what I have to do all the time. I can take care of myself."

Against a syringe full of heroin? Against a gun in your ribs and a hand between your legs? If this did not end soon, Lana thought she might be sick.

"You're very capable, Micki, I agree." Where had she found this phony, adult voice? "But we do need to talk. Go to your room and I'll be up in a few minutes."

"What about the party?" Micki's face was bright pink in the porch light. "What about my friends?"

"For you, the party's over."

Micki cried, "That is so stupid. You are so stupid."

"Be that as it may, I'm still your mother and—"

"You are not. You're not my mother." Micki charged up onto the porch, whirled, and screamed at Lana. "My real mother wouldn't treat me this way."

Behind her, Lana heard a sharp intake of breath from someone who had never heard Micki play her trump card—the potentially perfect birth mother. Micki's jaw muscles clenched. Some part of Lana felt sorry for her, for the mess of emotion she had got herself twisted up in; another part wished she and Jack had been patient enough to wait for their own sweet-natured and tractable Beth. Let someone else raise this temperamental spawn of strangers.

She didn't mean her thoughts—they were only thoughts. Jack would understand.

"That does it," Dom said. "We're going. Kids, get your stuff."

Lana turned to look at him and met the faces, gawking and curious, waiting to see what would happen next.

"I wish you were dead, not Daddy."

Lana turned in time to see Beth leap the steps two at a time, dart across the porch, and punch her fist into Micki's shoulder, banging her back against the screen door.

Stella screeched, Gala began barking.

"Leave me alone," Micki yelled and shoved Beth hard.

Beth staggered, teetered on her heels, circling her arms, lost her balance, and toppled backwards down the steps, arms wheeling and her back arched. Kathryn moved forward to break her fall and got halfway up the stairs. But Beth was Lana's twenty-first-century girl, her athlete and Valkyrie. When her strong, broad shoulders hit Kathryn square in the chest, Kathryn let out a whoosh of air and fell hard onto the cement. She curled into herself and lay still.

Chapter Five

The fall from the stairs did not kill Kathryn. After two or three terrifying seconds of stillness, she stirred and moaned and tried to get up, but Dom would not let her move. He had to get her to the hospital immediately and, of course, Stella had to follow after him in her own car. Dom shunted his three daughters off on Mars, who drove them back to the ranch in Malcolm's sedan, Malcolm following in her two-seater Mercedes. Lana said there was plenty of room at her house and there was no need for both of them to drive all the way out to the ranch; but Dom was not speaking to Lana and so that was that. In fifteen minutes they were gone, leaving Lana and the rest of her guests looking at each other, embarrassed and wondering what to say and do next. In another twenty minutes, most had muttered their thanks and apologies and commiserations and fled for home. A couple of Lana's run-and-read club friends stayed to help clean up. Wendy washed and bandaged Beth's scrapes. When Stella called near two A.M. to say that Kathryn had miscarried and Dom had taken her home, only Wendy and Michael were still at the house.

Lana hung up the phone, slumped against the kitchen wall, and slid to the floor. Wendy sat beside her and in silence they finished off a bottle of Pinot Grigio while Michael dozed in Jack's chair in the grownups' living room.

"Poor Micki." Lana said, "There's going to be hell to pay for this."

Wendy and Michael went home a little later and Lana prowled the downstairs, picking up overlooked coffee cups and plastic champagne flutes. It had been a good party while it lasted. She straightened stacks of magazines and fluffed couch pillows; she did whatever she could to avoid going upstairs and not until she felt afloat with fatigue did she check the locks, turn off the lights, and start up to bed.

Halfway up, she stopped and sat with her head in her hands. Not crying. She had gone beyond the country of tears into a wide, empty region where tears could not begin to express the desolation.

Lana looked in on Beth first. She had flung herself across the bed wearing sweats and a pair of Jack's old gym socks. She had appropriated all of these when Lana finally got around to emptying his chest of drawers. Beth lay on her stomach, her face pressed into the pillow so that her mouth was reshaped into the soft pout, the damp and seashell-pink, kissy mouth Lana remembered from her babyhood. She must have cried herself to sleep.

And I wasn't here, Lana thought. I didn't even nurse her scrapes. She had stayed downstairs cleaning and putting away because it was easier than being up here.

Micki sat in her windowseat, her comforter around her shoulders.

"It's late," Lana said, turning back the bed. "Here. Get in."

As if grateful to be told, Micki dragged herself and the comforter across the room and into bed. Her hair was tangled where she had been tugging on it, and her face, like Beth's, was rashy from crying.

"I'm sorry, Ma. I didn't mean . . . what I said."

Lana sighed.

Of course she meant her words. At the time she exploded she had meant every insult from the depths of her heart.

"I know you didn't." She touched Micki's hot cheek feeling on her skin the fire of her emotions, the burning coals ready to flare again.

"How's Aunty Kay?"

Lana told her.

"Omigodomigodomigod." As Micki's voice climbed the scale, she tried to sit up but Lana pressed her gently back into the pillows. "I didn't mean . . . I didn't know. . . ."

"Micki, listen, listen to me." Lana took a deep breath to keep from screaming the truth. "No one's blaming you, Mick. It was an accident."

"He'll say I did it. Dom will. He hates me anyway." She tossed her hips and legs from side to side, throwing off the bedcovers.

Lana held her shoulders. "He doesn't hate you."

Then again, maybe he did. He certainly disliked Micki, and had never made much effort to conceal it. In his last years Jack had only been civil to his brother-in-law because of Kathryn.

"Does this mean I'm a . . ." In the light of the bedside lamp Lana saw Micki's eyes dart in panic. ". . . murderer?"

Lana's stomach twisted.

"I started it, it was my fault." Micki rolled into a fetal position facing the wall. Lana slipped off her shoes and got into bed beside her, holding her around the middle and spooning into her as she had when Micki was little and too upset to sleep.

"I love babies, Ma, I'd never—"

"It wasn't a baby, Micki. It was a tiny thing smaller than your little finger."

"Tiff says it doesn't matter. She says even then they have souls."

"Tiff doesn't know that. No one knows."

Micki turned in Lana's arms; tears like moonlight danced in her deep-water eyes. "What do you think, Ma?"

Lana wanted to say that two A.M. on New Year's Day 2000 was not the time to discuss life and death, babies, fetuses, embryos, and the soul. Or maybe it was the perfect time. A new century, a new beginning.

"Close your eyes and I'll tell you." Lana closed her own. She knew what she believed. She had talked to Mars about it, to Wendy, to her friends in the run-and-read club. "I believe that just like the soul mysteriously leaves the body when someone dies, it just as mysteriously enters when a baby is born. Before birth, the mother and the baby share one soul."

"That's what happens?" Micki looked at Lana over her shoulder. "You're sure?"

Sure? She was barely sure of anything. "Yes."

"You think I shared my birth mother's soul?"

The knot in Lana's stomach felt calcified. "I guess so, Micki." She pressed her cheek against her daughter's straight, silky hair smelling of sweet shampoo, and kissed the nape of her neck. "When it comes to the soul, Micki, no one knows for sure."

"Do I have a soul now, Ma?" Such a small, uncertain voice.

Lana wanted to weep for the child who could ask this question.

It did not matter how much Lana and Jack had wanted Micki or how welcome they made her, a part of her would always be poor, colicky, cranky Micki, born like a coiled spring, a constant scratch along the blackboard, a girl whose mother had given her away to strangers because she did not want her. *Trash-can Baby*.

"Sometimes I think . . . I feel like I'm such a . . . such a fuck-up."

"You're a kid, Micki. A teenager. Every teenager screws up. It's a requirement." Lana slipped out of bed and tucked the blankets around Micki. "And you have a soul, no question."

Micki rolled onto her back and looked up at her. "Are you sure?"

Lana did not pause. "Absolutely. One hundred percent."

Before dawn a westerly kicked up, waking Lana from a tossing sleep. The window sheers billowed into the room, abloom with air that smelled of the garden; and on the balcony along the back of the house the bamboo chimes clacked and clattered. The touch of air on her bare shoulder, a tickle of hair at the back of her neck, thirst woke Lana suddenly, and for a moment in the gray light she was disoriented. She turned on her side to look at Jack. . . .

The blue-green numbers on the digital clock beside the bed told her it was almost five. She had slept less than two hours but it was pointless to stay in bed any longer. Jack had often awakened before dawn and taken Gala for a walk. Lately this had become Lana's habit as well. She occasionally wondered if Jack's spirit were urging her to get up and walk, live.

She rose and dressed quickly in jeans and a work shirt of pale blue cotton, softened by many washings. In the bathroom she brushed her teeth with the electric toothbrush, patted cream into her skin, and quickly combed her hair back and fastened it with a clip. Plain gold hoop earrings, and she was dressed for the day that had not yet dawned. Holding her athletic shoes by their laces, she tiptoed to the head of the stairs. From her customary place on the landing, Gala thumped her feathered tail but did not raise her pretty head. Lana crouched beside her and rubbed the long, silky red ears.

"No-good hound."

As she went down the stairs, Lana heard the dog stretch to her feet with a groan and then the click of her ID tags and her nails on the hardwood floor.

In the kitchen Lana tore a banana from a bunch hanging on a hook over the counter, and as she stood at the sink eating it and a handful of almonds, the dog finagled her wet nose under her hand. Lana opened the pantry and rummaged for a dog biscuit.

Lana believed Gala missed Jack. For many weeks after he died she was slow to settle down at night. The clickity-clack of her nails as she paced seemed amplified in the silent house. Once Lana left the closet door open and found Gala inside, resting her head on a pile of Jack's clothes collected for the thrift shop.

On the first day of the new century the gusty wind blew through the house and whistled around the corners and stirred up the old sounds and smells—laughter and little-girl squeals, popcorn and Toll House cookies just out of the oven. Lana hurried to escape.

From the hall closet she took a light down jacket and slipped it on, not bothering to zip the front. Gala heard the jangle of her leash and held her head and neck still while her back end went crazy with eagerness. A moment later, perched at the top of the veranda steps, she strained forward, tense, peering into the gloom for a glimpse of cat.

Up and down the street Lana saw only cars she recognized. No blue-green Jaguar convertible. Nevertheless she walked back to the front door and locked it.

Overhead the sky was creamy black, light enough to see the street and sidewalk, the familiar old homes on either side of Triesta Way. The palms in the Andersons' front yard bent in the wind, their fronds brushing each other with a sweet sound like rain falling. Lana thought about her neighbors peacefully sleeping, couples and families she had known for years; the Tillmans and Obregons had been at the party the night before. She assured herself there was nothing to fear on this street. The neighborhood owl hooted twice and lifted from its branch in the big pine two houses down. She glimpsed its wild-winged shape against the paling sky. Two blocks beyond the house, as she was about to turn left on Cabrillo, she stopped and stared ahead into the gloom.

A convertible was parked in front of the last house on the block. She exhaled. Not a Jaguar. A Buick.

Gala tugged on her lead. Lana let her off the tether. "Stay away from skunks."

Cabrillo ended in a cul-de-sac, a steep-sided canyon, and a trail down into darkness. From where she stood on the hillside, Lana glimpsed far below the long, straight line of I-8 running east to west through Mission Valley. The traffic sounds were as gentle and soothing as the pull and push of surf. A mile across the valley, silhouetted against the starless sky, the line of houses and condominiums were like a paper cutout. Perhaps over there another sleepless woman stood on a cul-de-sac overlooking the valley, another woman who appeared normal and even fairly happy on the outside but was really frozen dead inside.

In the canyon a coyote yipped. Coyotes were clever beasts who feasted on neighborhood cats and were said to lure domesticated dogs into their ring where the poor kibbled creatures were no match for their wild cousins. Lana was not sure this was true, but she whistled for Gala anyway.

As she turned back onto Triesta, Lana glanced up Cabrillo, wanting to reassure herself that the car she had seen was indeed a safe, Republican Buick. It was gone. Had she been mistaken? Had it been a Jaguar and had the driver taken off when he saw her? Or was she paranoid? She knew the difference between a Buick and a Jaguar. Even in the predawn twilight.

Lana thought about Micki's tantrum and Beth rushing in, Kathryn lying still on the sidewalk and Stella flying down the steps. The miscarriage.

Well, she had wanted fireworks, and now she had to pay for them.

She and the girls would have to go out to the ranch. Today.

Chapter Six

Above the stream of traffic on the Martin Luther King Highway, the sky was vivid blue as if God had given it a fresh coat of enamel to celebrate the first day of the New Year. Ahead, Lana saw a line of red brake lights, slowed, and after a moment came to a dead stop, boxed between a Honda van and a primered muscle car, a U-Haul truck to the right, and a red Porsche to the left. Her anxiety rose, her nerves winding tighter and tighter.

Throughout southern California the stores in all the malls were open for business on New Year's Day, offering unsold Christmas merchandise at hugely knocked-down prices. It was a big day for movie premieres, too, and at the College Park Multiplex the entrance ramp was backed up a quarter of a mile. She thought of all the city's ramps and highways and parking lots choked with drivers and passengers, half of them hung over and sleep-deprived; and she wondered what lemming instinct made people spend the first day of a new year trapped in their vehicles or crowded against each other in stores and movie theaters.

Beside her in the 4Runner's passenger seat Micki sat in a slouch, headphones affixed, most of her face concealed behind the fall of her long, white-gold hair, thick and glossy except for the broad streak of magenta down the right side. The nervous jerks of her tapping foot attested to the fact that she was awake and, like Lana, dreading what lay ahead. In the back, Beth appeared to be asleep, scrunched against the seatback and the window, using her jacket as a pillow, headphones in place.

Lana turned on the radio, pressed three or four buttons, heard nothing that pleased or interested her, and turned it off. At times

like this she wished she still smoked. Twenty cars ahead she saw
the blinking lights of cop cars and paramedics and for an instant, as
she thought of the body that might be lying on the asphalt, she felt
herself sinking into the marshy land that surrounded her life, that
wove itself in and out of every hour of her day.

Jack.

She jabbed Micki gently in the ribs.

"What?"

"Look out your side. How bad is it?"

"Ma-a." Micki managed to give the word two syllables.

"Please."

With a dramatic show of effort, Micki put down the window
and craned her neck to see what was happening up ahead. Five
lanes of traffic had come to a complete standstill.

"We'll never get there," she wailed, falling back onto the seat.
"There's cops and two para—"

"What?" Beth asked from the back seat.

"We're trapped in the middle of a—"

Lana's cell phone rang and she shushed the girls, who retreated
to their audio caves, grumbling about all the things they would
rather be doing.

"Hi, Ma." Lana forced a lilt into her voice even as it occurred to
her that she almost never got good news by cell phone.

Stella said, "Have you talked to your sister this morning?"

"Happy Y2K to you, too."

"Where are you?"

"On the MLK, headed for the ranch."

"I wouldn't go if I were you. You won't be welcome." Stella took
an audible breath and then started in on Micki. Lana held the
phone away from her ear so she could hear the sound of her
mother's voice but not the words. She knew the rant by now: no
impulse control, irresponsible. Lana had learned long ago not to
argue when her mother was on a bombing run.

Stella paused to breathe and Lana said, "I don't want to hear
this, Ma. I'm going to hang up if you don't stop." She glanced over
at Micki and in the rearview mirror at Beth. Both were oblivious in
their insulated worlds of music. "You're not allowed to talk this
way, not about my girls."

She had been saying this to her mother for fifteen years but it made no difference. Being a mother and grandmother gave Stella permission to say anything she wanted about anyone related to her, as many times as she wanted.

"And what was that girl doing? Talking to a total stranger? A man she didn't know from . . . Who was he? Has she told you yet?"

"This isn't a good time, Ma."

"She hasn't. Have you even asked her?"

"She didn't know him. He asked directions."

"You trust her?"

"Of course I do." Pretend, pretend, pretend. It was a way of life.

At Rancho San Diego the King highway became the old 94, a narrow, twisting road that wound first through expansive upscale "country" developments and after a few miles into the dry and rugged hills between California and Mexico. Homes were few and often no more than metal-sided trailers sitting beside a cistern with a few cows and a horse or two milling nearby. Overhead, the red-tailed hawks glided on the currents of air above the canyons, their fantails glowing amber in the sunlight.

The Firenzi ranch, *Tres Palomas*, was located in a small valley a few miles from the Mexican border off Snake Willow Road at the end of a graveled driveway cut through fifty acres of scrub-covered hills. A precious year-round spring fed a ribbon of creek edged with sycamores and silver-leafed cottonwoods that caught the light like coins. There had been a quarter-inch of rain in December, enough to whisker the dry hills with washes of lime green down the slopes and in the hollows. If the late winter rains came, for a few weeks in March and April the valley and hills would look like English countryside. A green so vibrant it was juicy.

At the top of a rise, Lana stopped the 4Runner and rolled down the window. The girls did not ask her why she stopped. Perhaps they knew she needed a moment to prepare herself. On a fence post ten meters from the car a mockingbird sang with its beak up-lifted. Lana watched its throat ripple as the music poured out.

Micki groaned.

"What?" Lana asked.

"Can we just get this over with?"

Below them in the shallow valley, rough-barked and rag-branched cottonwoods surrounded the long ranch house of redwood and stucco set in the midst of lawn and garden. The scene was pristine and peaceful: graceful house, red-painted barns, white-fenced corrals and paddocks, and horses grazing.

At the bottom of the hill an elaborate ironwork gate ornamented with three doves in flight kept strangers out. Lana keyed in the electronic code and the gates swung open. Reluctantly, Lana thought.

She parked the 4Runner at the side of the house and got out. Beth and Micki trailed her to the front door. She knocked and after a moment, Tinera opened it.

"Oh," she said. "Hi." She wore an apron and looked distressed. "Come in."

"Happy New Year, honey." Lana kissed her niece's slightly flour-dusted cheek. "What're you making?"

"Daddy said I should try to use the pasta machine. I'm making fettuccine." Tinera rolled her round shoulders and squinted.

"Where are Colette and Nichole?"

"At their friend's house."

"What about your dad?"

"He's with Mom."

"How is she?"

Tinera rolled her shoulders again.

"I'll go back and see her." Lana looked at Micki and Beth lagging on the threshold, still wearing their headsets. She gestured for them to take them off. "You two go with Tinera but come when I call you, okay?"

Lana walked back to the master suite at the far end of the silent house. For Lana's taste the house was overdecorated. She did not care for glossy ceramics, paintings of Gypsy girls—even very good paintings of Gypsy girls, as these undoubtedly were; and she thought dark, velvet-covered couches were ludicrously impractical in a family home in a desert climate, but maybe not, since hardly anyone ever sat on them. The living room was more for show than for living. Her boot heels rang on the copper-colored slate tiles.

She saw Dom at the end of the hall just closing the bedroom door. He looked exhausted. Above the blue-black stubble of his beard, triangles of shadow hollowed his cheeks.

"How is she?"

He put a thick finger to his lips. "Weak. She's been asleep all day."

Tears sprang to Lana's eyes and she hugged her brother-in-law. "I'm so sorry, Dom. What an awful—"

He pushed her away, barely contained anger bolting from his hands into her body, and jerked his head toward the little room, adjacent to the bedroom, which Kathryn called her study. They went in with an elaborate care for silence, as if they were spies on the edge of occupied territory—except Kathryn was the territory in question and Lana knew she wasn't the enemy agent.

"She's weak," Dom said again, brushing his hand across his brow, pushing back the thick wave of salt-and-pepper hair. "Bad night." Fleshy semicircles of fatigue cupped his large, moist eyes making him look more than usually saturnine. He smelled of sweat and Lana realized he still wore the slacks and shirt he'd had on the night before. "God, Lana, I love her so much and she was so brave. Her strength . . ."

When it suited Dom's purposes he made women the stronger sex, attributing to them extraordinary powers of endurance and suffering, but Lana had been present in the delivery room the night Colette was born. She had watched him and seen that the pain of childbirth carried an erotic charge for him.

Lana sank into one of two overstuffed chairs on either side of a bay window. The view was across the lawn to the white-fenced corral closest to the barn. Here in her sister's room Lana felt she could relax and get comfortable. She liked the old-fashioned striped wallpaper, the deep, very ladylike cushioned chairs, and tables covered with books—photo albums, cookbooks, picture books of horses and gardens. There were always roses in this room, even today, though they had begun to droop and fallen petals lay on the polished wood surface of the dresser like a scattering of tiny satin pillows. The petals would grow old and sticky and mark the dresser-top waiting for Kathryn to dust them up.

Dom refused to hire anyone to help her keep the big, rambling house. He believed housekeeping was her job, but even more, he wanted no invasion of the family's privacy. No stranger poking into drawers and closets and carrying tales into the world. What tales? Lana wondered.

She said, "It was an accident, of course, and the girls feel awful. . . . They're in the kitchen with Tinera."

"You brought them with you?"

"They need—"

"I don't believe their needs count for much under the circumstances." He did not sound angry, just worn out, worn down, done in. He dropped into the chair opposite Lana and covered his face with his hands. "It was a boy, Lana. A son."

He lowered his hands and Lana thought she had never seen such misery on any man's face. If he had moved toward her at that moment, she would have held out her arms to comfort him.

"A boy, Lana. At last."

"She was only a few weeks along. There was no way to tell—"

"I knew, I knew." He shook his fist. Not at Lana but close enough to make her pull back. "I knew in my gut since the afternoon we made him. When I came it was different, more powerful."

Enough with the details, Lana thought.

She said, "I know it's just words but honestly, the girls and I are so terribly sorry. But if it was a boy—"

"I said it was a boy, Lana. You don't believe me?"

"If you made a boy once, you can do it again."

"If?"

"Dom, I believe you. You made a boy."

"My brothers all have sons."

Lana stood up. "I'm going to see her—I won't stay long."

"She's upset."

"So are the girls. They need to tell her how sorry they are. Especially Micki."

She walked to the sitting room door and put her hand on the glass knob.

Dom said, "She's asleep."

"Then I'll just look in."

He stood in front of her, all five-feet-eight of him: a stocky, cement-solid Italian—and a stallion, according to Kathryn's innuendos.

"She's my sister."

"She's my wife."

A stalemate. And then, faintly, the sound of canned laughter.

"She's watching TV," Lana said.

"Before you do anything, we need to talk."

Maybe what she smelled wasn't sweat—maybe it was hostility.

Over his shoulder Lana looked out the window through a stand of untidy cottonwoods across a narrow strip of grass and garden and the turnaround where one of the illegal Mexican laborers Dom employed was raking the gravel. In the corral Jacaranda, Kathryn's tall bay thoroughbred, bent his forelegs carefully, dropped to the ground, and rolled in the scrubby grass, rocking from side to side on his back. Dom had no interest in horses, but Kathryn was never more comfortable than on the back of a fifteen-hundred-pound animal. For the first time this seemed important and Lana knew that later she would have to think about why her sister was both strong and weak at the same time.

"It's not just what happened last night," Dom said. "Last night . . . It's not you, Lana. Kathryn loves you and I don't want to get between you two. But your daughters . . ." He shook his head. "They're out of control. And a bad influence on my girls."

"Wait a minute, Dom. That's not fair." She blinked and focused on the thoroughbred, watched it lurch to its feet and swing off to the far end of the corral. "You and I, we have different ideas about raising kids. And that's okay, but if you want my opinion, your daughters—"

"I don't want your opinion," he said. And then he smiled and the charm came out like sunshine. He put his big hand on Lana's shoulder, close to her neck. She felt his heat on her skin. "This is so hard, this family stuff. You know I don't want to be harsh, you know how much you and your girls mean to me, but we've talked about this, me and Kathryn . . ."

"Kathryn loves Micki and Beth." She stepped away. "Whatever your feelings are, don't make her part of this."

"Hey-hey-hey, Lana, ease up. Let me say this, okay?" He moved closer and ran his hand up her neck and cupped her chin, turning her face toward his. She pulled aside and he smiled and she thought how this was what he had wanted, to get a physical reaction from her. "It doesn't have to be forever. Jesus, that's the last thing we want. Me and Kathryn just think that until Micki and Beth work out their problems, it would be best for everyone if the kids didn't spend time together."

"How long did you have in mind? A year? A decade? Maybe when they're grannies they can be best buddies." Lana rested her hand on the back of the chair and focused on the balls of her feet. "What are you talking about? Exactly."

"Lana, these things happen in families. Adolescence, it's a hard time. That's all I'm saying—don't get carried away." Dom folded his arms across his chest and looked down, pressing his stubbly chin back against his throat. "A kid like Micki, she's fightin' her way through it and believe me, I know what that's like. Me and my brothers, we wanted to kill each other." His gaze met Lana's. "But there's this peer pressure thing and for my girls to be around yours, especially Tinera at this time in her life, it's a bad idea."

Lana wanted to slug him. "What am I supposed to tell Micki and Beth?"

He half-smiled at her. "Tell 'em the truth. It won't kill 'em."

The truth: *Your uncle is a bastard and a son of a bitch. If he vanished off the face of the earth, I would never lift a finger to find him.* It was what she thought but she could never say it, not against her little sister's husband.

"I'm going to see Kathryn now."

"Lana, Lana, you're so angry. Why are you so angry with me?" He held out his hands as if to show he was unarmed. "I'm not the enemy here. I'm just doing what I have to, protecting my family."

"Well, good for you." Lana did not hear his response, just the bark of his voice behind her as she left the sitting room and went in to see her sister.

She closed the bedroom door behind her and pressed the button on the knob to lock it. If Dom wanted to interrupt he could break the door down.

The shutters were closed and the bedroom lay in deep violet shadow. The air smelled like rose potpourri, a heavy, sickish odor.

"Can't we open some windows?" Lana asked. "It's a gorgeous day."

The television flickered, there was laughter and the back-and-forth of sharp female voices; but Kathryn lay on her side, facing away from it. Lana walked across the room and turned the set off.

"Leave it," Kathryn said, not moving.

"After we talk."

"I don't want to talk."

"Yeah, but you still have to."

"God, you're bossy."

Lana walked around the room opening the shutters, sliding the windows back.

"It's cold," Kathryn whined.

"Put on a sweater."

Lana let the golden afternoon light into the spacious bedroom with the gilt mirrors and massive furnishings she knew Dom had selected. She knelt on the bed to prop and rearrange the pillows.

"Sit up."

"I don't want to."

"How do you feel?"

"Shitty, thanks."

Actually, Lana thought, for someone who had spent the night in the emergency room, Kathryn looked pretty good. Her fine blond hair was arranged in two stubby pigtails, she wore her diamond stud earrings—a half-karat larger than Stella's, Dom had made sure of that—and without makeup the natural roses in her cheeks made her look young.

"I have a killer headache."

"Let me get you some aspirin. Is there some in—?" Lana opened the drawer of the bedside table. "Oh my god, what's *this* doing here?"

She pulled out a .38 revolver like the one Jack had bought her years ago. Lana knew how to use the gun—Jack had made sure of that when they lived in the cottage on the grounds of Urban Greenery; but now her own revolver lived in its leather case on a shelf in her closet. The ammunition was in her dresser.

"Dom works late. He wants me to be able to protect myself."

Lana spun the chamber. "It's loaded. You can't keep a loaded gun right out where your kids could get it."

Kathryn groaned. "Why are you nagging me, Lana? The girls won't touch the gun. They aren't stupid. Anyway, it makes no sense to keep a gun for protection unless it's loaded. Dom says—"

Lana removed the bullets. "So don't tell him." She put them in a drawer under Kathryn's sweaters, then she went into the bathroom and came out a minute later with aspirin and a glass of water.

"How bad's the arm?" Lana asked.

"Not bad. Hardly hurts at all."

"God, Kay, I'm so sorry. About the mis."

"I know."

"Dom told me I couldn't come in."

"But here you are." Kathryn patted Lana's hand and managed half a grin. "That's my big sister."

"Do you want me to go?"

Kathryn shook her head. "Did you ever find out who the guy was in the Jag?"

Lana shook her head.

"She still isn't talking?"

"She doesn't know."

"And you believe her? You trust her?"

"You sound like Ma. Yes, I trust her. She's a good girl."

"If she were mine," Kathryn said, "I'd shake the truth out of her."

"You mean Dom would. He'd probably hold a gun to her head until she confessed."

Kathryn smiled.

"She and Beth are with Tinera in the kitchen," Lana said. "As we speak."

"You brought them?" Kathryn sat up straighter.

"She feels awful. They both do, but Micki 'specially. They need to apologize."

Kathryn shook her head and pulled the pink, satin-edged electric blanket up around her chin. "I'm not mad at them. Just tell them that."

"I'll go get them. You can tell them yourself."

"Don't push him, Lana. Please."

"All they need is—"

"It's not that easy."

"Kathryn, it'll take less than five—"

"Tell them I love them. Tell them anything you want to make them feel better."

"He says you think they're a bad influence on your girls." Lana fixed her with a stern look that came straight out of their childhood. "Is that true, Kay?"

Kathryn lay back, masking her eyes with her forearm. "Don't make me pick sides. Not you, too. Just believe me, I can't see them. If you love me, just tell them I'm not angry, and I don't blame them. Honestly." She lowered her arm and looked at Lana and in the wide, dry light of her blue eyes, in the parched sea of their color, Lana saw a survivor clinging to a shipwreck. It was one of those instants of vivid illumination that occasionally came to her like the flare of an ancient instinct; she knew with certainty that when she and Mars teased Dom, when they called him a retro-male, a throwback, and a fossil, he laughed along with them and played the sport, went home, and took his anger out on Kathryn. Lana could argue with her sister and eventually get her to agree to see the girls

and when it was over she would have been just as much a bully as
Dom.

"Okay." Lana rose from the edge of the bed. "I'll take them
home and I'll lie—"

Kathryn jerked forward and grabbed Lana's wrist. "It's not a lie.
I do forgive them. Totally. You can tell Mick I'm grateful. Tell her
she did me a favor." She spoke like someone trying not to scream.
"Tell her I never wanted that baby in the first place."

Chapter Seven

Lana told Micki and Beth the medication given Kathryn in the hospital had made her too groggy to visit with them. Their feet crunched on the gravel as they walked to the car; Lana felt Dom watching their departure and had a wicked desire to turn around and flip him the finger.

"What did she say about the baby?"

"It wasn't a baby," Beth said. "It was an embryo."

"She was philosophical, Micki." Lana had planned this answer as she left Kathryn's room and walked down the hall to the front door. "She said she'd get pregnant again. It's easy for her." Not precisely true, but it would make Micki feel better.

"She's not mad at me?"

"Not a bit."

But apparently Micki was unconvinced because over the next several days, she asked the same question several times. "It was an accident," Lana always told her. "Aunty Kay knows you'd never do anything to hurt her on purpose." Lana kept waiting for the next question—*Then why doesn't she call me?*—but Micki never asked it and Lana wondered if she was afraid to hear the answer.

In mid-January a series of Pacific storms stretched end-to-end like a wagon train rolled over southern California, deluging San Diego with as much rain in ten days as the region sometimes got all year and disrupting the city's relaxed Latin pace. Mudslides devastated housing developments in North County and storm sewers overflowed, contaminating miles of beaches. If you didn't own an umbrella there wasn't a store that could sell you one after the first day of downpour. Urban Greenery was a bog and everyone came to work in old clothes and heavy shoes or boots, cursing and blessing the rain in the same breath. The parking lot stayed empty all day. Lana used the time to clean and reorganize the showrooms and displays.

After several squally days the sky cleared for a few hours and shone like an enormous lapis dome on which someone had painted horizons of towering clouds backlit in gold. On such days Lana and Jack had walked on the beach bundled in parkas they wore only three or four times a year. A good storm brought up from the sea floor shells and colored stones and bits of smoothed glass as subtly colored as gemstones. They gathered these and brought them home for the garden. Lana could not go to the beach alone. Instead she left work after lunch and drove out to the ranch to see Kathryn, hoping to catch her at a time when she would have neither husband nor children for distraction.

She found her sister in the barn saddling Jacaranda. Kathryn wore a plaid flannel shirt and snug Levi's tucked into the top of a pair of expensively tooled leather boots. Her fair hair was tucked up under a watch cap Lana had knitted her in wool as blue as her eyes. Perhaps because of the season—no one had been spending much time out of doors the last two weeks—Kathryn looked paler than usual, and puffy-eyed as if she had been sleeping too much and too hard, late in the morning, in an overheated room.

"You're too thin," Lana hugged her. Through the flannel shirt, she felt Kathryn's ribs against the palms of her hands.

"Lets go for a ride, huh? While the weather holds?" Kathryn pointed in the direction of a tack room door standing open. "There's boots in there. And a helmet."

Lana did not want to ride, but she did want to talk to Kathryn and a trail ride was a good time to do it. Outside, away from the house and on horseback, Kathryn was always more relaxed than in her home.

"The horses have been crazy, cooped up inside," Kathryn said as she laid a western saddle across Graylight's back for Lana. She patted the mare's gray flank. "You'll have to watch her. She'll be twitchy."

"How about you?"

"Am I twitchy?" Kathryn smiled. "You know how it is. I love the rain but the gray skies make me blue." She laughed. "Sounds like a line from a song, doesn't it?"

"Are you taking your pills?"

"Yes, Big Sister." Kathryn made a face.

Kathryn hated to be reminded that she was under medication for depression. She resented the pills that lifted her spirit, felt taking them labeled her as crippled in some way. Lana believed Kathryn had been depressed most of her life, even as a small child when, to cheer her up, Stella had taken her shopping at Saks or to the hairdresser where she paid someone to paint her little girl's nails and backcomb her blond curls.

Mars said Stella would have done these things regardless of Kathryn's disposition because she was her favorite, the family doll. Kathryn smiled for everyone, passed around canapés, twirled and sang, *"Shine little glowworm, glow and glimmer;"* and when she was four, Stella and Stan and their friends thought she was irresistible, lisping through lines like *thou aeronautical boll weevil, illuminate yon woods primeval.*

Lana looked back now and felt a tug of sympathy for Kathryn, singing and dancing and smiling on command. But at the time it seemed her little sister got all the attention while Lana got none. So naturally she envied her, but she was too sweet to resent deeply or for long.

"How's Dom?" Lana asked as she adjusted the stirrups on Graylight.

"Furious. Construction stops in the rain."

On the way to the ranch, Lana had passed a ten-story office building with a sign out in front, FIRENZI CONSTRUCTION. These signs were all over the city. In the Golden Triangle the firm was building a massive complex for a German pharmaceutical company and near the Gaslamp a multistoried parking complex was rising from the rubble of an old warehouse. Lana thought how phallic this kind of construction work was and how perfectly it suited her brother-in-law.

It had been months since Lana last rode; she could not sort her way through the double reins.

"I'll do it for you," Kathryn said. "You just put on your boots."

The riding pants were two sizes too big and the blue denim shirt smelled and looked as if it hadn't been washed in some time. "I hope the fashion nazis aren't around," Lana said.

"You'll do," Kathryn said over her shoulder as she led Jacaranda out of the barn. "You smell good to Graylight."

They stood on hay bales to mount and then turned their horses up the gentle slope behind the barn along a narrow trail cut through rocks and scrub. Graylight and Jacaranda, accustomed to going out together, flicked their ears and tossed their heads in the sunlight, happy to walk and trot side by side, allowing Lana and Kathryn to talk. Occasionally Jacaranda remembered he was a stallion and nickered under his breath at Graylight but she was not interested, gave him no enticements, and so he mostly left her alone.

Kathryn asked how Micki was doing. "She knows I'm not mad?"

"She needs to hear it from you," Lana said. "But, yes, she knows you're not mad." With the resumption of school, Micki had begun obsessing about The Fives, the officially banned but blatantly active school sorority that had announced her as one of the candidates for membership.

"She's a sure thing, isn't she?"

"So it appears." Lana did not dare consider that Micki might be disappointed though she occasionally wondered how it was that, after years of being teased and hounded, Micki was now considered eligible for an elite sorority. "I feel sorry for Tiffany. She won't like being on the outside looking in."

"Maybe she'll get chosen too," Kathryn said. "She's on the list, isn't she?"

"Yes, but Mick says she doesn't have the kind of style The Fives are looking for."

Kathryn grinned. "God protect us from teenage girls with style."

As they rode the only sounds were the soft clop of the horses' hooves and the carping of crows in the scrub oaks. The sun was warm on the back of Lana's neck. After some time she asked the question that had been on her mind since New Year's Day and in the back of her mind for years. Once she had asked it, she knew it was the reason for her visit.

"Why are you afraid of Dom?"

"What?"

"Don't act like you don't get it."

"What brings this up all of a sudden? I'm not afraid of him. What a strange thing to say."

"It's not strange at all. If you don't think people know you're afraid of him, you need to come out of the fog and look around. It's

obvious." Lana reined Graylight to a stop. "Help me to understand, Kay. Please."

"This is just you and Mars making up stories."

It was true—Lana and her sister did talk about Kathryn, but not
in the trivial way that "making up stories" implied.

"He loves me, for God's sake."

"I'm not saying he doesn't."

"He'd never hurt me."

"And I never said he would, Kay." Lana felt a stir of alarm. Why
was being hurt even relevant?

They rode on to the top of the hill. Beyond lay another valley,
higher and shallower than the one that cupped *Tres Palomas*. At the
far end a few cows grazed in the tall grass around a clump of cottonwoods, but otherwise the valley was as empty and peaceful as it
must have been when Spanish soldiers first rode up from Mexico.
The rain had brought up fresh grass, making the meadow before
them a wash of green and gold.

Kathryn and Lana dismounted and tightened their horses' girths.
Graylight turned one brown eye on Lana and watched her, as if
amazed that she had caught on to her trick. That was the thing about
horses, the reason Lana never felt quite safe on one: they could be
tricky.

She heard a sound and looked around her horse's head. Kathryn
was crying.

"Oh, honey," Lana said and wrapped her arms around her.
"What's this about? Tell me."

"You'll get mad at him. You don't understand—"

"Just tell me what's going on. I won't let on I know."

"But he'll be able to tell you know something."

"No, he won't. He's not psychic."

"You have to promise." Kathryn looked at her, blue eyes glassy.
"This is just between us. Forever."

Forever was a long time but Lana gave her word. But as Kathryn
spoke, Lana realized these were things she did not want to know;
they shocked and angered her and she had nowhere in her mind to
put them.

"I feel so trapped," Kathryn said. "I can't breathe and if I complain he says he'll show me what it's like to be trapped and he
takes my keys away, sometimes for a week or more." More than

once he had stranded her on the ranch with only the phone and knowing she was too proud to call anyone, even her sisters. "Sometimes it's just because he's mad at the world and taking it out on me, or the house isn't clean enough, or I'm not cooking the way he wants me to. Sometimes he says I need to settle my mind, spend more time alone. He says it's for my own good." Kathryn looked hopefully at Lana, her eyes like blue glass medallions. Bright cheeked, blond hair wisping out from under her helmet, she looked hardly older or more in charge of her life than the little girl made to sing and dance for Stella and her friends.

Dom declared periods of silence when he forbade Tinera, Nichole, and Colette to speak to their mother.

"But why?"

"I don't know. Sometimes it's the market. Work. He gets these moods. . . ."

Once, after Kathryn had made him angry—"I don't even know what I did"—he made her stand in front of her daughters while he listed her faults and told his little girls he would rather see them dead than grow up like their mother.

"I'll kill the son of a bitch." Fury vibrated through Lana like a harp string. "Kay, he's sick. You have to leave him. You can come to me. I have room for all of you. It's not safe here."

Kathryn seemed surprised by Lana's reaction. "He'd never hurt me, Lana."

"What do you think this shit is? He doesn't have to punch you out to hurt you. You've gotta book it, Kay. Now."

"It's not that easy."

"I didn't say it was easy. Did you hear me say easy?"

"I'm not sure the girls'd come with me. They're crazy about him and I don't know what all he's told them." Kathryn shook her head. "I can't risk losing my girls."

"Well, that's another thing. His relationship with Tinera is plain peculiar."

"I'd leave him in a heartbeat if he laid a hand on one of the girls."

"Call Michael. He'll get you a good lawyer." In her mind, Lana began to make a to-do list—call a lawyer, go to the bank—and gradually she felt calmer as if some kind of internal gravity had been restored. Wendy's husband was a corporate attorney connected throughout the city. He and Jack had been best friends years before Lana met either of them. He had helped arrange Micki's adoption, and she had called him whenever the weight of minutiae connected to Jack's death threatened to overwhelm her. "He's like part of the family, plus he's a very wise and kind man, Kathryn. He'll help you find the right lawyer."

Kathryn dug the pointed toe of her riding boot into the rocky soil.

"You're an abused wife."

"You're exaggerating. He'd never put a hand on me."

Was that pride in her voice? Was she proud of the bastard's restraint?

"Kathryn, haven't you been reading the papers and magazines the last twenty years? Go on line. There are hundreds of sites devoted to Dom's kind of abuse."

For some reason, Kathryn laughed.

"Talk to me, Kay."

"I knew you'd hate him. That's why I didn't want to tell you."

"I don't hate him." Jack always said hating was a waste of energy. He told the girls to save it for the real evil in the world. "I don't like him but I don't hate him. He's sick." It would almost be better if he did hit her. "This kind of abuse is sick, it's . . . demented."

Kathryn pressed her face into Jacaranda's neck.

"Come home with me," Lana said. "We'll wait for the girls and then—"

"He hasn't been bad the last few months."

"Well, gee whiz."

"He was so happy when I got pregnant again. I know if he had a son, he wouldn't be . . . like he is. He wants one so much it makes him . . . strange. He wasn't like this when we were first married, Lana. He says he had more hope back then. You know how hard he works, all the good things he does. He was a finalist for San Diego Man of the Year last year."

"I know all this."

"Well, he says he just doesn't know what the use of it is, building a business and making a good name, unless he can turn it over to a son."

"And so you let him bully you, because you feel sorry for him?"

"I know how it sounds to you, but it's not so simple. It's not easy, living with someone who gets depressed like I do. I can't always be there for him."

"What's that mean?"

Kathryn dipped her head away.

Lana thought she might throw up.

Graylight swung her head around and lipped the shoulder of Lana's denim shirt. She pushed her away.

"Let me get this straight. If you don't want to have sex, if you're depressed or PMSing or—God forbid, just not in the mood—he takes away your car keys."

"Don't be mad, Lana." Kathryn's high, sweet voice broke. "I love him. And he takes good care of me. The bad times, they're not so often. Out of fourteen years?"

Lana did not like whiners and victims who made no effort to get out of the trouble they were in. But this was Kathryn, for whom she had always felt a weight of responsibility.

"Just try to forget I told you. I never should have. It's this being cooped up, the rain, it makes me even crazier than usual." Her sister had finished talking. She swung herself up into the saddle.

"You know what I wonder about sometimes?" Her voice was airy now, as if they had been discussing nothing more significant than movies or recipes. "I wonder how far I could get on horseback, just riding East, I mean. It probably wouldn't be hard to reach Arizona. And I could hide out in the hills." She giggled. "I wouldn't like the camping part, but I could do it, I could force myself."

Lana looked hard at her. "What are you planning?"

"Don't you ever daydream about getting away somehow?"

In the last year and a half? Daily. Sometimes twice an hour.

"Stop daydreaming and get real." Lana mounted Graylight and gathered the reins. Her hands were slick with sweat. She felt like telling Kathryn to grow up and take responsibility for herself and the girls. But she couldn't. Mars would say to Kathryn, "Get a life—sue the fucker," which was one of the reasons Kathryn never called or confided in Mars. Lana's role was to be supportive and receptive and pass Kathryn's confidences on to their older sister so that in the end, among the three of them, they knew the same things. Lana thought there must be a psychological term for this kind of triangular communication and she was pretty sure it wasn't healthy. But how did a family change habits frozen in place for decades?

"Either come home with me or call Michael. I know you don't like to think about divorce but the truth is—you know this—not all families are meant to stay together. No matter how much—"

"I'm not leaving him. I can't. Not now."

"Why not?"

Kathryn bent down to stroke Jacaranda's neck, sat straighter, and shifted her seat in the saddle. "What do you think I mean?"

"You can't be. It's too soon."

"Not for the Fertility Queen of the Great Southwest."

"You miscarried—what? Three weeks ago? It's impossible."

"I always know. The next day. I've never been wrong."

Lana focused on the far horizon, the rolling hills and cattle, the crows screaming. When she breathed in, the cool air seemed to burn her nose. She tried to think of something honest and supportive to say, but her mind was a blank. She turned Graylight toward home and kicked her into a trot.

Kathryn came after her. "Don't be mad, Lana. If I try to divorce him, he'll punish me in ways you can't imagine. *I* can't imagine." They slowed to a walk. Kathryn reached across the space between the horses and touched Lana's arm. "In the end, I'd be worse off than if I stay."

"You can get protection. A restraining order . . ." A great weariness filled Lana, as if the bolts of her back had begun to rust. "You have to take care of yourself, Kathryn. Do it for the girls. He's poisoning them. Not just against you but against being women. If this goes on, can you imagine how they're going to grow up? What kind of prehistoric men—" Kathryn's eyes had glazed over. Lana's words were not registering. "When we get back to the house I'm going to write down Michael's number. I want you to keep it. In case. That way you'll have someone to call."

"He'll find it."

"Well, shit, Kathryn, hide it where he won't. Are you saying he goes through your things? He searches your closet?"

"No. No, I don't think he does that."

"If you have to hide it, stick it in the toe of a shoe you never wear." Lana paused. "Will you do it? You won't throw it away?"

"I don't need it. I know Michael. I know how to reach him."

Chapter Eight

Lana's nerves were bopping. She could not go home or even back to work, so she parked her car in the first mall she came to and walked the length of it. She wandered through Crate and Barrel, looking at the dishes and glassware but not really seeing them. At The Pottery Barn she sat on a tapestry-covered display couch and immediately jumped up. If she had not she would have lain down, tucked her legs under her, and curled in a fetal position. As she hurried from the store she was pretty sure the saleswomen were whispering about her.

Lana was eight years older than Kathryn, and the joke between the sisters was that Lana had changed Kathryn's diapers more often than Stella. And shoved her stroller miles along Sunset Cliffs. And met her after school to walk her home, helped her with homework—Kathryn had never been a whizbang student—taken her to the doctor and dentist, to her dancing and piano lessons. But there was no way she could help Kathryn out of the mess she was in with Dom. So why wouldn't her mind leave it alone?

Lana left the mall and drove into town. As she turned off the Martin Luther King freeway, she was distracted for a moment by the sight of the city cut against the sky and water as clear and clean as an image in a child's pop-up book. And right there in the foreground she read a sign: FIRENZI CONSTRUCTION, BUILDING A BETTER SAN DIEGO TODAY FOR A BETTER TOMORROW.

What was it the kids said when they meant vomit? Hurl. Lana wanted to hurl all over that sign.

* * *

The next day Stella called Lana to say she had a headache and would Lana drive out to Lakeside and pick up the rent from Dora at the Hollywood Cafe. Lana arranged to do it at a time when Mars could come along, too; on the ride out, she told her everything Kathryn had told her.

"Wow, I had no idea he was so creative."

Lana reached across the front seat of the 4-Runner and punched her sister's shoulder. "This is serious."

"No kidding." Mars did not speak for a mile or so as Lana maneuvered the car into the fast lane and they drove up past the college and into La Mesa. The moon roof was open and the sun felt warm as summertime on the top of her head. On the radio Holly Hoffman played jazz flute softly. Lana thought how the notes must fly out the moon roof and confuse the birds.

Mars said, "Did you tell her he's crazy?"

"Duh."

"And what did she say?"

"She loves him." Lana sighed. "He'll change when he has a son. Yadda-yadda-yadda."

"I don't think he'd hurt her, do you?" It was unusual to hear doubt in Mars's voice. "I mean, crazy as he is, I still think he's mad about her."

"Or just plain mad," Lana said.

"Jesus," Mars muttered. She took a pack of Marlboros out of her purse and played with the box, passing it from hand to hand.

"Smoke if you want," Lana said. "I don't blame you." She shoved in the car lighter.

"I'm trying to cut down. My house smells like a saloon."

"You know what I can't get out of my mind? The image of her standing there while he dissed her. To the girls. Her own daughters. Just standing there, taking it. I don't know who's crazier, him or Kathryn for taking it." The night before, Lana had lain for most of the night, eyes closed, blanket up to her chin, her mind playing out scenarios of rescue and revenge.

"It's up to Kay," Mars said. "She's a grownup."

"Well, I think we could debate that and anyway, you two have never been all that close. You're almost old enough to be her mother."

Mars was fourteen when Kathryn was born a few months after Stella married Stan Madison. It was 1966 and Mars was already three-quarters out of the house, protesting against the war, smoking pot, staying out all night. The rages among Mars and Stan and Stella made Kathryn cry and no one except Lana seemed to hear her. So many nights she had taken the baby into bed with her. It got to be a habit, one that made them both feel better.

Mars said, "She's like Ma—she's got lousy taste in men."

"Yeah, but I don't think any man ever treated Ma like Dom does Kathryn." Lana grinned at Mars and they managed to laugh. "I'd pay good money to see one try."

The Interstate curved down into the El Cajon valley crowded with shopping centers and strip malls and houses and trailer parks and miles and miles of asphalt for driving and parking. During Lana's childhood it had been greener and more open, a wide valley of fields and streams cupped by dramatic mountains—not high but rugged and in some places made impassable by boulders and scrub-filled canyons. In the distance the rock face of El Capitan shone like rose stone in the westering sun.

Lana turned off Interstate 8 onto 67 and checked her watch. Almost four. She had meant to leave town an hour earlier but this and that had come up and she had not wanted to leave the job. Carmino had the flu and though Moises tried his best, managing the big nursery alone taxed his skills. Thank goodness she would be driving against the traffic on the way home, but even so, she would be late. She had left a note for the girls telling them where she was and asking them to put a pork loin in the oven. But they might not read the note in which case they would have to eat pizza again or order out. The list Lana kept in her purse was four pages long now and she was so fixated on crossing things off it that she often forgot about basics like paying the bills and putting a roast in a timed oven. Maybe she would bring something home from the Hollywood. Dora's chicken-fried steak was wonderful, and there was nothing wrong with having chicken-fried steak for dinner once or twice in a lifetime.

The Hollywood Cafe was on Maine Avenue, a four-block strip of boarded-up storefronts, a hardware store and a tack shop, a derelict movie theater and assorted short-term businesses: a hair-and-nail salon, a shop selling secondhand paperbacks. There were a few people on the sidewalks. The men wore Levi's, boots, and cowboy hats; the women were broad in the hips and high in the hair.

Maine Avenue, Lakeside, had been a great place to grow up in the days when everyone knew Lana and Mars, everyone knew Stella, everyone knew the Hollywood Cafe.

But only Stella knew how she had come to own the cafe and the cottage next door. It was the house to which Mars had been taken as a newborn, the house where, for a time, Lana had a father. But how she got the money to buy it . . . Stella never would say and Mars and Lana had stopped asking.

Lana said, "Did I tell you I heard from my Dad?"

One hundred dollars and a note in a Christmas card written in a deep backhand that said about the same thing as all the others Norman Coates had sent over the decades since Lana had last seen him. "Buy yourself something pretty in the New Year, Sweetheart."

Sweetheart. Lana wondered if he had forgotten her name.

Norman Coates and Stella had been married just long enough for Lana to get his name and put away a few blurred memories of a man with a bandido moustache, a ponytail, and a big laugh that made people turn around and stare and Lana feel shy. She hid behind him, peering out around his long legs while she gripped his belt studded with silver and turquoise. Jack had called her a cowboy's daughter, and she supposed this was true.

The invariably ratty yearly envelope and the frequent changes of address she had noted over time made Lana believe her father's hundred dollars was a hardship for him, and she wished he would not send it. Her thank-you notes were as cryptic as his messages. "Thank you for your generous gift. I am well and happy." Things she did not say: my husband is dead and my family is falling apart.

Slight though their connection was, she did not want to let it go. For reasons she did not understand, she kept the cards in their envelopes in a manila envelope in the bottom of her dresser. The way Norman Coates moved around, he would not be easy to find. Not that she wanted to. What would they say to each other after hello?

"Why don't you surprise him this year?" Mars asked as Lana turned into the parking lot between the cottage and the Hollywood Cafe. "Call him up or write him a real letter. Hey, I'll take care of the girls. You can go see him."

Lana felt a fizz of impatience with her sister, the way she felt when she had drunk too much coffee and there were still a dozen chores left on her list.

"What are you afraid of?"

"What about you? Why don't you go find your father?"

Mars grinned and tossed her head and her auburn kinks and curls bounced. "Alas, C.B. DeMille went to his reward some years ago."

"Ask Mom."

"Why bother? I've asked her a thousand times and she won't budge. By now I'm used to not knowing. And anyway, it's not the same thing as having a living, breathing father in Colorado."

"If he wants to see me he can find me himself. He's the father."

"So what are you saying? It's like dancing and he's got to lead? That's a stupid reason to cut yourself off from your own flesh and blood. Shit, Lana, you might like him. He might be a great guy."

"And then again," Lana said, "he might be a drunk or an excon."

"Is that what scares you? He'll be someone *unsuitable?*"

"This isn't about fear." And why, Lana thought, are we sitting in the car arguing about this right now? "Let's go see Dora."

"No, wait a minute." Mars put her hand on Lana's arm. She felt the weight of her sister's big jewelry—a wide turquoise bracelet, several silver rings. "Sure, it's about fear. You don't want to find out who—or what—he is because then you'll be stuck with it."

"Since when did you get to be such a fucking fount of wisdom? And what brought this on anyway?"

Mars shrugged and looked out the window, across the dusty parking lot to the cottage they had once lived in. A rag-leafed sycamore stood in the front yard, up to its knees in a lawn that was more weed than grass. But the house and shutters and the trim around the edge of the roof were freshly painted white and barn-red.

Mars said, "I liked your dad."

"So I gather."

"Mom was better off with him than Stan."

"That's not saying much."

"Do you remember when he used to take us out to the Gold Bar Ranch?" Norman Coates had been the manager of a thoroughbred breeding farm on the way to Julian. "I used to sit on his lap and steer the feed truck."

"If you're so crazy about him, you go find him."

Mars had an uncharacteristically misty look in her eyes that made Lana slightly uneasy. She wanted Mars as she normally was:

quick and sharp and unromantic. "He and Ma could really fight. Not as bad as with Stan, not mean like that—"

"Nothing was as bad as that."

"But he got under her skin and I think he liked to do it. Once he brought an old porch swing home from the Gold Bar. Do you remember it?"

Lana did remember that swing with its torn awning. "It squeaked so loud you could hear it across the street."

"Ma ripped into him when he brought it home, said it looked like it came off some sharecropper's porch. All the joints or bearings or whatever had rusted and your dad kept saying he'd oil them, only he never did." Mars laughed. "I think he left it that way to get a rise out of Ma. One day she hired someone to haul it off."

Mars pushed her sunglasses up into her thick hair. "Ma was a tyrant, wasn't she? Remember how she used to make me dust those damn venetian blinds every day of the year, rain or shine?"

The powdery valley dust entered the house on their clothes and shoes and in their hair, came in under the door and through the mesh of the window screens and coated everything in the house with a dull, sticky patina. Lana remembered being very small, holding her father's hand, kicking up dust with the hard, brown toes of her Buster Browns.

"I can't go see him, Mars. Or write him. Not now." The words were out before she thought them through. "I can barely manage the family I've got. I don't need anyone else."

"Lanny, you're doing great. You love the girls, they love you."

"I'm beginning to think love isn't enough. There's something else I'm missing."

"The trouble with you is, you want a storybook family—you always have. You've got an idea of the way things should be and nothing less will satisfy."

Lana's eyes filled with tears. "I had perfection."

"Bullshit." Mars leaned across the gearbox and kissed her cheek. "It wasn't perfection. Jack was a great guy but he could be a pain in the ass like any man. You guys had fights. You didn't always agree. He drove you crazy sometimes. Remember?"

Barely.

"Don't get like Ma. She's turned Stan into a saint."

Lana wiped her eyes with the back of her hand. "But life was good, Mars. Maybe not perfect, but it was very good."

"It'll be good again, Sweet Pea. Give it time."

The interior of the Hollywood Cafe looked much as it always had. Six large booths still lined one wall; five smaller ones and a desk for the cash register were on the other side. Dark blue vinyl had replaced the cracked, old brown leatherette upholstery on the booths and the seats of the hubcap-sized stools at the counter dividing the dining room from the kitchen. In the middle of the room, at three Formica-topped metal tables pushed end to end, a high school-aged waitress in pedal pushers and tank top, with plates lined up along her arm, dealt out hamburgers and home fries to a noisy crowd. The cafe walls were lined, as they had always been, with movie posters and pictures of movie stars. Dora had added new faces over the years but Jeff Chandler and Pier Angeli, Jane Russell, Robert Taylor, and Gregory Peck and a couple of dozen other actors from the fifties were still up there, smiling down as they had when Lana thought they were all friends of her mother. Why else would they have signed their photos with love?

Lana and Mars sat in a booth next to the window with Dora, a big-boned blonde in her forties. She was upset when Lana told her that Stella did not want to renew her five-year lease.

"Is she selling?"

Lana laughed. "No way."

"If she thinks she can get someone else to pay her more, she better think twice. There's lots needs fixing—"

"Dora, she isn't looking for anyone else, I can promise you that. You're a great tenant. Just sign the year's lease for now. I'll fix it for the five. Trust me."

A few moments later, as they walked to the car, Mars said, "You don't know, do you?"

"Know what?"

"She *does* want to sell it."

Lana's heart dipped. "She can't. She needs the income."

"She thinks she's got it all figured out."

Lana slammed the car door and squealed the brakes as she turned out onto the street. Neither she nor Mars spoke until they were on the freeway again. The stop-and-start lights of the oncoming traffic were like the eyes of sea creatures swimming at her in the late afternoon twilight. It got chilly and Lana closed the moon roof.

"Where does she think she's going to move?"

Mars raised her eyebrows.

Lana hit her forehead with the heel of her hand. "Wait, don't tell me. The beach. Right? Somewhere with an ocean view."

An ocean view meant money and the good life.

"I won't let her do it," Lana said.

"Oh-ho-ho, listen to you."

"I mean it. It's the stupidest thing I've heard in the last twenty-four hours."

Mars started to speak and then stopped. "Suit yourself, little sister." She put her head back against the headrest and closed her eyes. "And when you finish taking care of Ma and Dora and Kathryn and Micki and Beth and the job you can come over to my place, okay? I'm not in such good shape myself."

Chapter Nine

Micki cut across the strip of grass between Arcadia School and the Unitarian Church parking lot, through a hedge of oleander and into the alley going west. Behind her she heard yelling from the soccer field where she was supposed to be. No problem. Ms. Calvello hardly ever took attendance.

It was already the middle of January and Micki was still ragging over New Year's Eve. She still had not heard from her Aunt Kathryn.

She stopped walking and put down her book bag so she could pull off the navy blue vee-necked sweater that was part of the Arcadia School winter uniform. January was being very weird this year. Rain and then no rain and now clear and cold and so dry and windy the inside of her nose felt plastered.

She blamed her mother for the New Year's mess. Maybe she should not have pushed Beth and maybe it was wrong to yell all that stuff about being adopted, but the whole thing would not have gotten started if her mother hadn't got so torqued about the guy in the Jag. Did she really think Micki was so totally lame-ass dumb she'd get in a car with a complete stranger? He was in the neighborhood so she assumed he had been visiting someone. And all he wanted was directions, how to get to Old Town. Everyone who'd lived in San Diego more than twenty minutes knew how easy it was to get lost in all the cul-de-sacs and canyons. What was she supposed to say, "Oh, no, I can't help you without my mommy watching over me?" Fuck. She'd been standing right in front of her very own house with her grandmother in the living room watching TV and her family and friends coming up the road any minute. So what was the big deal? He asked a question and she told him. BFD.

It was a weird coincidence that his car had been over by the school a couple of times, but coincidences happen—everyone knew that. Maybe he knew one of the teachers or someone at the Unitarian Church. There could be lots of explanations.

But no way was he a perv. Micki knew what a perv looked like. Tiff lived next door to a guy who kept tropical birds in cages, and his backyard looked like a jungle with palms and ferns taller than she was. It smelled like bird shit so bad Tiff's parents had to call Animal Control and complain. She and Tiff sneaked in once when the guy was at work, and the birds looked all forlorn and downcast. They squawked like crazy and Micki knew they were begging to be set free. Now she wished she had opened their cages. Wouldn't it be cool to look up in the sky and see a macaw sitting on the phone pole? The guy who kept birds wore polyester shorts with elastic at the sides and Hawaiian shirts made of slinky nylon and the way he looked at Micki, he was absolutely and without a doubt criminally creepy.

The stranger in the Jag wasn't like that. He was just ordinary except that he wore his sunglasses even at night. She didn't know what brand they were but they wrapped around and looked like they cost about five hundred dollars.

But maybe she was wrong. That's what her mother would say. He might be a very cunning serial killer or molester who knew how to look like an okay guy. One of the girls Micki ate lunch with had passed around an article about Colombian drug lords who kidnapped blond teenagers and used drugs to turn them into sex slaves. When Micki considered this, fear overcame her curiosity; she hoped the man in the Jaguar was gone for good.

Besides, she had enough to worry about already without adding him to the mix. Even if his car was radically to die for.

She liked walking the alleys. Though the houses in Mission Hills were expensive, the lanes between them were unpaved and smelled of the deep dust her shoes kicked up so that when she closed her ears to the noise of traffic on the cross and parallel streets, it was easy to imagine she lived in a Tom Sawyerish kind of town; she would come to the end of a lane and see a horse and buggy going up the street. She would like to have lived in the olden days. For sure life was easier back then. No car accidents. No school sororities or strange guys hanging around, maybe watching you. She was pretty sure families had been simpler back then, too, but she was not sure in what way. Maybe they were just happier.

Along the alley a few of the yards had chain link at the back but most had tall wood fences or walls of cement block. Even so, there was almost always a way to sneak a peek. She could tell a lot about people by their backyards. Some houses looked great from the street but were like the Mojave out back, rickety plastic furniture and sorry-looking dogs in cement runs, even in Mission Hills which was supposed to be so upscale. Others were plain on the front but green and gorgeous in the rear. A house near the corner of Hawk was nothing but vegetable garden out back, winter and summer; in front there was just Pepto Bismol-colored gravel from stoop to sidewalk. You couldn't tell anything about a family by looking at the front yard alone.

Front and back, the Porter house on Triesta Way looked really good, like a happy family lived there. It was painted pale yellow, and every spring an old guy who'd been painting houses for a hundred years gave the doors and trim a fresh coat of white. In spring clumps of daffodils and ranunculus shot up in the front and her mother planted dozens of giant snapdragons, bright yellow. When she was a little kid Micki had helped her; it had been fun then to know the names of plants, and speaking the Latin names made her feel important. The spring after her dad died there had been no flowers, but by summer her mother had put in daisies and zinnias and marigolds, like she wasn't going to waste a minute of good planting time. Strangers driving by sometimes slowed their cars to look at the house and garden; once Micki saw someone with Minnesota plates stop to take a photo.

If they only knew.

Micki stopped under a pepper tree and dug deep in her pack for her cigarettes. She lit one and sat down in a weedy patch of green and leaned against the pepper's rough, spicy-smelling trunk.

She didn't want to go home. She never wanted to go home anymore.

Her mother tried to behave as if everything was okay now, with a fake smile on her face and so many "good ideas" Micki thought she'd puke from hearing them. Beth, Miss Bouncy-Bouncy Perfect Daughter, was just as bad. Neither one of them fooled Micki, though. Maybe her mother wasn't hanging out in bed anymore but she was still miserable. And she was so busy pretending she wasn't, she barely even noticed there was something going on with Beth. She had secrets now and she never did before. She was telling lies, just little ones about where she'd been and who with, but for Beth to lie about anything was weird.

Lately Micki thought she was the only person who knew what was really going on, and she did not like being alone with the truth. Why couldn't they all just admit how much they missed him and halfway wished they'd died with him? Or maybe her mother and sister did not feel the loss of him as she did. Maybe they had recovered already. Was there something wrong with her because she was still sad a lot of the time?

Tiff's grandmother told Micki that when her husband died after they'd been married almost forty years, his spirit hung around reminding her to do things, telling her it was Tuesday and she had to put the garbage out or it was April, time to register the car, and kind of making a pest of himself until she plain told him to leave and he finally did and then she missed him. It sounded a lot like nagging to Micki; still, she knew if she heard her father telling her to turn off the TV and do her math, she'd get right up and do it.

When Micki wasn't thinking about her father or the man in the Jaguar, she thought about The Fives. Actually, when she was at school, The Fives were practically all she thought of.

Officially, sororities were banned at Arcadia School, but that didn't stop The Fives; it just made them more exclusive and enticing. On December first a list of seventeen girls being considered for bidding had appeared on the door of the art room. Of this number, only five would be asked to join. That was the way it was every year—five new members drawn from the tenth-grade class. Micki's name had been third from the top which she thought was a pretty good sign. Tiff's was way down at the bottom. Since then the list was all she and her friends talked about. It would be boring if it were not so important.

One day right after the list came out, Micki's mom had been driving her to piano and she asked her what would happen if Tiff weren't chosen.

"You two have been best friends since you started at Arcadia. Do you want to give her up for The Fives?"

"We'll still be tight." As Micki had said this, she knew it probably would not happen that way. Fives hung with Fives—that's the way it was. It was a miracle Tiff got on the candidates list. For one thing, she was about ten pounds overweight, and for another, she did not have great clothes. Plus she acted silly sometimes and Fives were always cool.

Her mother said, "I want you to be happy, honey. If The Fives are what you want, if you'll be happy—"

Happiness was not the point of being a Five. The point was insurance. Fives dressed best, dated the coolest guys, drove the hottest cars, held most of the school offices and mostly got good grades and went to the colleges that counted. When Micki became a Five she would step into this hallowed and cushioned world and then she could finally relax. Being a Five was like a guarantee that even if she was adopted and her father was dead and she didn't have a normal family anymore, there was nothing wrong with her; she was not a reject or a trash-can kid.

A dog on the other side of the fence began to bark. It snuffled and scratched about a foot from where Micki sat at the foot of the pepper tree. She stood up, brushed off the back of her skirt, kicked the fence, and walked on. At the next cross street she flicked her cigarette into the gutter and looked left. Two blocks away, Washington Street was a four-lane boulevard lined with shops and restaurants. Sometimes she walked home that way, stopping in some of the antique stores to poke around for treasures. She had found a tortoiseshell comb for her Aunt Mars last Christmas.

Micki's mom would never have worn that comb in a million years but it suited Aunt Mars. Her mother, Aunt Mars, and Aunt Kathryn each had different fathers but when they were all together Micki could tell they were related. Especially Mars and Kathryn, who didn't even look alike until you focused on their eyes—not the color, but the heavy eyelids like Gramma Stella. And they both walked like her, with their toes out like ballet dancers or penguins. Genetics. The word seemed almost magical to Micki. If she had a real sister, even a half sister, it would be someone she could look at and see bits and pieces of herself, only mixed up differently. But still familiar—like a gerbera daisy and a sunflower were different but the same, too.

People said she and Beth were alike because they were both blond and tall. Ha! The older they got, the more the differences showed. Beth was younger than Micki, but she could do everything better. Beth said The Fives were zero units. She said they could crawl to her on their hands and knees, like at the Feast of Guadalupe, and she'd laugh at them. She wasn't just talking smack. Beth really would do that.

At the Miranda Street Park, Micki stopped for another cigarette over in the far corner where the old gravestones had been relocated and away from any patrolling cops. Micki didn't wear a watch but she guessed it was not yet three. School was still in session and sometimes the cops got bored enough to hassle kids ditching class.

The Miranda Street Park had been built over a graveyard that was more than a hundred years old; instead of tossing the headstones, which probably would have freaked a lot of people, the city had them moved and arranged in lines close to the fence that overlooked the Washington Street canyon. When Micki was in grade school, she and Tiff had sneaked out of their bedrooms at night and dared each other to walk among the stones. They grew older, lost their fear, and invented biographies for the deceased lying beneath the acres of lawn. Micki's favorite was *Jenny Sanchez, aged seven.* Etched in the square granite stone with her name was the figure of an angel bearing flowers. Micki ached with sadness when she saw that angel and asked herself why a girl only seven years old had died.

Micki was not a big church person—none of her family was, but as she sat smoking on Jenny's headstone she said a prayer for the little girl anyway and wondered what it had been like for her family when she died. Did her mother have a bunch of other kids or was Jenny her only one, maybe the only girl? Perhaps Jenny was her miracle baby, the daughter she had stopped hoping for and when Jenny died—tuberculosis or maybe typhoid, they were common in the old days—her heart was broken and her husband spent all his time at work. She wondered if they ever talked about it or if they were like her family and tried to pretend they were doing great.

Death screwed everything up.

Micki's father wasn't buried anywhere because her mom said he would not like being in a cemetery. He got cremated; then her mom, without telling anyone, sneaked off to Garnet Peak in the Lagunas and dumped his ashes out into the desert. Micki thought about this and she hated her mother so much her jaw ached. If he had a stone like Jenny's she could sit by it and talk to him. There were so many things Micki wanted to say and now she couldn't.

Micki stepped away from Jenny's headstone and flicked her cigarette butt at a puddle around a sprinkler head. She left the park and crossed Washington and turned up University. School'd be out pretty soon. Tiff and the gang might be at Bella Luna buying frozen coffee drinks.

Half a block away, Micki stopped and stared at the iridescent blue-green convertible in the Bella Luna parking lot, right next to the entrance; a few steps closer and she saw the side of a guy's head wearing wraparound shades like a rock star incognito. Should she turn around, go home, or walk in like she had a right to? Bella Luna was always crowded so why should she be scared? It was a free country. Besides she couldn't see the face of the guy driving so maybe it was someone else. There had to be more than one blue-green Jag convertible in the world. Iridescent?

To enter Bella Luna she had to pass right in front of the car and when she did she knew it was him without actually looking. She felt his shaded eyes like two warm hands pressing against her shoulder blades. She tried to act like she hadn't noticed him. She pushed open the door to the coffee bar as if he were invisible.

Bella Luna smelled wonderfully of coffee, and Micki liked the way the tight little space was crowded with tiny chairs and tables and a few fat, old chairs and couches. There was always lots of conversation going on, but no one talked too loud; even the laughter sounded respectfully subdued in Bella Luna so the women with their laptops (they always took the cushy chairs) and the men reading the L.A. and *New York Times* were not disturbed. The barrista, a girl named Andy with a peroxide blond crew cut, five eyebrow rings, and a labret asked Micki what she wanted but Micki barely heard her. She felt a draft raise the gooseflesh on the back of her legs as the door opened. She knew it was him.

"What, again?" Andy had the too-cool-to-live coffee bar 'tude, but for once it didn't tick Micki off.

"A double vanilla latte," she said. "With whipped cream."

"No problem." Andy waited for Micki to find five dollars wadded up in a corner of her purse.

It was stupid to be so nervous about the Jaguar guy when she was perfectly safe in a place like Bella Luna where she came almost every day. Her order was announced and she moved over to find a lid that fit. For some reason none of them did; then there he was, standing right beside her. She could smell his lemony aftershave. She was surprised by how tall he was.

He handed her a plastic top.

"Thanks," she mumbled, keeping her eyes down. Her knees felt like scoops of ice cream melting.

His voice was low, like the surf on a dark day. "You want to sit outside?"

That's what she had meant to do, yes; but now she didn't know if she should. Did he mean he wanted to sit with her? If he did, then she knew she should say no, but what if he were just making conversation? If she said no, she would sound rude. Or flakey. She looked around, any direction but his, and like being rescued by the Marines at the last minute, there was her godmother, her mom's friend Wendy, coming through Bella Luna's back door wearing a pair of paint-speckled overalls and a white sailor cap pulled down over her red-orange hair.

"Hi, Toots." Wendy hugged her and for an instant Micki wanted to cry, but she didn't know why. "Shouldn't you be in school?" Wendy looked from Micki to Jaguar man. She stuck out her hand. "Hi. I'm Wendy."

With Wendy beside her, Micki took a chance and looked right at him as she had never had the nerve to do before, even when he asked directions. He wasn't so old, maybe in his thirties, but a very tall and buff thirty. He wore his hair cut super short and his narrow wraparound, black-tinted sunglasses were pearlescent blue and hid his eyes completely. He wore Levi's and a loose-fitting blue Polo sweater and expensive leather sandals. Micki stared at his toenails. They were perfectly trimmed as if he'd just had a pedicure and he had a gold ring on his big toe.

"Eddie," he said and smiled as he shook Wendy's hand, a sparkling white smile like a toothpaste ad. Micki wondered if maybe he was a model. "Looks like you've been painting."

Wendy explained that she did residential brush painting only, very fine and careful custom work. "Today I'm finishing the gingerbread on a restored Victorian."

"That must be very satisfying."

"It is."

Micki squirmed in the silence.

Wendy looked at Micki. "So why aren't you in school?" She

placed her palms on Micki's shoulders and fixed her with an un-nervingly steady gaze. Wendy's blue-green eyes were almost neon sometimes and Micki had to look away, down at her sneakers. Wendy turned her toward the exit. "Go straight home, okay?"

Like she was a preschooler who needed to be told.

Chapter Ten

At about the same time, Beth Porter sat in the Mission Hills branch of the San Diego Public Library occupying space for four people on one of the long reading tables. Outside the picture window that fronted on Washington Street she watched the skinny eucalyptus seedlings planted at intervals along the sidewalk whip back and forth in the wind like pom-poms. The library was overheated and had a fusty, bookish smell Beth liked, even the occasional whiffs of disinfectant that wafted over from the bathrooms every time someone went in or out. It was comfortable and familiar and friendly.

On the table Beth had constructed a protective reef of history books, notebooks, papers, and half a dozen library books to keep away even the most intrepid of the many peculiar fish who occupied the reading room on weekdays. She watched one of the regulars at the next table pat the top of his long, matted hair, comb his fingers through it, pat it again as he read and muttered to himself. Hatching conspiracy theories, Beth thought. She didn't want him anywhere near her.

The hubcap-sized black-and-white clock on the wall over the checkout desk said it was almost four-thirty. School had been out since three-thirty and still no sign of Kimmie, who had passed her a note during fourth period saying she and her boyfriend would pick her up at the library at four. Beth would not have waited around if she had somewhere to go besides home.

Kimmie's taste in guys was the worst. This dude was stick-skinny, had piercings in creepy places—not that Beth had seen them and she never wanted to, either. His upper arms were covered with cheapo, all-black tattoos of devil heads and knives piercing a heart, blood dripping. So gross. Beth did not even like Kimmie most of the time, but she was the only person she wanted to hang with these days.

Which was weird.

Being with the girls she had known for years, especially Madison and Linda, who had been her friends since sixth grade, reminded Beth of the way things were before her father died. And more than anything else, Beth wanted to forget those times and get on with life. It hurt too much to remember. And scared her, too. When it came on, it rocked her with a feeling so powerful and huge and inescapable, she knew it would destroy her like a tidal wave if she didn't protect herself.

She looked down at the notes she had taken for her winter history paper on World War One, all printed, all the letters close together and the words the same distance apart. *Dysentery. Rats. Gangrene.* The numbers of dead in that war numbed her brain, and she hated to read about the English officers who didn't seem to care if a million guys died fighting the Germans. The gory details made a macabre sense, though, and helped explain why so many bad things had happened in the twentieth century; it got off to a really shitty start.

Her great-grandfather on her father's side had died at the Somme. At home there was a picture of him standing in front of a tent, one of dozens of tents in the photo, and he looked like such a dork in his tin hat and stiff brown uniform buttoned up to his Adam's apple, not like a real soldier at all. Yet he had killed men. And been killed. She wondered how he felt, leaving his wife and kids and a farm to fight across the ocean. It seemed almost insulting to the millions of dead that Beth would try to encompass so much suffering in twenty pages, Courier twelve, double spaced.

She didn't want to think about dying and getting killed but for some reason she had chosen this topic and the paper was due in two days. In two days the formerly perfect Beth Porter was going to present a winter project that was just a list of words: *dysentery, rats, gangrene, tin hats.*

All the while she'd been thinking, her hand had been doodling. She stared at the design of boxes within boxes within boxes like a maze or a labyrinth. Cages inside cages.

Maybe she could write a poem. Teachers were always impressed when you took a big subject and compressed it into poetry. They all thought poetry was the world's highest art form. Beth felt a lift in her chest as if she had been tensed for an attack and at the last minute the all clear sounded. She began to write quickly, listing every word that entered her head connected to war. Words that rhymed she put side by side and gradually a poem began to take shape. She forgot to be pissed off at Kimmie. She saw that with a little effort this might be a good project after all. Were there other pictures of her great-grandfather? Didn't her mother have a cardboard box full of old pictures?

But she didn't want to go home because it wasn't really home anymore. What she had was a house and a sister and a mother.

The house on Triesta Way looked the same as it always had, maybe better since these days her mother hardly ever stopped working, writing things down, crossing them out, moving around like a human example of perpetual fucking motion. And she talked all the time, chattered like everything was just great. Beth hated that phony smile, that false laugh when she knew her mother was broken inside. Like she was. And Micki. They were all shell-shocked and maimed as if they had gone to fight the Hun. She wanted to scream at her mother to stop pretending they were the same as they used to be. But fear shut her mouth, which meant that in the end Beth was just as phony as her mother. But at least she knew it. And she was afraid to stop. The world of artificial smiles and busy-busy would melt away like an iceberg towed to the Anza Borrego and abandoned. The phony world would vanish and what remained would be worse than phoniness. The truth. A world absolutely, starkly without Jack Porter. And Beth would have to learn to live with it. She was afraid if she did that she would in time forget him and then it would be as if he had never lived at all. As if, like Micki, she had never had a real father in the first place.

He had died on a Tuesday, on his way home to pick Beth up for dinner at the Big Bad Cat. That's where they always went on their special night out. Her father said the place served comfort food. Beth did not know what he meant by that, why he needed comforting, but she liked the huge hamburgers and piles of fries, golden and crisp on the outside, pulpy and steaming inside. He always pretended to read the whole menu like all the choices tempted him, but he ordered the same thing every time: meatloaf and a pile of mashed potatoes with extra gravy. He used to say, "Your mom's a great woman, but she has her limitations, and meatloaf and gravy is one of them."

These days she hardly cooked anything.

When the drunk driver slammed into his truck, Beth had been in her bedroom. She was drying after her shower and her clothes for the evening were laid out on the bed: a pair of striped hip-hugger pedal pushers and a new tee shirt with big eyes embroidered all over it. No one remembered afterwards that he had been coming home to get her. No one remembered Tuesday was their special night.

Beth folded her arms on the table and laid her head down. She got him in her mind and then she couldn't get him out. Except when she was with Kimmie, who was what her Gramma Stella called "a piece of work." The things she said and did were totally distracting. Kimmie said that in modern families the father wasn't really necessary because women could take care of themselves. She always made big-deal statements like that but she never asked why or how something was true. Her own father was a Realtor and lived up in Orange County with his second wife in a monster-sized house with an indoor swimming pool. According to Kimmie he had been having an affair with a Philippine dentist, but as soon as he got divorced he dumped her and hooked up with a practically anorexic aerobic instructor. Kimmie said their baby looked like Mussolini.

Life was crazy. If she were Kimmie, with a living, breathing father, Beth would go up to Irvine and pound on his door. She would demand that he pay attention to her. She would not let him ignore or neglect her. How could Kimmie stand it, knowing he was up there and did not want her?

The big secret was that Kimmie's mother had moved to Los Angeles during Christmas break, leaving Kimmie and her sister, Jules, alone until the end of the school year. Mostly Kimmie had the condo in the Gaslamp District to herself because Jules was in college and kept all her stuff at her boyfriend's.

Kimmie's mother had taken the living room furniture except for a vinyl-covered beanbag chair, a futon, and a television as big as the wall. The walls were bare and smudgy-looking and in the kitchen there was just a stainless steel refrigerator that hardly ever had anything but ice in it—it seemed like the ice maker was always going—a microwave, and a stack of plastic-covered, throwaway plates. Kimmie's room had a big bed covered with stuffed animals that smelled like cigarette smoke, a dresser, and some of the vertical blinds on the windows overlooking the street were broken.

The condo was the kind of place her father would never even want to go. And there, where no sign or scent of him intruded, where there was only Kimmie chattering like false teeth about her boobs and sex and partying, only there Beth could forget about her father. But then, back home, when she realized she hadn't thought of him for three or four hours, then she panicked. She was almost fifteen and might live to be ninety. When she was an old lady with a walker and a hearing aid would she remember how his hair got long and curled over his shirt collar? How he laughed all the time? Would she forget what was special about Tuesday nights?

Beth tried to think of more war words. *Panic. Shatter. Smashed. Bloody. Battered. Battered brown battalions.*

"Wake up, Bozo." Kimmie stood across the table. She was petite and skinny with small, regular features and long, dark brown hair which she wore in an intentionally lank style because she said it was very uncool to let on you messed with your hair. Her constant obsession was her breasts and the augmentation surgery she was saving for. Her mother had told her if she came up with half the cash needed, she would pay the balance. Beth thought if she would just eat a few regular meals she might get breasts that way.

"Put your stuff away. Let's book."

Five-fifteen. Beth had fallen asleep.

"I can't now. It's too late."

Kimmie looked at the wall clock. "I'm only fifteen—"

"You said four."

"I did?" Kimmie shrugged. "Whoops."

Beth stood up and began to cram books and papers into her backpack.

"I gotta go home," she said, feeling cross.

"What's your problem?"

"Why didn't you come when you said?"

Kimmie lowered her eyes, affecting an insinuating smirk. "A girl's gotta do . . ."

"Whatever."

"So, can you get out tonight? I promise," Kimmie crossed her heart elaborately, "we won't be late. Eight o'clock? At the corner?"

Beth felt torn. The condo was virtually guaranteed to get her mind off her misery; if she was careful, her mom would never know. But she also might get stuck down there. Kimmie and Strider smoked dope and took pills and often disappeared into one of the empty bedrooms, leaving Beth alone with the television. If Kimmie and Strider got too high or started doing it she would have to get a bus home and buses at night were creepy.

"Strider's buddy wants to meet you," Kimmie said as they left the library. "He's cute."

"It's not me, I just have these family things."

"That's punk."

They stood on the sidewalk and the wind twisted and tugged at their hair.

Kimmie said, "I am just so thankful, like on a daily basis, that my folks know when to leave me alone. Your mother is such a drag."

Beth wanted to say she wasn't a drag at all. That Kimmie might know all about sex but she was totally feeble when it came to mothers. But she could not be bothered. She might as well explain something to the television.

Kimmie looked down the block and waved in the direction of a battered Mustang. "You could just come with us now, call your mom from the condo, tell her you have to study."

Maybe Kimmie's mother was some kind of moron and that's why her husband dumped her.

"I gotta do my report. On the war."

"Oh. Yeah." Kimmie clicked her tongue ring. "When's it due?"

For a fraction of a minute Beth had an urge to scream. The instant passed and she said nothing, walked off toward home.

"Eight o'clock?" Kimmie called.

"Yeah. I'll try."

Chapter Eleven

L ana could not face going home. After leaving the Hollywood
Cafe she dropped Mars off at her house and went back to the
job. She knew single mothers. A father and husband were not essential to make a family, so why did she feel so disconnected from
her daughters that she avoided going home?

Urban Greenery occupied a little over twenty-five acres edged
with pampas grass next to the I-5 and beside the railroad tracks
connecting San Diego and Los Angeles. In a few years there would
be a parallel trolley line; Jack had wanted glassy-eyed commuters
to be enticed to visit the nursery that looked less like a business
than a big garden where visitors were encouraged to wander and
browse as they wished. That's why he wanted to buy up the land
next door, go into hock to do it. If he had persisted Lana probably
would have given in eventually. The idea of a garden nursery in the
middle of the city was irresistible. Jack had set up a couple of picnic
tables beside a California pepper and almost every day a few employees from the warehouses and factory showrooms in the neighborhood ate their lunches there. Eventually almost everyone
bought something. Browsers who lived in apartments with eighteen-
inch balconies found a reason to buy a multicolor windsock made
of parachute silk or a bit of iron statuary—an angel, or a bird dip-
ping its head into a seashell. The idea, Lana told her eighteen full-
time employees, was to make visitors to Urban Greenery believe
that the same wonderful effects created there could be recreated at
home. And most of them could: beds of succulents, herbs and an-
nuals, stunning perennial displays that required only water, light,
and nourishment. The trick was getting people to remember to pro-

vide these things with regularity; for some reason, this was difficult and customers tended to come back again and again, often purchasing the same plant two or three times in the hope that this year their neglect would pay off. Without Jack, some days it seemed all Lana did was give customers advice and support.

From the beginning they had made a decision not to try to compete with the huge plant retailers in their area and carved a niche apart by cultivating many of their own seedlings. Their plant stock included all the basic petunias, impatiens, and ivy geraniums, but they also sold many specimens that were rare or hard to find. If they didn't sell, Lana took them home and put them in her own garden or carried a care package out to Kathryn at the ranch. Urban Greenery also sold quality tools and equipment, much of it crafted in England and Germany. Five years earlier, Jack suggested they expand into statuary and lawn furniture and Lana had doubted they would ever sell the expensive art, tables, and chairs. The wicker was beautiful, but the price! No little boys pissing through cast-concrete penises, no mass-produced statues of St. Francis. What a pleasant surprise it had been to discover that there was a market for expensive, hand-hammered copper mailboxes, zinc pots, and six-foot steel étagères. The higher the price, the faster the merchandise seemed to leave the showroom.

In seventeen years Urban Greenery had gone from being a funky little plant-and-pot shop to a sophisticated home-and-garden store. Lana's office was in the fishbowl, a cube-shaped kiosk at the center of things with one-way glass on all sides that allowed her to work at her desk while keeping an eye on the premises. Wendy had redecorated it for her after Jack's death. Now her desk and computer occupied half the room and the rest was filled with a comfortable, overstuffed couch and a chair with an immense ottoman, bookcases crammed with landscaping books, and a long worktable. On the strips of wall dividing the windows, Lana had hung framed reproductions of some of Kate Sessions's original designs for parks and gardens in San Diego. Gifts from Jack.

On her desk Lana kept a photo of Jack taken when they had just bought the nursery and were living in the cottage on the property. Ponytailed, he stands over a hibachi grill, grinning from behind granny glasses as he turns hamburgers. Outside the picture's lens, Wendy and Michael and a half-dozen other friends were sprawled on plastic lawn furniture passing a doobie and trying to remember all the words to some Bob Dylan song. Sometimes when Lana looked at the picture she barely believed it was real, that she had not dreamed it up. At other times it was all so real and close she wanted to reach into the picture and tug her sweet, young husband's long hair.

In the office she lost herself in the black-and-white mathematics of bookkeeping and ordering and inventory. She was even getting good at handling personnel problems, an area of the business she had stayed away from until a year ago. Moises needed time off for the dentist. The Saturday cashier felt devalued by the full-timers and wanted all the perks: medical insurance, dental, her very own IRA. In your dreams, Lana thought.

Lana was engrossed when Wendy appeared in the door of her office. She stood up and they embraced as they always did.

"You smell like paint."

"Don't worry, I'm dry." Wendy pulled a straight-backed chair up to Lana's desk and sighed dramatically as she sat down. "I'm almost finished with that Victorian over in North Park. Gray with pink-and-white gingerbread. It's beautiful, but I think I'll have to sleep in the Jacuzzi tonight."

"I'll drive by tomorrow, take a look." Lana told herself to relax. Wendy was her best friend and drop-in visits were nothing unusual.

"I saw Micki."

Lana's stomach tightened a notch.

"At Bella Luna." Wendy made an *I'm-sorry-to-tell-you-this* face. "Cutting school again."

"Shit." Lana tossed a pencil across the room. It hit the fishbowl glass and bounced back onto the couch. "I bet it was last period. She hates her phys ed teacher."

"Lana, she was talking to that guy. Actually, that's not right. He was talking to her."

Breathe.

"His name's Eddie."

Lana waited. "That's it? What good is 'Eddie'?"

She walked over to the couch and retrieved her pencil. Without thinking, she shoved it into the electric pencil sharpener so hard it broke in two. She threw it into the basket beside her desk and sat down again. "What's that mean? He was talking to her, she wasn't talking, what?"

Wendy cringed dramatically. "Don't kill the messenger, Lana."

"Just tell me what happened."

"Nothing happened." She raised her voice. "I just walked in the back way at Bella Luna and I saw her looking down at her feet and him saying something. That's all."

"How did you know it was him?"

"That is one gorgeous car."

"Fuck the car. Did you ask him why he's following a fifteen-year-old girl?" Lana heard her voice grow strident.

"He offered her a ride home."

"In front of you?"

Wendy nodded and leaned forward, her elbows resting on the paint-spattered knees of her overalls. Lana caught a whiff of turpentine.

"You know how intuitive I am. If he were a bad guy I'd have picked up something, but I honestly did not get bad vibes off him. He just seemed like an ordinary—"

"You have sons," Lana said, angry with Wendy for dismissing her worry so easily. "You don't know. Girls are vulnerable."

"Hey, I get that," Wendy said, angry back. "I'm a girl myself, in case you hadn't noticed."

"You should've told him to stop or we'd call the cops. You didn't even find out his last name. Eddie. What good is knowing his first name's Eddie? Plus he might be lying. What am I saying? Of course he was lying. Perverts don't go around telling people their real names." Lana made herself stop. She pressed her feet hard against the ground. "Should I call the police?"

"There's nothing to hang on him, Lana." Wendy was apologetic now, as if the limitations of the California Criminal Code were her fault. "There's no law says a man can't talk to a girl in a coffee bar. Even a fifteen-year-old."

"He was also at our house. On New Year's. Don't forget that."

"He was parked across the street. He could park there every night for a week and it wouldn't be against the law. I'm sorry I didn't find out more. I was just so stunned to see him right out in the open in Bella Luna talking to her. So blatant."

"Did you get his license number at least?"

Wendy opened her mouth and closed it.

"If we had that, Michael could talk to one of the guys he knows downtown. We could at least find out the guy's last name." Lana put her face in her hands.

Wendy touched her wrist. "I think all you can do is put the fear of God into Micki. It's the real world, Lana, and she's got to learn to watch her back."

"Oh. Great. Thank you so much for that advice."

Wendy's sons were in college, and it seemed she had already forgotten that two parallel universes existed: one for adults and another for teenagers. In the teen's real world the perimeters of behavior were fluid and relative. Rules hard and fast on one day might be less so the next, depending on variables, the subtleties of which could escape an adult altogether. It was not enough to forbid behavior once or twice; it had to be continually referred back to and elaborated on, adapted to conditions, and tested for weaknesses. And even then there was no guarantee. With teenagers, nothing but uncertainty was sure.

"I can read her the riot act but if he's going to walk right up to her in broad daylight, the only way I can guarantee—"

"Comes a point, you have to trust her, Lana. Mostly."

"And I do. Sort of. If it were Beth, no problem. But Micki—you know Micki."

They sat in silence for a few moments.

Wendy said, "I don't think a stranger in a hot car would be able to compete with The Fives."

"Ha!"

"They're taking their sweet time with the list, aren't they?"

"Tell me about it." Lana stared over Wendy's shoulder. Through the window she saw Feliz with the leaf blower. He turned it on and the angry-giant-wasp sound of the thing drilled through to her brain. She got up and closed the office door. "I can't seem to move forward, Wendy. I thought, before New Year's, that things were getting better but now everything's a crisis. I know what I should do about Micki—lecture her on kidnappers and sex slaves and chauffeur her around until this guy gets sick of . . . whatever it is he's doing. Call the cops and at least go on record so if something does happen . . ." She waved the thought away. "I can't even go there." She reached into a desk drawer and withdrew a bottle of aspirin, wrestled the top open and knocked two tablets onto her palm, considered a moment and added two more. She washed them down with a swallow from the water bottle on her desk. "If I tell you something, will you promise not to think I'm awful?"

The corners of Wendy's mouth turned up a little. "You're the worst person in the world—we both know that."

"There's part of me that would just like to pack a bag and take off. Never come back." She thought of Kathryn riding her horse as far as he could go, hiding out in a lonesome town somewhere beloved by cactus and ocotillo. Lana wanted to walk away from her daughters and Urban Greenery to a new town, take a new name, scrub her memory until it was as bland as a death mask. Her mother had operated the Hollywood Cafe. Lana could do something like that and do an even better job than Stella had. She heard herself saying all this aloud and stopped, too embarrassed to go on. "It's the wind. It always fucks with my head."

Wendy said, "What you need is sex."

Lana snorted.

"I mean it. You need to get taken out to dinner and movies and then home to bed."

"I can barely handle the life I've got without adding a man. Think of the complications."

"That's the whole point. It would get your mind off your family. You're perseverating."

"Uh-oh, fancy shrinky word."

"It means—"

"I know what it means." Lana ran her fingers up through her hair and tugged on it as if she had picked up Micki's habit. "You think I should forget about Micki and this Eddie person. Think about something else."

"I never said that. What kind of a friend would say that?"

"You said I should get my mind off my family."

"I never said that either. What I *do* think is that you should stop going over and over the same stuff, wearing a groove in your brain." Wendy bit her lower lip and Lana waited for whatever she would say next. "Lana, I don't think this guy is dangerous. I don't know what this Eddie wants with Mick but I don't think he's dangerous."

"So what do you suggest? I have sex and forget—"

"Stop being so rigid and just listen to me. Maybe you don't need sex, maybe no one needs it. . . ."

Lana grinned. "I wouldn't go that far."

"I'm so sorry I dropped the ball about the license plate. That was really dumb but—"

"I know what you're going to say, Wendy. I know I can't be with her every moment, protect her every time she takes a breath, but she's so vulnerable."

"Maybe not. Maybe she's smarter and tougher than you think."

Lana's widened and burned. "Yeah, but what if she's not?"

Chapter Twelve

"Wendy saw you at Bella Luna," Lana said, trying to sound merely conversational as she and Micki loaded the dishwasher after dinner that night. Beth had gone to study at the library. "Were you going to tell me about the guy? Eddie?"

"My god, what is this? A police state?" Judging from her outrage, nothing in Micki's life experience had prepared her for the perfidy of adults. "What did she do, just go rushing to you, couldn't wait?"

"As a matter of fact, yes," Lana said as she rinsed a plate and set it upright in the bottom of the dishwasher.

"This is so embarrassing." Micki threw herself into a chair and covered her face with a dishtowel. Groaning.

Good, she wants to talk. She would have left the room otherwise. Lana leaned back against the sink, her arms folded across her chest. Uncrossed them. Now if she could just keep from sounding confrontational. . . .

She tried the intellectual approach, Problem Solving IA. "What do you think he wants?"

"How should I know?"

Okay, try being friendly. "You must be curious."

"So?" Micki picked at the green polish on her nails, peeling it off in sheets. Lana wanted to shake her until her teeth rattled.

"Got any ideas?"

"Rape. Drugs."

"Oh." Lana swallowed and ground her teeth into a smile. "Are you interested?"

"Ma-a."

"Give me a sensible answer, Micki. What do you think he wants?"

"How the hell should I know?"

"Don't be rude."

"What do you expect when you—"

"I expect you to keep a civil tongue in your mouth." So much for being nonconfrontational. I sound like Stella. Somewhere—in one of the many parenting books she had resorted to for guidance during the last year—Lana had read: with teens, pick your battles. What the article left out was that it took inhuman self-control to do it.

"You must have some thoughts. You must wonder what he wants."

"Why do you have to make such a big deal out of it?" Micki expelled a sigh and a groan on the same breath. "I think he just . . . wants to talk, Ma. I don't think he's a sex maniac."

Lana poured soap in the dishwasher, closed it, and turned the knob. The water rushed in and she imagined what it would be like to be small and trapped inside, drowning, with all that scalding water churning and knocking her sideways. . . . She felt like she had just described her life.

Micki said, "You remember that man who used to live next to Tiff, had the birds and all like that? Well, he used to try to get Tiff and me to go in his backyard."

"You never told me that."

"Calm down, Ma. Jeez." Micki patted her hand on the air.

"You should have told me. Tiff's mom—"

"We never went."

"I would hope not."

"Ma-a, let me make my point, will you? This guy, the Jaguar guy, he's not like that. He's never even asked me to go for a ride. Or even to sit in the car."

This information, intended to reassure Lana, only made her more anxious. Whoever this Eddie was and whatever his motives, he was not stupid. She stood listening to the shush of water in the dishwasher.

She sat at the table beside Micki. "You know, even if this Eddie is harmless, if he keeps hanging around I'm going to have to call the police and tell them he's stalking you."

"That is so unfair!" Red-faced, Micki stood up and began to thrash around the kitchen, slamming drawers. Gala stood in the doorway watching her a moment and then slunk away to a safer part of the house. "I don't know why I ever tell you anything—"

Lana didn't know what to say.

"You could like, ruin his whole life," Micki went on.

"It doesn't have to happen, Mick."

"You just said—"

"If you ignore him, he'll go away and then I won't have to do anything at all."

Did Micki have a larger role to play in this than Lana had first imagined? Did Eddie see in Micki what Lana saw? The wild wire in her, the sparks of reckless fire in her eyes? And how conscious was Micki of this quality in herself? Lana tried to remember when she had first become aware of her sexual power and all she recalled for sure was that she had been older than fifteen. But Micki was a television child, a movie kid. Had she learned from media what her body did not yet understand?

"I know all this strikes you as paranoid, but I'm doing what a mother has to do, Micki. It's my job." *And I'm not very good at it. I never had to be, before.* "Ignore him and the problem will go away."

"Are you saying this is my fault? You are so—you just don't get it."

Micki tugged hard on her hair. Lana's skull hurt.

"He's not old, you know. He's only like thirty or something."

"There are a lot of thirty-year-old men in prison for messing with underaged girls."

Micki drew a snarl of breath.

"I will ground you unless you promise not to talk to him."

"You don't even believe in grounding. You told me—"

"There are times."

Her cheeks flamed. "You are such a bitch."

"Don't speak to me—"

"Just because you're my mother, not even my real mother, you think you can make all these rules and I have to follow them like some kind of slave or something."

Not even my real mother. This was the big gun, the cruise missile, nuclear warhead. No, a kind of germ warfare that hit Lana's bloodstream, went straight to her heart and broke it. There was something about those nine months, the physical carrying of a life, that held sacred magic for an adopted child and elevated and sanctified even the most neglectful mother. Here she was, Lana Porter, who had done all the schlepping and cleaning up and worrying and yet she would always feel second-best to some hot pants, irresponsible fifteen-year-old.

Well, shit, maybe she was. That unknown teenager might have known how to handle this situation better than she. There were gentle ways to manage difficult conversations—Lana just didn't know any of them. She was like Godzilla crushing whole city blocks beneath her feet. Having started that way, she might as well flatten the whole damn town.

"Right now, Micki, I'm the only mother you've got and I'm telling you that if you don't do as I say, I will personally lock you in your bedroom and keep you there for as long as it takes."

Micki opened her mouth.

"No more talking."

Micki stared at her, no doubt thinking up a killer riposte. Then she shrugged, rolled her eyes, and walked out of the kitchen. "Whatever."

Lana looked down at her hands on the oak table. Trembling, of course. She wanted to thrash Micki, lock her in a convent cell, feed her bread and water until she swore to be agreeable.

What had ever made Lana think she would be good at mother-hood? And where the hell was Jack when she needed him?

That night the wind shifted and clouds rolled in off the ocean. Near dawn a veil of misty rain began to fall, and Lana awoke early with the weight of the long, gray day pressing down on her. She dragged herself out of bed and stood in a hot shower for ten minutes until she felt half alive. At breakfast Beth did homework as if she had not been in the library until it closed at ten the night before, and Micki sulked with a lip that could trip a trailer.

It was bliss to leave the house and get to work.

Lana intended to call Stella from work and talk about the Hollywood Cafe, but business at Urban Greenery was surprisingly brisk for a gray, midweek day; during the slow periods she worked in the back, ignoring the misty rain, down on her knees in the damp soil of the herb garden, her choppy nerves calmed by the smell of the dirt and pungent plants. By closing time, when she thought about her mother again, she was too tired to call her.

On the way home, she detoured for stops at the market and the dry cleaners; a true rain was falling as she put the car in the garage. She turned off the engine and sat a moment, crossing off lines on her to-do list and adding a couple of new things. When she could postpone it no longer, she dashed through the downpour into the house.

"Where have you been?" Beth's strident voice and the sight of her corded neck set off alarm bells in Lana.

"I called the job and Carmino said you left hours ago. Why didn't you have your cell on? Ma, the list went up today."

Lana dropped the grocery bags and dry cleaning on the oak table. "She didn't make it?"

Beth shook her head.

Rage hit Lana so hard it seemed to have velocity. She jerked the kettle off the stove and stuck it under a blast of water. She was going to need coffee. And food. Something starchy and satisfying like a cheese sandwich. But wine first.

"Tell me everything." She put the heat on under the kettle and went into the pantry for a bottle of Merlot.

"Tiff was on the list, Ma."

Lana stopped and turned. She knew what she had heard, but she did not believe it.

"Tiffany Watson got a bid and Mick didn't?"

"Are you listening?" Beth's forehead shone with sweat. "That's what I said."

Lana pulled a chair away from the table and sank into it. She dragged the cork out of the Merlot and drank right out of the bottle.

"Ma-a!" cried Beth, appalled.

Beth handed her a glass and Lana absently filled it to the top.

"When I heard, I said she should meet me at the courts and we'd go right home," Beth said. "I knew she wouldn't want to hang around. But she didn't show up so I came home and she was already here. . . ." Beth held out her hands in a gesture of hopelessness. "Ma, she won't even talk to me."

"Why'd it happen? I thought she was a sure thing."

"I heard it was cuz of New Year's. How crazy she got."

Lana took a slug of wine. "God damn those Fives."

Beth's blue eyes were suddenly wary. "Are you okay?"

"No. I'm not. I'm so fucking mad I can hardly breathe."

"It's just a club, right? Isn't that what you always say? How come now—"

"I can't go up there." She was talking to herself. "Not yet." She could not let Micki see how much she, too, had counted on The Fives accepting her. The Fives would get her mind off the Jaguar man; The Fives would give Micki a sense of belonging and she would stop nagging about public school. Her life—all of their lives—had been so miserable for the last year. Didn't any of them get a break? Ever? "I'll make her some soup."

Lana was sure she'd been goofy with hope. How else could she explain counting on a handful of teenage girls doing the right thing? The most useless race of creatures known to history. She swallowed wine without tasting. Before she could talk to Micki she had to get beyond feeling as if she were falling headfirst into a bottomless, scalding darkness.

Beth said, "You're not going to get drunk, are you?"

"Oh, for God's sake, when have I—" She stopped herself when she saw the mote of panic in Beth's eyes. She touched her daughter's arm. "You're right, it's just a club and if this had happened to anyone but Micki . . . Just give me a few minutes."

Beth said, "Why'd she even want to be a Five anyhow?"

Lana drew a deep breath and her head spun. She had not had that much wine, but then again she had gone without lunch so what did she expect? She stood and put her arms around her solid and reliable daughter. For just a moment she let herself be supported by the tensile strength of her young body, already so much like Jack's—wide, straight shoulders, strong, muscular back. She stepped away and patted Beth's cheek.

"Thank you, Bethy."

"For what?"

"Being you."

Beth looked as if she were about to say something but changed her mind.

"Get me a tray, will you? The one with the roses on it."

Preparing soup and arranging a tray with crackers and a handful of Oreo cookies took about ten minutes. Beth sat at the table and watched Lana as if she expected disaster at any moment.

"Order a pizza while I'm upstairs," Lana said. "I think we need a big one with everything on it."

"Even anchovies?"

"You bet. One quarter anchovies."

"Ma-a."

"Actually, tell them I want double anchovies."

"That is so gross," Beth said as she picked up the phone and dialed the number of the pizzeria. She knew it by heart.

Lana carried the tray upstairs with Gala tagging behind. The patter of rain was hard on the roof and Lana felt trapped inside the house, inside her life like that small person she had imagined in the dishwasher. She did not want to have another fire-and-fury conversation with Micki. She wanted Jack to take the tray from her and say he'd handle things from now on. Instead, she passed through Micki's room and looked onto the balcony that ran along the back of the house. Micki sat on the weather-beaten, plastic-wicker loveseat, bundled in her duvet, the pink angora watch cap Lana had knitted pulled down over her ears and eyebrows. After a long cry, her mouth looked bruised and overripe. She was smoking. The ashtray on the glass-topped wicker table brimmed with ash and butts.

"Put that out and come inside. I've brought you some soup." A curtain of rain blew across the covered balcony, wetting Lana's ankles. "You'll catch pneumonia out here."

"I don't see why I can't smoke." Micki stared across the balcony. "My life is over anyway."

"I guarantee you'll recover."

"Why do you always say stuff like that? Like it's a joke?"

Because I don't know how to talk to you, because I love you so much my tongue gets tied in knots and I'm afraid if I tell you the truth—that this was cruel and unfair and you will hurt for as long as it takes—I'll only make things worse. "Trust me, you will recover, Micki. Now come and eat and let's talk a while."

"I'm not hungry."

"Force yourself."

"Or what? I'll die? Big fucking deal."

Lana reminded herself to choose her battles and that swearing was one of Micki's techniques for derailing a conversation. Lana took the half-smoked cigarette from her and ground it out in the ashtray, turning her head away from the stink.

"You are fifteen. Smoking is a crime if you're under eighteen." She held up her hand, palm out. "And don't tell me it's no BFD. The way you talk to your friends is your business, but when you're with me—"

"You cuss all the time. You and Mars and Wendy. And anyway, I don't have any friends."

"Honey, you have lots of friends. This thing with The Fives—"

"You just don't get it." Micki sprang off the loveseat, uncoiling like a snake. Reflexively, Lana stepped back. "You think this is some kind of cheese-ass girls' club like in Nancy Drew or something. But it isn't, Ma. This is my entire life in high school. Totally fucked."

"Micki," Lana warned.

"See? That's what I mean. This is the worst day of my life and all you can do is tell me not to swear."

"I didn't tell you not to swear. I just . . ." Lana took a breath and looked out through the rain at the backyard. It fell straight now, glistening in the balcony light like strands of tinsel on a tree. She pressed down on the balls of her feet and said in her mind the names of the flowers that would bloom in her garden in a few weeks. Pansies. Johnny-jump-ups. Reciting the innocent names calmed her. The Carolina jasmine on the alley wall was already a cloudy mass of bright yellow blossoms. She could not see it now, but it was there, as it had been every January for a dozen years, as it would be next year.

She touched her daughter's shoulder. When Micki didn't flinch or pull away, she drew her close.

Micki stiffened against her and then something seemed to break loose and she began to cry. Pressing her face into the curve of Lana's throat, she sobbed, first gently and then with wet, gagging pain, her slender frame convulsed in grief. Lana held her closer, as if by doing so she could break the barrier between them and they would understand each other.

Micki tugged away and, avoiding Lana's eyes, went into her bedroom and threw herself on the bed, folding her arms over her face.

"Talk to me." Lana laid the tray beside her and sat.

"About what?"

"The list, Micki. The list."

"We all thought it was going up on Friday." Micki sniffled and rubbed her nose against her bare forearm. "Tiff kept sending me notes saying she knew I'd get chosen and she wouldn't and would I still be her friend when I was a Five and she wasn't. She made me promise all this shit." Micki sat up, drew her knees to her chest and rested her chin on them. "And there were these, like, rumors going around about how this year they only chose three because there weren't enough good candidates or they weren't choosing any at all."

A jury of Lana's peers, mothers like herself, would never find her guilty if she strangled the breath out of every Five.

"Eat some." Lana handed her the cup and Micki sipped the chicken noodle soup reluctantly, as if it were a strange brew and not good old reliable Campbell's.

"And then Marybeth Cooper stuck her head in the door right when Miss Young was talking about Martin Luther King and she's all yelling, 'The list's up! The list's up!' And Sophie Winslow jumped right out of her seat and went and looked. . ." Micki sighed and said nothing for a time. "It was tacked up in the little kids' locker room. How dumb is that?"

Micki finished the soup and cookies. Lana carried the tray to the computer desk Jack had built for Micki's tenth birthday when she got her own PC and printer. He had spent hours in his garage workroom, the mosquito sound of the sander skimming the birch boards he'd chosen so carefully.

She set it down. "What about Tiff?"

"She jumped up and down like she'd won the lottery or something. It was so embarrassing. She's a Five. Big deal." Micki pressed the heels of her hands against her eyes. "I don't want to talk, I just want to die. I can't go back to that school again." She grabbed Lana's wrist. "I'm not kidding, Ma. I can't do it. I'd be like totally mortified."

Lana certainly knew what it was like to want to pack up her life and move it somewhere new and anonymous.

"Can I go to Balboa?"

"We'll talk about it later, Mick. Now's not the time."

"You always say that."

Lana stood up and closed the balcony door. "What you need is a long bath. With candles and smelly stuff and—" The suggestion was such a platitude, Lana couldn't even finish the sentence.

Micki dragged her comforter up from the foot of the bed and rolled herself into it. She looked, Lana thought, like a pink caterpillar.

"Micki, what can I do? Let me help you."

"You can't do anything. My life is over." The sound of soft sniffles came from the silken carapace. "Just leave me alone—I don't want to talk anymore."

In her deepest heart Micki believed that her life was done up for good. Lana longed for permission to say that all this would pass, that eventually Micki would look back and realize how little The Fives mattered. She wanted to tell her that what she felt was a pain like any other, cousin to the pain of losing Jack. Micki had survived that. Just a day ago she had been laughing and lip-synching with MTV. It would take time, maybe a long time, but she would feel happy again. She would laugh as if The Fives never existed. The pain felt urgent and permanent because that was the only way it made sense. When the pain was no longer fresh, she would point out to Micki how time heals all wounds. And wounds all heels, as Jack had been fond of saying. Glory be, if there was a God, one day The Fives would get a taste of what they had coming. Later she and Micki would talk about all this.

They really would.

Lana stood at the foot of the stairs holding the tray and staring down at the whorls in the hardwood floor, trying to think why she and the girls had never really grieved together. Had they wanted to, her girls? Had she shut them out rather than let their pain be added to her own?

She remembered driving up to Garnet Peak with Jack's ashes in an urn on the passenger seat beside her. She did not want the girls with her. Casting Jack away, giving him to the wind and sun and sky, had hurt too much to share with anyone.

In the kitchen Lana watched the water run from the faucet across her hands and into the ceramic soup cup and down the drain. She did not want to hear The Fives mentioned again in her house. Ever.

Over the water sounds of the tap and dishwasher and the rain against the kitchen windows, from the kids' living room came the sound of television, a sitcom; there was no missing that canned laughter. When the doorbell rang a few minutes later and she took the huge pizza box from the delivery man's red insulated carrier, the smell of cheese and sausage and double anchovies gagged her and she knew she would eat nothing that night, no matter how much she craved the comfort of cheese and bread.

She heard Beth's laugh mixed with the laugh track.

"Shall I make a salad?" she asked, standing in the archway into the kids' living room where Beth lay on the floor doing leg lifts and watching a Seinfeld rerun. "We don't need a salad, do we?"

"Whatever."

"Come into the kitchen."

"Can't I eat in here? *Mistique*'ll be on in a minute."

In the old days the family almost always ate the evening meal in the dining room with the table set just so. Dinner in the kitchen was a rarity. Now she let the girls eat anywhere in the house.

"At least come in and get your plate," Lana said, walking toward the back of the house.

I'm not your damn servant.

She put two huge slices of pizza on a blue ceramic plate for Beth and poured her a glass of milk, but she nibbled her own right out of the box with another glass of wine and left most of it sitting in its own oil. Later she ground the leftovers in the garbage disposal, then dropped a lemon in to take away the smell. Beth went up to bed at ten and Lana followed soon after.

She went along the hall and knocked on Micki's door. When there was no answer, she opened it. The room was empty but the balcony door stood open.

Lana sniffed. At least she wasn't smoking.

"Time for bed, honey." She removed a folded sheet of lined school paper from Micki's pillow and placed it on the bedside table weighted down with a pencil tin. She gave the blue duvet a shake and let it fall to rest, hillocks and valleys of softness. "You don't have to go to school tomorrow. We'll see if there's a good movie playing somewhere. I'll ditch, too."

Lana waited for a response. There was none. She walked to the balcony door.

The chair was as it had been—the ashtray, too. The watch cap sat beside it on the little metal table. But Micki was gone.

Chapter Thirteen

Lana stared at the sheet of folded paper on Micki's bedside table and considered her options. Close the door and pretend... what? How far back did she have to go to reach what she remembered as the normal time before notes left on beds? The time when they were the Perfect Porters and assumed they would go on that way forever. Way back would be better, back when the girls were small and she knew how to be a good mother and the only problems that didn't go away were getting enough sleep and having two little girls so close together.

She didn't know it, but she had been pregnant almost three months on the day they signed Micki's adoption papers. It was like having twins, and she could not wait for them to be old enough to take care of themselves so she could have some adult time. She had longed to spend more time at the job but at the same time enjoyed caring for the girls. How simple it had been to teach them how to cross the street and to use a knife by practicing with plastic. Even toilet training had been a breeze. I've got motherhood nailed, she thought once.

Forgive me, she thought, addressing the universe. For pride and stupidity. For not appreciating what she had. For being good with babies and shitty with big girls. Don't let Micki pay the price. Better solid, bounce-back Beth, who could handle anything.

With shaking hands she lifted the sheet of notebook paper from where she had put it under the pencil tin, opened it, and read the words scrawled in red marker pen in Micki's jerky, backhanded script. *Don't blame me, Ma. I can't help it. I know I'm awful.* Lana stood still beside the bed.

I can't help it.

Help what? What was she planning?

I know I'm awful.

Had all Lana and Jack's praise and encouragement been for nothing? This couldn't be happening, not to Micki Porter, not to *her* Micki.

Lana didn't want to think about exactly what it was that could not be happening. She flung open the door to Micki's walk-in closet, saw the usual mess of Levi's and tee shirts and underwear, more clothes on the floor than hanging up, and swallowed back a bubble of irritation. In such a mess it was impossible to tell if she had taken anything with her when she left. Where was her back-pack? She ran downstairs to see if it was still hanging on the hook by the door. Gone.

That meant she put something in it. Back upstairs, Lana searched for the Lucite piggy bank Micki had been filling with quarters for the last year. Also gone.

She had taken her backpack and her piggy bank.

I can't help it.

Can't help what? Lana went through the girls' shared bathroom into Beth's room. The sound of Beth's steady breathing filled the silent room like the regular in and out of waves on a cobbled shore. Wherever Micki had gone she had not wakened her sister to tell her. Lana was sure of it. She closed the bathroom door carefully and walked across Micki's bedroom to the desk. On Micki's phone she pressed in Wendy's number. The answering machine clicked on. Lana clutched the handset, twisting her body from side to side. Finally the beep.

"Wendy. Are you there? Pick up if you are. Please. This is an emergency." She paused, praying for the sound of her friend's voice. "It's about Micki—"

"What about Micki?"

At the sound of Michael's voice, Lana began to cry.

The friendship between Jack Porter and Michael Cooper went back to high school years. Following Jack's stint with the Air Force, they lived in the same apartment complex in San Diego, dated in the same crowd, surfed and played pick-up basketball together. Michael said on the day Jack died, "Whatever you need, Lana, just ask."

And she was asking now.

Twenty minutes later, Michael and Wendy were sitting at the table in Lana's kitchen. Wendy's scrubbed face, clear of makeup, looked tight with worry around the eyes. Michael's hair was wet from the rain and she noticed that he was not wearing his watch.

"You guys were in bed. I got you up."

"It doesn't matter," Wendy said.

Lana looked at the concern in their expressions and she could hardly speak for the gratitude that filled her. "I didn't know what else to do." She managed to explain what had happened, beginning with Micki's rejection by The Fives.

"Last week I would have said she'd be at Tiff's, but now that Tiff's a Five—"

Michael took a small notebook and silver pen from his pocket and jotted a few notes. "She has other friends, doesn't she?" He held the pen poised above the paper.

"After I talked to you I called the ones I know." And swallowed her pride and tried to hide her fear as she admitted to the girls' mothers or fathers that she did not know where Micki was at almost midnight.

"What about Kathryn or Mars?" Michael tapped the pen point on the paper. "Could she be with them or your mom?"

Lana wanted to cry that this was a waste of time; she had tried all of the obvious possibilities. Her mother had gone to LA for the weekend and Mars had said she was being melodramatic but if Lana needed her she would come. She even called Kathryn, though she knew that was the last place Micki would go. Tinera had answered and Lana told her she should be in bed.

"I'm waiting up for Dad. He's at a meeting."

"Have you seen Micki?"

"Here? At the house?"

"Did she call?"

"You're the only call tonight. Except Dad. He checks in."

"Let me speak to your mom."

"She's asleep."

And you're up, Lana thought. The little wife.

"Can I take a message, Aunt Lana?"

"Never mind, Tinera."

"You want Daddy to call you?"

Lana wanted that least of all.

Wendy told Michael about the man called Eddie in Bella Luna.

"Shit." Michael threw down his pen and sat back, rubbing the nape of his neck.

"You think she's with him now?" Lana asked. "Do you think they might have arranged this?"

"Of course not," Wendy said. "I told you, Lana, I don't think—"

"Damn it, Wendy, she's gone. I don't care about your intuition."

Michael said, "Ease up, Lana. Anger isn't going to help us here." He sounded impatient.

Lana felt the salt burn of tears at the back of her eyes. At the kitchen sink she ran cold water and splashed it on her face. Looking down, the stainless steel sink reflected back a blurry vision of herself.

Michael stood behind her, his hands on her shoulders. "It's going to be okay, Lana. Micki's a good girl."

Those words: *Micki's a good girl. . . .*

"Damn Jack, damn him." She turned into Michael's arms and wept against his crisp, white shirt. She did not care if he thought less of her for crying and cursing Jack. "I want Beth," she cried, pushing him away, starting for the hall. "Beth should be here. I want my daughter."

"Let her sleep," Wendy put a restraining hand on Lana's arm. "There's nothing she can do."

The kettle whistled.

"Fix us some coffee," Wendy said.

Lana felt as if the hinges and bolts that held her together were vibrating and she might fly apart at any moment. Better to let Beth sleep, yes; Wendy was right. Lana did not want her daughter to see her so close to undone.

She put coffee cones over three cups, scooped French Roast into each, and added boiling water. Immediately the kitchen filled with the slightly skunky smell of the coffee; gradually the dailiness of coffee preparation, of opening up a package of ginger snaps and putting them on a plate, combined with Michael and Wendy's reassuring calm, eased Lana's anxiety enough so she could sit and listen as Michael spoke to her.

"There's no sense calling the police, Lana. Not at this point. I know that's what you want to do but believe it or not, it's not against the law for a kid to take off. Run away."

"Shouldn't the black-and-whites know to be looking for her?" Wendy asked. "How long does she have to be gone before—"

"If she's not home by tomorrow morning, I'll call a friend down-town. Someone'll come over and get her picture and—"

"But she'll be home by then, Lana. She's just gone somewhere to lick her wounds, and when she gets to feeling hungry—"

"She took money."

"—and grubby and wants a nice, hot bath and a soft bed, she'll come home."

Michael nodded. He had written almost nothing on his notepad. He had covered the page with dots and crosshatched lines.

"Do you want us to stay with you?" Wendy asked. She nodded toward the guest room off the kitchen. "I can make up the bed in there."

"No, you should go home. I'll be all right now." She needed to lie on the couch and close her eyes and wait out the dawn like a death watcher by a hospital bed.

As they prepared to go back into the rain, Michael said, "You call me if she's not home by noon tomorrow."

That was almost twelve hours away.

"Call me earlier," Wendy said, hugging her swiftly. "As soon as you wake up. You have something to help you sleep, don't you? I can go home and get something. You need to sleep, Lana. And it does no good to sit up, making yourself sick."

Michael held her at arm's length and spoke to her slowly and carefully, as if she were a child. "Wendy's right. You need the rest and she will be back. She's not the kind of kid who goes on the street. Believe me, Lana. She's not."

"But this guy, this Eddie . . ."

"She's got good sense. She's temperamental but she's not stu-pid."

Lana sagged in the middle. "That's what she says. She's not stu-pid."

"Well, there you are."

When she was alone again, Lana turned off the kitchen lights and those in the hall, and she went upstairs to make sure Beth was still safely asleep. She stood at the door of the bedroom, her hand on the knob, her mind full of a crazy fear that she would open the door and the bed would be empty. But when she looked in she saw Beth had turned on her side, her back to the light shining in from the hall. Her hair lay in a silken sheet across her pillow. Lana stepped softly to her bedside and leaned forward—careful not to touch the bed—and laid her hand on Beth's hair to assure herself that it was real.

In the grownups' living room Lana stretched out on the couch. She covered herself with the many-colored afghan she had spent one whole winter knitting from scraps and bits and closed her eyes and fell asleep suddenly and deeply for almost an hour. Rainwater rushing from the roof gutters woke her and she sat up, stiff and chilly. Micki was gone. The thought knocked her dizzy all over again. She needed fresh air. She walked slowly to the front door, unlocked it, and stepped out onto the porch.

The blue-green Jaguar convertible was parked across the street.

What happened next Lana would remember for the rest of her life. She screamed. Not a high-pitched cry of fear or surprise, but a roar that rose from her insides as if she were giving birth to a monster. Deep in its suburban slumber, the neighborhood's only response was the bark of a dog several houses away. Lana ran down the front steps. On the bottom step she tripped and fell forward on the path, dropped to her knees, and scraped her palms on the rough concrete. She ignored the sting and scrambled to her feet and ran across the wet street and slammed the bleeding heels of her hands against the window on the driver's side and her fists, too, and she kicked the door and she did not stop screaming.

A light went on in the Andersons'.

She screamed at the driver of the car. "Give her back, give her to me."

From his front porch, Jim Anderson called, "Lana, is that you?"

The man in the Jaguar's driver's seat, a young man, handsome in a faintly dissolute way, a young man with close-cropped hair and bruised circles of fatigue owling his eyes, a young man who stared at her hysterics without speaking, put his head on the steering wheel and wept.

Chapter Fourteen

"Can I help you out here, Lana?" Jim Anderson stood on the sidewalk by the Jaguar's taillight holding a tent of newspaper over his head. He wore his pajamas and dressing gown and the kind of slippers called scuffs.

She stared at her neighbor, her mind a sudden blank. And then, "Oh, Jim, no. Did I wake you?"

"I was just going upstairs. Is this man . . ."

The tear-streaked face of the man called Eddie shone in the glow of the streetlight. What the hell did he have to cry about?

"I'm okay, really I am."

"You're sure?"

"You're getting soaked, Jim. Please go inside. I'm fine out here."

He turned back to his house, growling over his shoulder, "You holler if you need me."

Lana looked at Eddie, pointed back at the house, and when he did not immediately open the car door, she gestured again and walked up the stairs to the front door without looking back, without wondering if she had lost her mind, inviting a weeping stranger into her house in the middle of the night. This particular stranger.

She heard the car door close—the warm, crisp click of an expensive car. His steps sloshed behind her. On the other side of the screen door, Gala watched with her auburn head atilt and her tail wagging. Anyone coming in the door with Lana had to be a friend, right? At the door Lana pointed to the stranger's feet. He unlaced his wet athletic shoes and left them beside hers on the porch.

Lana realized she had been holding her breath.

Inside she draped her wet coat and scarf over the coat rack by the front door and silently indicated he should do the same with his leather jacket. He followed her down the central hall to the kitchen with Gala tagging along, sniffing at his damp cuffs and stocking feet. Lana turned and said without looking at him directly, "Sit down." She pointed to a chair at the oak table. He sat and looked at her and she made herself look back.

She saw a man somewhere between twenty and forty with an unscarred, Marine Corps, All-American face. In the car he had looked vaguely threatening and used-up but this must have been the trick of shadows. In her kitchen he looked as young and harmless as one of Mars's adorable postdocs. Fear had addled her thinking. How else to understand bringing this man into the house and analyzing his appearance as if he were somebody's boyfriend?

Her hands trembled and she shoved them in the pockets of her jeans.

"Do you know where she is?" It surprised her that any sound came out from between her tightly clenched teeth. "I'll call the police if you don't answer me."

His eyes widened. "Michelle's missing?" He looked around the kitchen as if *missing* meant *hiding.*

"Micki. Her name is Micki."

"Oh." He nodded slowly, taking this in.

"No one calls her Michelle."

"I wasn't aware . . ."

"Are you telling me you don't know anything about this?"

"I don't even know what you're talking about."

Lana stared at him for a long moment. She heard the rain, a car on the street, and on another street the shrilling of a car alarm. She smelled lemon from the garbage disposal and kibble from Gala's dish, the old roses on the table in the hall, and Beth's Miss Dior powder clouding down from upstairs. She felt the grain of the hardwood as she pressed her soles hard against it. She read innocence in his wide open, blue-black eyes. She believed him. And she realized who he was and a new dread inched in around the edges of what she already felt.

She sat down opposite him. "She ran off. Before dinner."

It was almost two in the morning and still raining. Where was Micki at this hour, on such a night? Huddled in a doorway or asleep on one of those butt-breaking, contoured plastic chairs at the bus station? Eating a hamburger in an all-night Denny's? Fear for her daughter pressed against her ribcage and she told herself again: breathe, breathe.

Eddie said, "Dinnertime. That's not too long."

Fuck you. Who are you to have an opinion?

He smiled—to reassure her, she supposed—and Lana saw braces shining on the top row of teeth. Why hadn't Wendy told her? Had she been so distracted by meeting him at Bella Luna she failed to notice he had as much tin in his mouth as a fourteen-year-old?

"Why were you crying?" she asked.

He bit his thumbnail and rubbed the torn edge against his cheek. "When you came out the front yelling and started pounding on the door, I just lost it." Another metallic smile. "I don't know why, maybe relief? I've been wanting to talk to you for a long time, only I never had the nerve."

Lana let this sink in.

"Who are you?" The question was a formality.

He leaned forward and pulled an alligator skin wallet from the back pocket of his Levi's. He opened it and withdrew his driver's license. She read his name, Eddie French, and an address in Los Angeles.

"I didn't want it to happen this way," he said. "I thought I could do it gradually but after a while—"

She looked at him straight on, taking in the dark blue eyes, the high cheekbones and square chin. Even his mouth, with its slightly swollen lower lip, was tender like Micki's.

Lana put her elbows on the table and rested her face in her hands. She thought how a girl like Micki could get lost in many ways. There was the wandering-off kind of lost, the kidnapping kind, and the seduction. And this kind of lost: the real father, the true mother.

"What about her birth mother?" Might as well know the worst. "Where's she?"

He shrugged.

Well, thank God for something.

"We lost contact after the baby was born. Barbara moved to Texas with her family. For a while her friends told me things and then I moved away from Modesto, went to college." He took a square, white paper napkin off the lazy Susan in the center of the table. "I never stopped thinking about her, though. Micki."

He folded the napkin in half and half again, making it smaller and smaller. His fingers were long and thin with thick knuckles. Micki had the long fingers, too, but not the knuckles big as walnuts.

"I wanted to get married," he said. "I thought that was the right thing to do."

But they had never been in love. She was an easy girl, and he was a horny virgin boy scared he'd run out of luck if he stopped to put on a condom. When she told him she was pregnant he wasn't sure at first that he was the father but there was a blood test. His parents demanded it.

When Eddie French was seventeen he might have been scrawny and dorky, but he wasn't anymore. He had gone from geek to what Mars called a hunk. Micki's father was a hunk. Why did this seem so wrong to Lana?

"When the adoption went down, I just signed some papers. Didn't pay much attention. Except for some reason I did remember the name of the lawyer." He looked apologetic.

"And that's how you found her."

He leaned forward and, thinking he meant to touch her, Lana pushed her chair back. Confusion clouded his face for an instant. He sat back and when he spoke again his voice and manner were restrained, less boyish. "I never meant to cause trouble for you, believe me. I didn't even have any plan to meet her. But I was curious to see what she looked like. Then I saw myself in her." He looked down at the open palms of his hands and then up at Lana, his expression forlorn as a foggy day. "She ran away because of me?"

Lana surprised herself by laughing.

"Micki has quite a full life without you."

He flinched as if stung.

Lana laughed again and shook her head. She stood up. "What can I get you, Eddie? Coffee? Milk and cookies?" She sat down. If he wanted something he could get it for himself. She was acting crazy but under the circumstances, who could blame her?

"Why'd she run away?" he asked. "You must know."

"Must I?" She heard the mean, arch tone of her voice. "You have no idea what it means to be a parent. Certainly not of Micki. She's a

complicated girl and you've come along at a very bad time for her."
She told him about The Fives. "You should have had the lawyer
contact me. There are ways to do this, proper ways, not skulking
around—"

"I never meant to—"

"I don't care what you *meant* to do, it's what you did." She let
her voice rise. On the floor beside her cold, bare feet, Gala pricked
up her ears. "I'll bet you didn't give five minutes' thought to how
your sudden . . . appearance would affect her. Especially under the
circumstances."

"Circumstances. Yeah." He rubbed his knuckles as if the size of
them caused him pain. "See, that's what I was thinking. If her dad
was still alive, that'd be one thing. But since he isn't and I know she
must be hurting on account of it and now there's this Fives thing,
you say—"

"Stop, wait a minute." Lana waved her hand at him. "How did
you know about Jack? My husband?"

"Research." He shrugged. "On line."

As simple as that?

"I want to know her, Mrs. Porter."

He had never finished college. He went to work with a software
company that made video games. He was, he told her, blushing, a
kind of computer genius. "I can't spell and I'm a slow reader, but
computers make sense to me."

With friends he had formed a video game company—Delphic—
and begun to create and sell games. "Ghost" was Delphic's first big
hit, a whole-world game of skill and strategy and carnage that had
taken off on all the college campuses. Even Lana had heard of it
and its television spinoff, *Mistique.* After that came several more
successes.

"But I sold my shares in Delphic a year ago."

"And now you're rich."

He laughed softly and looked embarrassed. "Jesus, yes."

Lana heard the refrigerator click on and purr. Gala stood and
went to her water dish for a noisy drink. Lana was conscious of the
rain coming now in squalls as the tail of the storm moved east.
Behind the house and across the alley a motorcycle started up,
revved, and squealed off.

Dawn.

Lana saw how it would be for Micki, the allure of Eddie French with his money and his glamour. She looked around her kitchen, the most comfortable and familiar room in her comfortable and familiar house, and thought that it would be forever after the room through which Eddie French first entered their lives. Not the room where she and Jack had once made love against the counter, not the room where the girls had learned to read.

"It's my fault she ran off," Lana said, surprised by her candor. "She wouldn't promise not to talk to you again and so I said she was grounded."

"That's all it took?"

"All? You think that's nothing?" Righteous anger. She held onto it and felt more confident. "A stranger stalks her—that's what you were doing, by the way, stalking a teenage girl." He held up his hands defensively. "A stranger stalks her and tries to entice her into his car—"

"I never did that." He planted his palms on the table and his chin jutted forward as Micki's did when she was indignant. "You make me sound like some kind of pedophile. That's crap. This thing just happened, like it grew, you know?"

He was a kid, that's what she knew. A kid who struck it rich building games, a horny kid who got lucky and made Micki. And it was easier to get mad than acknowledge the fear that lay deeper than her anger.

All this thinking and feeling—too much, it was too much. Lana wanted to be numb, grayed-out, bland flour-and-water. She walked to the sink and for a moment stood observing the dawn twilight fill her back garden. The rain had stopped and pools of water stood everywhere and water dripped from the eaves and sang down the rain-chain in shimmering dawn-lit drops.

Eddie French tapped a cigarette on the tabletop.

"You can't smoke in here."

"I wasn't going to."

"Look . . ." She sat again, leaning toward him with her hands on her knees. Looking at the garden had given her a little clarity. "There may be a time when you and Mick can get to know each other. I'm not ruling that out. And anyway, in three years she'll be eighteen and then it'll be up to her what she does. But not now. Now I'm in charge and it's the clearest thing in the world to me that you just don't know how to be a father. You stalk her, you frighten me. A father would know how wrong it was to do those things."

Lana stood. Up-down—she must look like a jackass to him, but so what.

"I want you to go home." Lana crossed the room to her cluttered kitchen desk, opened a drawer, and dug around in the mess until she found an Urban Greenery business card. "If you need to get in touch, don't call here. Use my e-mail. Legally, I have the right to keep you away from her and I will do it. I promise you, I will."

He took the card and she put a hand on his arm to urge him out of his chair. He was compliant, as if relieved that she was taking charge. On the porch they put on their shoes. She handed him his soft leather jacket and walked him across Triesta Way to his car and he got in. At its gate, the Tillmans' Newfoundland woofled amiably.

"Will you let me know she's all right?" He reached across the seat and opened the glove compartment. He found what he was looking for, another business card.

How very civilized we are.

"Mrs. Porter, I'm going to worry if I don't know." His expression—the brows lifted and knit at the same time—was so like Micki.

"But you're going to stay away."

"I said I would."

"All right then. I'll let you know when she comes home."

In her bedroom she lay under the duvet, still wearing her Levi's and sweater. She had slipped a CD of hypnotic Navajo-ish flute music into the disc player beside the bed and willed the music to take hold as she watched dawn fill the room and the gradual emergence of detail. Line by line, the family pictures on the wall gained definition, the ruby-red-and-turquoise-blue-beaded lampshade grew lustrous, and she made out the tiny figurines on a shelf above her dresser. The dancers were only a few inches tall but perfect in their particulars—forever on pointe, forever waiting for their curtain to rise, having no other function than to wait. Jack had brought them home from Hong Kong for his mother after the war and now they were Lana's. The light revealed more functional items. The rucked-up rectangle of Tibetan carpet, the wastebasket needing to be emptied, a little overstuffed chair where Lana had held both Beth and Micki when they were small and grumpy. She saw where it had worn at its base from the constant rubbing of her heels. Behind the side window's silhouette of an olive tree, the sky changed from apple-green to a creamy yellow full of curded clouds. She thought of buttermilk and how she'd never liked the slimy feel of it against the back of her throat.

Norman Coates drank buttermilk. She had forgotten that. Indeed, it was a fact she did not know she knew until that instant when she remembered him standing by an open refrigerator door, drinking from a carton. Micki's father was a rich computer wizard. What was Norman Coates and why did she resist finding out? Afraid, Mars would say, *had* said, any number of times. But what did she fear? That he was an ordinary man or a terrible man, a drunk or an ex-con? With a part of her mind, she knew that if all these things were true it would not change who she was. But another part knew that just by knowing him she would be forever changed. As knowing Eddie French would change Micki. She would not be Jack's little girl anymore. Nor even simply Lana's. A belt of fear tightened around her, and she brought her knees up against her chest and lay like a baby until the flute music did its stuff and she slept and awoke at just after eight to a quiet house. Beth might have overslept. More likely, she had left for school already. Lana knew that she must get up and make herself walk down the hall to Micki's room.

In the hall she heard Gala scratch her claws against the wall as she stretched. For her own reasons the dog spent the first half of the night at the foot of the stairs, moving to the upstairs hall near dawn to be near her carelings. Perhaps that was when the wolves came, at first light. Lana imagined her beautiful Gala, vigilant through the long darkness, and was knocked back by an unaccountable rush of grief for all of them, for everybody, for the vulnerability of all living things.

Micki's door was closed. Lana could not remember if she had closed it herself the night before. She turned the knob and stepped in.

Chapter Fifteen

Dressed in Levi's and a black hooded sweatshirt, feet bare, Micki stood at the balcony door looking out on the backyard. She turned around.

"Hi, Ma." She grinned sheepishly.

Relief, coming so fast on fear, paralyzed Lana.

Micki shrugged.

"Where were you?"

"Down at the job."

Lana put her hand on the doorjamb to steady herself. "The dogs—"

Three Dobermans—Buster, Boz, and Freya—worked nights behind the chain link fence surrounding the nursery, gardens, and shop.

"They like me," Micki said. "But I think there's something wrong with Buster. He barely got up the whole night."

"How did you get in?"

"I have a key."

Lana had forgotten that both girls did. She had also forgotten that some nights Jack went to the nursery when he could not sleep and came home at dawn with dirt under his nails and a happy report that while the world slept he had pulled a bushel of weeds from the native plant garden. Urban Greenery was the first place Jack would have looked for Micki.

She pressed her hands against her eyes to hold back tears of rage and relief and told herself she could collapse later if she had to. "Do you know what you've put me through?" Her voice quivered. "Not just me. I had to call everyone—"

Micki's eyes widened. "You called people? Who?"

"Your friends."

"You called Tiff? Omigod, I can't believe you'd do that." Micki shoved past Lana on the way to her closet. "She's a Five now and you called her? Now everyone in the world's gonna know. You have, like, totally humiliated me."

"I don't care if you are!" Lana grabbed her arm. "Damn it, Micki, you ran off! I did what any parent—"

"Not Dad." Crimson bloomed in Micki's cheeks. "Dad wouldn't."

"You left that note. You knew how I'd react." Micki had manipulated Lana's emotions, run them through a shredder. Reason vanished, and propelled by a black, bilious anger, she charged across the bedroom and slammed the door shut. "You're in big trouble, little girl, let me tell you. I don't know who you think you are that you can do whatever you want, think of no one but yourself, but what I *do* know is it's got to stop because I can't, I *won't* let you sling me around like a—"

"I hate you, you don't understand, you don't get it at all!" Micki uttered a stifled scream and fell back on her bed, arms stretched wide like a sacrificial object. "I can't go back there," she moaned. "It'll kill me. I'll feel like a freak."

"Give it up, Micki. You're not a freak, you know you're not. Stop telling yourself that story."

"It's not a story, and besides you're not my mother." Micki tugged on her magenta hair. "Like you really know!"

"Don't push me, Micki. I am very tired this morning and . . . just don't push your luck."

Had parenting always been this difficult? If it were, why would anyone do it? When Micki was a baby, Lana had looked forward to mother-daughter conversations, side by side on the bed, talking about life. What bullshit. She and Micki never talked, they argued. They vied for power, that's what Jack had said. Micki toe-to-toe with the little girl in Lana.

Micki sat up. "You think I'm exaggerating but you don't know the kind of shit they talk."

"Stop being a drama queen. The Fives aren't everyone."

"Everyone who counts." She fell back again.

"But why?" Lana cried, almost yelling. "Why do they count?" She crossed her arms over her chest to keep from exploding with exasperation. "Why do they count if they say terrible things about people? Why do they count if they're mean and shallow?"

Lana thought, I sound like I leapfrogged adolescence, avoided it altogether, like I don't remember what it was to be young and never pretty enough or talented or funny. Smart—that was the word that had defined her. Lana had been smarter than anyone else she knew except Mars.

"They're bitches."

Micki's eyes narrowed. "You think Tiff's a bitch?"

"Honey, I wasn't talking about her."

"Well, you better because she's one of them now." Micki sat up, grabbed a pillow, and hugged it against her stomach. "And Tiff doesn't want anything to do with me."

"But you've been friends for so long. I can't believe . . . It'll take more than The Fives to break you up." As Lana said the words, she knew they were dishonest. But the truth—Lana did not want to look at it, forget saying it aloud. "I think after a few weeks—"

"God, Ma, you are so out of it. Listen, from tenth grade on, there's like two groups of people, you know?" Micki jumped off the bed and moved around the room in jerks and starts, picking up knickknacks and putting them down, tugging at her hair. "There's The Fives and they're in everything and give all the cool parties and like that. Then there's everyone else and what they all want is to be . . . Fives. Only they aren't. They're second best. I don't want to be second best at that crappy school. I'd rather be at Balboa High with the tweakers."

Micki fell backwards onto the bed again and cried to the ceiling, "How come nothing ever goes right for me? I feel just like that kid who shot up his high school."

Lana said quickly, "That boy had no friends, his father was an idiot about guns, and his mother was—"

"They have an honors program at Balboa. It's a big deal, Ma." Pleading.

"Micki, I won't consider it. Your dad and I—"

"What the fuck does he care? He's dead."

Lana caught her breath.

Micki threw her pillow across the room. It banged against her desk chair, knocking it over. "I should just go kill myself."

Lana grabbed Micki's arms and pulled her up, her voice quivering with fear and fury. "I don't want to hear this kind of talk, Micki. About shooting people or killing yourself. You're not allowed to say that kind of stuff."

"If I killed myself all The Fives would come to my funeral and act like I was some kind of celebrity. Tiff'd be so happy, her mom'd finally let her buy a black dress."

"Stop it!" Lana shook her, felt her fingertips press hard into Micki's arm and her head wobble. If she had to, Lana would hurt her back to sanity.

Micki collapsed against her, sobbing. "I want to die. I wish I were dead."

Lana went limp with relief as she smelled cigarette smoke in her hair and she remembered Eddie French tapping the tobacco end of a Marlboro on the oak table. If she told Micki about him now, The Fives would instantly shrink to zero units. She could do it.

But the risk was huge, too great by far. There was only so much room for grownups in a teenage girl's life. To make room for Eddie, someone would be shouldered out. She felt a surge of loyalty to Jack. If the tables were reversed—if Jack, not she, were alive and if Barbara the birth mother waltzed out of nowhere—Lana knew he would protect her memory no matter what it took.

"Listen to me." She held Micki before her at arm's length, tried to meet her gaze, but Micki cut her eyes away. "I don't want to hear any more talk about killing or dying, do you understand? Look at me, Mick. Now.

"You're going to school today and it may feel like the hardest thing you've ever had to do, but you *can* do it. Because you have to. You've got more brains and class than any of those Fives and when you go back to school and hold your head up and show them you will not be humiliated—they can't humiliate you unless you let them do it, Micki—they're going to be sorry they didn't give you a bid. But if you just pick up your skirts and mouse off to Balboa, it's like telling them they're as important as they think they are." She bent her head to get a look in Micki's eyes, smudgy and still shimmering though she had stopped crying. "You don't want them to gloat, do you?"

Micki sighed and Lana hugged her again. "You're stronger than you know you are. And I have faith in you, Mick, more faith than you have in yourself."

Micki snuffled and leaned away from Lana to get a tissue from the box beside her bed. "I wish Daddy were alive. He'd know what to do."

Later in the morning, when she finally got to Urban Greenery, Lana found Carmino in her office perusing the ledger spread out across the worktable, an intent expression on his dark face.

"*Ola,*" she said without enthusiasm and tossed her bag and umbrella on the couch where the scrunched and tumbled pillows indicated Micki had spent the night. "So, we broke?"

Sarcasm and irony were not Carmino's humor. "Oh, no, no," he rushed to assure her. "Everything looks good. Real good." He gestured to the ledger in front of him. "You want to see?"

"I know what they say." She sank onto the couch and wrapped her arms around a fat cushion covered in nubby, gold-and-green tapestry fabric. "Micki slept down here last night."

"That explains why the coffee was made." He smiled uncertainly. "Like Jack, huh?"

Carmino was too gallant to say a beautiful teenage girl had no business sleeping on the office couch. He was one of nature's gentlemen in whom tact and discretion were qualities bestowed by grace. The work staff at Urban Greenery—most of them Mexicans who crossed the border every morning and rode the trolley from San Ysidro—respected him and when Lana recalled the year since Jack's accident, she knew Carmino was one of the reasons she had survived.

"Micki says there's something wrong with Buster."

Carmino thought a minute. "He was here when I started working. Gives him eight, nine years maybe. Getting old for a dog."

"I think I'd better take a look at him." She stood up. "Come with me. We can talk about where we're going to put all those new seedlings. Maybe we should buy out Toys R Us and extend the garden." Carmino's expression made her smile. "I'm teasing," she said and patted his arm.

The three Dobermans spent their days in a chain-linked kennel at the back of the native plant garden, in a generous space around a pepper tree and several ten-foot clumps of pampas grass, well away from customers. In the breezy morning full of shadow and light, as the last of the clouds passed overhead, the grasses were noisy with tiny finches and their white fronds moved like fans of ostrich feathers.

Two dogs—Freya and Boz—leapt up from their slumbers in the watery sunlight as Lana and Carmino approached. They were ugly dogs, oversized and deformed by inbreeding, with massive shoulders and blunted, bullish heads; the ears of each had been mutilated by kitchen-table crop-jobs done with scissors and knives. Their salvo of barks stopped when they heard voices they recognized. Still, they approached the fence cautiously, their ears half up, half down. Lana stuck her hand through the fence, knuckles first. Taking one whiff of her, the dogs whined and twisted, and Carmino opened the gate and he and Lana stepped into the kennel.

Jack had brought these dogs home from a Doberman rescue shelter north of Los Angeles. All three had been guard dogs at a factory somewhere in the barren wastes east of the I-5/210 interchange. The business went bust and the dogs went to the pound and had been on the death list when the rescue worker found them. They had been fierce and terrifying in those days; Jack had worked with them for weeks before giving them the nighttime run of the nursery. Over years the family had grown fond of the animals, and in a restrained way the affection was reciprocated. As little girls, Beth and Micki insisted on bundling up packets of kibble and biscuits for them every Christmas. Micki had designated Memorial Day their joint birthday.

Buster stayed inside the shed and did not come to greet Lana. She crouched in the doorway and called him out of the shadowy interior. He staggered to his feet and walked unsteadily to her, his head hanging inches from the ground. Sorrow swelled in Lana's throat as she rubbed his poor ears. She couldn't bear to think of the pain he must have suffered as a puppy, and a part of her wished for revenge against those who had abused him. An ear for an ear.

She looked up at Carmino. "Can you take him to the vet today?"

"Sure."

"Call ahead and talk to the receptionist. Her name's Tobyn. She knows us."

"What do you want me to do if he says he's sick?"

"Get him whatever he needs and then drop him by the house. Moises can manage here for a couple of hours." She stood up. "We're going to have to think about getting another dog. I'll call rescue in a day or two."

Carmino's swarthy Indian face looked sorrowful. "All this time, he's been doing good work. Protected the property good." As they walked back toward the shop, he asked, "You think they'll have to . . . you know, put him down?"

Maybe it was the accumulated worry of the last month. Maybe it was the pain of the last year and a half. But now the life and death of a dog she barely knew, a dog she regarded as an employee and not at all a pet, was important to Lana. It occurred to her that if in some way she had handled Jack's death badly, she might make up for it by being good to Buster.

Back in the office she called Wendy and Michael to tell them Micki had come home.

"So that's it?" Wendy said.

"No," Lana admitted, reluctant to go into details yet. "I'll tell you the rest but not now." Eddie French and Lana had talked about so much the night before; she needed time to rethink the conversation before she shared it with anyone. This was what she told herself.

She worked for a while and then ran errands, checked a half-dozen items off her list, then drove up into Mission Hills. She still hadn't called Stella about her intention to sell the Hollywood Cafe, but now a nap was all she could think of. Micki and Beth wouldn't be home for a couple of hours; if she got lucky, she might sleep for an hour or more. She parked the car in the driveway and was surprised to find the back door unlocked. She knew right then that whatever happened next, it would not be a nap.

Chapter Sixteen

"Micki?" Lana entered the kitchen and dropped her purse on the table. She walked down the hall and called up the stairs. "You home, Mick?"

"It's me."

She turned at the sound of Beth's voice. She stood in the arch between the two big front rooms.

"You're early. What happened to basketball practice?"

Beth walked across the hall into the second living room and dropped onto the couch. She pressed her mouth into an angry line and glared at Lana.

She wants me to ask what's the matter. She wants me to drag the latest teenage misery out of her. And I can't do it. I'm too fucking tired of teenage angst.

"I'm going upstairs—to take a nap. If I don't sleep, I'm going to pass out." Lana started up the stairs. "If you need to talk to me, you can do it later."

Beth followed her. "You shouldn't stay up all night if you don't like being tired."

Lana stopped on the stairs, resting her palm on the satiny oak banister. Sighing—she could sigh forever and the tightness in her chest, the lump halfway up her throat, would not budge—she sat. "Out with it."

Six steps down, there was no missing the anger on Beth's face as she pulled a hank of hair over her shoulder and began to braid it.

Both her daughters played and fiddled with their hair. Was there some significance in that?

"I heard you."

Lana didn't know what she was talking about.

"You know what I mean."

Beth grated on Lana's already raw nerves. "Sorry to disappoint, but I do not know." And whatever she wanted to say, Lana was not going to help her.

"That guy. Eddie French. Micki's father."

Suddenly, the part of Lana's mind where thoughts connected up logically stopped working, and she said the only thing that came to her. "Where's Micki?"

"Why are you always asking that? You've got more than one daughter, you know."

"Did you tell her?"

"No way."

"Well, that's something." Lana stood and climbed to the top of the stairs.

"But *you're* going to, right?"

"This isn't your business, Beth."

"She's my sister."

"Just let me handle it."

"Great." Beth spoke with ragged bitterness. "That's reassuring."

Lana turned and stared at her. When had Beth become insolent? "I'll decide when I decide."

"Shit."

Maybe Lana should just give up the fight against cursing. Everyone said these words now—*fuck* and *shit* and *pussy* and even *cunt* had begun to crop up in fairly polite conversation. And every night on network television couples made love, women took off their blouses, men put hands on them right there with the camera ogling. Was it worth the energy it took, all this no-saying? And did it accomplish anything?

She walked into her bedroom, closed the door behind her, and fell on the quilted bedspread, facedown. It smelled of washdays and sunshine, but she was not so easily comforted. Walking away in the middle of a confrontation wasn't good parenting, but what was she supposed to do when she didn't have a clue, not a clue, how to handle the situation? She thought of Jack with a rage that tied her up inside. He had abandoned her. He had left her with more than she could ever handle well. She turned enough to see the photo of him on the bedside table, framed in pewter. Jack stood beside the rustic entrance to their favorite little hotel in Baja. The print was black-and-white but she remembered the screaming bougainvillea colors, the hot purple against scarlet and orange. In any other context it would have been too garish but there it had been perfect.

With a swipe of her hand she knocked the picture off the table. It hit the carpet with a gentle thump and the back fell open. She picked the photo up off the carpet, stared at it for a moment, and then tore it in half. And then quarters, eighths, pieces so small she couldn't make them any smaller.

She hated Jack for not going home the usual way. Through Old Town and up the Juan Street Hill—that was the safe route. She would never forgive him for changing his pattern and leaving her to do a job that confounded her. And what the hell was a father anyway? She had never really had one herself so how was she to understand? In Micki's case, Jack hadn't even provided the sperm. That honor belonged to a game maker in wraparound shades. So what precisely had been Jack's function in the family, what had he provided that she and her girls found so particularly difficult to do without?

She heard the bedroom door open. Beth stood in the opening, her hands shoved into the pockets of her Levi's.

"Yes?" Lana said.

"Don't you think it's weird? That she's his daughter?" Definitely there was a goading note in Beth's voice.

"She's *my* daughter," Lana said calmly. "And Jack's."

"Yeah, but you know."

No, she did not know. And this was the problem. What did it mean that Eddie French had given her his genes? Did this biological fact mean they were spiritually connected or were people like plants and regardless of the stock, what they needed most was nourishing soil and water and sunlight? Had she and Jack been the soil and water and sunshine in Micki's life? And more to the point, could Lana now be those things by herself? This was what frightened her. That she wasn't sufficient. Jack had provided the secret ingredient without which the family was rotting at the roots.

"I can tell you what Daddy'd say." Beth, the All-wise, All-knowing, Valkyrie Teen Queen of Justice and Retribution. "He'd say you have to tell the truth."

Lana sat on the edge of the bed. "Well, Beth, your father's not here right now. But I am and you can just stop talking long enough to listen to me. We both know how Micki is. This is the kind of thing that could potentially—"

"Big deal, Eddie French is her father."

"Jack is her father. Same as you."

"Her blood father."

"Keep your voice down."

"Why? You act like this is something shameful. Or dangerous."

"You're right. It *is* dangerous."

"I think you're afraid of this guy," Beth said. "You never knew your own father. Mars doesn't even know who hers is. You're all weird on the subject." Beth spoke to Lana as if she were a feeble-minded toddler. "There's nothing wrong with him. I sat on the stairs and listened to you guys talk and he's a regular guy." A smile pinched the corner of her mouth. "She'll like him, too. Is that what scares you? He'll take her away?"

The words made the skin at Lana's jawline tingle. "It might happen."

"You're serious?" Beth laughed. "Get over it, Ma. There's no way Micki's gonna leave us. This is the only place she feels safe."

How could that be true when Lana felt threatened on every side?

"You think he was telling the truth," she said. "Well, suppose he was. But what did he leave out? Maybe he's a drug addict."

"You're only saying that because he designs video games and you think they're a waste of time." Beth slouched against the door-jamb, braiding her hair again. "If he wore a suit and tie you'd invite him to live with us."

"I'm going to have Michael run an information check on him."

"If you don't tell her, I will."

"This is for me to do. I forbid you."

"Forbid all you want, Ma." Beth turned away with a cocky toss of her head.

"I'll punish you. I'll ground you. I'll make you sorry." An idea flashed into Lana's mind. She stood up, her hands clenched into fists at her side. "I won't let you get your license. I won't sign for it."

Beth turned and gawked at her and then, unexpectedly, laughed. "That is so lame, Ma. We're talking Micki's birthright and you say I can't get my license?" Her mouth dropped open in an exaggerated show of disbelief. "I can't believe you said that."

"Believe it." Lana's jaw ached from clenching her teeth, but if she relaxed she would say all the thoughts pricking at the edge of her mind. *I hate being a mother. I don't want to be a mother. I wish you and Micki would both go away and leave me alone.* "I will do what I must and none of it is up to you."

Beth shrugged, feigning boredom now. "I'm going to Kimmie's."

"No."

"Why not?"

"I don't have to give you a reason."

"But it might be nice. It might be the honest thing to do."

"Honesty has nothing to do with it." Lana's body felt heavy and flaccid as if she had stayed a year in bed. "You're a growing girl, you have to eat something." It took a huge effort to stand and walk. "Come down to the kitchen."

"I made a quesadilla when I got home."

"That's not enough. Make some of that vegetable soup."

"I hate soup."

"Since when?"

"Ma-a."

"You're an athlete. You've got to eat to stay strong."

"Hah!"

In the kitchen Lana took a plastic container of homemade vegetable soup from the freezer. "You play soccer and basketball—"

"Yeah, well, not this year." Beth took the soup from her and put it into the microwave, setting the controls with impatient jabs of her index finger.

"You love basketball. You told me last year—"

"People change." Beth leaned against the counter and stared at the floor.

"What about your friends? Madison and Linda?"

"What about them?"

"Your best friends are on the team."

"Kimmie's not."

The microwave rang like an alarm and Beth removed the steaming soup. Lana caught a faint aroma of carrots and onions and beef broth but not enough to make her hungry. That was the problem with microwaved food—it lacked the sensory pleasures of a simmering pot. In truth, she didn't blame Beth for not wanting to eat it. Still, a growing girl needed nourishment. Like a plant. She handed her a spoon and dropped an ice cube into the soup to cool it down.

She watched Beth take a mouthful and thought of the thousand-and-one meals she had fixed for her family and that effort seemed like a thread, a continuity she could hang onto.

"I don't want you to quit sports, Beth." She buttered a piece of sourdough bread and laid it on a plate with a wedge of cheddar beside it. "You've been an athlete since you started playing soccer. Remember? You were four and the star of the team because you were the only kid who figured out the point of the game."

Beth looked pained. "Why do you always haul out that story, Ma?"

Because I knew you then and understood you.

"You're five-feet-ten. I thought you wanted to get a basketball scholarship."

Beth tipped the plastic container of soup forward so Lana could see that it was empty. "Can I go now?"

"No. Yes. Be home by ten. It's a school night."

"Whatever."

"How're the reflectors on your bike?"

"I put new ones on last week." Beth grinned her wide, impish smile full of fun; it surprised Lana like a gift she had given up hoping for. "See? You don't have to worry about me."

"Oh, baby," Lana laughed. "I'll worry about you until I'm in my grave and probably afterwards, too." She reached for Beth, wanting only to touch her cheek as she had a thousand times before, but Beth would have none of it. Ducking away, she leapt for the back door, calling, "*Hasta,*" over her shoulder.

When she was alone again, Lana went out onto the front porch and leaned against a pillar. Here and there at the western horizon, rain fell to the sea in fraying, silken floats; but overhead the sky was watery blue behind puffs of stormy gray clouds blowing east like a stampede of flying sheep.

She wished she could follow the clouds to a new life. She remembered thinking much the same thing on the night of the fireworks that didn't happen. Talk about a portent! No wonder she was having such a lousy 2000. She did not want to go away forever, just long enough to figure things out. She already knew she had to do more than mend and patch her family. Something at the core needed fixing. She and Beth and Micki had to learn how to be a family without a father. She knew that. But how? What would the new family look like, feel like?

All her life she had done what was required of her and this time would be no different. She patted the porch pillar with the flat of her hand as if to reassure the house on Triesta Way she would do whatever she had to. Once she figured out what that was.

Later in the afternoon Lana scrambled eggs for Micki, who hated school food and refused to carry a lunch from home. When she had money she ate off-campus with her friends; when she was broke she came home ravenous, her blood sugar somewhere below sea level. Now that she was on the outs with Tiff, Lana did not know what she did at lunchtime.

"How was it today? Did you talk to Tiff?"

Micki looked at her like she'd lost her mind.

"So what did you do?" Lana did not look up when she asked because with Micki she was more likely to get a straight answer if there was no eye contact. She slid the eggs from the frying pan to a blue plate.

"You said I had to go to school so I did it. I went."

"And?"

"It sucked the big one."

Micki opened her backpack and began flinging books onto the table. History of Europe since 1900, a tome to challenge a body builder; American literature since who knew when, another massive volume. Even at an expensive school like Arcadia, the lockers were too small to hold the number and weight of books the girls carried around with them, so they carted their education on their backs and grew up strong as weight lifters or bent as dowagers.

"What's your homework?" Lana buttered four slices of toast. "Want some ham?"

"I don't care."

Lana took a heel of ham out of the refrigerator, sliced two pieces, and warmed them in the microwave. She laid them on the plate beside the toast. For a moment she watched her daughter eat.

A car pulled into the driveway beside the house and a moment later a door slammed. What now, Lana thought with irritation and dread, and then saw Carmino at the back door with Buster. Gala came running and barking from somewhere in the front of the house and slid to a stop at the porch.

"Come on in," she said to Carmino. "Both of you."

Buster and Gala approached each other cautiously, circled, and sniffed. Gala cast a condemnatory look at Lana, dropped her red-feathered tail, and slunk out of the kitchen.

Carmino explained what the vet had said. It came down to old hips, old back, old age.

"He looked at his teeth, says he's got more'n ten years. That's a long life. For a Dobie."

Buster did not look happy, sitting on bony dog haunches, head low. Lana saw how gaunt he had become and remembered that when Jack brought him back from Doberman rescue, she had recoiled from the sight of his mangled bullet head. An ugly dog, she had said. A junkyard dog. But now, to her eyes, there was something poignantly sweet in his ugliness. She crouched at his level and called him to her. He let her rough his ears, more like a pit bull's than a Dobie's.

"He'll be fine here," she said, looking up at Carmino.

"Cool," Micki said with more enthusiasm than she'd shown in several days. "He can sleep in my room."

"Let's let him sleep where he wants. A bedroom might not seem right to him." Lana straightened up. "I'm going to have to go get some more food, a dish and all."

"I can do it," Carmino said.

"No, you go on back to work and check on Moises. He's good but he's not you."

In the car driving down the hill to Petco, Lana did an inventory of her motives. There was plenty of dog food in the house and spare pet dishes in the garage. She just wanted to get out of the house and avoid further conversation with Micki.

Outside Petco, she called Michael on her cell phone and told him about Eddie French. Before she could ask him to do it, Michael offered to run a check on him.

Then she called Wendy, who answered from a perch halfway up a housepainter's ladder.

"I'm just finishing the trim on the west side. Pink and gray and really pretty."

"You want to call me later?"

"Nope, this is perfect. I'm due a break."

It took fifteen minutes for Lana to tell Wendy the whole story of Eddie French.

"I'm glad you called Michael. You gotta know what you're deal-ing with here." Wendy's voice sounded brisk and confident.

"And you have to do the telling," Wendy said. "I don't trust Beth's motives."

"What do you mean?"

"Well, think about it, Lana. She's just lost her own father and now her adopted sister's got a new one and not only is he her fa-ther, he's also rich and hip."

"You mean you think she wants to hurt Micki?"

Wendy laughed. "Beth's not a saint—she's a good kid but not a saint."

"I never said she was. But she's not unkind, that I know for sure."

"Uh-huh," Wendy said.

Lana made a few purchases at Petco—food and a bowl and leash—then drove up the hill to Bella Luna for a cappuccino to go. As she waited for her order she looked around her at the coffee bar clientele, the young professionals bent over their laptops, the friends in conversation, the untidy girls and boys dressed in their signature black and charcoal gray. For every girl with combed hair and a touch of makeup, there was another slouch-shouldered and kohl-eyed. Lana thought of Beth giving up basketball because of her new friend Kimmie and realized she had never met the girl and that in an emergency she would have no way of reaching Beth. Beth and this girl were spending hours together every day and Lana had no idea who she was or where she lived. She put her purse down on the counter and dug out her list. She wrote *talk to Beth about Kimmie* at the bottom, crossed it out, and crammed the same words at the top between *call Ma re HC* and *check on Kay*.

Driving home, Lana thought about Wendy's words: *She's a good kid but not a saint*. Was she not seeing Beth as clearly as others did? Should she, on top of everything else, begin to worry about her, too?

Chapter Seventeen

Kimmie Taylor's bedroom was long and narrow with one set of windows and a sliding door leading to a perilously small balcony overlooking Sixth Street two blocks south of Broadway. The only furniture in the room was the queen-sized bed Beth had never seen made, a dusty exercise bike, and a chest of drawers. A huge poster of Johnny Depp hung over the bed.

Though still early, it was dark out; Beth heard the happy-hour racket issuing from bars and restaurants in the Gaslamp District. Kimmie sat on the floor in thong panties and a midriff tee shirt giving her toenails a third coat of blood-red polish. Her bony knees and elbows looked too large for her small body. Her skin had a blue-white transparency that, with her dyed black hair and gray eyes encircled with black liner, gave her a ghoulish look she admired in every window and mirror. From where Beth lay on the bed, she could smell her. An odor like stewed chicken.

"They'll be here any minute." Kimmie's boyfriend and someone called Damian. She blew on her toes. "This guy really wants to meet you—"

"Which I totally don't get."

"He saw you with me and he says you're hot."

Which meant what? That she was cool? At school Ms. Hoffman talked about using precise language. When she said *precise* she sounded like a snake and at lunch all the girls imitated her. But Beth liked it when words meant something.

"If you go, Strider'll be pissed off. He promised Damian you'd be here."

"I hate his name. Did you ever see that movie?"

"Remember the Rottweilers?" Kimmie asked. "They were so-o rad."

"Who'd name a kid after the child of Satan?"

"It's not his real name," Kimmie stood up and walked to her closet. Like the rest of the room, it was almost empty. Through Kimmie's eyes, Beth saw the clothes in her own closet, the rainbow colors, the boxes of shoes, and the hook on which her comfortable, old dressing gown hung. Kimmie would laugh at all this. She didn't own a dressing gown and her closet was a bat cave of black and gray. "He named himself. Like Strider. His real name is Robert."

"He chose that name? Of his own free will?"

Beth wished she were home reading a book, wearing her dressing gown. A gift from her father, it was tight across the shoulders and too short by several inches, but she would wear it until the seams burst because nothing else felt quite as snug. She grabbed a hank of hair and pulled hard, like Micki did, so she wouldn't think about her father. Instead she thought of Eddie French.

Maybe he and Micki would go off and live in his house in L.A. Her mother would fight it, of course; but he was rich and maybe Johnny Cochrane was his attorney. Micki would leave and Beth and her mom would be alone in the big, haunted house on Triesta Way.

Beth had not mentioned Eddie French to Kimmie. She wanted to talk about him but her thoughts felt intensely powerful and too dangerous for casual conversation. It was like being a government agent carrying a secret formula with the capacity to destroy the world.

Beth lay back on the bed and groaned.

"Stop worrying."

She sat up again. "I'm not worried."

"He'll be your first, right? You want it to be, like, perfect."

"My first what?"

Kimmie's look was meant to wither.

"Oh. That." Did Kimmie actually think she would have sex with a stranger in this apartment where the germ level was probably close to toxic? Hadn't she heard of HIV and all the other bugs buzzing around between people's legs? Kimmie was not stupid so why did she act like she was? Beth had figured out the answer to that one. She could see that life would be much simpler if she were able to turn off her brain the way Kimmie could.

"I've gotta be home by ten. I promised my mom."

"Jeez. She's like that Hitler guy."

Beth swallowed back a defense of her mother.

Kimmie stripped out of her thong and tossed it into the corner behind her open bedroom door where she put all her dirty clothes.

Beth looked away, embarrassed. In her house no one walked around naked. She looked back, pretending to look at her magazine. Kimmie had a thick triangle of dark brown wool between her legs. Nothing like Beth's sparse growth. She wondered if there was something wrong with Kimmie. Or with her. She had never seen an adult woman naked from the front, not even her mother, who was even too modest to walk around in her underwear. She had no idea what was normal and what excessive. Maybe blondes didn't have as much hair as brunettes. Just a few months ago she would have asked her mother to explain all this, but they did not have that kind of relationship anymore.

It was not all her mother's fault they had stopped talking. If Beth asked her a private question, a female question, she would be thrilled and probably give Beth more answer than she wanted. If she had been with Madison and Linda, they would have gone off on the idea of a book about pubes. Kimmie wouldn't get that it was funny. She did not have much sense of humor, and if it wasn't about her, conversation did not interest her. Kimmie was in love with herself like the guy in the myth who kept looking at his own reflection in the water. The spotlight and the microphone were always aimed at Kimmie, and for hours on end that was fine with Beth. It helped her forget her father and how much she did not want to be home now that he was gone. She used to love her house. She and Madison and Linda had spent about a thousand Saturday night sleepovers in her bedroom where everything was just so, the way she liked it. And shooting baskets in the driveway. That's where she perfected her hook. Now she could not wait to get away from home, and she hated her bedroom with its old-fashioned bed and the shelves crowded with mementos she was supposed to keep to remind her of family trips to Yosemite and San Francisco and the time her father took her to the circus and they sat in the front row and an elephant almost stepped on her toe. If she threw them all away, would she forget?

Kimmie pulled on tights without underwear and slipped her feet into sandals.

"I think I'd die if I had a mother like yours. She is such a nag."

Lana was not a nag, but why explain when Kimmie would not listen?

If she went home she knew exactly where she would find the book that had a picture of the guy looking at his reflection. And on the inside front cover she would read *To Beth from Santa* written in her father's big, looping scrawl. In the grownups' living room there was an easy chair with wide arms and a square footstool the size of a table, both covered in a soft, knobby, oatmeal-colored fabric. This had been her father's chair—her mom preferred the matching couch where she could stretch out full length. To sit in it with him, talking and reading, falling asleep—Beth thought she would give up years of her life to do that just one more time. Over a period of weeks they had read the myth book cover to cover, and her father had told her about Freud and Jung and how no one said or did anything without a reason, even if they didn't know it. That was one of the things she had loved about him. He never thought she was too young to learn.

Beth saw that it was going to be one of those nights when nothing, not even Strider and someone named after the son of Satan, could distract her. How did her mother manage to act like nothing was wrong? Maybe she didn't care anymore. This answer seemed unlikely, for she knew her parents had loved each other. There had been times when Beth felt like a fifth wheel around them.

"Thank God my mom knows not to ask too many questions," Kimmie said.

Why don't you shut up, Beth thought. Your mom's not so great. She left you alone in this dump.

Beth had never met Mrs. Taylor nor had she seen a picture of her, though Kimmie had said repeatedly that she was totally hot-looking, which, when Beth applied Kimmie's standards of style, probably meant she dressed like a hooker. Tight skirts, spikey heels, and too much hair gel. Beth tried to imagine a mother who would leave her fourteen-year-old daughter alone in a condominium while she moved herself and all but a few sticks of furniture a hundred miles north to Los Angeles.

"Where's Jules?" Beth asked. "She's supposed to live here, isn't she?"

"I told you, she stays at her boyfriend's over by the college."

"Does your mom know that?"

Kimmie shrugged and opened her eyes as wide as eggs. "You think I'm going to ask her?" She slid open the door overlooking Sixth Street.

"I can't hang around forever."

"So leave."

There must be a convention in town, Beth thought, as the sound of traffic, of honking and brakes and music and laughter, rose from three stories below.

"Watch this." Kimmie walked to the railing and yelled down to the street. "Hey, you guys, how do you like this?" She turned around, pulled down her tights, and mooned the sidewalk.

Beth heard hoots and whistles from the street. "I'm outta here," she said, and began to gather her jacket and book bag as the doorbell rang.

"You can't go now. Don't be a flake. I was just having some fun. It didn't mean anything. Jesus, Bethy. Lighten up."

She was right, mooning strangers did not mean anything.

So why not stick around and meet the spawn of the dark angel? It would be wrong to abandon Kimmie when she had promised to stay.

But her heart sank when she saw Damian. He looked exactly as she had feared he would. Pallid and pierced, he and Strider dressed like twins in black Docs, black Levi's, black tee shirts, and black leather jackets. Strider's hair was long and stringy; Damian's head was shaved except for a cap at the top dyed pure white.

"What d'you mean, you didn't get any food?" Kimmie punched Strider in the shoulder. "I gave you forty fucking bucks."

"Lay off, bitch." Strider grinned and held up two plastic grocery bags. He grinned at Beth. "This is Damian." He upturned one bag, and cheese crackers, Oreo cookies, graham crackers, extra-creamy peanut butter, and a can of chocolate frosting spilled onto the stained carpet. Out of the second bag he took two six-packs of beer and a fifth of Jim Beam.

Kimmie looked at Beth. "Didn't I tell you these guys were cool?" She said to Strider. "Beth wants to go home."

"I never said that. . . ."

"You're not going anywhere," Strider said. "We is gonna party." He mimed a drumroll and strutted off toward the kitchen, moving his shoulders and hips exaggeratedly. Kimmie followed him, leaving Beth and Damian alone.

"We got all that for forty dollars." Damian had a froggy voice, part high, part low as if it had not finished changing. "Not bad, huh?"

"Okay." Beth began to braid her hair.

They were standing in the middle of the living room furnished with an oversized television, CD player, a couch, and a beanbag chair.

Should I sit down? Beth wondered. If she sat on the couch he might sit next to her, but would it seem mean if she sat in the beanbag? So what? She sat on the chair and felt it envelop her protectively.

Damian rocked back and forth, bending his knees like he was plugged into some kind of music.

"You're Beth."

Nope. I'm the Queen of England.

"Damian," he said, looking down at her. His legs were skinny as two-by-fours.

"Yeah. Strider said." She paused. "How come you chose that name?"

"You know the movie? With the dogs?" He waited for a response. As if everyone hadn't seen *The Omen* about a thousand times. She nodded her head. "I know this guy—he's called Lucifer."

"You're kidding me. That is so dumb."

"Yeah," Damian said. "You got it." He sat on the couch, crossed his legs, uncrossed them, and leaned forward. "You go to that girls' school? Like Kim?"

Beth nodded. "You?"

"Hoover," he said. "What year are you?"

"Ninth," she said. "Same as Kimmie."

"You're big."

She glared at him.

"Tall."

I wear shoe size nine and a half, and I could beat up your skinny ass and walk away whistling. She remembered the way her friend Madison used to blow on her palms, brush her hands together, and say, "Gotcha!"

Beth asked, "How old are you?"

"Sixteen."

"When's your birthday?"

"November."

"Do you have your license?"

He took out his wallet—she saw he had three one-dollar bills—and withdrew his driver's license from its plastic window. In the picture his hair was long and Beth could tell he had tried to look dangerous for the camera.

"It says you wear glasses."

He shrugged.

From the kitchen came a squeal of delight and Kimmie danced out into the living room, holding her hand outstretched.

"Honest to God, isn't he a great provider? Look here what we got." Three fat joints lay on her palm.

Strider appeared from the kitchen and walked to the CD player on the floor beside the monster television set. He crouched and examined a stack of discs, chose one, and put it in the player

A female rapper.

Beth couldn't understand the words but the beat got to her immediately.

"You dance?" Damian asked.

"Not really," Beth said.

"Me neither."

Kimmie held the joint between her thumb and forefinger, struck a match, and lighted one twisted end. It flared, illuminating her huge, penciled eyes. She inhaled deeply and passed the joint to Strider. As he toked, she exhaled with a sustained "ahhh" and lay on the floor on her back. "What great shit."

Damian was third and Beth almost told him what she had read about soldiers in World War I, how the third man on a match was a dead man.

The joint came to her. Beth smelled its deserty aroma and knew she must be taking secondhand smoke into her lungs, but not enough to get high. She imagined the newborn pink of her lungs and thought how good it felt to run up court for a basket, but she did not want to be out of the circle, either. So she would pretend. Like the President had. Or maybe she would inhale just a little bit. If she got a little high, maybe she would forget about her father and Eddie French. She didn't have a father anymore and pretty soon Micki would be gone, too. But grass was a drug. Illegal. On an IQ test it would be sorted into the same column as heroin and cocaine.

She thought of Nancy Reagan shaking her finger, like in one of those old Uncle Sam posters, telling her to say no and Lana saying that pot was bad for brains that were still developing.

"Are you going to smoke it or fuck it?" Strider asked. He sneered as if he knew she was chicken to do it.

She closed her lips on the joint and pretended to inhale and hold.

She thought her brain must be pretty well developed already. She was a good student. Her history teacher had practically made love to her World War One project. And everyone knew the shit they taught in drug ed was two-thirds exaggeration. She wanted to stop thinking and remembering and bliss out for a while. Not check out of life completely like Kimmie and her friends. They were losers, she knew that; they were temporary friends until she could get herself on the other side of whatever was making her so miserable now. What was that stuff in the Constitution about life, liberty and the pursuit of happiness? That's what she wanted. To pursue a little happiness.

Kimmie and Strider lay on the floor. They had taken cushions from the couch and rested their heads on them. Kimmie had her arms stretched up and over her head and her eyes were half closed. The inside of her arms was skim-milk white. Strider moved his torso from side to side with the music. On the couch, Damian looked at Beth and grinned. She had a feeling he did not even see her.

To him it did not matter who she was. None of these people cared if she had played on the county's traveling basketball team the year before and could again if she wanted. It did not matter to them that her father was dead and Micki's wasn't or if she used to have a perfect family, and now she didn't even want to go home. Strider tore apart the Oreo package and the cookies spilled out on the carpet like chips at a poker game. Kimmie grabbed one and took it apart. Beth watched, fascinated, as she ran her tongue across the white filling.

The tongue seemed to be an intensely weird body part. Beth giggled. She sat back down and giggled until her stomach hurt.

"What?" Kimmie asked.

Beth shook her head. She could not stop laughing.

"Happy shit," Strider said, and tickled Kimmie's stomach.

Damian nudged Beth with his foot and held out the joint. So

soon? She blinked several times before she took it. Squinting in the
smoky room, she held the damp end to her lips, pretending to inhale. Her thoughts wandered off again.

She and Micki once sat on the stairs eavesdropping on their parents and godparents, Wendy and Michael, who were in the kitchen
drinking beer and getting rowdy. They heard Jack talk about
Thailand, about being on leave and totally, absolutely wrecked the
whole time, having no memory whatsoever of what happened
over a space of three days. Beth thought he must have been drunk,
but then Michael said something about Thai sticks as thick as his
thumb and all bud, and Beth realized her father had been out of it
on drugs. For three days.

That night she could not sleep as she tried to reconcile her father
the druggie and her father the man who listened to classical music
and read myths and sang old-fashioned love songs to her mother,
the man who watched from the audience when she gave her first
public speech. "What Democracy Means to Me." She was eleven
and terrified, until her gaze found him sitting in the middle of the
fifth row, wearing the striped tie she had given him for Christmas
just that year. Not smiling at her—that would have been too embarrassing. He focused on her like a laser beam the way he promised
he would so that all the energy in him zapped right into her and
she wasn't afraid at all.

God, how she hated these memories.

She passed the joint.

"You smoke it?" Damian asked.

"What?"

She was the loneliest girl in the world, but Kimmie and her
friends didn't care. Her mom was happy as Ms. Pacman and when
Micki found out about Eddie French she would be out, gone. All at
once Beth wanted not to care, to zone out. Tired of thinking, she
reached over and grabbed the joint back from Kimmie and took a
long draw, sucking the burn down her throat and deep into her
lungs.

Chapter Eighteen

"You're stoned," Micki said when she walked into Beth's room that night.

"Didn't anybody ever teach you to knock?" Beth lay on her bed and closed her eyes. After a minute she raised her head and looked at Micki. "You're still here. Why is that?"

"I've got that geometry test tomorrow."

"So?"

"You promised, Beth." Micki had seen her sister at school and Beth had said she would help her study. "You never break your word."

"I said I would. Now I can't. That's not the same as a promise."

"Does Mom know you're stoned? She's gonna be so pissed."

Beth sat up, brushing her hair back off her face. "Who's gonna tell her?"

"You look awful," Micki said.

Beth fell back again. "Jeezus."

Micki stared at her sister, the perfect Beth. It crossed her mind to tell on her, but she thought of the hell she'd catch for that and gave away the idea. Still, she felt she ought to do something. Beth was her younger sister.

"You shouldn't hang with Kimmie Taylor. You've got good friends." *Not like me,* said a voice in her head. "How come you don't go around with Madison and Linda anymore?"

Beth's eyes were shut. She made a sound like snoring. On her way out the door, Micki said, "Go ahead, ruin your life, see if I care."

* * *

Micki left home early the next morning, telling her mother she had to study for a geometry test. She entered Arcadia School by the north entrance, the main entrance that everybody called the kiddie port because students under fourteen were forbidden to enter or exit by any other door. The tenth-grade entrance was on the south side of the school. Every morning of the school year, tenth-graders gathered there on the picnic benches and under the magnolia trees to copy homework and talk about boys, clothes, teachers, and each other. Micki could have used some help on her math but not even the threat of a failing geometry grade would make her use the south entrance. She had done it yesterday, and she still felt the places where girls' stares burned into her back.

"Well, Micki, this is a surprise." The teacher's aide at the kiddie port had been around Arcadia since Micki started in the sixth grade. She checked the little kids in every morning. "What brings you 'round this way?" Her smile was so chirrupy she had to be putting it on.

Micki felt her cheeks heat up. The aide probably knew about The Fives. Her shame was probably what the staff and student body talked about every chance they got.

She mumbled something about convenience and ducked her head as she scurried down the long hall lined with trophy cases and class bulletin boards. There was no one around and her feet rang noisily on the linoleum tiles. Tenth-graders had their lockers in the new wing that was about as far away from the kiddie port as you could get, but she had planned for this and if she hurried she would avoid everyone until class began. Then it would be the same humiliation as yesterday, and she could not even use the bathroom without fearing she might encounter a Five.

It was no good saying she should put their rejection behind her—her mother's words; it dug into her dreams and during the day it was like a sponge that absorbed every other thought. When she went to bed the shame of her friends' dissing sat on her chest like a hundred-pound tomcat with maggoty breath.

Every day she wished her father were alive, but especially now because she knew he would find a way to help her not care about The Fives anymore. He would tell her honestly what was what and her eyes would open. When he was alive nothing was horrible or scary for very long. Well, one thing had been, but it happened a long time ago.

A little kid in a red sweater came out of the school office at a run and peeled past her, down the hall. Micki remembered being that young, and when she did she remembered what was even worse than getting dumped by The Fives.

Fifth grade had been the most horrible year of Micki Porter's life.

Probably because it had been the setting for a nightmare, Micki remembered Ms. Winston's fifth-grade class at Forrester Elementary in almost cinematic detail. The cursive alphabet that ran along the top of the green board, the chart of the Presidents of the United States, and beside it—twice as large—the chart headed "Reading Marathon" on which Ms. Winston kept track of their book reports. Every book was worth one hundred miles and the challenge was to run from San Diego to Washington, D.C., between September and June. Every kid in the class had a drawing of a sneaker with his or her name on it. Micki's shoe had been around Wichita, way out in front of the rest. She loved to read and it came easily to her. In the fifth grade her favorite books were myths and fairy tales and Agatha Christie.

In Ms. Winston's large, public-school classroom, students sat at square tables placed close together, one person on each side so that when they moved their chairs they were always knocking into each other and getting into fights. Under the tabletop was a shelf where she kept her books and the colored pencils she got for Christmas and which someone stole the first week. Things were always getting stolen at Forrester Elementary. At her table there had been two boys, JD and Sebastian. Sebastian was a chunky African-American with a corkscrew laugh. JD was a Jehovah's Witness; on Halloween and Valentine's Day and other special holidays, he had to go into the office and read while Ms. Winston's class ate chocolate chip cookies the room-mother brought. The girl at her table was Tanya Waterman.

Even now, so many years later, when Micki thought of Tanya she felt a tightness in her throat that would turn into tears if she let it.

In fifth grade Micki had sometimes felt like a little girl, sometimes an adolescent. She and Tanya giggled about boys on the phone every night and had sleepovers every weekend. One Saturday they persuaded their parents to let them ride the bus to Fashion Valley, where they tried on clothes and hung out at the food court watching the high school kids and then went home and played

Barbies. In school they wrote notes back and forth, and at recess they hid out in the bathroom with the other fifth-grade girls and Lonnie Palmiri showed them the picture she had drawn of a man's thing.

One spring afternoon when the wind was blowing hard and the sun was hot, Micki and Tanya lurked on the edge of the school grounds under a pepper tree playing a folding paper game that was supposed to tell you who you would marry and if you would be rich. Tanya told Micki her mother and father were getting a divorce and she might have to live with her grandmother in Colorado. Micki, wanting to share something just as important, told Tanya she was adopted.

It took a minute for this to sink in.

Tanya asked, "Who's your mother? You mean you don't know your mother?" Tanya's mouth opened like she was going to bite into an apple.

The question puzzled Micki. "You know my mom."

"Yeah, but she's not the real one. What about your real mom? What happened? Why didn't she want you?"

Micki began to feel prickly all over.

"What was wrong with you?"

"Nothing."

"I knew this lady, she used to live on our block, and she had a baby with this big, old foot. You could hardly even see her toes."

"But there was nothing wrong with me," Micki said, raising her voice. She stood up, brushing the peppercorns off her shorts. "Let's go play tetherball."

Tanya followed Micki as she ran off, ran fast. Instead of stopping at the tetherballs, Micki kept running up over the asphalt rise to the top level where the boys in the sixth grade played softball. She heard Tanya far behind, yelling her name. She ran straight through the sixth-grade game; the boys screamed at her and someone threw a ball and it hit her in the back but that did not make her stop. She ran around the flagpole where the school said the Pledge of Allegiance every morning, ran down the open halls of the school past the teachers' room and the office and the janitor's closet and the supply room and the workroom, and down the alley at the side where the school vans parked and the custodians smoked and around the portable classrooms and back onto the asphalt again. When she stopped, the air burned in her throat and chest, sweat poured off her face, and a bunch of fifth-grade girls were staring at her: Tanya and Lonnie and the nasty little girl who never washed her feet and Jerrianne, whose mother was in jail.

Micki looked back at them. Tanya whispered to Lonnie. They laughed behind their hands, looked at Micki, and scampered over to another clutch of girls. By day's end everyone in the fifth grade knew Micki was adopted. Sebastian took her pencil; she grabbed it back and he said, "Your mother didn't want you so she gave you away. Like to Goodwill." He thought this was hilarious, and high-pitched laughter twisted out of him and corkscrewed around the classroom, making everyone laugh with him. Ms. Winston rapped her shoe on her desk like she always did when the class got crazy, but the sight of her bare foot only made it worse.

The next day Micki's adoption was all Ms. Winston's class talked about. Not only had she been given away, she had been given away because there was something wrong with her and everyone had a theory about what that was. By the time Ms. Winston knew about it, the game of the season was Make Micki Cry.

That time, even Micki's father could not make the pain go away because it was easier to believe the kids than fight them. She was weird, she was messed up, she was stupid; no wonder her real mother couldn't wait to dump her. She was a reject—unwanted and unlovable. Her parents sent her to a kiddie shrink with basset hound eyes who gave her a book about adoption. They read it together and talked. She knew—logically—there was nothing wrong with her, and she had not been abandoned. Her birth parents had talked to a lawyer and out of hundreds of couples, chose Lana and Jack to be her parents. After a week or so, the kids in Ms. Winston's class turned on someone else and Micki's wound scabbed over and only hurt when she scratched and made it bleed. Occasionally someone got bored and brought it up again. Micki knew they did it because she got upset, but she did not know how to hide her feelings so it kept happening over and over.

For most of the fifth grade she had felt as she did now, mousing through the corridors of Arcadia School to avoid attention. Like Tanya, The Fives had recognized something out of whack about her.

At the end of the main hall, Micki hurried down the ramp and ducked into the corridor that went past the gym. Anyone who saw her there would think Micki had come to school early to use the exercise equipment; girls did that sometimes. Fives never did, but hey, she wasn't a Five. By minute increments she was getting used to the idea.

Outside a teachers' cloakroom, she met Ms. Hoffman.

"You're early, Micki. Is there anything wrong?"

Ms. Hoffman's eyes could see into you like a hawk's.

"I had to do some things," Micki said, and made herself look right in the teacher's eyes because if she did not, Ms. Hoffman would get suspicious. "I'm cool."

"I'm glad to hear that."

Ms. Hoffman had been teaching English at Arcadia School for twenty-three years, almost since the school opened. Six feet tall and shapeless, she nevertheless carried herself with the hauteur—a vocabulary word—of a runway model. Wings of gray framed her dark hair, which she wore parted in the middle and wound in a braid at the top of her head. Her features seemed to belong to three different faces: small, sparkly yellow-green eyes, a beaky nose, and a large, rectangular mouth enclosing big, very white teeth. By any set of standards Micki possessed, Ms. Hoffman was a homely woman; and yet there was something so special about her appearance that there were times when she appeared almost beautiful to Micki. In a cockeyed way.

Ms. Hoffman perspired prodigiously and addressed the class in stentorian—Micki loved vocabulary drill—tones that begged to be mocked. When she talked about "the great women of lit'rature," she raised her eyebrows and flexed her nostrils so that if you sat in the front row as Micki did they looked like black holes with hairs.

Her classroom was at the end of the building. She said seniority had to have some reward apart from exhaustion and despair. This was a joke but the first time Micki heard it she just stared at her teacher and wondered what kind of despair Ms. Hoffman meant. Micki imagined if she could see into her heart, there would be an image of Ms. Hoffman's only lover, probably a writer killed in Korea or Vietnam before he could finish his novel. She probably kept the pages in her house and took them out once a year and read them and maybe cried although it was next to impossible to imagine Ms. Hoffman actually crying tears.

Her classroom was extra large and had two walls of windows. On the gloomiest day it was airy and full of light. Unlike other classrooms, where the desks were lined up like chocolates in a box,

Ms. Hoffman arranged the desks in a long oval, open at one end to make space for her to stand near the white board.

Micki liked Ms. Hoffman because she made her feel it was important to be female. She dismissed most male writers with a set speech at the beginning of tenth grade. "We've been reading the lit'rature of men for so long, they have very little left to communicate to modern women." They still had to read men but only the best of them.

Micki sat in her class that morning, slumped deep in her desk so the base of her spine was on the edge of the seat. Tiffany sat beside her, doodling pictures of girls with long hair and Bambi eyes. Teachers at Arcadia were required to use seating charts set up at the first of the year and positions rarely changed. This meant Micki and Tiff sat next to each other in almost every class. But they didn't talk anymore.

To introduce the works of Emily Dickinson, Ms. Hoffman talked about the time way back when there were hardly any women writing books.

"If you had eight children and never learned to read or write, you would not contribute to lit'rature either. But if you and I could eavesdrop on those times, we would no doubt hear stories spoken mother to child, friend to friend, poems invented on the spot—perhaps in the form of prayers. Who knows?" Ms. Hoffman looked down at Micki. "Micki Porter, can you tell us in what other ways your female ancestors may have expressed themselves creatively?"

The eyes of the whole class drilled her. She sat up, chewing her lower lip, trying to think of something to say.

"Once, I went with my family . . ."

"Speak up, Micki. Let the back row hear you."

". . . on a trip and we went to a museum in this, like, real small town and there were these sort of pillow things woven out of hair. Human hair."

Someone behind her said, "Gross."

Why had she told about those stupid pillows? They had nothing to do with poetry. She slumped again, letting the magenta hair fall forward. She tugged it and stared at the floor.

"Not lit'rature, certainly. But a highly creative use of materials at hand, though by today's standards, somewhat ghoulish. Why do you think they did that, Micki?"

She wanted to look at Tiff and have Tiff make a face and both of them giggle. She wanted the moment to be funny and over with, not a drawn-out misery.

Ms. Hoffman tilted her head to one side. "Micki?"

"I think . . . it's like, sometimes you want to make something and you don't have any cool supplies?" She watched Ms. Hoffman's face for a signal that she had said enough. "And maybe they didn't think they could write good poetry. Or couldn't write at all, never went to school. Or maybe they wanted to do something really personal, like for someone in the family?" She swallowed and sat on her hands. Ms. Hoffman smiled without showing her teeth, which Micki took to mean the answer was satisfactory if not excellent. "Plus they all had a lot of hair back then."

Someone laughed. Micki recognized it as coming from a fat, braying creature who never would have dared to make a sound if Micki had been a Five.

After Ms. Hoffman's class came lunchtime. The worst part of the day. The time when Micki wanted to evaporate. She stood in the hall outside the upstairs bathroom and through the window watched Tiff walk off campus in a group of Fives. All blondes, all talking—probably about her. She imagined they were going to Naturally Good or for coffee at Bella Luna; they would be talking about their diets and their 'dos. And what a dork Micki Porter was.

Micki went to the library, as she had every day since she was dinged, and sat on the floor back in a dusty corner where the librarian stacked the books with torn covers. She dug a granola bar out of her purse and tore a corner open with her teeth. She had brought a book from home, snitched it from her mom's old paperbacks. This one was called *Fear of Flying*, only it was not really about flying. It seemed more about sex and women who were afraid to be themselves. Micki knew authors really liked this subject, but she did not think any of them had a Tanya in their lives. Or got totally dropped by their best friend and a whole club.

The year before, Micki had told Tiff about what happened in the fifth grade. She already knew Micki was adopted but she had never heard the gory details of her revelation to Tanya. They were smoking a joint Tiff had boosted from her mother's stash. It was a summer Sunday afternoon and they had Tiff's house to themselves and a half-gallon of Rocky Road ice cream on the coffee table between them. Even though Micki had long before sworn she would never tell the whole story, the tale had poured out of her in such a way that it might have made Ms. Hoffman smile and say that women are natural storytellers. Ms. Hoffman said that for thousands of years women had no other source of entertainment than themselves and if they were accused of gossiping, that was just another name for a certain kind of storytelling.

As she listened to Micki's storytelling, Tiff's eyes filled with tears and she swore to hold sacred what she had heard. They had kissed on the lips to seal the truth between them. A strange thing to do, but it had made the vow more profound. As she leaned against the stack of musty-smelling books scheduled for recycling, she supposed Tiff had told the story to The Fives by now. She wouldn't dare mention the kiss, though.

Sometimes she missed Tiff even more than she missed her father. Tiff could listen for as long as it took to get something said, and she knew the right questions to ask and when to laugh. But now, as she watched the motes dance in the thin winter sunlight slanting down through the library's old-fashioned sash windows, burnishing the maroon-and-buckskin-colored bindings of the old books, it seemed humiliating that an ordinary person who was neither Micki's mother nor father could be so important to her.

The first class after lunch was music. All that month they had been studying Russian composers and today they were going to listen to Stravinsky's *Firebird Suite* and write a two-page impression of what they heard. This was a no-brainer. The *Firebird* had been one of her father's favorite pieces of music and thanks to him, Micki knew all about the myth of the phoenix rising from the ashes. During class Ms. Levine walked around, tapping girls on the shoulder with a ruler when they looked like they might doze off.

When Micki got to class, Tiff was at the front of the room gesturing a lot as she talked to Ms. Levine, who listened intently, puckering and unpuckering her lips like some kind of fish. The classroom filled up and they were still talking. Micki could tell by the way Tiff moved her shoulders from side to side that whatever she was saying was important to her. Once or twice Ms. Levine looked over at Micki and gradually Micki began to feel a weight as if a heavy coat were slowly dropping down on her shoulders. Finally, Ms. Levine nodded and Tiff walked to the back of the classroom. After a moment a girl who had entered Arcadia with the New Year and to whom Micki had never spoken—she didn't even know her name—came to the front and slid into Tiff's seat.

Micki started to say something but the girl interrupted. "Hey, don't blame me. I like the back of the room."

The strains of the *Firebird Suite* washed over and into Micki, rose in her and flooded her with shame, filled her lungs and pressed against her heart. She heard someone moan and recognized her own voice.

The new girl nudged her. "What's wrong with you?"

A sharp pain darted through her stomach. She grabbed her book bag and escaped.

She had no particular plans when she left the school, nowhere she was heading for sure, but eventually her wandering took her along Fifth Avenue, past the bookstores and boutiques, through Hillcrest and into the green expanse of Balboa Park. The parking lots were full and the tourists out in force. She recognized them by their pale skin and the maps and guides they clutched. At the Mingei Museum she stopped long enough to run her hands along the curves of the huge Nicki St. Phalle sculptures. Her father had let her climb them when she was small, holding her lightly with his rough, gardener's hands. In the organ pavilion someone was practicing, filling the air with the same repeated bars. She knew where she was going now.

Balboa High School was on the far side of the park, across the wide boulevard that ran straight into the middle of downtown. It was one of the city's oldest schools, having been established at what was once the edge of town. Tiff called it the fortress because of the forbidding, windowless exterior cement walls. Micki crossed the parking circle and pushed open the front office door. The long front counter was crowded with kids and adults and she had to wait ten minutes for a student aide to ask what she wanted.

"I heard about a special program . . ."

The girl was Hispanic. She wore blue eye shadow and her black bangs had been combed straight up and sprayed stiff. No one at Arcadia wore her hair in that style. Micki wondered how she looked to this girl in her plaid uniform skirt and navy blue blazer.

"We got lots of programs. You mean sports or—"

"Academic," Micki said.

The girl sighed. "You gotta be more specific."

"An honors program?"

"Oh, yeah." The girl looked under the counter and brought out a bundle of brochures. "You're talking about the International

Baccalaureate." Her gaze assessed Micki. "You gotta have really good grades to get in."

"How good?"

The girl made a face. "The tests are like way hard. Teachers here don't even correct them. They get sent off somewhere like ... Sweden, I think."

"Wow," Micki said.

She took a handful of brochures and stuck them in her back-pack, and she did not look at them until she was back in the park, where she stopped at a refreshment kiosk and bought a fruit drink and sat on a bench in the Organ pavilion. The sun was warm on her head and shoulders and she slipped off her blazer.

The International Baccalaureate Program was only available at Balboa High School and the brochure made a big deal of how it was open to any student who could handle the work. At the end of twelfth grade there were massive tests, and some of them were sent off to Switzerland to be corrected along with tests from students in dozens of other countries. If a student passed those tests she could get advanced placement in college.

Thinking about all those tests depressed Micki.

Atop the worn, gray plaster facade of the Organ Pavilion, over the flowers and leaves and birds and curlicues, lines of pigeons perched liked robed judges, black silhouettes against the blue sky. A plane passed overhead, orange and brown. Southwestern.

She wished she were on a plane going somewhere far away. She felt trapped, her options as limited and grim as poor old Ken Allen, the orangutan who used to escape from his cage in the zoo every chance he got and was always brought back and the walls of his en-closure built higher. The sun dipped below the pavilion and violet winter twilight filled the park with shadows. Micki dropped the brochures in a trashcan, put on her blazer, and walked out of the park fast. It was creepy there at night and everyone knew the homeless slept in the gullies among the palms and ferns and eucalyptus.

She wished that Eddie, the man in the Jaguar, would come by and offer her a ride. Despite her mother's admonitions, she would ride with him gladly to get out of the park. Maybe not. Anyway, it didn't matter. She had not seen him in days and days and she felt stupid for caring.

Chapter Nineteen

In the hour before dawn when the winter light in Lana's bedroom was the color of oysters and the only sound a ripple of breeze through the garden wind chimes, Jack had slept beside her, warm and smelling of soap and bed and dreams. Lana's consciousness drifted outward to the edges of the day, moved from her own dreams into the thin, gray light. Eyes closed, she pressed her body against his back, reached around his slim hips and flat stomach and cupped his penis in the palm of her hand until it hardened and he made a sound, a kind of pleased woofle, and turned to her. Eyes shut, hands and body with their own intelligence. Sex in the morning, sex without thinking, sex a drowsy segue from sleep to pleasure and back and then awake. Quick sex, no fancy stuff, and afterwards lying together in a sticky union, drowsy as warm wolf cubs entangled with each other, drifting back into sleep.

She would never have sex like that again. She might go to bed with someone, sometime, but never as easy, never as much fun. It had taken Jack and Lana almost twenty years to perfect the movements of their private dance. She would never have the desire or patience to devote twenty years to anyone again. Mars said buy a vibrator, said she owned one and the inventor should get a Nobel. For a while Lana lay in bed thinking about sex, about whether Jack would be her last lover. At this point, it did not matter to her if he was, so maybe she should buy a . . . device. She giggled at the unlikely image of herself walking into a sex shop in broad daylight. She did not care to think of who frequented such places after dark. If sex was the best way to begin a day, giggling came a close second.

After lunch, Lana left the job and drove north on 805 to talk about bareroot roses with a wholesale grower. She crossed that off her list and drove to a little Del Mar perennial nursery and had coffee with the owner, whom she had known for years. Another item crossed off. On a whim, she detoured off I-5 going home and drove out Carmel Valley Road beside the wetlands to the long stretch of beach that separates La Jolla and Del Mar. To the west against a computer-screen-blue sky, the black silhouette of a line of pelicans skimmed the water, intent as bargain hunters. Beyond the roll of breakers, surfers dotted the water in their black wet suits. She liked the way they straddled their boards and waited for the perfect wave. She liked their implied confidence that there was such a thing as a perfect anything anymore.

She turned the 4Runner left and down into the deserted parking lot facing the estuary, parked the car, and sat. The late-January day was cold and bright with sharp, reflected light that tossed coins in the water and heated up the car's interior and made Lana sleepy. She pushed her seat back as far as it would go and propped her feet up to one side of the steering wheel against the instrument panel. A pair of snowy herons flew across her line of sight and came to rest on a muddy islet just up the estuary. She sat up and watched them poke in the muck with their pointed beaks, thinking of what they found in the tarry goop, the worms and crabs and minute creatures that may not have evolved much since the dawn of life. In the parking lot she was sandwiched between the traffic on Torrey Pines Road and the interstate a mile east. Overhead a contrail zippered the sky above the bluffs of the Torrey Pine Preserve. Her mind could not stretch the distance between the creatures in the mud and those with intelligence to design cars and planes and all the other necessities of the year 2000. The immense differences in life forms that managed to coexist in the world astonished her. If Jack were in the seat beside her they would have a conversation about this.

She dialed Kathryn's number on her cell phone and after a few minutes her sister answered.

Lana asked, "How are you?"

"I believe all my limbs are intact. I am consuming sufficient calories—"

"You sound sleepy."

"I've been halfway watching TV and dozing." Kathryn yawned. "What's up?"

"Are you still pregnant?"

"Mmm."

"Do you know for sure?"

"If you're asking have I been to the doctor, no, I haven't." Nor had she taken a home pregnancy test. She did not need to; she knew. She always knew immediately. Lana believed she did not want to take a chance of being wrong because when she was pregnant Dom treated her like a Belleek cup too precious and delicate to do more than look at. She might not want any more children, she might be sick of being pregnant and not care if her baby was a pony or a platypus, but she did like to be pampered.

Across the estuary, the Torrey Pines grade wound through the preserve's beautifully sculpted, eroding sandstone cliffs the color of gold. Lana and Jack, each with a baby in a kid-carry, had often hiked and picnicked in the preserve. She shut her eyes and let Kathryn talk.

Dom wanted no risk of another miscarriage so Kathryn was to stay in bed all day like a Victorian heroine, and he had enlisted Tinera to cook and clean. He would never hire anyone to help in the house, would not have his privacy invaded. *And in a family of females*, Mars had once said, *who needs a maid?*

"It's not fair to Tinera," Lana said.

"She doesn't mind," Kathryn said. "She likes to work around the house. Plus we spend a lot of time together. Anyway, it's only until the end of the first trimester."

"That's three months you're taking her away from school and her friends." Sometimes Lana actively disliked Kathryn. "To a kid Tinera's age, three months is a long time."

"Well, what do you want me to do?"

"Tell him she has to be in school. Hire a maid."

"She goes to school."

"How often?"

"Lana, Dom goes by her class every Friday and picks up her work. He makes her study where he can see her doing it. I work with her, too. She's practically getting home-schooled, for God's sake. She's doing well. And even if she weren't, do you really think I could change Dom's mind? You know how he is," she whined. "Why do you always fuss at me?"

"After our conversations—"

"I exaggerated."

"I don't believe you."

"Lana, you have to forget what I told you. We never had that conversation."

A gull settled on the parking sign a foot from the front of the Toyota and peered at the windshield. Lana peered back, making a face.

She said, "Lying around isn't good for you or the baby. If there *is* a baby, which I sincerely doubt."

"That's not fair."

"Then why won't you take a test? What are you afraid you'll find out?"

"I know when I'm with. I always know."

"Kay, you told me you wanted to leave him. What happened to that?"

"I was depressed. You know the way I get."

"Are you taking your meds now?"

"I don't know why you call me if all you can do is nag."

Another gull settled on the parking sign a few feet away, lifted one clawed foot, and scratched like a dog.

Lana said, "It's a gorgeous day. I'll come and get you. We'll go for a walk."

"Tinera's here."

"So?"

"I'll get up, I promise."

"I'll come for tea, then."

"She'll tell him you were here."

"I'm your sister, Kathryn, and even if I weren't, you have a right to do whatever you want."

A gust of wind rocked the car. The gulls fluffed their wings.

"I know." That peaked, little-girl's voice. "It's so complicated, Lanny."

Lana bit her lip and told herself what Jack had always said: *She's a grown woman. She has to take care of herself.* Silence stretched for so long, Lana was able to follow several bits of the television conversation playing in the background. A cook talking about Cajun spices.

"I'm okay," Kathryn said, finally. "Honest to God, I am. I'm thinking about stuff."

"What stuff?"

"I'm figuring things out."

"What's to figure? You either stand up for yourself and get a life or you don't. You either grow up or you don't." Lana spoke through clenched teeth. "I want you to know there is so much I am not saying right now."

"That makes two of us."

Another silence.

Lana broke it. "He's sick, you know. This obsession with keeping you barefoot and pregnant like some Sicilian peasant. It's not the goddamn tenth century."

Kathryn laughed. "Tell Dom. I dare you."

Lana knew that without Jack's support she would never confront Dom. He frightened her. Not by what he did—he had never hurt anyone physically as far as she knew—but by the sense Lana had that there was inside Dom Firenzi someone none of them knew, a person contented enough to stay hidden so long as he got what he wanted. She had never seen him really angry and never wanted to. Her horseback conversation with Kathryn had only increased her wariness.

"Kathryn, I'm not going to be around to care take of you for the rest of your life. One of these days you're going to need me and I might not be available. It's not like my own life is so easy right now."

"Have you told Micki about her father?"

Jack is her father, Lana thought. Jack. Jack. Jack.

"Michael's still investigating."

"What about The Fives thing?"

"She seems to be adjusting."

"You hardly mention Beth these days."

"What do you mean?" Lana felt her hackles rise.

"Just what I said. It's always about Micki."

Lana took her feet off the dashboard and lifted the lever that brought the driver's seat forward. "They're both doing okay."

A few moments later, they said good-bye; Lana put her phone back in her purse. As she watched the gulls lift and bank, turning toward the long, open beach, she thought about the lie she had told her sister. *Okay* was not a word she could honestly apply to either Micki or Beth. The previous week Micki had cut school, walked right out of music class, and gone down to Balboa High School. It seemed this desire to change schools was more than a passing whim and Lana would have to put her foot down. Meanwhile,

Beth stalked the house, her anger palpable. Lana felt like a criminal under surveillance when Beth was in the house and just as glad when she was out.

"What shall we have for dinner?" Lana asked Micki, who sat at the kitchen table that evening with her school books around her. "Spag with white sauce or red?"

"Whatever."

"I'll make red. With sausage." She watched Micki for a response. "Honey?"

"I'm not really hungry, Ma."

Lana walked into the pantry and pushed jars and cans around until she found a sixteen-ounce jar of spaghetti sauce she had canned the summer before when Big Boys overran her garden. She came out of the pantry with the sauce and a large kettle.

She said, "Tell me about your day."

"You know."

"I *don't* know. That's why I'm asking."

"Same old same old."

"What does that mean, Micki?"

"It means it was okay. O. K."

Under the circumstances Lana had no more idea what *okay* meant than she had understood *you know* and *same old same old.* Someone could make a bundle publishing a dictionary that clarified the vagaries of teenage responses. All Lana knew for sure was that Micki wanted her to shut up. Well, she wasn't going to do it.

"Beth's having dinner at Kimmie's." Lana looked up in time to see the corners of Micki's mouth turn up and quickly down. "What? Why were you smiling?"

"I wasn't smiling."

"Micki, I saw—"

"Jesus, Ma, if I'm moody, you worry, if I smile . . . Get a grip, will you?"

"And will you stop using that tone with me? This family isn't a TV show, Micki. We're polite to one another."

Not wanting to see Micki's reaction to this, Lana turned to the counter and sliced the sausage into bite-sized pieces that would brown quickly in the oven. She focused on pressing the balls of her feet into the floor. When she turned around, calm as the Sargasso, Micki's fair head was bent over her books.

Lana thought of interrupting her with the story of how when she and Mars got out of school they had spread their books on a table at the Hollywood Cafe. Just months ago Micki would have wanted to hear how the waitresses brought them toasted cheese sandwiches with French fries and milk shakes. Lana always got butterscotch and Mars had chocolate and they'd sit there and whoever was in the Hollywood would shove up next to them and try to help with their spelling or arithmetic.

There had been a waitress who could add up whole columns of numbers in her head and knew the times tables through nineteen. When they got good grades the dentist down the street gave them quarters, and Lana was read to by a ragged man whose shoes made a sound on the linoleum like steel wool on the grill. She was only seven and read better than he but he loved doing it, she could tell.

Lana said to the top of Micki's head, "How would you like to go shopping on Saturday?" She laid the chunks of sausage in a roasting pan. "We could have lunch at the Cheesecake Factory."

"I don't care."

"Does that mean yes or no?"

"It means I don't care if we go shopping or not."

"Damn it, Micki, look at me. Your life isn't over."

"Too bad, huh?"

Lana sank into a chair opposite her and laid her head on her arms.

"Ma-a."

Lana felt marooned, the last in her platoon, tossed up on the sands of Iwo Jima and told to defeat the entire Japanese army.

"You can't mourn The Fives for the rest of the school year. You're giving them power over your life. They rule you. You have other friends. You've always had friends."

"I did something stupid," Micki said. Buster lay on the floor near her. She bent and stroked his ears. "Yesterday, I went over to Tiff's."

Lana waited a moment and then asked softly, "Why was that stupid?"

"I don't know. . . . I was thinking, like, maybe she'd want to do something. Those music awards were on TV—last year she stayed over so we could watch them."

Micki looked up. Micki's flawless skin and innocent eyes—a shiver of amazed joy went through Lana to see such beauty.

"I almost didn't and then I thought what the shit . . . sorry, Ma."

"Never mind."

"It was like we hardly even knew each other. She acted like I was a stranger." Micki began to imitate Tiff in a high, airily affected voice, " 'Oh. It's you. Hi. I can't invite you in because I'm really busy now doing important things. Me and my important friends . . .' "

Micki picked up her pencil and broke it in half.

Lana said, "I can't understand. . . ." Don't lie to this girl. You *do* understand. Every girl who had ever passed through school understood what Micki was going through. "Girls can be the meanest creatures on earth." No advice, no solution, just the truth. "They'll tear your heart out if it suits them."

Micki put her head down on the table and sobbed and Lana crouched beside her chair, stroking her hair and gently patting her back.

No advice, no solution, just strokes and pats. Lana had never felt more inadequate.

The phone rang.

Lana heard Michael's voice over the speaker and she hurried to pick it up before he could say too much. She took the phone out into the yard. In the half-light, the olive trees along the back wall were twisted and spidery shapes. Like swarms of white stars, the jasmine climbed their trunks and their boozy fragrance filled and thickened the twilight air.

"I'm sorry this has taken so long, Lana. The guy I had do it's real busy. The attorney sends his regrets. He'd like to share the adoption file with you but it's an attorney-client thing. Locked up tight."

Lana looked back into the kitchen through the greenhouse window. Micki stood at the stove stirring the spaghetti sauce. "Did you tell him about Eddie French?"

"I did."

"And?"

"Lana, he wouldn't say anything for sure."

"Did he say anything for *not* sure?"

"He said you should talk to the guy. That's all."

"That means he is who he says." Not that she had ever really doubted it but she had hoped. . . .

"Seems probable." Michael paused. "My investigator ran the name Eddie French through the Internet—"

Damn it, I could have done that, Lana thought. It had not occurred to her.

"If this is the real Eddie French, he's a big deal."

"Shit."

"He's got hundreds of sites."

"He really invented that game?"

" 'Ghost.' Yeah. But that's not all. He's supposed to be working on some hot new game idea that's going to revolutionize computer learning."

"Great. That's what I really need, a fucking genius saint."

Michael chuckled softly. "He's not quite that. My guy expanded his search to Lexus and that's when it got interesting. Whole slew of newspaper articles about Eddie French. He's been in and out of rehab a couple of times, had a few tangles with the cops. A couple of years ago he punched one out and tossed his camera."

Lana felt a surge of validation and relief, followed almost instantly by another emotion she could not identify. She disconnected the call and took several deep breaths to dislodge the congested feeling trapped above her lungs. When this did not make it go away she crouched and tugged several spears of nut sedge that had poked up around her favorite Mr. Lincoln rose. It was a tenacious weed, sending out its invasive runners even in the wintertime and was virtually impossible to kill. Buster wandered over and looked at her, teetering a little on his weak hindquarters. She shoved the weeds into the pocket of her apron and perched on the edge of a landscape boulder and stroked his head.

The question she had been asking for weeks had taken a new slant. What would it do for Micki's spirits to learn she was Eddie French's daughter? Lift them, no doubt, no doubt at all, at least for a while. The guy was somebody and when the word got out, being his daughter would carry cachet at Arcadia. But he'd been in trouble with the law and had drug problems. Wasn't a man like that almost certain to hurt Micki? Wasn't it begging trouble to bring him into their life?

Lana went back inside and put the phone back on the wall.

"Who was that?" Micki asked as she gathered up her school things.

"Michael."

"What'd he want? Looked like big secrets."

"Oh, yeah," Lana said. "He wants to plan something special for Wendy."

"Cool," Micki said. "I'm glad somebody's having a happy life."

In the upstairs hall an oversized utility closet with a window had been designated as the girls' playhouse when they were small. There was a television there, one that Dom had found too small-screened for his family, and Jack had built a wall of shelves on which were stacked games and art supplies, books, and the essential junk of young lives dating back several years. Lana would put it on her list to clean the place out, send a bunch of stuff to Goodwill. Beth and Micki had decorated the walls with posters of rock and television stars; the furniture was old pillows and an orange beanbag chair one of them had dragged home from a junk store. The room gave Lana claustrophobia but the girls and their friends loved it. Micki retreated there right after dinner while her mother sat at her kitchen desk writing bills, listening to the jazz station from City College.

When Beth came in the back door just after ten, Lana said, "You're late."

Beth looked at the wall clock. "Five minutes." She slung her book bag onto the oak table where it slid off and onto the floor. She stared at it a moment.

Lana wondered if she planned to pick it up.

"Be more careful."

"Sor-ry." Beth hefted the bag onto a chair.

"Did you have enough dinner? I made spaghetti. Want some? Only take a minute to warm it up."

Beth considered this for what seemed a long time to Lana. "Nah. I'm wiped."

"Are you sleeping okay?"

"I'm just tired. No biggie. Why're you putting the smack down on me?"

Lana stared at her. "I don't even know what that means."

"Just leave me alone, will you? I gotta go to bed."

"I only asked you if you wanted something to eat."

"You think I'm a moron? I don't get what you're doing?" Beth flounced across the kitchen, throwing up her arms. "It's not what you say, it's the way you say it. You ask me if I want food so I'll tell you I ate from all the food groups tonight. You ask if I'm okay means you want me to spill my guts. Well, I don't have any guts to spill, Ma. I'm just really, really tired."

Lana's vocal cords had frozen. She stood up, her hands busy stacking the bills into two neat piles, paid and unpaid. She crossed the kitchen and began to wipe down the counter, wondering how many millions of women felt as she did right then, sick to their souls of wiping down the same slab of counter space just to give themselves something to do to keep from screaming at their children.

When she could talk, she said, "I want to meet Kimmie." She stopped herself from explaining why. She did not need to give a reason.

There was silence and then Beth said, deeply blasé, "Whatever."

"I don't like the way you act since you started hanging out with her. I don't like this new attitude. It isn't you, Beth."

"Maybe you don't really know me."

"Don't be ridiculous. Of course I know you. You're my daughter."

"So?"

"Beth, what's happening to you?"

"Nothing is happening to me. Jesus, Ma, has it slipped your attention? I'm fourteen."

Lana thought about this answer.

"Look at me, Beth." She put her hands on either side of Beth's face. Beth tried to duck her head away and Lana held her with the pressure of her hands against her cheeks. "Are you telling me everything is okay with you? Really and truly okay? Because if you tell me that, I will believe you."

"I'm fine, Ma." Beth smiled, tossed her head back, and then hugged Lana.

Her hair smelled dusty, like the herb garden. Not right somehow. But she felt wonderful in Lana's arms, solid and strong and warm.

"You believe me, don't you, Ma?"

"Oh, Beth." Lana patted her daughter's cheek and felt the fire of life burning in her; and from nowhere, tears stinging in her own eyes. "Of course I do."

* * *

We tell the truth, Jack used to say. *It isn't always easy, but we do it anyway.* Once, when she was nearby, Lana heard him tell the girls that every family has core beliefs, and honesty was one of theirs. That night as she prepared for bed Lana wondered if that, like everything else, had changed in the last year and a half.

Chapter Twenty

"Beth's telling you something. I think you should listen," Mars said the next day when Lana met her for coffee at the university's Price Center. They took their cappuccinos outside and sat on a bench facing the sun. At midmorning, crowds of milling students in Levi's and tee shirts filled the stone-and-concrete, amphitheater-shaped food-and-activity court. A few wore shirts and sweaters and there were one or two women in skirts and high heels whom Lana took to be staff or faculty. For the most part, the students were a scruffy bunch. In dramatic contrast, Marlene was in her expensive, hippie-poetry-professor mode, wearing a russet wool cloak matching her wild auburn hair that fought against the combs holding it up and back, chunky amber earrings, a black sweater, and a black skirt cut on a swirling bias. High-heeled boots made Lana's feet hurt just to look at them.

"Beth's growing up," Mars said. She lifted the lid from her coffee and blew on the foam. "But you keep treating her like a little kid."

"I don't think it's outrageous to want to know what she eats."

"So many kids have issues around food."

"She doesn't have issues—she's just gotten secretive all of a sudden and I don't like it. If you had children you'd know what I mean."

Mars looked at her.

"Sorry."

"You know, there's a whole theory about the kids being born today. Kind of interesting."

Mars pursed her lips and took a sip of coffee, giving rise to a familiar pinch of envy and admiration in Lana. No one else in the family had her sister's lippy, sensuous mouth, so glamorous and expressive. "The writer says these kids are radically different from previous generations, much better able to take care of themselves, way more independent *by nature*. It's an evolutionary thing. And parents don't know how to raise them because they're using antiquated methods." Mars looked sideways at Lana. "Just a thought."

Lana let the New Age theory rest in a corner of her brain while she watched three workmen building a wall to enclose an outside eating area. Rebar—an iron bar, to strengthen the cement. Her daughters, children of the New Age, had rebar running through them. That she knew to be true.

"Even if you don't buy the evolution thing," Mars said, "what you don't realize—or maybe you do but you don't want to accept it—is kids are different from when we were growing up."

"I'm not a troglodyte, Mars."

"Great word."

"Ms. Hoffman." Lana sipped her coffee and wished she still smoked. "It's not a generation thing. It's since Jack died, they've changed. I feel them getting away from me."

"Look at their ages." Mars tossed her hand blithely. "Beth's poking her nose out into the world—that's good. Mick can be a bit fractious. . . ." She paused. "You better tell her about her father, though. That's a time bomb you're holding."

She went on talking in this vein and Lana beamed up a few feet, watching her sister's animated hands that continually shaped and accented her words as she spoke.

Unlike Lana and Kathryn, Mars had never wanted to be married. When she was seventeen she told Lana that marriage tied a woman to a Hoffa-sized cement block. At eleven Lana had no idea who Hoffa was, but as usual, Mars's conviction impressed her. Lately, though, a wistful hint of uncertainty had crept in around the edges of her sister's personality, like algae at a pond's edge. The hint of green longing made Lana love Mars even more.

"When I started teaching twenty-five years ago, they were respectful of authority, malleable as putty. Not anymore. If you don't give these kids autonomy, they take it. Yours are just showing how normal they are."

Frankly, thought Lana, I wish they were a pair of oddballs.

"I still want to meet this new friend of Beth's."

"Oh, absolutely. I'm just saying, why don't you trust her—"

"I do trust her. Pretty much." Sort of. The qualifications were new and made Lana sad. "I was thinking last night how Jack used to say honesty had to be a core family value—"

"Sweet Jesus, sounds like a sermon from the Crystal Cathedral!"

"—and I wondered, what d'you think were the core values in our family?"

Mars looked at her and laughed. "Just one: whatever Stella wants, Stella gets."

"Be serious."

"I mean it. So long as Ma was happy, anything went. She didn't really mind my running around playing hippie, you know. But it upset Stan. That man was Mr. Republican. And when he was unhappy, that made her unhappy because when he was pissed off he yelled and drank and ran around."

Lana had been too young to understand the alternation of screams and silence, the slamming doors that had characterized the house on Sunset Cliffs. She remembered shielding Kathryn from the explosions and, when she could, running along the cliffs, sometimes as far as the lighthouse. She recalled the flash of sunlight on the waves far below, the shock of the cold salt air in her lungs, and the plans and promises she made herself to the beat of her feet on the sandy path. She would have her own family and they would love each other; there would be laughing and no yelling.

"Speaking of running around," Lana said, happy to change the subject, "how's the boy biologist?"

"You mean Malcolm?" Mars made a down-mouth, tilted her head to one side, and combed her fingers through her corkscrew curls. "I had to let him go, I'm sorry to say. I tired of the lad."

Lana poked Mars gently. "Tell me the truth."

Mars picked a long, curling hair off her black skirt and sighed. "The truth is that no matter how well preserved and wickedly inspired in bed, a fifty-year-old poet will always lose out to a tight pussy from Big D."

Lana laughed as she was supposed to, but her heart ached for her sister having to save face with humor. "You did make that New Year's resolution, about finding an older man. How old was Malcolm? Twenty-five? Six?"

"Actually, he was thirty. But the problem is, Lana, I never meet anyone who isn't young. No one interesting, anyway. I meet sixty-year-old English profs still trying to seduce women with the poems they wrote thirty years ago." Mars put down her coffee cup. Her voice was low and throaty. "Can you remember how a young man's skin feels? I bet you can't. Well, it's like warm leather, smooth and supple, and it always smells clean. Even their sweat is sweet. And the muscles—God, Lana, the muscles are incredible. Even the boys that don't work out have this wonderful tone to them." She paused to watch a pair of male students in snug Levi's and tees. "They are angels of seduction, Lana. Irresistible. I'm telling you, thinking about it makes me all frothy."

Lana stared at her sister and then they burst into laughter so tickly that the students nearest them stopped talking and stared.

Two old bags acting like schoolgirls, Lana thought. Tired eyes and blotchy skin and hair that requires *product* to make it shine. Time had stepped in to repossess their teeth and abdominal muscles.

Someone coughed. Lana looked up at a pretty Asian face and straight black hair with peroxide yellow tips.

Mars composed herself. "Yes?"

"Dr. Madison, excuse me for interrupting but my name is Nancy Song and I just want to tell you I bought your book. Of poems? And they were so awesome. Especially the one about the bridge? It just broke me down. So totally. And so I was wondering, if I brought the book by your office—during office hours—would you sign it?"

Mars smiled graciously. "It would be my pleasure."

"Do you have a new collection coming out? I hope so because I think you're a truly great poet."

"Well, aren't you lovely to say so."

Lana watched her sister playing the star as if it were her birthright, using the canned phrases, and the old question came into her head. Who was Mars's father?

Kathryn said he had to be a movie star, a Fifties heartthrob who swept Stella off her feet back in the days when she worked at Bullocks Wilshire. Lana had in mind a mogul or a politician, the CEO of a vast financial empire. Mars had no doubts. She was the bastard daughter of a movie giant. C.B. DeMille, maybe. Stella herself had nothing to say on the subject. Never had. In her nastier moments Lana thought it was possible she just didn't know.

"I am working on something now," Marlene told the girl. "Poetry can't be rushed, of course, but I'm pleased with the progress."

When the student had passed on, Lana asked, "Are you actually writing, Oh, 'truly great poet'?"

"You know me, Lana. I don't lie."

"I forgot. Honesty's a Madison family core value, right?"

It was convenient to stop at Stella's on the way home from the university. Her town house was part of a small complex of vaguely Spanish-styled homes halfway up Mt. Soledad and faced east across mesas and canyons toward the mountains. It was a view Lana had always loved as she loved the morning light, but Stella had never been satisfied. She associated an ocean view with wealth and everything else with the Hollywood Cafe.

In a rare act of forward thinking, Stan had paid cash for her unit and put it in her name three years before he died. As a rental it had earned a decent income but when Stella moved in it required extensive interior work. New carpets and paint, all new fixtures in the kitchen, and remodeled bathrooms had eaten up most of the insurance payout so she lived carefully now, depending on revenue from the Hollywood Cafe and a small portfolio of investments.

Stella was having a martini and watching the five o'clock news when Lana arrived. She offered her a drink.

"Water, Ma."

For a few minutes they watched the news of local disasters, car wrecks, and police chases. Stella loved it.

"We need to talk," Lana said. "Can I turn this off?"

"I want to watch the weather."

"I'll turn down the volume for now."

Stella looked irritated but she sat back in her chair and gathered the skirt of her bronze-and-black caftan around her legs.

"So?" she said. "I suppose you want to hear about my plans." Lana nodded and let her mother talk about why the house on Mt. Soledad irritated her, the problems with her neighbors, the lack of afternoon sun. "I want to be at the beach again, Lana. I want to see the sunset on the Pacific."

"So drive."

"You know what I mean."

"What I know is you're dreaming. Have you actually looked or done any research? Places at the beach cost a million dollars. Minimum."

"You exaggerate." Stella peered around Lana to watch the silent television.

"A fixer-upper maybe you could get for eight hundred. Thousand, Ma. Eight hundred thousand."

"The secret is a good Realtor. A savvy real estate broker can find the bargains." Stella admitted she had not yet found this miracle worker.

"You haven't really done anything, have you? This is all in your head."

"Watch your tone, Lana."

Lana thought of herself saying much the same thing to Beth and Micki and knew how it made them feel. She walked to the square picture window overlooking the city's northern suburbs. In the distance the outline of the Cuyamaca Mountains rose like a hazy graph line against the sharp blue of the darkening winter sky. Below streets lined with apartments, condominiums and town houses quilted the mesas between the sharply etched canyons, intersected occasionally by velvet green parks and landscaped "clean" industries—the dozens of electronic and pharmaceutical companies that had come to San Diego when the war industry left. Streetlights had begun to come on.

She looked back at Stella. "Why do you want to move, anyway? This is a lovely house and the view's breathtaking. You'll never be able to afford anything nearly as nice. You'll end up—"

"I'm going to sell the Hollywood."

Lana sat down again. "Ma, Dora's leased the Hollywood for years. She pays her rent on time every month. That's guaranteed income. That's what buys your groceries." And your French manicures, and puts high-test in your Cadillac, and sends you off to the Caribbean every other year.

Stella fiddled with the pearl buttons down the front of her caftan, a voluminous garment that reminded Lana of Las Vegas. And must have cost a bundle. Her mother, tall and willowy as a showgirl, favored the kind of glitzy outfits that had made much of her movie star glamour when she was forty, and from several feet away she still looked stunning. Close up, she made Lana sad, hanging onto powdered and rouged illusion by the tips of her perfect manicure.

"Dom has offered—"

"You'd take money from him?"

"That man has a sense of family, Lana."

"Since when has *family* become a holy word?"

"You're prejudiced against him."

"Is that what he says?"

"It's his culture, Lana. You don't like that he's Italian."

"Ma, being Italian's the best thing about Dom. Apart from that he's a bully and he's cruel to Kathryn. That's what I don't like about him."

"Oh, you exaggerate. He wouldn't raise his hand to Kathryn. He adores her."

"Yes, he does. In his way. But he's still abusive."

"And those girls, the sun rises and sets in Tinera."

"I'm not going near that one, Ma." Lana shook her head. "The relationship between him and Tinera is sick."

Stella looked at her fiercely. "What are you saying?"

"There's something unnatural—"

"What do you mean, *unnatural?*"

"Not incest, not the usual kind, anyway. But it doesn't have to be physical. There's such a thing as emotional—"

"Well, he's not easy, I'll grant you that, but that's not the same as abuse." Stella rubbed her index fingers in the corners of her lips. "And it's certainly not incest. I don't even like to say that disgusting word, Lana." Stella used to inhale a cigarette when she needed to think. Now she fluffed her hair and fidgeted with her earrings. "You've put a halo around Jack. You've forgotten how he could make you so angry sometimes. There's not a man born isn't a pain in the neck half the time."

It was just too much that Stella would speak of Jack and Dom in the same breath. Lana walked into the kitchen and poured herself a glass of tap water. In theory, Stella was a grown woman and did not need a caretaker. Ditto for Kathryn. Why couldn't Lana just walk away?

She returned to the living room and sat beside her mother on the gold-and-white brocade couch.

"Dom doesn't want it to be a loan," Stella said, watching herself in a mirror across the room. "It would be a gift."

Lana shook her head. "No, Ma, it wouldn't be a gift. It'd be a bribe in advance. In case you ever realize what a son of a bitch he is, he wants the money there to keep you quiet."

Stella widened her blue eyes in apparently genuine bewilderment. "How did you get so cynical? When you were a little girl you had the tenderest heart . . ."

"Just hold off, okay? Don't take a loan from him, okay?" Lana waited for her mother to makes some sign of agreement. "Promise, Ma?"

"But I want to move." She sounded like a disappointed four-year-old. "I'm tired of this old place."

"You're bored. Take a class in something or go on a trip. Just don't sell this house or the Hollywood."

"I don't know why you're so fond of that place."

"Those were happy years for Mars and me."

"Is that so?"

"Meaning?"

"Well, it just seems to me that if it was all that wonderful living in a two-room cottage next door to a diner, you would have bothered to make contact with your father. Norman Coates." The weather anchor came on and Stella unmuted the television.

Lana expelled a long breath and sat back, feeling an ache between her shoulder blades.

"Just wait a little longer, Ma. Please."

"Well, look at that. No rain for a while."

Lana left her mother's and drove to Mission Bay Park, where she parked near the visitors' center. She went inside and changed into the running clothes and shoes she kept in the back of the 4Runner. On the path beside the bay she ran south toward the Hilton Hotel, the water to her right. The path was full of other twilight runners in shorts and skimpy tops. First she heard their shoes hitting the cement path behind her and then their breathing. She drifted to one side to let them pass her. She was in no hurry and had not run in ten days so her quads felt puny and sent messages to her brain that she should sit down, go home, do anything other than pound along the pavement in the half light.

As she ran she thought about her sisters and her mother, her daughters. This was her family and she wanted to hold them all close to her, protect them and nurture them. Why did it have to be so complicated to do that simple thing that mothers probably did when they lived in caves? And what about Eddie French? How did he fit into all of this?

He did not fit in, she thought later as she stood in the kitchen, staring out the greenhouse window. Absently she deadheaded the glazed pots of pink and white impatiens, dropping the limp, brown, slightly sticky flowers into the mouth of the garbage disposal. She raised her arms above her head and bent to the side, first left and then right. The run had made her ache all over but she didn't have a backache anymore.

At the back of the yard behind the olive tree, the yellow Carolina jasmine had begun its two weeks of vivid bloom. By the garden lights she could see that the brick back wall appeared to be draped in a bright shawl. On the slab of cement by the gate out to the driveway, Buster slept in the pool of porch light. Lana had provided him with a comfortable cushion on the porch but he seemed to prefer the kind of hard bed he had always known.

He had adapted to domestic life with surprising ease although most of the time he preferred the backyard to being in the house. He and Gala ignored each other. At night he moved through the pet door inside and out and back inside. Lana heard the click of his nails on the hard floors as he patrolled. He was more feeble now than on the day Carmino brought him home from the vet's, and two nights earlier he had left a puddle on the kitchen floor. Every day he moved more slowly. Lana had seen this before in dogs—the slow, stoic decline. She would wait for his eyes to tell her it was time to go.

The house felt empty without the girls, the sound of their voices and music and footsteps pounding along the hall overhead. They were so often gone these days. She would surprise them with a treat when they got home. Where had she put the recipe for the lemon pudding cake they both loved?

Maybe I am getting used to being alone, she thought. At least I'm cooking again. Occasionally.

In the midst of grief so much had slipped through the gaps and not been retrieved. Lana had bought the girls bus passes so she wouldn't have to drive them whenever they wanted to go to a mall or sports events. And to avoid cash hassles—which Jack had always managed, of course—she had given them their own charge cards with monthly spending limits. What had changed the most was their mealtimes. They no longer ate in the dining room. Once it had been important to Lana and Jack that the family eat together in a rather old-fashioned and traditional way—china plates, cloth napkins, an all-food-groups meal, homemade desserts like lemon pudding cake—and that there be conversation at these meals, that they share the daily up-and-down of their lives. For more than a year now she and the girls had eaten meals at the table in the kitchen. Paper napkins, pizza, take out Thai or Chinese, occasional spaghetti or tuna casserole. And what passed for conversation at these meals just barely qualified. Dialogue with teenagers was not easy, not if it mattered what was heard and said, and Lana rarely had the stamina to make a real effort. Sometimes she sent them up to the playhouse with their meals, let them eat while they watched *Jeopardy*. That first year she had so little appetite she dropped fifteen pounds without thinking about it. Some nights she could barely swallow what she set before herself.

She stepped onto the back porch and called Buster. He hobbled slowly to her. She sat on the stone steps and ignored the cold percolating through her Levi's to her thighs and buttocks as she rubbed his head and neck and talked to him about the day, the weather, the garden, and asked him how he felt. Did his hind quarters ache, or his spine? She had a few aches and pains herself, he might like to know. Gala padded out of the house and onto the stoop and hung her head over Lana's shoulder.

The tears came before she could stop them.

The ringing of the phone brought her back to herself, and she jumped up to answer, rubbing her eyes with the back of her hand. She recognized Eddie French's voice immediately.

"You said you'd call me. How is she?"

"She's fine."

"Why didn't you tell me? I've been so worried—"

She knew she should say she was sorry but she could not make herself do it.

"Look," he said, "I'm scheduled to go to Europe in a few weeks and I'm going to be there for a while and I was hoping . . . You said you'd think about it."

"And that's what I'm doing. Thinking."

"Mrs. Porter, I don't know what you think of me—"

"I think you're a young man who made too much money too fast and got in trouble. With drugs. And the law."

Of all the reactions Lana expected, she did not anticipate his low, soft laughter.

"You've been doing your research," Eddie French said. "Good."

Condescending bastard. "What do you mean, *good?*"

"I mean I'd do the same thing. Did do it."

"You didn't find out Jack and I had been in trouble with the police. And neither of us had or ever did have a problem with drugs. Or alcohol, either."

"And I did. I admit it."

What did he want? A medal? Full access to Micki just because he didn't bother to deny the truth?

"Would you have told me if I hadn't found out for myself?"

"Absolutely."

"Easy to say now." She looked at the clock over the back door. She expected Micki home soon and she did not want to be caught on the phone talking to Eddie French. "Why don't you just tell me what you want?"

"To spend time with my daughter. To get to know her."

From the second floor of the house came a wail, a scream, a cry from the heart. Gala began to bark.

"Oh, Christ—oh, God, no." Lana dropped the phone and ran along the hall and bounded up the stairs, taking them two at a time.

Micki stood in the door of the playhouse holding a phone. Her mouth was open and her eyes wide as she stared at Lana.

"Was that my father? It was. That was him, wasn't it? The guy in the Jag?" She threw the phone down; it clattered on its edge, almost hitting Gala, who had followed Lana up the stairs and now slunk away with her tail between her legs. "I hate you," Micki screamed. "I'll hate you forever for this."

Chapter Twenty-one

Micki looked at the card in her hand and then at her cell phone lying a hand-stretch away on the bed. Her mother had given her Eddie French's business card as if she could ever make up for not telling her the truth.

How much she hated her mother came over her like nausea, like when she and Tiff got stoned and ate a super-sized pizza and a whole half-gallon of Rocky Road ice cream. Micki got off the bed and went into her bathroom and stuck her finger down her throat as she had done that night. Nothing came up now.

Back on the bed, she lay on the small mountain of pillows piled at the headboard—florals, plaids, and polka dots in shades of pink. Did she really love pink or had her mother shoved the color down her throat? She threw the pillows off the bed, scattering them across the blue carpet. She stared at the ceiling and thought about ways to hurt her mother, ways to teach her a lesson.

Had she actually believed she could get away with such a huge lie? Just pretend Eddie French didn't exist? All her talk about honesty and being trustworthy had been bullshit, every word of it. While she was upstairs, before the phone call came, Micki had been thinking about telling her mom that Beth was getting into trouble, smoking dope at Kimmie's and maybe worse stuff, too. Now she wouldn't say anything. Let her find out how much it hurt when people hid the truth. And so what if Beth did get in trouble? Why should her life always be easy? It wasn't like they were real sisters.

She tried to remember what Eddie French looked like and she realized she did not even know the color of his hair. He was her father and she did not know if his eyes were blue or brown or gray.

She remembered a pair of good-looking wraparound glasses and expensive clothes but his actual face was a blur.

Her own father. How bad was that?

She spoke aloud to the ceiling. "Eddie French is my father." She looked at the card in her hand. "Edward French, President and CEO, French Electronics." She should feel excited or nervous or something but she didn't. Except for being angry with her mother, she felt hollow.

"I hate you," she said.

Her father—her adoptive father, Jack—used to say that hating took energy away from the good part of life. Why bother hating anyone, he would say. "Save your hate for something that counts." Didn't her mother count? After what she'd done, didn't she deserve to be hated?

In the direction of her bedroom door Micki yelled as loudly as she could. "I hate you."

She rolled over on her stomach and began to pick at the stitches on her duvet. It was getting old and if she wanted to she could probably shred it with her fingernails. But it was silky and warm and she liked it. Eddie French was rich. She might go to live with him and he would buy her a whole new bed. She could have all new bedding and pillows instead of the dorky-looking pink things her mother had made. It excited her to think of starting new. She imagined walking out the door with only the clothes on her back, stepping into the blue-green Jaguar and a fresh life; she got as far as opening the door and sitting down, closing the door, and doing up her seat belt, but after that it all got vague and sort of scary. How would she have a conversation with the stranger driving the car and what would it be like to wake up in the morning and walk into his kitchen looking for breakfast? She would have to tell him that her favorite cereal was oatmeal with butter and milk and brown sugar. Or maybe he slept late and she would be alone opening cupboards, looking for something good. Did he live in one of those apartments a mile up in the sky—no pets allowed, no garden possible? Would they eat dinner together? What would they talk about?

It would be like a first date.

It was easy to talk to Jack. Sometimes he walked into the house and the first thing he said was, "If it isn't good news, I don't want to hear about it," but that was only if he'd had a bad day himself.

Mostly he listened to everything and if she wanted advice, he gave it. So different from her mother, who was too busy to sit down and listen, who had to be doing stuff all the time, knocking items off her list.

Eddie French might expect her to dress and act a certain way. What if he were a born-again something with a list of rules and he made her go to church with him and study the Bible. This did not seem likely but anything was possible.

An hour ago he had been a mysterious man in a Jaguar and now he was her father.

Did she want to go and live with a stranger?

She got up from the bed and opened her bedroom door a crack. Gala lay just outside, looking sorrowful, and Micki quietly urged her in and up onto the bed. She lay down beside her and pressed her face against Gala's warm stomach, inhaled the comforting funky dog smell, felt the tiny bumps of her nipples against her cheek.

If she went with Eddie French she would never see Gala again.

Micki wouldn't miss Beth much but there would be times, like Christmas morning and getting ready for school, borrowing each other's clothes. It was good to have someone to talk to at night. And Beth was smart. Micki would have flunked Spanish every term if not for her. And she had been right when she said not to trust The Fives.

God, The Fives. They seemed like nothing now.

Right this minute, Beth was down at Kimmie Taylor's some-where in the Gaslamp District, probably smoking weed. Why was she hanging out with such a weak link? Micki felt uneasy about her, like she was in some kind of danger. But, hey, smoking a little mj might do her some good, loosen her up a little.

Maybe he wouldn't even want her with him. He might get to know her and not like her. Judging from her history, that seemed to be something she could expect. She should prepare herself, at least.

One thing about her mom. She might be a deceitful bitch but Micki knew she loved her. Was it possible she really meant it when she said she knew she had made a mistake not telling the truth? How much did being sorry count for? How much sorry was sorry enough?

Another thing Micki's father—Jack—used to say: love is the most powerful force in the world.

Gala groaned and rolled onto her back, wanting Micki to rub her tummy. She sat up and did this for a few minutes. The velvet softness of her skin was so familiar beneath Micki's fingertips, almost as familiar as her own skin. She smelled her fingers and tears sprang to her eyes.

She could not just suddenly get up and go away from Gala. She imagined her dog wandering the house, puzzling out her absence. Sniffing in the corners, whimpering outside her bedroom door, and maybe, when she got a chance, lying on the bed. Her mother would turn the room into a sitting room for herself so that if Micki decided she wanted to come home there would be nowhere for her except the guest room off the kitchen. Her mother had always wished for her own little room to make a mess of—well, if Micki left she'd have one for sure; Gala would walk around it, looking for the bed, wanting to climb up and nestle on the pillows and whimpering because she couldn't. Someday she would die and Micki might never know.

Micki could not stop crying. She had the saddest and most disappointing life. This day should have been exciting, learning the identity of her birth father. Instead it was a maze and she did not know how to get out of it.

An hour or so later she heard a noise outside the door and a gentle knock.

"I've left you some supper," her mother said.

"I hate you," Micki yelled. "I don't want your food."

Gala hopped off the bed and pointed her Irish setter nose at the doorknob. When Micki did not immediately let her out, she bumped the knob with her nose.

"All right, all right," Micki said, and got off the bed. She felt stiff and hungry and miserable as a homeless girl living in a rescue mission. She was exhausted and ached all over and she could not think clearly.

But she was still madder than she had ever been in her life.

She opened the door for Gala, then picked up the tray and carried it into her room, slamming the door with her foot. Hard enough to make the the pictures on her wall rattle.

Besides baked potato and hamburger, which Mickie loved, her mother had made the best dessert in the world, lemon pudding cake, and she had given her an extra-large serving.

Which was bribery and she wasn't going to fall for it.

You can cook anything you want, Micki thought, but I'll never forgive you.

She put the tray on her desk. She was not going to actually sit down—that was too much like capitulation. She walked around her room, looking at things. She walked onto the balcony and back inside. If she went to live with Eddie French, would she take the trophy she won in track and field last year? What about the stuffed porcupine her father, her adoptive father, gave her and the little suede bag he brought home from New Mexico filled with interesting rocks and a coyote tooth? From time to time she paused at the desk to eat a mouthful. Almost immediately, she felt better. With something in her stomach, she plotted her next move.

Obviously, she was not going to leave home with Eddie French. Not right away, when she did not even know his hair color. But she was going to call him and invite him to come down to San Diego to sleep over. She wasn't going to ask permission, either. She wanted to try out what it was like to eat meals with him, find out if he liked dogs and get used to the way he looked. But she wanted to do it on her own turf where she knew she could go to her own bedroom and shut the door and not come out. Unless she wanted to.

Micki finished eating and moved back onto the bed and picked up her cell phone.

This was crazy—her hand was shaking. She took a deep breath and dialed the number her mother had written on the business card.

It rang twice before he picked it up.

Micki swallowed and wanted to change her mind. "Is this Eddie French?" Whose voice was speaking? It sure didn't sound like her own.

"Micki?"

"Oh," she said. "Yeah. Hi."

"Hi."

The pause on the line was like a long, straight road across the desert. "I got your number from my mother." Adoptive mother.

"Okay."

"So." Micki held the phone away from her, took a deep breath and forced herself to expel it slowly.

He was talking. ". . . know you."

She cleared her throat. "I'm sorry?"

"I said, I want to get to know you."

Her heart beat so hard now she thought she might have a stroke. "Okay."

"But I don't want to make your mom unhappy."

"She's jealous," Micki said, and felt inexplicably guilty. She added, "You know."

"Sure," he said. "Makes sense."

When he said it, Micki saw how her mother's reaction, the secrecy and the jealousy, did make sense in a mean kind of way. But not the dishonesty. Micki would not forgive her that.

"So how do you want to do this?" he asked.

She took another breath. "Well, I was thinking you could maybe come down here. Stay at our house."

"Really?" he sounded surprised. "Your mom doesn't mind?"

"No," Micki said. "She thinks it's a great idea."

Chapter Twenty-two

"He's coming Saturday." Micki's voice and posture dared Lana to deny her this. "And I told him he could stay overnight so he didn't have to drive all the way back to LA."

Heartsick, Lana said, "No, Micki. We don't know him. You've invited a stranger to sleep in our house." It was as if she patrolled a rampart and the lives of everyone depended on her keeping the enemy out.

"He's my father."

Lana turned from the anger in Micki's eyes. The sun had fallen into the sea but still burned beneath the blue-black waters.

"Don't you care?"

Jack, poor Jack—so quickly disposed of, so lightly dismissed.

"Let's go outside." Lana held the back door open.

"I don't want to."

"Please." Lana led the way and sat on the back stairs.

"It's cold," Micki complained as she sat beside her. "Can I at least go get a sweater?"

Lana took one arm out of the baggy, mended-at-the-elbow, blue wool cardigan that had warmed her through a dozen winters. It had been her first knitting project and was full of mistakes. She stretched it around Micki's shoulders.

At their feet, Buster lay on his side on the cement, his cloudy eyes open, watching them. The porch light made a pool of warm yellow in the darkness of the garden. No crickets in the cold weather, no birds. Lana heard something skitter across the garage roof—probably a wood rat—and music from across the alley.

She said, "Before we talk about Eddie French—"

"Don't apologize because it won't do any good. I'm not going to forgive you so don't bother asking." Micki wrenched herself away, taking the sweater with her.

"I did . . . a bad thing," Lana said. "Worse than I ever realized."

"You lied to me."

"I'm not asking you to forgive me—"

"I never will."

"At least try to understand. While you were in your room, I was thinking over and over, trying to figure out what I might have done differently—"

"You mean, like, just tell me the truth?"

Truth. The way Micki used the word only proved how young and inexperienced she was. She had no idea how complicated the truth could be, mixed up as it always was with motive and fear and equivocation, so many variables that actually finding the truth in any situation required a piercing vision. To a child like Micki it sounded easy—*just tell the truth*—but at that moment, sitting beside her angry daughter, it came to Lana that telling the truth was the greatest challenge of love.

"I admit, I wasn't thinking about you. I mean, I thought I was, but really . . . Micki, my heart hurts—"

"What about me?" Her voice rose. "What do you think my heart feels like?"

Gala ran to the corner of the yard, barking at something, probably the wood rat's cousin, and Buster rose and loped awkwardly after her.

"I'm afraid for our family," Lana said quietly. "I feel us pulling apart from each other."

"So you lied to me? How much sense does that make?"

I didn't lie, Lana thought. At the time it had seemed like the right thing to do, and if you had asked me outright who Eddie French was, I would have told you. Was this a small point in her favor? She remembered reading there were two kinds of sins, those of omission and commission. Either way, she was guilty. Zero points.

"Well, he's coming to dinner," Micki said, "If you don't want to be here, you can just go away and I'll do the cooking."

Lana wanted to prepare Micki for disappointment, for Eddie French being a tease who would make her love him, and when the novelty of parenthood wore off, vanish into cyberspace. Lana did not think he was a bad man—she didn't think he was a man at all; he was a boy living a boy's video game life. It did not matter that Mars routinely had sex with men his age. He was young—that's how Lana saw him. How could he function in any way even vaguely approximating the father of a fifteen-year-old girl, a girl as temperamentally sensitive as Micki? She wanted to tell her daughter about all the casual cruelty there was in the world, the evil and the ignorance, and that she must protect herself against anything that brought her too much joy because in the blink of an eye, the beat of a heart, in no more time than it took for a truck to scream through an intersection, it could all end.

But she could preach until she was hoarse and get nowhere because Micki was like every other human being—she had to learn about life for herself. Eventually she would even understand how slippery truth could be.

"All right," she said, resigning. "I won't make you cook. He can come."

Micki grunted, stood up, and went inside, dropping the old sweater beside Lana, who stuck her arms through the sleeves and wrapped it around her as she sat a little longer, staring at her garden.

The next day, late in the afternoon, Wendy surprised Lana at Urban Greenery. One look at her friend's Halloween hair and Lana's spirits perked up. Wendy wore corduroy slacks and a cotton shirt; a constellation of white paint speckles bloomed on her forearm and more on her neck just above the button-down collar of her shirt. She slung her heavy purse over the corner of the couch and sat down with an expansive sigh.

"I have come to tempt you out of your den. I left messages on your machine."

"I haven't cleared it in days. Sorry." Lana gave a quick summary of events. "He's coming to dinner on Saturday."

Wendy blinked several times.

"Spending the night."

"Holy shit."

Lana passed a hand over her face as if she could wipe something away. "I just gave up," she admitted. "I got tired of being the enemy and fighting her on everything."

"Did you tell her about his drug history and all?"

"She heard it over the phone."

"Well, maybe it's a good thing. Get it all out in the open? Honesty the best policy. The truth never hurt—"

"Yeah, yeah."

"You should have called me."

"She's so full of *will*. I mean, put hers against mine and she'll beat me every time. Remember that time we took her to the zoo and she got mad and said she'd walk home alone? How old was she? Five? Jesus, she was all the way across the parking lot to the stoplight before I caught up to her."

"This is way too heavy to handle without alcohol." Wendy stood up. "Leave your car here and we'll go tie one on at the Bay Club."

"I can't. The girls are expecting me."

"I'll get you home at a decent hour."

Lana said she couldn't, she had too much to do, but as she made excuses she was clearing her desk, putting papers in her in-basket. Yes, it would be a relief to relax in the company of an adult, bliss to let gin manage her thinking for a while. She found Carmino helping a customer in statuary and called him aside, apologizing to the woman who could not decide between trios of copper or zinc planters. She gave Carmino her keys, and he promised to drive the car up to her the next morning.

In Wendy's black BMW, Lana sank back into the satiny burgundy leather upholstery and closed her eyes. She would have liked it fine if Wendy had turned the car and driven due east, on and on until they reached a place where accidents never happened, children behaved themselves, and the natives had no word that meant disaster.

"Damn," Lana said, "I forgot my phone. It's in my car."

"Use mine." Wendy leaned behind her seat and dug into her purse.

The phone on Triesta Way rang three and then four times. Before the fifth ring, she heard her own voice on the answering machine. She waited and then said, "I'm going to have a drink with Wendy. Eat up the cold salmon in the refrigerator. You can make salads. I won't be late."

Wendy cocked an eyebrow at her. "Will they actually do that? Make salmon salads?"

"Oh, probably not. It just makes me feel like a better mother if I make the suggestion. There's frozen pizza."

"Do you ever wonder what kids ate before pizza?"

"God knows. Nuts? Berries?"

"Grubs."

Wendy swung the car into a parking space at the Bay Club and turned off the ignition. She held out a comb. "Drag this through the rat's nest."

Laughter lived near the core of their friendship. Bless Wendy; she had a vein of spontaneous and irreverent lunacy that could almost always lift Lana out of whatever bog she had fallen into.

The Bay Club was an old—which in San Diego meant seventy years—and shabbily elegant establishment perched on a spit of land between the submarine base and the airport. Though primarily a sailing club, it had racquetball courts, exercise facilities, and a small dining room and bar that extended out over the water. Membership was expensive and limited by the size of the marina. Wendy and Michael did not sail, but her family had belonged to the club when she was young and membership had passed on to her at an irresistible price.

A chill westerly was gusting, kicking up whitecaps as they entered the bar. The sail and power boats tossed in their moorings, flags flying. Wendy and Lana found a quiet corner inside, near a window. At the bar, three men in chinos, cotton sweaters, and topsiders drank beer while a basketball game played on the television behind the bar.

Wendy ordered gin martinis with double olives. "Who's the sports guy you'd most like to have sex with?" It was a game they had played for years.

"Michael Jordan," Lana said. "No question."

"Rock singer?" Wendy asked.

"Sting."

Wendy looked disgusted. "You are so boring. You've been giving the same answers for ten years. Why don't you choose someone young?"

"Young guys don't tempt me. I like a guy with seasoning. Besides," Lana said, taking her drink from the waiter, "I'm faithful, like a dog."

"How would you like to be Sting's dog?"

Outside, the late-afternoon sun flashed on the wavelets, off the white of the boats and metal masts and cleats. In a pale blue sky, clouds ran east before the wind, their tails lit with gold.

"I'll sip," Wendy said. "You guzzle."

"Since when are you my pusher?"

"Since you started avoiding me."

"I told you, I haven't had a chance to clear the machine." The astringent gin bit and iced Lana's throat, the fragrant juniper berries buzzed the inside of her nose; together they sent a rush to Lana's brain. Jack always said she was a cheap drunk.

"Talk," Wendy said.

"I told you everything."

"Shit, girl, you barely touched it. You're having him to dinner, but what are you feeling? And what does Beth think of all this?"

Lana slipped the green olive off the toothpick with her teeth and bought a little time chewing it. Wendy's snake-eyed look meant she would not give up until Lana answered her questions.

"I'm so tired of analyzing everything, Wendy. Half the time I don't know what I feel . . . except I miss Jack and I'm sick of pretending I don't."

"Then stop pretending."

"You were the one who told me—"

"I didn't mean for you to make it a twenty-four/seven way of life. I didn't mean for you to hide—"

"If I fall apart, the girls will, too."

"Maybe that'd be a good thing."

Lana shook her head. People always knew what was good for her.

"What about them—what are they feeling?"

Lana started to answer an automatic *fine . . . okay . . . no problem,* then stopped herself. "I honestly don't know. I think they're okay. Beth's being more teenage, getting a little mouthy, but basically she's steady. And Micki hates me and she's planning her new life around Eddie French."

"Has she told you that?"

"Wouldn't you be?"

"I don't know. I don't have a clue what I'd do."

Lana lifted her shoulders and let them drop. "What can I say then?"

"She's over The Fives thing?"

"She's still bugging me about going to Balboa." Feeling pleasantly buzzed and talkative, Lana sipped the fresh drink that had miraculously appeared before her. "Over my dead and decaying body." She went off on a rant about Grace Mamoulian.

Wendy said. "If you dislike La Mamoulian so much, why not take Micki out of Arcadia? Give her what she wants?"

"I worry what'd happen to her in public school."

"She might be happy, Lana. What about the birth mother?"

"Vanished, but he's looking for her. No doubt she'll show up on the doorstep one of these days."

"And when that happens?"

Lana held up her glass and peered into it like a crystal ball. "I'll kill her."

A cheer went up from the bar and the men dug in their pockets for their wallets and began handing bills around. The bartender switched the channel to another game in progress.

"You have no faith in yourself," Wendy said. "Micki loves you. No one can replace you."

"It's so unfair to Jack. It's like one night of hot teenage sex is somehow equivalent to fourteen years spent raising the most turbulent, the most challenging—"

"Would he say they were equivalent?"

"Who? Jack?"

"No. Eddie French." Wendy looked at her. "He wouldn't, would he? This is you, making it all up when you don't even know the guy."

Lana pushed her drink away; she was through. "You've brought me here to lecture me and now you've done it and I've had two martinis and I'm not even slightly high."

Wendy laughed.

"I want to go home and go to bed." Lana stood and the room rocked like a sailboat.

"Don't be angry with me, Lana."

"What do you expect?"

"Just do what I said. Relax about Eddie French. Trust in Micki's good sense. You don't have to fear this guy." Wendy leaned forward and the waves of her persimmon hair swung out, quoting her face. "Promise me you'll think about it, okay?"

"Oh," Lana said. "Yeah. Ceaselessly."

Chapter Twenty-three

"Constantly, ceaselessly." Lana slammed the door of Wendy's BMW and walked up the steps to the porch, calling back over her shoulder, "Neverendingly, interminably, endlessly."

At the sound of her key in the lock, Gala bounded and slid to the door, barking wildly. She danced and spun around as if Lana had been gone for weeks. Lana pushed aside the tennis shoes and folded laundry waiting to be taken upstairs, and sat on the bottom stair. While Gala licked her and nuzzled her face, Buster emerged from the kitchen, head lowered in submission and uncertainty. He retreated to the far side of the entry and lay down with his head on his paws, watching her.

Micki spoke to her from the second floor landing. "Tiff's here."

Lana looked up, grabbing the newel post for balance. Tiff. Tiffany. The name made a few circles through Lana's brain before it attached to any feeling. Brat. "Nice to see you, Tiff." Not a hint of sarcasm.

Tiff hung her streaky blond head over the rail. "Isn't it cool about Mick? About her dad? He used to go out with that really cute actress on *Mistique*." Tiff paused, apparently expecting a reaction. "You know that show about the witch coven? They go to this high school in L.A. and they're at war with another coven, only it's all adults and really bad?"

Lana had no idea what Tiff was talking about. She also felt dizzy.

"What's the matter, Ma?" Micki came down the stairs and peered at her. "Omigod, are you drunk?" She looked up at Tiff and they began to giggle. "You are. You are totally blitzed."

She wasn't blitzed, just slightly off center for the time being and a bit dizzy. Her daughter's face was almost, but not quite, out of focus. She held onto the newel post and spoke carefully. "First, I am not drunk. I am just a little high. Second, even if I were—as you say—'blitzed,' it is none of your business. Third, I'm going to have a drink of water and then—fourth and finally—I'm going to take a shower and when I get out I want you to be in bed." She focused on Tiff—traitorous, back-stabbing teen scum. "How are you getting home?" *Oh denizen of septic tanks.*

"My mother said I could spend the night."

"We did our homework, Ma."

Lana thought she would sort out the turn and return of teenage friendship when she could think more clearly. "You have fifteen minutes to get into bed. Turn off the video and go to bed. Go to bed."

Tiffany and Micki held each other and collapsed in laughter.

Buster stood at the kitchen door and watched Lana pour a glass of water from the cooler on the back porch. She took one swallow and felt ill. It was years since she had drunk martinis . . . and on an empty stomach. What had she been thinking?

She went outdoors and took a deep breath of the bracing air. The sky was blue-black and cloudless and even in Mission Hills a few stars were visible, a handful of salt scattered across the night. No moon. She thought she might throw up.

When her eyes became accustomed to the darkness, she walked along the crunching gravel paths between the raised garden beds where a patchwork selection of plants grew: roses in semi-dormancy, forget-me-nots, pansies, and snapdragons already ripening at their tips. A cherry tomato, planted by the birds the summer before, bore tiny green fruit, hard as marbles.

Nothing and no one could stop spring. It would come because the planet spun and to prove it, all she had to do was close her eyes. The world tilted on its axis and the days lengthened. The alternation of the seasons could not be stopped by drunk drivers and birth fathers. The turning of the planet and the movement of the stars had never failed Lana. In a world of instantaneous change, any one or thing capable of creating the galaxies, ordering the comings and goings of comets and meteors, the falling of stars and the rising of the sun and moon, must be—before all else—constant. Utterly dependable. This was the god Lana believed in. She had been a bust as a Methodist, but God was still there, down deep, lodged and immovable in her.

When she went upstairs, she looked in on Beth and found her bed empty. Micki stood in the door of their shared bathroom, wearing a 10K tee shirt of Jack's. Tiff stood behind her.

"She went to Kimmie's."

Behind Micki, Tiff nodded her head. "She said you wouldn't mind."

Carmino came with Lana's car the next morning, and she drove him back to Urban Greenery and then turned up the hill to Arcadia School. She was not wearing her work clothes, the sporty Urban Greenery polo shirt and slacks. Instead she had taken particular care to choose an outfit that was stern, professional, and meant business, a wool skirt and blazer in a shade the saleswoman at Nordstrom had called *crème anglaise,* and a pale yellow pullover. No jewelry and her hair sleek. Her head hurt and she felt mean.

She went directly to Grace Mamoulian's office. Grace looked up from behind a large bowl of narcissi, her plucked and arched brows rising like sash windows.

"Lana, what exciting news for Micki." Grace came around from behind her desk with her manicure outstretched. She wore her signature brown, a knit suit with a high collar and brass buttons the size of half dollars. "It's about time something good happened to her. Sit down, sit down."

Grace moved the arrangement of narcissi aside. Their fragrance hit Lana's brain like a blackjack. She stayed on her feet and clutched the leather strap of her handbag so hard she felt the stitching press into her palm. "I'm not here about Micki."

"Oh." The eyebrows dipped and came together. Grace went back to her desk chair.

She feels safer with four feet of walnut between us, Lana thought. Well, she isn't. No one was safe around Lana that morning.

"What can you tell me about Kimmie Taylor?"

"Kimmie? Oh. You're here about Beth?"

"Tell me about this girl."

"Well, she's new this year. Transferred from The Bishop's School."

"What kind of a girl is she?"

Grace's guard went up almost as visibly as if she had drawn a brown cloak around her shoulders and over her head. "She and Beth are thick as thieves, aren't they? They've always got their heads together, plotting. I'm surprised you haven't met her."

There was a note of censure in Grace Mamoulian's voice. Lana sat down, composed herself, her hands in her lap, both feet on the floor as she awaited the answer to her question. From the next office she heard the secretaries and aides talking, their voices like murmurs in a theater as the curtain rises.

Grace cleared her throat and reached for a pen on her blotter. She turned it end over end. "Well, let's see. She's a fairly good student. Quite pretty. She seems . . . nice." Grace Mamoulian's laughter barked at Lana. "Girls this age aren't easy to read, but then I don't have to tell you that, do I? You have two of them, and so close together. I don't know how you do it. And now this new . . . father."

Lana was not aware of looking surprised but she must have.

Grace said, "Oh, the upper classes can't stop talking about it. They all play 'Ghost' and that actress from *Mistique* is a great favorite with them."

"What about her family?"

Grace pressed her lips together. "What's happened, Lana? Why the questions?"

"I have two daughters here. I pay thousands of dollars a year in tuition and special fees. I contribute generously and regularly to the Arcadia endowment. I want you to tell me about this girl Kimmie."

"Lana, there's no need to be hostile. There are privacy issues. I'm sure you—"

"I don't care what kind of issues there are, Grace. We've known each other a long time. You know the kind of woman I am and you know my girls."

"Well." Grace Mamoulian sat back, still playing with the pen. "Let me think a minute." She patted the tip of it against her lips and then pressed the intercom button and asked her secretary to bring in Kimmie Taylor's file.

Silence.

The atmosphere of the large and elegantly furnished office, with its wide walnut desk and built-in bookcases, the deep pile rug and shuttered windows, and the arrangement of expensive furniture, was both academic and feminine and intended to impress parents. Lana wondered how much of every tuition check was spent to ensure that impression.

"Here we are," Grace said as she took the file from her secretary's hand and opened it on the desk before her. She ran her gleaming, blood-brown fingernail down a page and looked up. "Her father fairly recently remarried. He lives in Orange County. A Realtor, very well to do, I think. Her mother is a makeup artist."

"In San Diego?"

"Mmmm, yes."

"What else?"

"She has a sister, Jules, who attends San Diego State."

"What about her grades, disciplinary problems. Does she get into trouble?"

Grace Mamoulian looked affronted. "These files *are* private, Lana. I can't tell you anything else without breaking confidentiality."

"She could be wanted in five states and you wouldn't tell me?"

Grace Mamoulian laughed, jolly as a toothache. "This is Arcadia. Our girls come from good families. There are problems occasionally, of course. We do live in the modern world. But there's nothing in Kimmie Taylor's record you need to worry about." She sat back, closing the folder, and it was clear that she meant for their conversation to be over. "Is there something else?"

"I want to see Beth." Lana stood up. "And Kimmie."

"They're in the middle of class. . . ."

"I know that but I still want to see them."

Two deep hash marks appeared between Grace Mamoulian's eyebrows and her squinched mouth made a fist. "I can let you see Beth, of course, but Kimmie . . ."

"I won't take them off the school grounds. We'll go outside and sit on the front steps."

"No. I don't think so. That would not be appropriate." Grace Mamoulian looked trapped, and Lana felt better than she had all morning. What she asked was unusual, perhaps, but not outrageous. She was a parent and being a parent gave her certain rights. It flashed across Lana's mind that this was what it meant to be a parent, to recognize her own legitimate authority and exercise her power where she had to. Score one for the embattled army of mommies.

"Grace, I have a family situation here that I can take care of quickly and painlessly if I see both girls together."

"Very well. There's a conference room, across from the front office. Why don't you go and sit down in there and I'll get a monitor to summon the girls." Grace added coolly, "Will that suit you?"

When Beth and a slender, dark-haired girl came into the conference room about ten minutes later, Lana was standing at the window, watching the sunlight flash on the long, curving fronds of the palms that marked Arcadia's main entrance. She had found a couple of aspirin in the bottom of her purse and swallowed them dry.

"Hi, Ma," Beth said. It gratified Lana to hear the quiver of apprehension in her voice. "How come you want to see us?"

"Sit down. Both of you." She waited a moment. "Introduce your friend, Beth."

Beth sighed and slumped in her chair. "Ma, Kimmie. Kimmie, Ma."

Lana looked at Kimmie Taylor and in that moment witnessed something extraordinary and chilling. The girl's expression—which had been somewhere between sullen and suspicious when she entered the room—lifted and opened in a perfect imitation of what Lana later defined to herself as "charming youth."

"Mrs. Porter, I'm so glad to meet you. Finally. My mother keeps saying, *Have you met Beth's mother, have you met Beth's mother?* Now I can finally say yes."

Lana knew she had trouble on her hands.

"I need to talk to you both."

Kimmie made a terrible strained and apologetic face. "Oh, gee, Mrs. Porter, I'm in the middle of a math test."

"What about you, Beth?"

"Whatever." She fidgeted, grabbed at her hair, and began braiding it. As she pulled the hair over and under her fingers, she turned her head away from Lana and stared at the floor. Her skin had a yellow, slightly greenish cast and her blue eyes were cupped by circles of fatigue. Unhealthy. Lana felt an instant twist of guilt as she thought of meals unprepared and conversations deferred.

"I didn't give you permission to stay out last night." Beth looked at her hands.

"It's my fault, Mrs. Porter, I begged her to come. I've been so worried about this math test because I just totally don't get the theorems. I mean the first ones, yeah, I learned those but since Christmas it's gotten so hard and I feel like my brain's exploding. D'you know what I mean? My mom'd help me but she's an artist, not a math genius." Kimmie smiled. "Don't blame Beth, Mrs. Porter. Honest to God, she said she was supposed to stay home but I begged and begged."

Lana could not prove Kimmie lied but she knew cunning and deceit when she heard them play a duet on a sour piano.

"Beth, from now on and indefinitely, you are forbidden to go to Kimmie's house. She can visit at our place. If you have to study, you can do it at home." Lana watched Beth; her gaze remained fixed on the floor. "We have a big house, Kimmie. Which you would know if Beth had ever invited you over."

Kimmie giggled and rolled her eyes. "My mom will be, like, so glad to get us out of her hair."

Beth folded her arms across her chest and slipped lower in her chair.

"Tell me about your family," Lana said.

"Ma-a."

"Well, my mom's a makeup artist." She chirped like the finches in the bottlebrush tree. "She commutes to L.A. a couple of days a week which is like such a bore, as you can imagine. She and my sister, Jules, and me live in a condo downtown. You guys are so lucky to have a house. I would give anything not to live downtown."

Kimmie rolled her eyes and chirruped on while Beth watched and Lana listened with reluctant fascination.

"My dad lives in Orange County. He's a real estate broker. And he's got this new baby who is just the most adorable thing.

"My dad and me are real close, though." Kimmie tossed back her limp, dark hair. "He's super busy, of course. Plus having a baby—he wants to spend a bunch of time with him. Bond, you know? But he calls me at night and we have these great talks and he gives me advice about stuff. I can totally trust him to be straight with me."

"Well," Lana said. "You're a lucky girl, then."

Kimmie grinned and sat back like an attorney resting her case.

Outside the room Lana heard students passing in the hall, the rise and fall of excited female voices. She glanced up at the clock.

"Is that it?" Beth asked.

"No." Lana's hands tingled with the temptation to slap Beth for her insolent tone of voice. "You are forbidden, Beth—I am saying this now in front of Kimmie so there will be no misunderstanding—forbidden to go to Kimmie's house. Under any circumstances."

"Ma-a, you already said that."

"Gosh," Kimmie said, "is that forever, Mrs. Porter?"

Kimmie had a small, black tattoo on the back of her left hand between her thumb and forefinger. A cross. Otherwise she looked just like Beth in her plaid uniform skirt, white blouse, and navy blue vee-necked sweater. Probably she was just another girl, harmless and confused and growing up awkwardly in a sad family. It troubled Lana that she had only an instinctive dislike of her and could find nothing concrete to object to. She couldn't blame her for not washing her hair, and half the girls at Arcadia had tattoos. Even Wendy had a flower inked on her ankle and a small star on her shoulder—the latter a birthday gift from her boys.

Relax, she told herself. Don't overreact.

"Not forever, Kimmie. But until I've had a chance to talk to your mother."

"That seems fair enough," Kimmie said, standing up.

Beth stood beside her.

"Sit down, Beth—you're not going anywhere."

"She has a test, too," Kimmie said.

"I do, Ma, honest."

"You're going to have to make it up."

"Mrs. Porter, Dr. Williams isn't going to like that. She is, like, so rigid."

"Leave us, Kimmie." Lana added, "Please."

The minute the door closed behind Kimmie, Beth cried out, "Oh, my Jesus Christ, that was so horrible, that was just the worst thing you've ever done to me." She sank as far down as she could in her chair, laid her head back, and stared at the ceiling. "You mortified me. You totally humiliated me in front of my best friend."

"I thought Linda and Madison were your best friends."

"You're not going to turn into one of those mothers who tells their kids—"

"Be quiet, Beth, and listen to me." Lana paused. "Sit up straight and look at me."

Beth sighed, sat up, and stared at her, opening her eyes so insolently wide they looked ready to pop out.

"I don't believe half of what Kimmie said. And even if it's all true, you knew I didn't want you to go out and you deliberately disobeyed me. What did you think my reaction would be? Just shine it on?"

"Well, I wasn't going to hang around the house with Micki and Tiff. All they could talk about was this Eddie guy, her *father*, and how rich he must be and who he dates. Like Tiff's all of a sudden her best friend all over again because supposedly this guy fucked . . ."

"Stop it."

Beth gawked at her and laughed.

Lana looked down at the palm of her right hand. She rubbed her thumb in a circle at the center. Outside the window a gardener used a whining leaf blower, and the drone tunneled into her head and amped up her headache.

She spoke carefully. "I want you to cool off this friendship with Kimmie."

"Why?" Beth sat up, tossing back her hair, jutting her jaw. "What's the matter with her?"

"I don't like the influence she's having on you."

"You don't know her, you don't know anything about her."

"I don't have to explain myself to you, Beth."

"You are so unfair. So . . . arbitrary."

Lana almost smiled. Inside this new and defiant Beth there was still a girl who loved words. It wasn't much to give her hope, but it was something.

"I'm sorry you feel that way, but I'm not going to change my mind."

Beth folded her arms across her chest and looked at the tabletop. "You want me to cut her. Just like Tiff did Micki? People have the right to choose their own friends, and I choose Kimmie. I like Kimmie and she understands me."

If Lana tried to ground her, she would run away. Kids thought nothing of running off nowadays. They had seen everything on television and had the courage of fools.

"You're hung over. That's why you're so pissy. Micki told me you went out last night and got smashed. She said you humiliated her in front of Tiff." Beth sneered. "If Dad were alive he would be so mad at you."

For an instant the fluorescent light in the conference room blinded Lana. She stood up.

"He never would have let the family get so fucked up."

"The family isn't—"

"We're as bad as all the rest of them. We used to be perfect and now we're shit. I wish it was you died, not him."

Lana's hand lashed out before her brain engaged. She felt the sting of her palm against Beth's cheek, instantly pulled back, and covered her mouth with her hands. Stunned, Beth touched her cheek with her fingertips.

"Beth, I'm sorry—"

Cry, please cry, and then I'll hold you and it will be as if . . .

Beth sniffed and shook her head, reached back, and lifted her hair off the back of her neck and then gave it a rebellious little toss. She was out of the room before Lana could think of anything to say.

Chapter Twenty-four

Sixty minutes later, Lana burst in on Mars in her office at the university. Reading her e-mail, she was dressed in aubergine sweats. Through the window behind her there was a view of an open, grassy space bordered by the campus's signature eucalyptus trees. Without sitting down, Lana told her sister everything—about drinking with Wendy, Beth going to Kimmie's overnight without permission, and the scene at the school.

"She said she wished I was dead." Lana wiped her eyes with the back of her hand. She had begun the day perfectly groomed; now she felt like a bag lady. "And she meant it."

"Right then, she did."

"She's right. I *have* screwed up. I've made a terrible mess of everything."

"Stop feeling sorry for yourself." Mars pulled a box of tissues from her lower desk drawer and slid it across the desk. "So you aren't perfect. Big deal."

Lana stared at her sister. "Have you been listening to me? Are we even in the same room?"

"Lana, Beth isn't going to hate you forever for one slap."

"It's child abuse—neglect, too. I should have stayed home last night."

"Spare me the breast-beating. You went out with a friend. And Beth took advantage and cut out on you." She leaned across her desk. "Think back, Lannie, think of the times I broke curfew and stayed out all night, think about the dope I smoked and guys I fucked before I was eighteen. I'm not recommending any of this for Beth, believe me, but I'm just saying it's not the end of the world if she gets a little wild." Mars ran her fingers through her thick curls, shaking her head as if she needed to dislodge something. "What did you think was going to happen? Jack dies, you bawl and mope for a few days, and then get over it? It wasn't just Jack that died. It was your old family that went with him. Now you've got to rebuild."

"You think I don't know that?"

How do you rebuild a family? If she could slow her mind down and take each item one at a time, turn it over in her thoughts and examine it from every side, then she could make some kind of orderly list. When she could do that, she would have the answer.

The rest of the week passed without incident. Stella called daily to lecture her about real estate and Realtors. Lana promised to have a friend in the business call her. "Someone you can trust, Ma." Kathryn called to talk and then had nothing to say though Lana was sure something was going on at *Tres Palomas*. Beth sulked, stayed out of Lana's way, and spoke to her only when she could not avoid it. Micki was cool like a card player holding onto her trump as long as possible. The dogs liked Lana just fine but she figured they'd go for her throat if she stopped feeding them. On Friday night Tiff invited Micki to spend the night. Beth snarled that Kimmie would be over later.

Lana remembered Kathryn's idea about escaping on horseback and imagined how far she and her sister could get away together.

The run-and-read club met at Lana's on Friday night. She filled two vacuum pumps with regular and decaf coffee and mixed a batch of toffee brownies as her contribution to the refreshments, ran the vacuum quickly through the front rooms, and checked the little downstairs powder room tucked in under the stairs. As usual, a pile of teen magazines crowded the cramped counter space. The magazine lying open on the top of the mess caught Lana's attention. She sat on the toilet seat cover and looked at the article about Eddie French and the witchy teen idol on *Mistique*. She gathered the magazines in her arms and carried them onto the back porch.

By the time the run-and-read group had arrived, Kimmie had also appeared dressed in black, eyes outlined in charcoal, her lipstick the color of blood. She and Beth were enclosed in the playhouse upstairs. Planning new ways to make me suffer, Lana thought, and surprised herself by smiling.

The run-and-read club had begun as an informal group of friends. Gradually its numbers had increased and now there were eight in the club though they were rarely all present at the same time. They ran occasional Five and Ten Ks, met at the bay or out on Harbor Island to run, and every month they got together to talk about the books they were reading and to exchange copies. They were an odd mixture. Joan Lang was a one hundred percent Republican Catholic; Jessie Ward supported every liberal cause that came her way and marched in the annual MLK parade with the members of the Blue Sky Commune to which she once belonged; Jilly Pepper worked for the *Union-Tribune,* and Lorna McCoy was a CPA to her marrow.

That night's leader would be Susan Weinstein, a high school principal. She was a tall woman in her early fifties with a springy cap of salt-and-pepper hair, a nervous manner, and a determined sense of humor that amused and exhausted Lana.

With glasses of wine and cups of coffee, they settled into the couch and chairs in the grownup living room and for more than an hour talked about the novels they were reading. Around nine they moved to the kitchen for refreshments.

Beth and Kimmie came through the back door, laughing, just as the break began. Their cheeks were a healthy pink.

"Where have you been?" Conversation around the table stopped.

Beth shrugged. "Out back, with Buster." She picked up a toffee brownie. "Can I have one of these?"

"I made cheese crisps," Wendy said. "The kind you like."

"Cool," Beth said. She and Kimmie began to load their plates.

Something itched at the corner of Lana's mind.

Joan said, "Leave some for the rest of us."

Kimmie laughed, "You would not believe how hungry I am."

"Mmm, I think I would," Jessie said. "I think I would."

Lana watched as the girls said good night over their shoulders and went upstairs. She heard the sound of their giggles as they climbed the stairs and felt her friends looking at her. She looked back at them.

Susan said, "Every night I go down on my knees and thank God I don't have teenagers anymore."

"Even Beth," Joan shook her head in disbelief. "I never thought it would happen."

Jessie said, "Once upon a time, even you were obnoxious and ill-mannered, Joanie."

Obnoxious and ill-mannered. This was how Lana's friends saw her daughter. Lana wanted to defend her, except that the description fit. And Jessie, a psychologist, said it was normal and nothing to worry about by itself. "Humans are programmed to rebel," she said. "If we don't do it when we're young, we do it when we're old."

"I never rebelled," Joan Lang said. "I never had anything to rebel against."

Jessie looked at her over her half frames. "You're the kind who runs off with a TV repairman when she's sixty years old."

Having spilled everything to Wendy at the Bay Club, it was not so difficult for Lana to tell her friends about bringing Eddie French into the house, about Micki inviting him to dinner and overnight. Even the slap. As she spoke they drew up chairs and stools, poured more wine and coffee for themselves. When Lana finished the story there was a moment of silence.

"Wow," Lorna said. "You must feel awful."

Lana blinked back tears. Was she so starved for understanding?

"Oh, honey," cried Elsie Diaz, wrapping her fat arms around Lana, "you've been having a time."

For a few moments everyone commiserated with Lana and then they started talking more or less all at once, every woman with a different take on the situation.

"I don't think you should have invited him to come," Susan said. "Next thing, you're going to meet the mother. When she shows up, there's going to be big trouble. I don't think you're ready for that."

"Forget the mother," Joan said. "What about him? My God, my boys would spend all day playing Ghost if I let them. It's the most incredible video game. This Eddie's like a . . . star."

"Plus, you say he dates the black-haired witch from *Mistique?*" said Jilly Pepper, the youngest of the group and noted for her lack of tact. "Shit, Lana, you got big trouble."

Elsie glared at her.

Jilly held up her hands defensively. "Well, it's true. She can't compete with him. He comes in carrying a ton of baggage and all of it glamorous."

"I'm not trying to compete," Lana said forlornly.

Joan laughed. "Of course you are. He's a frontal assault on your authority, not to mention Jack's memory and your role in Mick's life."

"I have this friend," Jilly said. "I went to school with her—she went off with her birth mother, never looked back."

"Shut up, Jilly," Wendy said.

"You know, there's a tremendous psychic wound in every adopted child, even the happiest," Jilly said. "My friend's still in heavy-duty therapy. Whatever happens with this guy, all kinds of deep and serious shit is going to get stirred up in Micki. "

"I know that, Jilly, but I didn't have any choice." Lana was glad now she had not mentioned Eddie French's two trips to rehab and his scrapes with the law. "There wasn't anything else I could do."

"You could have told him to stay out of your lives, and forbidden Micki—"

Susan, the mother of three, laughed.

Wendy said, "Jilly, you don't know what you're talking about. You can't forbid teenagers. You do that and you're asking for trouble. Personally," Wendy looked at the women around the table, "I think Lana did the right thing, the only thing she could. She invited him and now she can set the terms."

"Plus," Susan said, "you can keep an eye on them."

"And you better do that," Joan said, wagging her head. "How old did you say he is?"

"Thirty-one or two, I think."

"Oh, my dear, an undomesticated male." Susan said, laying her hand on her heart. "Be still, be still."

"Is he good-looking?" Joan asked.

Lana thought a minute. "In a young kind of way."

Lorna said portentously, "He's a young man and you have two very pretty and innocent daughters."

Lana laughed. "He's her father, Lorna."

Across the room, Susan groaned.

"What?" Lana asked her. "What?"

"Sex, Lana. Sex. You've heard of it?"

Lana put down her coffee cup. "What is this, a gang bang?"

"You think incest only happens in novels?"

"Why is he so interested in her?" Jilly wanted to know. "What's in it for him?"

"Hey, fathers love their children. Just as much as mothers," Wendy said. "And I think its totally fabulous this guy has always wanted to know Micki, that he's never forgotten her."

"I think it's kinda creepy," Jilly said.

"Jesus Christ," Wendy said. "What kind of family did you grow up in?"

Jessie said, "I hate to say it, Lana, but I think you've got another problem."

"Great. Birth mothers, runaways, incest—what could be worse?"

"Beth's smoking dope."

"No." Lana shook her head so hard she felt her earrings swing and hit her jawline.

Wendy said, "You're kidding, Jessie. You're crazy."

Out of all of them, only Lana knew Jessie was right. It was this that had been itching at the edge of her thoughts the last week or two; this explained the vaguely dusty smell, the peculiarities of appetite, the sleepiness. "That's why they were outside."

Jessie nodded. "Sorry to be the one to tell you, kiddo."

No one said anything for a moment or two. Outside, the wind had risen. The wind chimes clanged against the side of the house and the Tillmans' Newfoundland howled mournfully.

When her friends had left and Lana had cleaned the kitchen, she went upstairs to say good night to Beth. She knocked on the door to the playhouse and when there was no response, she opened it, not trying to be quiet. The television was on and they were asleep on the floor, covered by a pair of old blankets. They looked as if they had fallen asleep in midsentence, still in their shoes and socks, the crumbs of toffee brownies scattered around them. In their sleep all hint of resentment and deceit vanished from their faces. Beth's mouth was open slightly; the sweet rosebud of her inner lip glistened in the television's flickering light. She lay slightly on her side, exposing the small of her back where her skinny tee shirt had ridden up. Between it and the top of her sweat pants, her skin was a lovely, warm pinkish caramel and Lana's palms tingled with the longing to lay her hand there. Motherhood's sublime cruelty was deprivation. She had gone from having permission to touch and know this other body as well as her own, to being forbidden to touch without permission—and half the time being laughed at for wanting to. And so it seemed Lana's life grew narrower with every day. She could no longer touch Jack, she was not allowed to touch either Beth or Micki. Motherhood, of all the roles she might have chosen, seemed the most thankless and bitter.

Later in the night she lay in bed, unable to sleep. The events of the last two days, capped by Jessie's revelation that evening, replayed in her mind and demanded that she do something.

Aloud she said, "I will but I've got to sleep." She had to rest for what lay ahead.

She got out of bed and opened the old cedar chest in her closet in which she kept extra blankets and all the family's photo albums. She checked the date on the spine—1989—and carried it back to bed with her, then sat propped in her pillows until after three, her eyes burning with fatigue. There were photos of the cottage on the grounds of Urban Greenery, of Wendy and Michael and all the children at Sea World and the zoo, on camping trips and at La Bufadora down in Baja. On one page all the shots were of Jack and the girls when they were two and three. Their little faces shining with hopeful potential broke through Lana's self control. She pressed her face into the pillows and let her heart break. Alone except for Gala, who stood with her chin resting on the edge of the bed, dark copper eyes never leaving Lana's face, she wept until she no longer felt any pity for herself. Exhausted, she felt nothing and closed her eyes without troubling to reach up and turn off the light. Sleep opened its door and as she was about to step through, she paused on the threshold and had two clear thoughts.

She would not give up. She would confront Beth tomorrow. She would keep on being a pain in the ass to her girls, a nag and a burden, and someday they would thank her for being steadfast.

And she would invite Mars to have dinner with the family and Eddie French. Mars knew about young men. She would make it easier.

Chapter Twenty-five

On Saturday morning the sky was a flat, dimensionless ceiling of high clouds the color of pancake batter, and there was static in the air as if someone were trying to send a message along old, stripped lines. The garden was full of the noise of birds when Lana awoke; she listened to them for some moments, isolating the species. The mockingbird, of course, loud and clear, probably up on the roof. The dither of the pink-breasted finches drawn to the feeders in the olive trees, the mourning doves. She felt good. Glad that book club was over and she would not have to host for another eight months, glad it had gone well and there were not too many delicious leftovers to tempt her. Then she remembered the conversation around the table and her mood sank like the barometer.

She had to confront Beth about the marijuana.

But not immediately. Not while Kimmie was still here.

She dressed and went downstairs and looked around the untidy kitchen. She had refused Wendy's offer to help clean up. She had wanted to be alone.

She called Mars and invited her to dinner.

"You mean you trust me with *him?*"

"Don't be a wise ass," Lana said. "I need your moral support."

"I'll be there. You better believe I will."

Next she made a cup of coffee and while it dripped through, she went upstairs and into the playroom where Beth and Kimmie still lay, zonked to the world. The room smelled sourly female. Lana opened the room's one small window and roused them, trying not to sound too abrasive.

"Good morning, ladies, time to rise and shine."

Kimmie groaned and rolled onto her stomach. She lifted herself onto her forearms and squinted at Lana. Blurred mascara made misery of her eyes.

Fifteen-year-olds aren't supposed to look like this, Lana thought.

Beth lay curled into the beanbag chair, her face half covered by a blanket. Lana nudged her shoulder gently to get her moving. "I know it's early, but I have a ton of stuff to do today and I need your help.

"I'll be happy to drive you home first, Kimmie."

Beth groaned.

"It's half past eight now. I want to be in the car by ten. That gives you plenty of time for a shower and something to eat."

"Can't Mick help you? It's her—"

"She'll help, but I need you, too."

Groans of protest and complaint followed Lana downstairs. While she drank her coffee she loaded the dishwasher and cleaned up the kitchen.

Marijuana, marijuana, marijuana. The pretty word sang through her thoughts, and when she shoved it aside, back it bounced. She had to talk to Beth, but first there was the dinner with Micki's birth father to think about.

What a cheery life she was having. Any more laughs and she'd be forced to shoot up a post office.

She made another cup of coffee, peeled a banana and ate it as she thumbed through her favorite stained and dog-eared book of family recipes, deciding finally to fix a party lasagna using the last jar of marinara sauce. She made a shopping list: ricotta and mozzarella cheese, parmesan, mushrooms, roasted red peppers, raisins, and walnuts. Maybe Eddie French was allergic to walnuts. Maybe he'd keel over and solve half her problems. The makings of a Caesar salad, a long loaf of French bread, and a couple of bottles of good red wine. Fair red wine. There was no reason to blow the budget on this event; she did not want Eddie French to think she had tried too hard.

Good red wine. She did not want him to think she was cheap.

She sat back and warmed her hands on her coffee cup, staring at the lazy Susan in the middle of the table, cluttered as always with notes and pencils and bills. Gala came through the pet door and put her nose under Lana's elbow. Absently, she petted the silky, auburn head.

Jack said she was a contradiction. A disorganized woman who made lists compulsively and lived amidst islands of clutter while longing for order. She worried about time and yet she was always late. A good cook who rarely cooked. A loving mother whose daughters smoked dope and ran away from home at night.

As much as she wanted Eddie French to be a jerk Micki could not wait to be rid of, Lana hoped he was special.

Had she ever thought this before? She actually hoped he would be a nice guy and that Micki would feel better-connected to the world because of him. She sat back in her chair, slightly breathless with the realization that something in her had changed over the last weeks. After scrambling up a cliff for the last month, after skinning her knees and cutting her hands on every rocky obstacle, she seemed to have reached a plateau of sorts, a level place.

A little before ten, Beth and Kimmie dragged themselves into the kitchen, both still looking exhausted. They had taken showers; their damp hair clung to their hairlines and dripped down the back of their little black tee shirts. They made a mess where Lana had just cleaned—cereal bits on the oak tabletop, sugar and drops of milk. The only bread in the house was an unsliced loaf. Beth cut two irregular slices more than an inch wide but Lana said nothing. Kimmie smiled excessively and made sit-com conversation. Beth moped with her shoulders slumped and her feet shuffling on the floor like an old woman's.

Lana poured two glasses of orange juice and set them on the table. Kimmie thanked her.

"I'm making that special lasagna for dinner," Lana told Beth. "What shall I get for dessert? One of those cakes from Costco?"

Beth looked at Kimmie and rolled her eyes. To keep her irritation down, Lana pressed the balls of her feet into the floor. Her right foot cramped.

"Damn!" She sat down, took off her shoe, and massaged her foot.

"What's wrong?" Kimmie asked.

"Cramp," said Lana, gritting her teeth against the pain.

"Maybe you need calcium. My mom used to be a dancer and when she got cramps the doctor gave her injections. Calcium, I think."

"I'm going to need your help today," she told Beth as she retied her shoe and gingerly put some weight on it.

"We were going to the mall, Mrs. Porter."

"I'm sorry, Kimmie. You'll have to go alone."

"But I really need Beth to help me pick out a dress. See, I've got this big thing coming up with my dad and he's given me a ton of money for a new outfit but I don't want to waste it, see, so I thought if Beth—"

"No," Lana said, not caring if the story was true or a lie. "I'll drop you off at your place and then Beth and I have some errands to run."

"Ma-a. Can't you leave me at Kimmie's and pick me up after?"

"No."

For a second she thought Beth would resist, but a night sleeping half in a beanbag and half on the floor had taken some of the spunk out of her. She muttered something about what she would do when she graduated and slunk out of the room under a hot, black cloud.

"We're leaving in ten minutes," Lana called after her. "I don't want to wait for you."

"Omigod, she is so scary!" Kimmie closed Beth's bedroom door and leaned against it, crossing her arms over her stomach, bending over as if she were in pain. She lowered her voice. "That was so incredibly bizarre."

"What?" Beth wished everyone would just disappear and leave her alone.

"Why does she want to drive me home?"

"So you don't have to take the bus, I guess. Or walk."

"You believe that?"

Beth said she did but in fact she thought the offer of a ride *was* a little peculiar. The Gaslamp District was way downtown, nowhere near her mom's usual haunts. And she had seemed a little too cheerful at breakfast—smiley-smiley, like a doll with happy lips painted on.

Beth walked into the bathroom she and Micki shared and looked at herself in the mirror. Her hair was almost dry but it hung limp and weedy—and where had the shine gone to? She opened the shower and looked at the shampoo and saw the word *Conditioner* on the bottle. Now she remembered Micki saying they were out of shampoo. She had washed her hair in conditioner and been too crapped-out to notice.

"Shit," she muttered, turned her back on her image, and rested her butt on the vanity.

Kimmie came into the bathroom.

"We washed our hair in conditioner," Beth said. The look on Kimmie's face made her laugh. "At least it's soft."

They burst out laughing, as if this were the funniest thing they had ever heard and Beth remembered the night before, how they had laughed at everything they saw on television. A little grass out in the backyard by the shade house and then watching movies, eating the good stuff from the run-and-read club. Kimmie had explained how there were different kinds of marijuana. There was happy grass—like last night—and munchie grass, and talky and philosophical, and so on. Whatever kind it was, Beth liked it because when she was stoned, she forgot about her father and she didn't care about her mother or Micki or anything.

They were in the Toyota by ten-fifteen, Kimmie in the front seat so she could direct Lana to her condo. They took the freeway south from Washington Street, through the "S" curve to Tenth Avenue. From her seat in the back, Beth glimpsed the fortress facade of Balboa High School one block up.

They caught every red light. South of Broadway, the traffic hardly moved.

"Is it always this busy on Saturday mornings?" Lana asked as if she had never been out of Tinytown. "It must be noisy at night."

"Oh, there's always lots going on. You get used to it." Kimmie pointed to a parking place in front of the lobby of her condo. "This is me here."

"I'd like to meet your mother. I could park—"

Beth sat back, braiding strands of sticky hair.

"She went to L.A. this morning." Kimmie said with a poor-me whine. "It is so hard to get makeup work in a place like San Diego so she's gone most Saturdays and Sundays."

Lana tilted her head slightly, looked at Beth and then at Kimmie. "You stay alone?"

"Oh, no. God, no. My sister Jules is here. She's in college."

"I see," Lana said.

"Can Beth walk me to the elevator? Just take a minute?"

"Make it snappy."

Beth followed Kimmie into the stark white lobby and stood beside her as she pressed floor three on the elevator.

Kimmie made a face. "So listen, can you do it? Will you come?"

The night before, Kimmie had told Beth that Strider's old friend, Tex, was coming in from Tucson the next week and there would be a party.

"He's bringing some great stuff."

"I don't know."

The truth was that Beth was almost glad Lana had forbidden her to spend time at Kimmie's. If she and Kimmie were alone like last night they had a good time, but at the condo there were always people hanging out and not just kids. Sometimes even Kimmie did not know who walked in the door. These parties were kind of pitiful. No one ever said anything interesting or really funny, the food was packaged cookies and crackers and day-old pastries.

"Your mom isn't going to let you out of her sight, Beth, so you're gonna have to figure something out if you want to have a life."

"Maybe I ought to back off a little. She seems like she's getting suspicious."

"Why would she be suspicious when you're so perfect?"

If she were perfect she would not be with Kimmie right now. She would be playing basketball or washing her hair with honest-to-god shampoo.

Kimmie tugged on the sleeve of Beth's sweatshirt to get her attention. "Here's what you do. Just tell her you're back with your old friends. She thinks they're like saints, right? She wants to believe you so she will and then if you say you want to stay overnight with one of them . . ."

Beth thought about how easy it had become to lie, the ease with which the stories came into her mind and flowed out as convincing words.

"I don't know, Kimmie . . ." It was not that she wanted to stay home, just the opposite; but even when she and Kimmie were alone with Damian and Strider, the atmosphere in the condo freaked her. What if something happened? One of them could pass out and die and there could be a fire or a robbery or a broken leg. . . . "Who is this Tex guy, anyway?"

"Strider's known him since they were like babies, toddlers." The elevator opened and Kimmie stepped across the opening to block it. "I think their moms hung out. Plus he's got friends, too, and they're all coming and bringing great shit."

"Great how?"

The elevator groaned and Kimmie mouthed one word, "Crystal."

"Jesus, no, Kimmie, that's bad stuff. You don't want to mess with that."

"I'm not saying make it your life's work, for crissakes. Just for a treat." She stepped into the elevator and as the door began to close, she punched the open button. "It's my birthday."

"You didn't tell me that."

"I'm telling you now." Kimmie's large eyes filled with tears. "You're my best friend. I can't have a party without my best friend." She grabbed both of Beth's hands. "Say you'll come. Promise you will."

"I don't know. . . ."

"You really are my best friend. I never had someone I could depend on like you before."

"I thought you said your birthday was in May."

"Beth-y."

The look on Kimmie's face reminded Beth of an illustration in a book at home, one of the fairy tale books she had loved so much and her father had read aloud to her in his big chair. *Myths and enchantment tales*, he called them. She recalled the pen-and-ink illustration of the poor little match girl staring in at the happy family celebrating Christmas together while the snow piled up around her bare feet.

They left Kimmie's and drove to the big Ralph's in Uptown where Beth trailed after her mother as she filled a shopping cart.

"I thought you said you were just getting stuff for tonight."

"Be stoic. I'll take you to Fresh Mex for lunch."

The bill for the groceries came to almost two hundred dollars. Beth watched her mother give her charge card to the checker and thought about how she had been coming to the market since she was a baby and loved to ride around in the cart singing out the names of food items she saw and recognized, like Jell-O and soup and eggs. Now it was a drag and she hoped she wouldn't see anyone she knew.

At Fresh Mex they ordered tostadas and diet soda and sat at a table in the back. Good, thought Beth, less chance of being seen. She felt her mother's eyes on her. Shit, what now?

"I need to talk to you about last night."

"What'd I do?"

"You tell me."

"What?"

"I think,"·her mother rolled her lips together and Beth saw how nervous she was. She felt a little rush of pleasure in the midst of her wariness. "I think you're smoking grass."

"Me?" How to handle this? What would Kimmie say? "You think I'd do that?"

"Tell me the truth."

"I am telling you the truth."

"No. No, you're not."

"Jesus." She tossed down her plastic fork. It bounced on its tines and fell to the floor. Good, a distraction. Beth started to get up but her mother put her hand on her wrist.

"Leave it for now. You can use mine."

Beth leaned back and folded her arms across her chest. She would not look at her mother, would not give her the respect of eye contact.

"Just tell me."

I'll wait her out. But as the minutes ticked by, she grew restless. In silent combat her mother usually gave in first but this time she was sticking with it. Every now and then she looked at Beth and raised her eyebrows.

"Everyone smokes," Beth said. "It's no biggy."

"You're the only one who matters to me."

"It's recreational, Ma. Like Dad's martinis."

Her mother smiled. "Exactly. And if I heard you were drinking martinis I would be upset."

She seemed calm, which was strange.

"You did it. Plenty."

"I was an adult."

"It's still against the law," Beth said.

"Well, that's another point—we'll get to that."

Her mother walked to the condiment bar for another fork, handed it to Beth.

"Marijuana impairs your judgment. Like martinis. It's not healthy for a developing brain."

"Ma, that's all propaganda. Aunty Mars told me she smoked, like, a bushel of dope. And look at her. She's got her Ph.D." Beth thought she saw a pinch of irritation around her mother's mouth. *Gotcha.* "Besides, I only do it once in a while."

"I don't want you to do it at all."

Beth picked up her tostada and took a bite. It broke in half, spilling lettuce and cheese onto her tray.

"Shit." She looked at her mother, daring her to object to the word.

"You may not smoke marijuana, Beth. You can argue all you like and some of what you say I might even agree with, but I still won't permit it. When you're living away from home you can make up your own mind—you'll be responsible for yourself then. But now—"

"You haven't given me one good reason why."

Her mother laughed.

"You haven't."

Beth watched as her mother used her fingers to count off the reasons pot was bad, all the stuff about her brain and her concentration and her short-term memory. None of it mattered. None of it was true one hundred percent of the time. Besides, Beth wanted to get stoned.

"It helps me." She picked at the bits of crisp tortilla.

"What do you mean?"

"You know."

"You tell me."

"I don't think. About him."

She heard her mother sigh. "Why don't you want to think about him?"

"You don't." It came out an accusation and angrier than Beth expected.

Her mother looked at her, her mouth slightly open so Beth could see a little bit of cheese on the inside of her lower lip. "I think about him all the time. He's in my mind constantly."

"You sure don't act like it."

"What are you talking about, Beth? Do you expect me to walk around the house in tears and sobs? Have you any idea how many days a week I'd just as soon not get out of bed?"

"You don't have to yell."

"I'm not yelling. I'm making a point."

"Yeah, well, I get it."

"No, you don't." Her mother spoke in a soft, harsh voice Beth had never heard before, stretched out and thin. "You think you're the only one who's sad about Daddy? I keep my feelings to myself. If I didn't, this family would disintegrate."

"It's doing that already."

Her mother said nothing.

"You went out and got drunk. And you lie."

"I don't."

"What about Micki and her birth dad?"

"That was different."

"I was hanging with Kimmie for weeks before you even noticed."

Her mother's jaw moved from side to side in a strange way. She covered her mouth and coughed.

"We didn't even have a funeral for him. You couldn't wait to throw his ashes out."

"Beth, that's enough. And it's not true. We'd talked about it, he and I, and I knew his wishes. He wanted to be spread up at Garnet Peak. That's why I went there."

"Yeah. By yourself."

"I should have included you. Yes, I admit that was a mistake but oh, Beth, I could barely do it alone. If you and Micki'd been there, I couldn't have managed—"

"So what?" A man at a nearby table turned around and stared at Beth. She lowered her voice. "This is all bullshit, Ma. You closed us out. You wanted him to yourself, only you never could say it. That was like acting out a lie, Ma."

Beth watched the words sink in. Her mother pressed her thumb and index finger against her nose. For a long time she seemed to stare at the speckled, plastic-covered tabletop. Then she puffed her cheeks and blew out a long, sustained breath. "Well," she said, "I guess this has been a long time coming."

Cautious, Beth said, "What do you mean?"

"This conversation. It's a little hard to swallow but at least I know how you feel about me." She stood up, brushing taco crumbs off the front of her sweater. It was an old one, Beth noticed, with a darn near one of the cuffs. She suddenly felt sorry for her mother and wanted to put her arms around her there in public and tell her that she loved her and she was the best mother ever. But it was a passing thought. Mostly she was glad they weren't talking about marijuana anymore.

Chapter Twenty-six

Beth was fifteen years old and at that age it was easy to be honest and straightforward. Simple questions with absolute answers was one of the gifts of youth. But with the years Lana had found there were fewer questions to which she could respond affirmatively; she always wanted to add a little caveat.

Yes, the world is round *but* there are times when it appears flat. Yes, murder is wrong *but* I think I'd kill to protect my children. No, I don't believe in spirits from the afterlife, *but* there are times when I almost feel Jack near me, almost.

Clear, pure truth—she was no longer sure she believed in its existence which did not mean she'd given up on honesty, but Beth did not understand that if Lana had been honest after Jack died, her vital systems would have shut down one by one, leaving her in a coma of grief for which there was no doctor. At that time, to be honest was to open herself to a suffering so huge she could not bear to look at it. So that, in a very real way, Wendy had saved her life with her words. If Lana had not gotten out of bed and pretended to be all right, she would have been sucked down into her pain. And then what would become of Micki and Beth?

Had Beth forgotten the mornings when the milk was sour? When no one did the laundry and she and Micki lived half the time at Wendy's? Did she really want that time back again?

Lana's palms left damp smudges on the steering wheel. She braked too fast and sent a bag of groceries onto its side. She heard the navel oranges rolling back and forth in the way-back. She looked over at Beth. Her face had set like plaster into stubborn anger.

Self-centered brat.

Lana was sick of her life being ruled by the wishes and demands of adolescent girls who could not trouble their airy heads to consider what it was like for her. They had lost their father. Yes, she knew this was bad, but she had lived her whole life without Norman Coates. Lana had lost her friend and her lover and her guide and helper and playmate when Jack died.

You closed us out, Ma.

She pulled the Toyota into the driveway and the brakes squealed when she slammed her foot down on them.

"Get out of the car," Lana said. "Go up to your room and stay there."

Beth slammed the door behind her.

Lana watched Beth walk between the car and the garage door and she hated her; she wished she had never been born and then she hated herself for thinking such a terrible thought.

Beth was all she had of Jack. She must remember that.

She got out of the car and opened the way-back. The angle of the driveway had made the oranges, two avocados, and a ten-pound bag of Yukon Gold potatoes roll to the door. An orange rolled out and down the driveway like a tiny sun. She left it and carried the groceries in and put them away.

The house felt empty and crowded at the same time.

"Here's the truth," she told Gala. "If I could, I'd leave tomorrow." The girls were old enough to take care of themselves. They'd only miss her when it came time to pay off their charge cards.

Had she really closed the girls out? No. Then why had she put the urn with Jack's ashes on the passenger seat of the Toyota, nested in a pillow off their bed so it would not roll? And why had she buried the memory of doing this so deep that she had not remembered until Beth's anger brought it back?

She had put the urn in the car and driven to the Laguna Mountains early on a clear, cold November day less than two months after Jack's death. Before then his ashes had been in her closet, on a shelf. That day she walked the Garnet Peak Trail, where she and Jack had been a dozen times, her back to the mountain, her face to the Anza Borrego. The long side of the mountain, boulders and talus as steep as if God had set his shovel in the ground to separate the mountains and the desert, and far below and beyond the expanse of blue-gray and pale gold desert fading at the horizon into a dusty mauve mist; she remembered it clearly now. To the right of her there were hang gliders, their blue and red sails like flowers drifting on the updrafts a thousand feet above the desert floor. The wind blew her hair backwards until it hurt. Her wind-parched eyes watched the empty air, the gliders, the occasional hawk with its wings glinting red-gold in the sunlight. After some time had passed she walked back to the 4Runner and got the little ceramic urn. She discovered later she had left the car door open and buzzing like a wasp. She had returned to her aerie and stood with her toes at the cliff's edge, too close for safety. Now that Lana remembered, she did not blame Beth for being angry. Maybe it was wrong to dispose of Jack's ashes without the girls beside her. A shame as wide as the desert filled Lana, desiccated her heart.

She had gone to Garnet Peak and without a thought of Beth and Micki, she had opened the urn and lifted out handfuls of Jack—coarse and gray-white, like eroded sea shells at the edge of the surf. It was a strange, sad thing that a man, tall and strong, should amount in the end to so little: two cups or three of something rougher than sand, finer than rock. By chalky handfuls she had tossed Jack's remains into the wind, the wind that blew constantly where the mountains met the desert. And the wind carried him up and out like dust. A grain lodged in her eye and she had to finger it out as if it were just a bit of grit. She remembered so clearly how that bit of bone felt at the corner of her eye, like a boulder. But on her fingertip it was a speck she could barely see. A dot of white. She put her finger in her mouth and sucked it off and thought, her eyes too wind-dried for tears: *this is the last time I will take him inside me.*

When the urn was empty she swung her arm out wide and tossed it out over the escarpment as far and hard as she could. She did not hear it break hundreds of feet below.

She remembered driving back along the Sunrise Highway and down I8, reaching home and climbing into bed. Where she stayed until Wendy told her to get up.

Lana grabbed her gardening basket off the shelf on the back porch and went outside to cut snapdragons and stock for the dinner table. Around the corner of the house where she had trained pink Cecil Bruner rosebushes over the wall that separated their house from the Tillmans', she sank down and leaned her back against the cold bricks.

She pressed her forehead against her knees, wrapped her arms around her knees and pulled them tightly against her body; a little tighter and she might be able to shut off her own breath.

I must make it up to them, she thought.

Can't be done.

I must.

Too terrible what you did.

I must try.

Back in the kitchen, she carried the basket of cut flowers to the sink and ran tepid water over their stems, leaving them to drink it up while she went upstairs to Beth. She found her daughter in the playroom, in the beanbag chair, reading a book.

From the doorway Lana said, "I've been thinking about what you said, Beth."

"Uh-huh."

Lana could not see Beth's face and was just as glad. "I can't make it up to you, I know that. But I wanted you to understand that what you said, it got through to me. I heard you, Beth."

"Uh-huh."

An hour later as Lana put the final touches on the lasagna, Billy Joel playing loud on the CD player, loud enough to muffle her thoughts, Micki slammed through the back door and flung her backpack down the hall toward the foot of the stairs.

She dropped into a chair at the table and reached for a toothpick, a bunch of them standing up in a tiny cup like bits of kindling. Her expression was stormy.

"Hello to you, too," Lana said, trying to sound pleasant. "How'd it go at Tiff's?"

Micki lifted her shoulders and let them drop.

"Want some chicken noodle soup?"

"Do we have any saltines?"

"In the pantry."

Lana ladled out a bowl of soup made from leftovers several weeks earlier and defrosted that morning. Micki sat down again, opened the saltine box and crumbled several squares in her hand, dropped them into the soup and began to eat.

"Did you have a good time?"

Micki made a disgusted face. "Some of The Fives came over." She slathered butter on a saltine. "They are such honest-to-god phonies, Ma. They wanted to know about Eddie and how rich he was and who he dated. Like I know that stuff. Like it even matters."

"Did they all spend the night?"

"Pretty much."

"What a crowd."

"I felt like a bug under a microscope. Like they don't see me every day at school. What did they think, I'd grown pointy ears? Like Spock?"

"So you don't care that you're not in the . . . club?"

Micki gawked at her. "Of course I care. Being a Five *means* something, Ma. It's not about friends. You never can get that."

Lana turned away and poured the rest of the sauce over the lasagna. It seemed she did not get a lot of things, at least not until too late.

"Ma? You okay?"

No, but she wasn't going to say so.

Lana heard Micki get out of her chair and walk up behind her. She felt her daughter's chin rest on her shoulder and she swallowed down a sob.

"Can we eat in the dining room tonight?"

"Of course. I've already cut the flowers."

Lana waited, hoping she would say more. A simple "thanks" would thrill her.

Micki set the table because she wanted to make sure she did not have to sit next to Eddie French. She put Beth on one side and him and Auntie Mars on the other and herself across from them. Her mother sat at the end nearest the kitchen as usual. She brought out the heavy cherrywood box in which the family silver rested, sixteen place settings with old-fashioned curlicued handles. As she laid each place in careful symmetry she remembered how heavy the knives and forks had felt when she was little and how she had worried about dropping one. She put salad forks to the left of the dinner forks and dessert spoons to the right of the knives as she had been taught. The table napkins were heavy cotton with faint lines of green and gold to match the cloth she had taken from the cupboard upstairs. For the centerpiece she arranged snapdragons and stock in a cut glass bowl—Waterford, like the water glasses she set to the left of the forks. If Micki had once been afraid of dropping her knife and fork, she had been even more terrified of breaking one of the Waterford glasses that Grandma Stella told her were worth more than she was. She thought about these childish fears, and the time when they had worried her seemed far away not just in time but geography as well, as if that little girl had not only lived in another century but in another country.

Her mother came in to set the table and was surprised to see it done already.

"Thank you, Mick. That's a help."

She had tears in her eyes. Weird.

Micki supposed that her mother was nervous about Eddie French. She could have told her that she understood and felt the same, but she was still mad at her for keeping him a secret. Micki had taken it for granted that the woman who told her to tell the truth would hold herself to the same standards.

She went upstairs and into her bedroom, where she found her sister standing in front of her closet.

"Can I wear your turquoise sweater tonight?" Beth asked.

"I got chocolate on it."

"Shit."

Micki lay back on her bed and hugged one of the pink-and-white-checkered pillows.

Beth looked at her. "You excited?"

"I guess. Kinda." She rolled over onto her side, pulling the pillow closer. "Actually, I feel really strange. I sort of wish he wasn't coming." She hadn't planned to say that but it was true.

Beth sat on the edge of the bed. "Remember when we were little and you just got this bed and we bounced so hard it broke? Before you even slept in it one time?"

Micki laughed. "Ma was so mad. She wouldn't fix it. She said I'd have to sleep on the floor until I graduated from high school."

Micki thought about her father coming up the stairs with his tool belt on and she imagined the same kind of images filled Beth's mind. She said, "I'm never gonna stop missing him. Do you think she does?"

"What?"

"Miss Daddy."

Beth nodded slowly. "Yeah, she does."

"You'd never know it."

"Yeah. Then sometimes I think she's really sad," Beth said. "You can't tell with her."

"Do you? Miss him?" Micki felt happy they were talking again.

"What d'you think? Of course I do."

"You don't act like it, either." Micki was thinking how Beth was never home anymore, how she had become secretive. "You're at Kimmie's all the time."

"That doesn't mean I don't miss him."

"How come you like Kimmie so much?"

Beth got up and browsed through Micki's closet some more. "Sometimes I don't so much."

"I liked your other friends better."

"Look who's talking. I already told you what I think of The Fives."

Micki closed her eyes and the movie in her mind fast-forwarded to last night at Tiff's. She had been excited to be invited for a sleepover. It had been the answer to all her yearnings. Then she walked into Tiff's bedroom and saw three old Fives from the class ahead and two girls Micki had known since sixth grade. She felt awkward and shy, as out-of-whack as she had been in the fifth grade. Sissy Lindstrom had a photo of Eddie French she had cut from some style mag. He'd gone to a premiere with a sitcom airhead who wore glued-on white satin cutoffs and a sequined halter top and her hair—like Micki's mother would say—a rat's nest. It was embarrassing to think of her birth father actually asking a skank like that for a date. Did they go back to his place and do it? The thought had made her want to get up and walk home even though it was dark outside. The Fives could not stop talking about how Micki was going to have famous friends and go to premieres, stuff she had never thought of and did not care about. She tried to explain that she only wanted to meet him and find out what he was like, that Jack was her true father, but they didn't listen so she shut up.

"You have more clothes than I do." Beth held up a red tee shirt with navy blue and white tabs on the sleeves and stars around the scooped neckline. "Can I wear this?"

"What's wrong with your own clothes?"

"Jeez, I'm sorry I asked."

"Wear black—that's what Kimmie'd wear."

Beth pulled the red tee off its hanger and dragged her sweatshirt over her head. She was skinnier than Micki remembered. Her pelvic bones were the only things holding up her baggy pants.

Micki said, "I heard you got a bad grade on your geometry test."

"Big fucking deal," Beth snarled as she pulled the tee shirt on.

"It will be when Ma finds out."

"I don't care what she says. I hate her. She's such a liar. Look what she did to you. If you hadn't picked up the phone—"

"What about you? Why didn't you tell me?"

"I was going to, only she made me promise I wouldn't. She said she wouldn't let me get my license next year."

Micki did not blame her sister. At the same time she felt alone in the world, abandoned by everyone.

"I was going to tell you." Beth admired herself in the mirror. "This is hot."

After a few minutes Micki got off the bed and took a shower and dressed carefully, taking time to become absorbed in drying her hair. She wore a pair of Levi's and a fuzzy blue sweater that was almost as dark as her eyes. And the earrings her father had given her for her twelfth birthday, tiny, white opal studs with electric blue veins running through them. She could have worn makeup but she didn't. She could not say why but she wished she were ten years old again.

She walked through the bathroom into the bedroom, where her sister was holding a magnifying mirror up to her face as she applied mascara.

"You're like Elvira, Queen of the Night," Micki said. "You're not a Goth, you know."

Beth put down the mirror and glared at her. "You don't know what I am." She jabbed the mascara wand at Micki.

Micki turned and walked away but at the bathroom door she stopped with her hand on the knob. It felt big and solid in her palm and she was glad to have it to hold onto.

"You're gonna get in big trouble, Beth. And I don't mean just Ma."

"So? It's my life."

The doorbell rang and Beth made a face.

"Go say hello to your daddy, why don't you?"

Chapter Twenty-seven

It was strange having him there, first in the kitchen and then in the dining room. There did not seem to be enough oxygen in the air and Micki wanted to open a window but her mother said they'd freeze.

The evening did not start well. Her mother had bought wine and Eddie reminded her that he did not drink so there was nothing for him except some half-flat quinine and a two-litre bottle of Coke which he didn't care for. Aunty Mars poured him a glass of bottled water and squeezed half a lemon into it. Eddie French seemed happy but her mom went on and on about being sorry she forgot and having a lot on her mind until it got embarrassing and Aunty Mars hugged her and told her to calm down and shut up.

Things were not so tense by the time they sat down to dinner, thanks mostly to Aunty Mars, who looked fabulous in a long, slinky green dress and heels that made her six feet tall. She was totally on, telling stories, asking questions and, of course, she had opinions about everything. Some of them were so off the wall they made everyone at the table laugh, which was what she wanted. Halfway through the lasagna, Micki finally relaxed and sometimes found courage to get a clear, cool look at her father. Birth father. Whenever she forgot to apply the adjective she felt guilty.

Eddie French dressed like a GQ model and he was good looking—not spectacular like a movie star, but handsome enough so if Micki were to walk with him down the street, she wouldn't mind if people saw them. She could not tell if they looked alike except for the eyes, the navy blue eyes were the same. One time she looked up from her lasagna and he was looking right at her and when their eyes met, he did not look away and neither did she. The strangest sensation came over Micki. He's mine, she thought. I am his.

Beth was a jerk through the whole meal. She hardly said more than "Pass the salt."

Then, just when Micki had begun to enjoy herself, her mother had to bring up alcoholism and drugs. Micki wanted to sink through the floor. Would the woman never give up?

"When did you stop? Drinking?" She spun the stem of her wineglass as she spoke so it was obvious to everyone she was uncomfortable. "We should talk about this, I think. I want Micki to know."

Micki and Beth looked at each other and rolled their eyes.

"I don't mean to embarrass you. . . ."

Not much, Micki thought.

"Doesn't embarrass me at all," Eddie said.

"How come you wear braces?" Beth asked.

Her mother glared and said, "We're talking about something else now."

Eddie said, "When I was drinking and using, I couldn't track the plot of a first-grade reader, but these days I can handle two questions at a time."

Aunty Mars laughed. Lana patted her lips with her napkin. Micki had never seen her look so awkward and embarrassed.

"I wasn't implying—"

"—and I wasn't inferring."

He told Beth, "I got the braces because I've always been ashamed of my lower teeth. Tops are okay, but on the bottom they were crazy, going in all directions."

"Don't you feel sort of weird," Beth asked, "when you go out with stars and all?"

He leaned on his elbow. "Tell you the truth, Beth, most of those girls have a lot worse things than braces." Before anyone could ask what he meant, he said, "And I just don't get embarrassed unless I feel I've done something wrong." His eyes crinkled at the corners and Micki could barely see the pupils, just a flash of light in them.

"Like I told you on the phone, Mrs. Porter, I made a lot of money fast and you know what they say about cocaine, it being God's way of telling us we have too much money?"

Beth said, "You used cocaine?"

He smiled at Beth. Micki wanted to grab his arm and remind him that *she* was his daughter. "I did a lot of drugs and drank. Got two DUIs before I wised up."

"What do you mean, wised up?" Beth could not take her eyes off him.

"I went into Betty Ford, stayed a month, came out and joined AA."

"How long have you . . ." Lana asked.

"Three years, five months, fourteen days and," he looked at his watch, "about nine hours."

Most people would have been mortified by the questions and the silences, but Micki's birth father seemed unfazed.

"Look," he said, resting his elbows on the table, "I don't mind talking about it. Everyone makes mistakes, I figure, and what counts is if you catch yourself in time. Before you get in too deep to get out. And then if you learn something in the process."

"So young and yet so wise," Aunty Mars said, halfway joking.

"Everything I know that's any good comes right out of AA, believe me. I didn't know jackshit before I got sober."

Jack. The silence around the table got heavy and Micki felt the sweat under her arms.

Aunty Mars to the rescue.

"Did you have a famous roommate at Betty Ford?"

"A car salesman from Gardena."

The conversation moved on to famous people who had drug and alcohol problems and Aunty Mars talked about some of her students. Then she asked Eddie French to tell them about his new company.

"I got sick of making games. After I got sober, I looked at my life and I didn't think it amounted to much more than a bank account. I figured video games could be used for education as well as fun if I could just get the right gimmick going." He speared a cherry tomato and put it in his mouth. As he chewed, his eyes crinkled again and disappeared, becoming reflections of the candles on the table.

"You did?" Lana asked. "Get a gimmick?"

He nodded. "I think so. I'm going to Europe in a couple of weeks to talk to some folks."

"How long will you be gone?" Micki asked, struck by a spasm of dismay. It was the first thing she had said directly to him that night. As soon as she spoke she felt shy, afraid her alarm showed, afraid he would think she cared.

"Couple of months, maybe three. After that I'm going to Japan to talk to some design guys I know. Thought I'd go around the long way. Stop in India. I've never been to India."

"Must be nice," Lana said dryly. "All that time and money."

Micki stifled a groan of mortification. What was wrong with her mother anyway? Why couldn't she just be nice?

They ate dessert in the kitchen, at the round table. Beth said she did not want any and went upstairs while the rest of them sat at the table eating and talking, beginning to sound like friends. Micki sat next to Eddie French and a couple of times his shoulder touched hers. She jerked away and then wanted to dig a hole for herself. What kind of idiot was she? They talked about all kinds of things—video games and traveling and even Lana relaxed and told a funny story about the time she and Jack drove down Baja to Cabo and camped on the sand.

"My dad and I used to camp," Eddie French said.

Omigod, thought Micki. I have grandparents. Not just Stella. She hadn't thought of this.

"They live up in Modesto. Dad runs the Ace Hardware up there and they've got a little fruit ranch."

Do they know about me, Micki wanted to ask.

"I was an only child. The folks would have liked a whole basketball team, but I'm all they got."

They like children—they might like me.

He turned to Micki, "Are you always so quiet?"

She looked away and then back at him, ducked her head, looked up and smiled, shook her head.

"Well, I'm gonna be here tomorrow. If you think of something you want to say." He was teasing her.

She blurted, "Can you come back next weekend?"

"Micki . . ."

Aunty Mars said, "He's got a trip to plan, Micki."

"Actually," he said with a lazy smile, "I don't have a thing to do." He lifted his hands from his coffee cup and spread them before her. "Not a thing."

Micki looked at her mother and her mother looked at Aunty Mars and her face looked hard and the muscles in her neck were like ropes.

"Sure," she said. "Why not?"

Chapter Twenty-eight

As Lana walked Mars to her car that night, they talked about Stella and decided to wait another week or two before confronting her with the impossibility of moving to Bird Rock. They both hoped a sane Realtor would give her a dose of reality. It was a strange, still January night. Lana could have stood barefoot, wearing shorts, and not been chilled. Overhead the sky was blue-black and bright with stars like bramble roses in the spring. From the north a plane approached, blinking its warning.

"You were not what I'd call the soul and spirit of graciousness tonight." Mars unlocked the door of her cinnamon-red Mercedes coupe and tossed her bag and shawl across to the passenger seat.

"I said he could come, didn't I? What more do you expect of me?" And next week, too. What else could she say with all of them looking at her?

Mars slipped into the driver's seat and attached her seat belt. "You're brave and I'm proud of you." She put her key in the ignition but did not turn it on. "He's a nice guy, don't you think?"

Lana could not disagree. And obviously Micki felt the same, though Lana had noted that she rarely looked at him directly, but from the corner of her eye as if out of shyness or some distrust. It was good, Lana thought, that she was being cautious.

"We'll see," she said. "It's not too hard to make a good impression at dinner."

Mars said, "I feel sorry for Beth."

"You should feel sorry for me."

"Micki has a father now and Beth doesn't," Mars said, "When I went to the bathroom—"

"I was doing the dishes, as I seem to recall." Micki and Eddie French had gone into the kids' living room to watch a video, leaving Lana marooned and morose amidst the remains of dinner.

"—I went upstairs. Beth was in the playroom watching television."

"And let me guess." Lana looked up at the stars as if words were written there. The plane was overhead now, its engine noise a low backdrop to the night's silence. "She told you what a terrible mother I am. How I'm dishonest and a liar and no one understands her anymore. How alone she feels and she only has one place she likes to be and that's with her friend Kimmie but now I—"

"She talked about that scene at school."

The turbulence of the day had put a great distance between Lana and the meeting at Arcadia School, so great that at first she did not know what scene Mars was talking about.

"Oh. That. I told you all about it. I wanted to meet Kimmie. Before Beth started hanging out with her she played basketball and she didn't smoke pot."

"As far as you knew."

"I knew."

Lana took a deep breath of the mild night air, fragrant with jasmine and, from the Tillmans', mock orange. Somewhere someone had a mesquite fire burning. "Did she tell you what I did with Jack's ashes?"

Mars nodded.

"And did she tell you I admitted it was wrong?"

Mars nodded again and gently tapped her leather steering wheel cover. "I always wondered what happened. Why we never had a ceremony—"

"You blame me, too?"

Mars's expression was tender. "Lana, one thing I know is you always do the best you can. I don't blame you for anything."

Lana watched the lights go out in the Andersons' house. First the porch light, then the living room, then the upstairs front spare bedroom where old Mrs. Anderson did her needlework every night. Down the street in the big pine the neighborhood owl hooted twice.

"Give Beth some space—she'll come around."

"Too much space and she'll get lost," Lana said. "That's what

happens with adolescent girls. Especially those who have no father."

"You didn't have a father. Neither did I."

"Beth isn't us, Mars."

"Maybe not. But she's also not who you think she is."

"And I suppose you do?"

"Don't get huffy, little girl. I'm saying maybe *no one* knows who
Beth is anymore, least of all Beth."

"All the more reason for me to hold her close."

Mars sighed and turned on the ignition. "I'm outta here. Thanks
for dinner." She started to put the car in gear and stopped. "I like
him, Lana."

"Yeah, so I gather."

The neon-green numerals on the bedside clock swam before her
in the darkness like a species of strange fish. Four A.M. and all hope
of sleep had gone south. Lana pushed back the covers and got out
of bed. From her spot at the top of the stairs, Gala thumped her tail.
Lana pulled on sweat pants and shirt, picked up her trainers and
socks, and tiptoed out of the room. At the top of the stairs she sat
and pulled on her shoes and socks, then went downstairs, Gala following. In the kitchen she encountered Eddie French just coming
out of the guest room.

"Oh."

He was barefooted and wore a pair of abbreviated boxer shorts.
The stove light cast shadows on the contours of his broad shoulders and narrow waist, the sculpted pecs and stomach, the long,
powerful muscles in his thighs.

"Can't sleep," he said, and walked over to the sink.

Don't bother being embarrassed, Lana thought. Don't bother
putting on clothes. I'm just the mother of your daughter. The *adoptive* mother. And what if I'd been Micki? What if she'd walked
down here and seen you in your underwear?

Looking at him from behind, she was more conscious of his
wedge-shaped torso and his butt like a soccer ball. Such a slim
waist. She remembered what Mars had told her, how a young
man's body is hard but warm, that the flesh gives beneath the fingers but just a little. She wanted to touch him, to feel the tone of
him, the warmth of his skin against her palm.

"I'm making coffee," she said, and got busy.

"You always up so early?"

His voice was low, clouded and drowsy. Lana thought of Jack bending over her in the dark bedroom to say that he was off early, he'd see her at work, the way his voice filtered in through the lattice of her dreams.

"I couldn't sleep," she said, tapping her nails on the stovetop as she watched the blue flame lap around the bottom of the kettle. "I'm taking the dogs for a walk."

"Want company?"

"Not really." Just now he frightened her a little. He was young and she was old and tired. "I'm sorry, that was rude. Please come along."

"I don't want—"

"Forget it. My social skills aren't so good before dawn." She poured water through a single-cup filter cone. "Shall I make you one?"

He thought a minute. "Yeah. Thanks. I'll go put something on."

Do that.

She watched him walk into the guest room. Even in the dimly lit kitchen, she saw the definition of the long muscle that ran down the back of his thighs and the teardrop shape of his calves. Wendy said she liked having sons because there were always young male bodies around the house to admire. Yes.

He came out of the room wearing Levi's and a loose sweater.

"This is the coldest time of the night," she told him. "Look in the hall closet. There should be an old jacket of Jack's."

As he came back into the kitchen a moment later, he was pulling on a dust-colored windbreaker with a tear in the sleeve just below the elbow. Jack had caught it on some barbed wire and she said she'd mend it but never had. She kept it because it smelled like Jack where the lining rubbed against the back of his neck. Now the smell would be spoiled.

She made Eddie French a cup of filtered coffee in a thermal mug and they went out the back door, Gala eagerly following to where Buster lay on the cement slab beside the house, eyes open, head on his paws. Lana clipped the leash to his collar and he seemed happy to come along so long as they didn't move too fast.

Near the eastern horizon the sky was blue, filtered through gold, but overhead it was still dark, the color of Micki's eyes, and

Venus, the morning star, shone like a miracle. The temperature had dipped slightly from earlier when she stood beside Mars's car, but it was still unseasonably warm for a midwinter night. There was hope of rain for another few weeks but soon the scarlet and gold ranunculus bulbs would sprout their frilly leaves and on the liquid ambar tree the buds would grow plump and ripe. If she had been alone, Lana would have stopped and leaned against the neighbors' wall and cried, she missed Jack so. This would be her second spring without him and as she cast her thoughts ahead, she thought she could not bear to face the season alone. She looked sideways at Eddie French and felt a surge of dislike for him.

Under the Lexus parked in front of the Wilsons' house, their old gray tom crouched and watched. Gala saw him, stopped and pointed, her tail quivering. Buster walked on by, unimpressed by cats. Gala barked once, the Wilsons' sound-activated porch light went on, and the cat flew out and up the carob tree in their front yard.

"Gala," Lana called softly. "Get over here." Reluctantly the setter obeyed. Lana pulled a leash out of her jacket pocket and attached it to the dog's collar. "You can't be trusted."

In silence she and Eddie French walked across Fort Stockton toward the Miranda Street Park. Lights were on in a few houses. A few cars were on the streets.

Eddie French said, "I want to thank you, Lana, for your kindness. For letting me get to know Micki." He laughed softly. "The name suits her, better than Michelle."

"We always liked that Beatles song."

"She seems like a terrific girl." After a pause he added. "I want to thank you for that, too."

Don't think by showing me your good manners and your gratitude I'm going to let you into our life. You don't automatically get a part of Micki because you know when to say thank you. Her brain was gummy from worry and lack of sleep. It wasn't the time to talk.

"I finally got in touch with Barbara," he said.

"Barbara?"

"Micki's birth mother?"

Here it comes. First Eddie French and next the mother, the woman who did not want Micki but now feels she has a right to her. She clamped her jaw shut.

"She lives in Texas. Some little place you never heard of." His tone was derisive. "She didn't want to talk to me on the phone so I flew down there. I went to her house. Not right off—I didn't want to cause her trouble."

So you stalked her? Like Micki?

His voice grew distant and thoughtful and she understood that he had been saving up this story; it had taken restraint for him to wait until the right time to tell it. She was interested, of course. How could she fail to be? But angry, too. Lately everything seemed to make her either teary or mad.

"Her house was okay. Neat and all, and there was a big red truck in the driveway. One morning I saw a man come out the front door and get in it, drive away, and then a couple of kids—a boy and girl—leave. For school, I guess. After that, nothing happened so I figured she was alone. I didn't want to get her in trouble."

He had said this before, and Lana felt he wanted a response from her but if he wanted reassurance that he was a good boy he could go home and ask his mother. His mother. My god, Lana thought. Am I old enough to be his mother? She did the math and was relieved. Though he seemed a boy to her, he was only ten years her junior.

"Man, I thought she'd slam the door in my face, the way she looked at me like when we were kids and she was after me to do things for her and I wouldn't."

In Texas, Barbara had grown plump but her face was still pretty and her hair still as fair and thick as Micki's. "Her maiden name was Aandahl. Norwegian. I remember her mother was called Gunhild and I always thought that was such a great name, like a Norse goddess or something." He looked at Lana. "You ever play 'Ghost?' "

For a moment Lana did not know what he meant. "The video game," she said, catching on. "No. Never."

"Well, I named one of the Viking queens Gunhild."

"A Viking ghost?"

"Yeah, right. In the game there's this world where all the great mythic and historic figures live in ghost form and when you play it you're trying to populate the world with humans and you have to learn to do it without offending the ghosts. Of course, most of them want to kill you but a few can be allies and they have special powers and strengths and you can earn these to give you a better chance against the bad guys."

"That's a video game?"

"Yeah. 'Ghost'."

He told her more about the game and she listened because she was grateful not to have to hear about Barbara for a few minutes. His friend from community college had done the hard programming for "Ghost" because in those days Eddie French had known very little about computer languages. He had come up with the patterns, the strategies, the intricate interplay of power, ambition, and violence. She guessed that as much as he wanted to talk about Barbara, "Ghost" was a diversion they both welcomed.

At the Miranda Street Park, Lana let Gala off her lead, and she raced away toward the trees while Buster, the guardian, stayed close by, pressed against Lana's leg.

Eddie French got to the end of his explanation about "Ghost" and there was a long silence.

"What happened when she opened the door?"

Barbara would not invite him into the house but finally, after he had begged her, she agreed to meet him that afternoon in a nearby town where there was a mall. They could appear to meet by accident.

"I was sitting on a bench in front of The Gap and she came by. Didn't even sit down. I never saw anyone so nervous." She had dressed up and applied makeup, and she was not as pretty as that morning when her face was plain and scrubbed. But he could tell from the way she outlined her eyes, the blue mascara, and precisely drawn lips that appearances were important to Barbara.

His tender observation puzzled Lana and made her watch his face more closely in the half-light. Did he feel empathy for Barbara? Lana would not have guessed this was within his repertoire, did not quite believe her perception; and yet—she kept coming back to this thought as he spoke—he sounded as if something in his old girlfriend's efforts touched him.

"She told me her husband didn't know she'd had a baby. None of her friends knew. They all attended the Four Square Baptist Church in that little town and if it ever got out about Micki—she put her hands over her ears when I said her name—she'd be ruined and her husband would never forgive her."

In the midst of relief, Lana felt a sink of grief for Micki.

"I admit I was pissed at first. I think since Micki was born I must have thought about her at least once every day. Not like obsessing but just curious and worried for fear, you know, something might have gone wrong. I couldn't understand how Barbara could live as if our baby never happened. Plus I felt sorry for Micki, you know? To have a mother like that?"

"I'm her mother," Lana said. "She has a mother like me."

"When I got to thinking about it, though, mostly what I felt was relieved. This way I get her for myself."

It was light enough to make out his features clearly and to see how Micki looked like him, and how she did not. "You don't get her at all."

"I didn't mean get like *have*. I meant—"

"I know what you meant, Eddie. You meant that now you're in her life. But you're not. For as long as she is living in my house and dependent on me, you will be peripheral to her life."

She said the words and for an instant, as they were coming out of her mouth and filling up the cool morning, she believed them. Eddie French could go away now and their lives would return to normal. But the words were mist and all their power vanished in the air, leaving a familiar groaning emptiness inside her.

She sat at a picnic table. There was no going back, no pulling back the ashes, no mending the urn that had held them. Part of the family, but not *of* the family. It sounded like the metaphysical jibberish philosophers debated. Well, she didn't like to argue, never had. Pressed against her leg, she felt Buster's labored breathing.

"I don't want to take her away from you," Eddie French said softly. "If I could just make you believe that, Lana."

She gestured for him to sit down beside her. He straddled the bench.

"I don't think you understand—you don't get what a family—" Something broke in her and before she could mend it, the words tumbled out. "I love her so much, Eddie. She and Beth, they mean everything to me."

"I know that, Lana. And I'm so grateful. I wish I could've known Jack, too."

She began to talk about Jack's death and how when he was taken from them, an essential ingredient went with him and she didn't know what it was. Eddie did not interrupt her even when she stopped long enough to wonder why she was revealing so much and so freely. His eyes never left her face.

"I always thought Micki was the difficult one," she said, "But now it's Beth I'm frightened for. Love doesn't seem to be enough anymore."

He said something in response but Lana did not listen. He played with a cigarette.

"Go ahead. Smoke it."

He lit the cigarette and smoked for a moment, staring at the smoke rising from it. "Beth's right—lots of kids smoke grass and they do fine in life. And if they mess up, sometimes that's good, too. Lots of times we have to do the wrong thing in order to figure out—"

His easy answer irritated her. He wasn't really a father, not a parent. He didn't know.

"It's not your problem, Eddie. Forget about it." She stepped away from the picnic table and whistled for Gala. She felt him watching her, waiting for her to say more. She took a breath. "And about next weekend."

"Thanks for letting me come. Micki kind of put you on the spot, didn't she?"

"You are invited to dinner on Saturday night but you'll have to go home afterwards. I don't want you to stay overnight again."

He looked at the burning end of his cigarette.

"I'll do whatever you want, Lana. Just let me be Micki's father."

"No. I won't let you. Micki had a wonderful father. She doesn't need you. She wants you but she doesn't need you."

Chapter Twenty-nine

At first Lana could not make out what Tinera was saying and twice she had to tell her to slow down. It was Monday evening after dinner, and she was wearing shorts, sitting on the front steps making a list for the week. In the wind the copper tube wind chimes had gone beyond music to cacophony.

"You gotta come, Aunty Lana. Come now, right away, come nowcomenowcomenow."

Across the street Mr. Anderson had turned on his sprinklers and the water spread in a wide arc out onto the street. The winter evening felt oddly like summertime and put Lana's nerves on edge.

"Mama's gonna kill my daddy. She says she will."

Lana's hands began to sweat. "Let me speak to your father."

Tinera lowered her voice and Lana realized this was a secret phone call. And a rare act of initiative. "He's in the closet. If he comes out she says she'll kill him."

"Your mother would never—"

"With a gun."

Lana remembered the .38 revolver she had seen in the drawer of Kathryn's bedside table.

"Okay," Lana said stupidly since nothing was okay. "Can you get Kathryn for me? Can you take the phone to her?"

"Oh, nononono," Tinera cried, "she doesn't know. . . . Please, come. I can't talk anymore. Please just come."

"Tinera, I'll tell Aunty Mars. She'll—"

"No, not her. Please *you* come, you've got to come."

"But, honey . . ." Dial tone.

* * *

Lana keyed in Mars's number and let the phone ring, tapping the point of her pencil into her bare knee as she waited. The answering machine clicked on and at the same moment she remembered her sister taught a three-hour seminar on Imagist poets on Monday nights.

In the laundry room she pulled clean Levi's out of the dryer and put them on. She called up the stairs to Micki and Beth and when they came to the kitchen she explained about Tinera's call, omitting mention of guns and killing, making it out to be only a three-star emergency.

Micki asked, suspiciously, "How come you're going over there and you don't even know what's going on?"

"You know Tinera, she never would have called me if it wasn't important." Lana opened the hall closet and grabbed her blue parka vest and had pulled it on and snapped the buttons down the front before she remembered how warm the night was. But the weather might change.

"Can I study with Kimmie tomorrow night?"

Lana looked at Beth, slouched against the doorjamb, dressed in black with raccoon rings of mascara around her eyes. "Is she all you can think about?"

"It's crazy here. You running off, Tiff and The Fives in and out—"

"I said no, I meant no."

The gates to *Tres Palomas* were closed and for some reason the code to open them had dropped out of Lana's mind, but as she rummaged through the papers in the 4-Runner's glove box for the card on which it was written, she heard them creak and swing wide, and she imagined Tinera down the hill in the house watching from behind the curtains for her arrival. She let herself feel the apprehension that had been circling her like a buzzard ever since the call. Violence was so out of Kathryn's character that Lana could not imagine what event or series of events had led her to threaten her husband. And with the three girls right there. She felt a vibration of fear in her ribcage, like a bird beating its wings.

Instead of parking in front of the house, she stopped fifty feet away and got out, closing the door softly. In the paddock a pair of horses trotted to the fence and hung their heads over in curiosity. The leafless sycamores and cottonwoods groaned in the wind—the smell of horses and sage was strong and pleasant. The front door swung open when she touched it. The house was uncannily silent. She turned down the tiled corridor and walked toward the master bedroom. She heard crying from the first bedroom, Nichole's. Lana tried the door but the big glass doorknob did not turn. The children's bedrooms did not have inside locks, which meant someone had locked Nichole in. Quickly Lana moved to Colette's door and tried its knob. The same thing. She pressed her ear against the thick paneling but heard nothing. At eight and nine, Colette and Nichole were old enough to climb out their bedroom windows but too cowed and docile to try. Had Kathryn locked the girls in before she threatened Dom? Had she made Tinera do it? Or had Dom locked them in and started something with Kathryn? If so, why was Tinera at liberty?

She opened the door to the master bedroom.

Tinera sat cross-legged in the middle of the California king-sized bed wearing her nightgown—a blue paisley with spaghetti straps. Her hair was in tangles. She looked at Lana with large, frightened eyes. On one side of the bedroom, the drawers of Kathryn's dresser hung open; articles of clothing were scattered on the floor. The television was on, volume off, two news anchors going on and on. Lana realized it must be after eleven. At the foot of the bed, Kathryn sat backwards on a straight chair with her feet in fuzzy, white slippers flat on the floor, her back to Tinera and facing the closed door of the big walk-in closet. Perfect posture. She held the .38 revolver in two hands, resting her wrists on the chair back.

"Big sister to the rescue," she said when Lana entered. "I wondered when you'd show up. Tinera said she had to go to the bathroom but she used the phone to call you. Covered up the noise with running water. Pretty smart, huh?"

"Kay," Lana said softly from the doorway. "What's happened?"

"Tinera? Tell your aunt what's going on. Same as I told you."

Lana felt sick.

Tinera began to cry.

"She's a little girl—don't involve her in this. Send her out of the room."

Kathryn shook her head and sat up straighter. "Oh, no, she's Daddy's favorite, she's the little mother so she has to know." Her voice was as perfectly reasonable as if she were explaining some mundane matter at a parent-teacher conference. "Don't worry, Lana, I'm not crazy. I haven't had a breakdown."

That was a matter they could debate later.

"Tell me what he did."

"Let's see. Where to begin? How about this." She yelled at the closet door. "I'm not pregnant. I had a miscarriage."

Lana saw a bullet hole in the wall above the closet.

"Jesus, Kathryn, you fired—"

Dom cried from the closet, "She tried to kill me, she's crazy, Lana. Take the gun away from her."

"Shut up!" Kathryn grinned at Lana, apparently enjoying herself. "Don't worry, he's not hurt. I just did it to scare him, just to let him know I wasn't kidding. He didn't believe me, Lana. He thought it was just poor old Kathryn moaning and groaning, same old, same old." She faced the closet again and adjusted her grip on the revolver. With the back of the chair supporting her wrists she could stay that way for hours. "I went out on Jacaranda and I did jumps and I galloped and trotted, we trotted a lot, and then we jumped some more and then I got a pain so I got off the horse and I squatted down in the dust. . . ."

"Oh, Kathryn." Love and sorrow flooded out on Lana's words.

There was a sudden pounding from inside the closet. "Grab the gun—she won't shoot you, Lana." Dom's voice was muffled but she heard the rage and fear in it. "She won't hurt you. Take the gun away."

"Don't even try," Kathryn said to Lana.

"Trust me," Lana held up her hands, palm out, "I won't."

"She's crazy," Dom cried. "Make her tell what she did, see if she isn't crazy."

Lana looked at her sister's eyes. They were not wild with madness. She saw calm and a hint of amusement in her expression.

For once she has the upper hand.

"I had a miscarriage right there. In the dirt. And afterwards I found a stick and I dug a hole and I buried it."

On the bed Tinera began to wail, a frightening, primitive sound.

Kathryn raised her voice sharply. "It was blood, Tinera, that's all it was. Just a little blood. No tiny fingernails or beating heart. No soul." Kathryn looked at Lana and went on as conversationally as if they were having lunch at the Harbor Inn. "You know what I've never understood about the right-to-lifers? The way they make out like an abortion actually damages a soul. It seems to me that if a soul doesn't make it into the world one way, it'll find another."

"Kathryn, that's not the point now."

"I beg your pardon, but I think it is. I didn't kill a soul, I killed," she raised her voice, "a little male embryo."

"You bitch," Dom yelled. "You fucking cunt bitch."

Lana darted across the bedroom and slammed the heel of her hand against the closet door. "Shut up, Dom. Your daughter's here."

"Tinera, honey, go call the police, okay?" Even muffled by the thick door, his voice wooed and purred. "Call the sheriff's number, baby girl. You know that number."

Lana shook her head at Tinera, who put her hands over her ears.

"She's not going to do it, Dom. We don't need the police here."

"I came home," Kathryn continued as if the interruption had not occurred, "and I told him and he began to cry. He cries as easily and effectively as a woman, did you know that, Lana? He can turn on the waterworks like a nineteenth-century heroine."

"Give me the gun."

"Don't you want to hear?"

"Yes, but give me the gun first." Lana held out her hand.

"Then he'll come out of the closet. Then it'll start all over again."

Lana dropped her hands and crouched beside the chair, whispering, "What d'you think? He's never coming out? You're going to let him starve in there? Think ahead, Kathryn. What have you gotten yourself into?"

Kathryn rested her chin on the butt of the gun.

"My god, be careful." Lana reached for the gun and Kathryn jerked away.

"I didn't think, I couldn't think." Her eyes seemed lost in their sockets. "I just had to do something or I was going to explode."

Lana tried to swallow but her mouth and throat were dry. "So tell me then, what happened after he started to cry?"

"He said he was going to sell all the horses. Except Jacaranda. He said he was going to go outside right then and shoot Jacaranda." She looked down at the gun in her hand. "He got the gun out of the drawer and when he saw it wasn't loaded he went into the closet to get his Luger."

"He's got a Luger in the closet?"

Kathryn giggled. "He forgot he took it to the gun shop to be cleaned. Too bad, huh? We'd all be dead."

Lana went to the bed and gathered Tinera into her arms. The girl was clammy-cold despite the warm wind blowing through the bedroom windows. She pulled a blanket up from the end of the bed and wrapped it around her shoulders.

"He put my gun on the dresser and I picked it up and loaded it." Kathryn smiled again. "You put the bullets in my drawer, remember?"

"And you made him go in the closet?"

"He was in there already, cussing because he couldn't find the Luger. He started to come out and I kicked the door shut. He opened it and I shot. Over his head. Like . . ." she sighted down the revolver, "this." She pulled the trigger.

Tinera screamed. Dom yelled. Lana fell back against the bed, her heart drumming in her head.

Dom screamed, "She's insane, Lana. You can see—"

"You're both crazy. Shut up and let me think."

There was now a second bullet hole just above the closet door, inches from the first. She's a good shot, Lana thought. If she weren't, Dom might be dead now. She went to Tinera and held her, sobbing, and tried to think.

The first thing was to get Tinera out of the bedroom.

"I told you, she has to be here. She's the little mother and she needs to understand everything. Him and me. Everything."

"She's a child—"

"No."

Lana whispered to Tinera, "I'll get you out soon. Just try to hold on." She kissed the girl's damp forehead and went back to sit on the bed near her sister. "Listen," she said, "I won't let him kill your horse. It won't happen, Kathryn, do you believe me?"

"It wasn't Jacaranda's fault, Lana. It was me. I rode him hard because I wanted to miscarry. I'm tired of being depressed all the time, staying in bed and being an invalid. I want to have a life. I don't want any more babies." Kathryn eyes shone with tears. "I don't even like babies. I never did."

Lana glanced at Tinera. She was lying down now with the pillows around her head. Perhaps she hadn't heard.

Lana said, "Is that right, Dom? You were going to kill the horse?"

"Damn straight. And what does she mean, she doesn't like babies?" His anger burned through the door. "She's a woman, for crissakes."

"Fuck you!" Kathryn screamed. "I told you when we got married I didn't want to have children and you said it was okay but you were lying. From the beginning you were lying. You made me have babies. You made me." Kathryn turned toward the sound of Tinera's sobs and pleaded to be understood. "I love you now, honey. I didn't before when I was pregnant, when you were so small and all you did was cry and there was so much to do and this big house, but I love you now. I love you all now."

Tinera flew off the bed and dropped to the ground at her mother's feet, hugging her legs. She spoke through streaming tears. "Put the gun away, Mama, try, please." She lowered her voice. Lana barely heard her whisper, "Make a deal with him. Say you'll do things and then he won't be so mad. You know."

Kathryn shook her head. "I won't do that anymore. I can't."

Lana pulled Tinera up and into her arms. Her hair smelled sour and oily. Poor little girl, Lana thought. Neglected and abused and adored all at the same time.

"Your mom's through making deals, and your dad's just going to have to get over being mad. She's not making any more promises." She looked at Kathryn. "Am I right?"

"Bingo, Lone Ranger."

Lana led Tinera to the bedroom door, thinking all the time of the revolver behind her, feeling its barrel like an index finger prodding the hollow of her back.

Kathryn said, "I told you I want her—"

"No." Kathryn would not shoot her; still, Lana's legs felt weak as she walked Tinera to the door and out into the hall. She let out a relieved sigh and leaned against the wall.

She asked Tinera, "Do you know how to unlock Nichole and Colette's rooms?"

"Daddy has the key."

"Did he lock them in?"

Tinera nodded.

"Why not you?"

Tinera looked miserable. "He wanted me to see. To learn."

"He told you that?"

She nodded.

Lana thought she would throw up. She swallowed hard. "Here's what you do. You go help the girls climb out their bedroom windows."

Tinera backed up a step, shaking her head.

"Honey, you have to do it."

"He'll get mad."

"I'll take care of your father."

"What if she kills him?" She began to cry again.

"She won't. You know she won't."

"Then why—"

"Tinera, it's not the time to talk now. I want you to take your sisters out into my car. And then you stay with them."

"What about Mama?"

"Just wait for us there."

"But Daddy—"

"Do as I ask, Tinera. I won't let anything bad happen to you, not to any of you."

Kathryn watched Lana come back into the bedroom. "Now what?" she asked and smiled sheepishly. She whispered, giggling, "To tell you the truth, I haven't figured how to get out of this situation."

"It's a doozy, all right," Lana said.

The Santa Ana blew through the open windows and from across the lawn and driveway Lana heard the sound of a horse. She drew aside the pale rose organdy sheers to see Jacaranda chasing his imagination around the paddock in the starlight, his luxuriant mane and tail catching the moonlight, flying as if he sensed he was in danger.

She spoke to the closet. "You can't kill the horse, Dom."

"I can do what I want. I own him."

"Well, not exactly," Lana said. "I don't know how it is in Rhode Island, but here in California you only own half of him. And even if you ignore that, you still don't want to kill him." Lana felt as if she were reading from a script. The words just came to her and she said them. "Think about this, Dom. If you kill the horse, I'll go to my friend who works for the *Union Tribune*." Jilly's beat was entertainment but Dom didn't need to know that. "I'll tell her the whole story and you probably won't be on the front page of section one, but I'll bet you make it big, maybe headlines and a picture, in the city section. Lots of people read that section, Dom. Thousands and thousands. Your pal Father Kelly reads the city section. If you're lucky, you might even get on television. One of those human interest pieces with Kathryn crying and Tinera and poor Jacaranda . . ."

Something slammed against the closet door. "Get out of my life, you bitch. This is my house and you're trespassing—"

"I was invited, Dom. And what I'm doing is called mop up—this is called crisis management."

"And I didn't start it," Kathryn screamed. "You said you'd kill him. You said you'd blow his brains out."

"You used that horse to murder my son."

"It wasn't a son," Kathryn said. "It was an embryo."

"You don't know."

"But I do," Lana said, yelling over both of them. "I've had miscarriages, Dom. I had four of them so don't tell me what's a son and what's a daughter. It's blood and slime and a clot of cells, that's it."

After more than fifteen years the loss of those children, who for days or weeks had lived so brightly in Lana's imagination, still brought a stab of pain like no other. But they were never really children except in the way a dream or a wish is real.

She heard a car door slam. The girls were in the Toyota.

She leaned down and whispered in Kathryn's ear. "You go."

Kathryn shook her head and Lana wanted to throttle her.

"Look, I'm giving you a way out. Otherwise you'll sit here until you dry up and blow away. You and the kids can come to my house. We'll figure something out after that."

She stretched out her hand for the revolver. Kathryn still would not give it to her.

"Now," Lana said.

Kathryn lowered her eyebrows and tried to look fierce, but it wasn't hard to understand why Dom did not take her seriously. Even angry, she looked pretty and vulnerable.

Lana wiggled her fingers.

Kathryn engaged the safety and slapped the revolver onto her palm. As Lana felt its cold weight, a lead ball dropped in her stomach and her knees knocked as she walked to the corner of the bedroom farthest from the closet, broke the gun, and removed the bullets from the cylinder, then closed the gun as carefully and quietly as she could. She stuffed the bullets deep in the pocket of her parka vest as she walked back to Kathryn, who still sat on the chair in front of the closet. She gestured for her to get up and go into the hall.

"The girls are in the car," she murmured, close to Kathryn's ear.

"Go out to them and lock the doors. Don't let anyone in except me."

Kathryn nodded, turned to go, and Lana grabbed her forearm.

"Quietly. I want him to think you're still here."

Lana returned to the bedroom and sat as Kathryn had, resting her hands on the back of the chair, holding the revolver steady. It probably was not normal to feel so calm under such circumstances. Maybe she was in shock. No, she was just calm. And confident. Which might mean she was just as crazy as her sister, but she did not think so. Dom was a bully and the one thing a bully could not handle was someone who refused to be bullied. She looked at her watch. It was almost midnight. On the television Jay Leno was talking to someone Lana did not recognize.

Dom said, "Kathryn?"

"I have the gun now."

She watched the knob of the closet door turn. Dom's shoulders and gray, drawn face appeared. He looked around the room.

"Where is she?"

"In my car."

He stepped out of the closet and moved toward the bedroom door, fast for someone so stocky.

Lana yelled, "Stop right there."

He turned on her, an icy fury in his eyes.

Now's the time to get nervous, Lana thought. But her senses felt clear and acute like a hawk's, diving.

"I will shoot you. I won't kill you, Dom, but I'm as good a shot as Kathryn and you know it. I will shoot and I will hurt you if you give me any trouble."

"You and Mars. If it weren't for you—"

"What? You think if it weren't for us, Kathryn'd be your brood bitch?"

"You'll never shoot me." His mouth twisted to the right in a spasm of humor. "She would. My Kathryn's got fire but you're too busy hosing everything down to have any of your own." He swaggered out into the hall. Lana followed and caught up with him and jammed the muzzle of the .38 into the small of his back.

He stopped.

"People change, Dom. Even good old dependable Lana. I might surprise you and turn out to be an honest-to-goodness firecracker." She hoped he believed her because if he didn't he could turn around fast, grab the gun, and it would all be over. A turn-and-grab move was the kind of thing gangsters did in movies all the time. It helped to think of Dom as a henchman out of *The Godfather*. "Go into the living room and sit down. Let's see if we can deal."

I'll make you an offer you can't refuse. If I can think of one.

Dom walked into the big living room with its heavy drapes and velvet couches and sat on the edge of a couch under an oil painting of a Gypsy girl with a cart and pony.

Such bad art. How could Kathryn tolerate it on her walls?

Lana sat on an ornately carved wooden chair Kathryn had told her was a bishop's chair and a valuable antique. Mostly it was uncomfortable, which was good. She did not want to relax. The situation might be terrible in its particulars, but it was almost worth it for the exhilarating run of ice through her veins. She could not keep Eddie French out of their lives. She could not figure out what to do about Beth. But *Tres Palomas* was a rare vision of the black-and-white world, and black and white was like order forms and inventory and accounting ledgers. She could handle black and white.

She reached under a tasseled shade and turned on a lamp that spilled a circle of yellow light in their corner of the room. In the lamplight his face looked more saturnine than ever. Ten feet of Persian carpet separated them.

Lana said, "I'm going to take her home and get the kids calmed down. I'll talk to her, find out what she wants, what would make her happy."

"What about me? Don't I get to be happy?"

Lana thought a moment. "Why can't you both be happy? Or at least try to be? Seems like it's been all about you, Dom. If you were to work with a professional—"

"You don't know what you're talking about." He shook his head with such determination that his thick hair moved from its smooth wave and fell across his forehead. "Stuff like this, personal, we keep in the family. It's nobody else's business. That's our way."

The revolver was heavy and Lana's wrists had begun to hurt.

"Dom, you may not believe it, but I value family as much as you do. And this thing you've got going here, it's not a family, it's a dictatorship. If you want to save anything, you're going to have to get help."

"I could divorce her. After today she wouldn't have a chance in court."

"But you don't believe in divorce. You told me no one in your family has ever been divorced."

He scratched his stubbled, blue-black jaw.

"You're a well-known man in San Diego. Father Kelly thinks you're Mr. Catholic San Diego. And I know you have competitors who'd like to see you in trouble. Remember the bidding war you got into with the Vegas Company? Made the paper, big time." Her gun hand felt ready to cramp. She shifted her grip minutely, hoping Dom would not notice. "I think I could ruin your reputation if I really tried."

"I'm not afraid of your threats."

Maybe he wasn't, but neither was he foolish enough to take a chance.

Lana watched his eyes move from her face to the gun and back again. "Go ahead, take her, take 'em all. I'll be over tomorrow."

"And you won't kill Jacaranda."

"How can I? You've got the gun?"

She looked at the revolver shining in her hand. This was not the only gun in the house. He might have plenty of firepower elsewhere. At the least, a rifle. "If you really want your family back, you'll swear."

She saw his Adam's apple bob.

"On your mother's name. On Tinera's name." The two Tineras.

"Jesus, woman—"

"You'll lose her forever if you hurt that animal."

"Goddamn it, she killed my baby. A father has rights in this society."

"Tell it to the shrink."

He closed his eyes and tipped against the back of the couch.

"Swear, Dom. On the two Tineras."

He looked at Lana with such precise and undisguised loathing it struck her that, until that moment, she had never been hated. People disliked her sometimes but this was hate and it felt like a weapon aimed at her head. She forced herself not to cringe.

"I swear."

Chapter Thirty

For fifteen minutes Micki had been watching the perspiration circles under Ms. Hoffman's arms grow to the size of salad plates. She wore shields under her blouse—Micki could see their outline—but apparently she just soaked right through them. Why? Hot flashes? It couldn't be nerves because the class was discussing *The Scarlet Letter,* which Hoffman could practically recite from memory. Was all that moisture streaming from her pores just an unfortunate biological fact? God, she thought, life is unfair.

People die, people sweat, your aunt and cousins move in with you, and there's some huge disaster no one really talks about. And Micki was supposed to concentrate on *The Scarlet Letter.*

She couldn't get behind Hester Prynne. Why didn't she just move to New York or New Amsterdam—whatever? Did she have more than one blouse? Did they all have the red "A" on them?

And what did it matter anyway?

Micki's home had turned into a boarding house since Aunt Kathryn and all came to live with them. At first Micki felt sorry for her cousins, especially Tinera, but when she tried to say so, Tinera blew her off. Aunt Kathryn was meeting with Uncle Dom today at Jessie Ward's office. Accidentally on purpose, Micki had heard Kathryn on the phone telling him they could only talk to him with a third person present. Like a referee. Micki had been surprised to hear her aunt stand up for herself, and even more surprised that her Uncle Dom agreed to her terms.

She was glad Dom was not her father.

As far as Micki could tell, crummy fathers far outnumbered the good. Tiff's mom had raised her alone since she was two and her father went off to sail around the world. They were still married, and he came back to San Diego every now and then. Tiff barely knew him. There were girls whose fathers lived at home but never talked to them or drank too much or yelled all the time. Worse than beating and drinking had been the story her grandmother once told about *her* father. She had been the youngest of fourteen children, raised on an apple orchard in Idaho. Her father called her "the little one" because he could not remember her name.

Micki's father—Jack—had lots of names for her: Tricky Micki, Michelle ma belle. He had been the best dad; there would never be another like him.

Ms. Hoffman was talking about sin and temptation and retribution, making *The Scarlet Letter* more complicated than it had to be. The way Micki saw it, the story showed what happened when people didn't tell the truth. If the Rev loved Hester, he would have told the truth and saved them all a world of trouble. Forget all the sin stuff. Micki wasn't even sure she believed in it, and she wasn't going to worry about it now. She had enough going on between her ears.

Fathers—good, bad, dead, alive—they filled up her brain and never gave up. The night before, she barely slept at all for thinking of Eddie French. She wished she had words to describe the feeling in her stomach when he looked at her. She saw him, and at the same time she saw herself—not exactly the same, but deeply familiar. Scary.

On Sunday they had gone to brunch alone at the Catamaran. Micki felt happy and self-conscious at the same time. She wondered if people at other tables knew they were father and daughter. He had reserved a window table overlooking Mission Bay. She ate a whole plate of lobster chunks off the buffet and told him about the family trip to Maine where she saw a cook drop live, squirming lobsters into a pot of cold water to cook them. She had asked her father why they didn't scramble out—what good were those claws if not to rescue themselves? Jack said the lobster didn't know he was cooking until it was too late.

Micki worried that her mother was a bit like a lobster. If she didn't stop pretending everything was okay, she might never be able to get real again. And if Beth hung out with Kimmie and her lowlife friends much longer something bad would happen to her, too.

Eddie was easy to talk to. Time went quickly over brunch and later, walking beside the bay dotted with sailboats and the sand where children built castles like it was June, not January. But she still did not understand what he wanted. To know her, he said. To be part of her life. Sometimes this made sense and other times—like when she remembered fifth grade and thought about The Fives—it amazed her and made her suspicious.

She wanted to trust Eddie but maybe he was a liar, a cheat. Maybe a player.

Her father, Jack, never hid things or disguised them or pointed her in the wrong direction. What she learned from him was that so long as she knew the truth, it was as good as finding the North Star. The truth kept her from getting crazy lost, boiling up in a pot like a lobster.

Her mom seemed to believe that if she kept on acting like everything was fine and they were still the perfect Porters, it would magically happen that way. Like a fairy godmother waving her wand around. Micki had decided that her mom was just generally afraid of the truth; she must have been this way when Micki's father was alive, but no one noticed then because he balanced her out. Like on scales.

Micki heard her name.

"Are you with us today?" Ms. Hoffman's yellow-green eyes sparkled in Micki's direction.

Micki blinked and nodded.

"Then will you give us your opinion, please?"

Micki cleared her throat and looked at Tiff beside her, doodling Audrey Hepburn faces with big eyes and thick bangs.

Ms. Hoffman asked, not unkindly. "Did you enjoy the book, Micki, or did you simply rent the movie version as most of your classmates seem to have done?"

"I didn't see the movie," she said honestly.

"Is it too much to hope that you actually read the book?"

"I couldn't understand parts of it." Like most books written before 1950, *The Scarlet Letter* had too many words. This was not what Ms. Hoffman wanted to hear. "The sentences were hard. Too long."

Ms. Hoffman lifted her eyebrows.

"I liked what it was about."

"Would you care to share what that was? In simple sentences, of course."

Her mom said Ms. Hoffman spoke archly. To Micki she was just sort of sarcastic all the time.

"If you don't tell the truth you can get sick and ruin your life. Even die."

Ms. Hoffman smiled, showing her large, white teeth. "In part, you are correct. What else? Anyone?" She raised her eyebrows and scanned the class. When no one volunteered, she walked to the windows and for a moment watched the eucalyptus bordering the school grounds rock in the wind. "I think we should just shut the school during Santa Anas."

Someone behind Micki cheered softly.

"I wanted Hester and the minister to get together," Tiff said.

"Me, too," said Nancy Challen from the back of the room in the drawling way all The Fives spoke. Even Tiff had begun to speak as if she were too bone-lazy to breathe right. "And what was that thing on his chest about, anyway? Was that sick or what? If he was going to confess, he should have done it way sooner, before he was ready to die."

Ms. Hoffman looked at Micki. "Why do you think the Reverend Dimmesdale took so long to acknowledge his guilt?"

Micki looked down at the book on her desk, open to one of the hundred-plus pages she had skimmed the night before. No matter. She knew the answer without reading. "People only change when they can."

Like Eddie couldn't come find her right away. He had to be ready. He told her on their walk, "I was a boy for longer than most." Micki had asked him why he and her birth mother—she knew her name now, Barbara—didn't get married. He hedged a bit and then just said, "We didn't love each other." Micki thought she knew the rest: Barbara did not want to marry him; she did not want a baby. Her. Micki.

So the kids at Forrester Elementary had been right, after all. Micki had been given away because she was not wanted. Micki thought about Barbara handing her over to the care of strangers, and a chasm opened up inside her the size of the Grand Canyon with no pretty river at the bottom. No bottom at all.

The bell rang. Micki gathered her books and headed out into the hall. Tiff caught up with her, and they walked together to their next class.

"Did you really read that book?" Tiff asked. "It was so boring."

"Once I got into it, it wasn't bad."

Tiff groaned. "God, you're smart. Can we study together next weekend?"

Next week she wanted to spend time with Eddie.

She asked, "How 'bout tomorrow, after school?"

As expected, Tiff looked away. After school she would be with The Fives at Bella Luna.

"So what's he like?" Tiff asked as they slipped into their seats in Señora Dominguez's Spanish classroom. Micki did not know for sure, but she imagined that Tiff had requested a desk change and been turned down.

"Who?"

"*Him.* Your father."

Micki glared at her. "My father is dead."

"You know what I mean. Did you talk about *Mistique* and Melany Anderson?"

As a matter of fact, Micki and Eddie French had talked a lot about Melany Anderson, the star of *Mistique.* At brunch he answered all Micki's questions about her, the premieres and the parties. He did not seem really interested, though, and when Micki's questions ran out he changed the subject.

"Is she really pretty up close?"

"We never, like, got around to that stuff," Micki said with studied condescension. "We had a bunch of other things to talk about."

Señora Dominguez entered the room, bringing with her heavy perfume and rigid discipline. Although Micki had been speaking border Spanish to the men at Urban Greenery since she was a toddler, she struggled for a passing grade in this class. Señora Dominguez said she spoke Spanish like a hillbilly spoke English. Restlessly, Micki shifted around on the hard desk seat, trying to find a comfortable position. She should have gone to the bathroom instead of talking to Tiff at the break.

She raised her hand.

"May I be excused?"

Señora Dominguez looked at her as if to say a girl getting a C-minus should learn to hold her bladder, but she gave her the nod anyway.

As soon as she was out in the hall, Micki didn't have to go anymore. She also did not want to return to Spanish. First looking both ways to make sure no one was in the hall, she shoved through the emergency door into the stairwell, where two options presented themselves. She could go down to the ground floor and ditch the rest of the day, or she could ignore the No Entry sign and duck under the chain blocking the stairs to the roof.

Originally this part of Arcadia School had been an office building, and the flat roof was territory strictly forbidden to students. But when Micki was a sixth-grader, she had discovered the roof and used it as her private hideaway. It was hot on the tarpaper-and-gravel-covered roof, and the dry wind made her cheeks shrink and tighten and her eyes feel hot and squinty. She sat behind an air conditioning unit and got a cigarette out of her purse. She used her hands to cup the match as she lighted it. She checked her watch and saw that she had almost thirty minutes until her next class, physical education. She didn't dare ditch that again.

Beth was the athlete in the family, or had been before she turned into a Kimmie-clone. For the first time Micki could ever remember, she felt like Beth's older sister, wiser since The Fives dinged her and Tiff got two-faced and Eddie entered her life. Maybe he would talk to Beth. He didn't mind talking about how low-down and miserable he felt when he hit his bottom. That's what he called the worst time: his bottom. She could feel the honesty in him when he talked about what it was like to be an addict and an alcoholic, and it made her feel safer than she had in a long time. Maybe her mom would tell him she was worried about Beth.

Micki almost laughed.

No way her mom was going to tell someone she didn't know, and was halfway scared of, that they weren't the perfect Porters anymore.

She heard the stairwell door open.

"Micki Porter?"

She recognized the voice of one of the monitors, Ms. Popelli.

"I know you're up here. I can smell the cigarette."

Shit, Micki thought. More trouble.

Chapter Thirty-one

As she sat facing Grace Mamoulian, stiff as a bookend on the cruelly right-angled chair to which she had been directed, Lana wanted to kick a hole through the woman's gleaming walnut desk, right through to her Donna Karan-clad shins. The air conditioner hummed a monotone in the bright, chilly office. An hour earlier the sun had been hot on Lana's back when she was down on her knees transplanting Early Girl tomato seedlings and heard Carmino's voice on the PA system summoning her to the telephone.

Grace Mamoulian wore a chocolate brown suede jumper, very simple and expensive. Gold jewelry, hoops at the ears and a thick, punitive-looking bracelet. Lana noticed that her nails had been manicured since their last encounter. Today her polish was a rose-red so dark it was almost black.

Lana glanced down at her own hands. As she suspected, there was still dirt under her fingernails. When the call came she hadn't stopped to wash her face or comb her hair.

Beside Lana, Micki sat on another straight, hard chair, her hands shoved beneath her thighs—probably cold. When Lana walked into the office, Micki had not looked up at her, but Lana had paused briefly to kiss the top of her daughter's head just to let Grace know this would not be a slam-dunk for the side of authority.

Grace Mamoulian relaxed into the depths of her own chair of tufted cowhide and smiled with chilling benignity. "Tell your mother why I've called her away from work, Micki." Lana suspected this would be payback time for the scene she had pulled the week before. "Look at your mother and tell her," Grace said.

"I was smoking. On the roof." Micki looked at Lana through a curtain of magenta-and-gold hair.

That's it? Beth's smoking dope, my sister wants to shoot her husband, and you got me down here to talk tobacco? Since official-dom had demonized them, cigarettes had become the rebellion of choice for most of Micki and Beth's friends. Lana did not like it that her fifteen-year-old daughter sneaked cigarettes, but neither did she think it was a crisis. Micki would stop smoking when acting-out became less important than staying healthy. Lana had done it, Wendy and Jack and Michael, too. Starting and stopping were middle class rites of passage.

Grace folded her hands on her spotlessly gleaming desktop. "And you knew when you did it that here at Arcadia we regard to-bacco in the same way we do other drugs? That tobacco use is absolutely forbidden? Do you know the punishment, Micki?"

Micki's hair shimmered when she nodded.

"Tell your mother what it is."

"Suspension," Micki said, and cut her navy blue eyes at Lana.

Lana heard *suspension,* which could not possibly be right. Lana looked at Grace and pressed the balls of her feet onto the floor. "That's ridiculous." Her feet were anchors holding her down when what she truly wanted was to fly across the desk and throttle Grace Mamoulian.

"It's in the school handbook, Lana. Arcadia has a no-tolerance policy."

"And you knew this, Micki? Why did you do it? Did you *want* to be suspended?"

"Everyone goes up there, Ma. To smoke."

Lana looked at Grace. "Is that true?"

"She exaggerates. The stairs are blocked and the girls know the roof's out of bounds. Except for a few rule-breakers . . ."

Guess who.

". . . we have perfect conformity."

"Perfect conformity always worries me, Grace."

Lana's right foot spasmed; she felt a pull up the back of her calf and for a few seconds she concentrated on not letting it cramp. When she spoke again, she sounded calm. Actually she *was* calm.

After Monday night with Kathryn and Dom, being called to the principal's office was an irritating gnat bite.

"Suspended for how long?" she asked.

"One school week."

"I think that's way excessive. What about her work? Tests?"

"Arrangements will be made vis-à-vis tests. She can pick up the week's homework assignments tomorrow afternoon."

Lana bent her toes hard against the plush carpet. "Micki, the car's parked out in front. Will you go wait for me there?" She reached into her bag for her keys.

Micki stood up.

"I think it would be good for Micki to hear what we have to say about her deportment," Grace said.

"I don't. It's okay, honey, go along."

After a pause that went on a moment too long to be comfortable or natural, Grace said in a voice so sweet and light she might have been wooing forgiveness from an angel, "I know you feel bad, Micki, but let me reassure you that when you get back to Arcadia, no one will hold this incident against you. It will be in your record, of course, but your teachers and the staff will all be supportive. And maybe after a while, you'll realize this is for your own good."

Without expression, Micki looked at Grace Mamoulian and then took the keys from her mother and left the room, saying nothing.

Insolent brat, thought Lana, and grinned to herself.

Grace and Lana faced each other across the great walnut divide. Grace tipped her chair back a little, laughing softly as if over a joke only she could fully appreciate.

"These girls," she said, patting her fingertips together. "They *will* push the rules."

"Especially bad rules."

Up went Grace Mamoulian's umbrella eyebrows.

"It makes absolutely no sense to treat smoking tobacco as if it were on a par with smoking crack."

"I didn't compare tobacco to crack."

"You did—you said it's school policy to treat tobacco like any other drug."

"With suspension for the first offense, yes, that's true. But of course with crack we'd insist on counseling and mandatory drug testing as well."

"But not for cigarettes? Which means they aren't the same."

Lana watched Grace Mamoulian rub the two deep lines between her eyebrows. She wore a small, gold ring on her thumb. Strange.

"Has anyone ever challenged the legality of the policy?"

"Is that your plan?" Grace looked surprised. "To take Arcadia School to court?"

"How many girls smoke off the school grounds?"

"Good Lord, Lana, I have no idea. What concerns me is what goes on at school."

"So if you knew a girl was a tweaker every day after school you wouldn't speak to the parents?"

"It isn't the same."

"Before this policy, what was the punishment for smoking?"

"Oh, it varied. Detention, usually."

"But since September, tobacco and crack are the same. Heroin, too, I suppose. Marijuana, Ecstasy, LSD?" When had Lana's foot and calf stopped cramping?

Grace Mamoulian stood up, spidering her fingers on the desk as she leaned toward Lana. "I don't think we should continue this conversation right now, Lana. If you want to take this up with the Board, then of course you must suit yourself. Or, I'd be happy to give you the number of Howard Cortez, the school attorney. However, for children like Micki, isn't it best to hold firm on this? Isn't her well-being what we have to consider first?"

"What d'you mean, 'children like Micki'?" Lana stood up, eye to eye with Grace Mamoulian.

"This has upset you, Lana. You're not yourself."

Lana laughed because Grace Mamoulian had it all wrong, one hundred and eighty degrees of error.

"You seem to like to label people, Grace. I'm not sure that's a good trait in a school administrator. Wouldn't you be better at your job if you treated people as individuals?"

"Are you questioning my qualifications?"

"I'm asking what you meant when you said 'children like Micki'."

Grace sighed and patted her smooth hair. "She is a difficult girl, rebellious. She doesn't take direction well."

Lana laughed. "You bet she's difficult. She's a wonderfully difficult girl and she's had to put up with some pretty rotten stuff at this school so that, frankly, if she goes up on the roof to smoke once in a while, I don't blame her."

Grace's mouth snapped into a line. She looked down at her pristine desktop, and Lana knew she was fighting to compose herself. "If you would like to meet again next week, I can have Mr. Cortez here to discuss this. I know we all want the same thing, what's best for Micki."

"I'm the only one who can speak to what's best for Micki. And what I think is, she would be better off at another school."

Cash registers had appeared in Grace Mamoulian's eyes and once again her voice was creamy. "We value Micki—you know that, Lana. If I sounded harsh . . ." Lana wondered if she had any idea how transparent she was. "She is a difficult girl, no question, but she is also smart and charming and all her teachers admire her energy."

"Well, that's too bad because they're going to lose all that charm and energy." It meant losing Ms. Hoffman, but maybe she would invite her to dinner, sort of keep her in the family. Lana slipped her leather bag over her shoulder and walked to the office door and opened it. "I'll tell your secretary. She can do whatever's necessary to release Micki's files."

Ten minutes later, Lana slipped behind the wheel of the 4Runner and expelled a long breath as she leaned her head against the Toyota's headrest and closed her eyes. She had wobbled down the main hall and out of the school on gelatin legs and now she seemed to be quivering all over.

"What?" Micki asked.

Lana opened her eyes and looked at her daughter.

"Am I suspended?"

"Do you still want to go to Balboa?"

For a fraction of a second, Micki looked confused and then her face opened in a sunflower smile that heated up the car ten degrees. She threw herself across the gearshift and hugged Lana.

"We'll go down there tomorrow and get you enrolled, but first you have to empty your locker. Make it fast. I want to ditch this place as soon as I can."

Micki skipped off and Lana watched her go.

On the way up Washington Street in response to Grace Mamoulian's summons, she had decided to give Balboa some serious thought. She had planned to visit and talk to the teachers, but now . . .

Beth would stay at Arcadia, where she seemed to be thriving despite her recent fall from grace. Lana laughed aloud at the pun. That woman was a piece of work who would have to be mollified before she took her resentment out on Beth, who had four more years before graduation. On second thought, Grace would realize it was not politic to be hard on Beth, for if Lana had withdrawn one daughter from the school, she might take another out even more easily. Who knew if other parents would follow her example? Probably at the next meeting of the Arcadia board of directors the no-tolerance policy would be amended not to include suspensions for cigarette smoking. She had done the right thing. Without Jack. Without asking advice of anyone.

Of course, there would have to be consequences for Micki; she could not be rewarded for breaking the rules. Lana tried to think of something that would register as truly onerous. She would also talk to her about right behavior and the dangers of smoking.

If only Lana's other problems could be as easily settled.

Lana's day had begun with a warm east wind. A January dawn too warm to sleep. She had been out before sunup with the dogs. From the rim of the canyon she had watched the sky turn from black to deep turquoise shot with streaks of pink and gold, a rococo sky reminiscent of Stella's favorite decorating colors. She took deep breaths of air and felt her lungs shining like pink toenail polish.

Dom's calls began a couple of hours later as Lana stood at the counter looking out the greenhouse window as she beat eggs and cheese together for scrambled eggs. Kathryn had burned an English muffin but was eating it anyway and drinking her third cup of coffee. The kitchen smelled brown but outside, in the back-yard of the neighbors across the lane, the acacia trees had broken into bloom overnight, their golden-globed pom-poms another proof that spring would come.

Lana answered the phone and at the sound of her brother-in-law's assertive voice, her good mood shrank. She handed the phone to Kathryn. "You want me to leave?"

Kathryn shook her head.

Lana lifted a frying pan off its hook near the stove and set it down over the heat. After resisting the temptation for a few seconds, she gave up trying to be discreet and listened openly.

Kathryn showed surprising muscle.

"I told you last night, I won't talk to you alone." A long pause, and Lana could not hear what Dom was saying but the grumble of his voice carried across the room. "I don't care if you think it's too personal—I won't talk to you without someone there." Another, shorter pause. "Because you're a bully, Dom, and I'm tired of being harassed into doing things I don't want to do."

Lana grinned and gave Kathryn a thumbs-up before she poured a tablespoon of olive oil onto the hot skillet and swirled it around until the bottom shone. She waited another few seconds and then dropped in a handful of chopped ham.

Over its sizzle she heard Kathryn say, "For starters, I don't want any more babies. I don't care. This isn't 1700 and we aren't Catanian peasants. I want my tubes tied."

Lana turned around in time to see Kathryn holding the receiver out from her ear and rolling her eyes.

Micki and Beth clattered down the stairs and a moment later came into the kitchen, arguing about music and the Grammys. Micki wanted to know since when was Beth into Goth.

Lana shushed them and all three eavesdropped.

"I don't want to get divorced, I never said I did." Kathryn's voice softened. "The gun was to get your attention, Dom. You were going to kill Jacaranda."

The girls looked at Lana. She just shook her head.

"Honest to God, if you ever threaten me or anything I love ever again . . . Dom, I never said that, don't say I did. You know I never would have hurt you."

We are our mothers all over again, Lana thought. Mars knew how to get what she wanted, and from whom had she learned that if not Stella? And exactly like Stella, Lana had become adept at putting a bright coat of paint over bad moods and miseries and going on about her business as if she were the happiest woman in the world. Beth had called her dishonest. Lana had said the same of her own mother more times than she could count. Stella bent and twisted and avoided the truth to escape blame or get what she wanted, to make the world into what she thought it should be.

As Kathryn continued to argue and Micki and Beth continued to listen, Lana's two or three square feet of the kitchen, the area right around the stove and greenhouse window, suddenly seemed apart from the rest of the room. She stood in a patch of morning sun and felt a fingery heat, a palmy warmth on her shoulder. For a flying moment, Jack was right beside her.

"Forget breakfast, Ma."

Beth's voice shattered the glass ball around the moment, whiplashing Lana back to reality. She looked at the frying pan and stirred the ham.

"Just a few mouthfuls of egg." Her throat felt tight. "And a piece of toast."

"I'm not hungry."

"You will be if you don't eat."

"Jesus H. Christ." Beth threw her pack against the back door. "I'll eat, I'll eat."

Lana stood where she had been a moment before; she had not moved. She tried to think herself back into the protected moment and to feel again the hand on her shoulder.

Nothing.

Into the phone Kathryn said, "I married you because I love you and I still love you but I'm telling you, Dom, we have to have a different kind of marriage. I just can't live like that anymore. . . . See? That's what I was saying. You're mean. That's why I want us to see Jessie. She can help us both. . . ." Her voice rose. "This isn't just about you, Dom. I'm not saying I don't have faults, too."

Lana fed the girls, trying to ignore Beth's petulance, and saw them off to school. Tinera, Colette, and Nichole were staying home. Earlier she had sent them into the playhouse with a tray of cinnamon toast, oranges and bananas, and milk. And just as well. Kathryn's conversation was none of their business. She made more toast and two more cups of coffee. All the while, Kathryn and Dom went over the same, cratered territory. No sooner had she hung up than the phone rang again.

"If it's him, I'm through talking."

But it was Jessie Ward calling to say she had a cancellation and could see the Firenzis at ten A.M. Kathryn got on the phone again to tell Dom.

Next came a call from Stella.

"You've been on the phone for over an hour."

"Don't blame me, Ma."

"I hope you're going to do something."

"Me?"

"Kathryn listens to you. She's always trusted your opinion."

"She knows my opinion."

"Which is?"

Lana looked directly at her sister sitting three feet away across the table drinking coffee. "I think she should leave the son of a bitch. I think he's beyond redemption. She should get as big a settlement as she can and start over."

"Don't be ridiculous."

"You don't know," Kathryn's eyes filled with tears. "You just don't understand."

Lana made a loony-face at her.

Stella said, "She wants to stay with him—not a bone in her body wants to take those girls and go off on her own. Do you think she could run a Hollywood Cafe somewhere? Not a chance. Kathryn is not an independent woman."

And whom should we thank for that?

"This is just an upset. All marriages have them."

Though Stella thought she and Kathryn were tight as tuna in a can, she knew nothing about the gun, the miscarriage, or Jacaranda. Lana had not said a word about the subtlety of Dom's abuse. Her mother changed the subject and told her how encouraging Lana's Realtor friend had been when she explained her financial situation.

"Make sure you tell her the truth," Lana said. "Don't cover things up to make them look good."

Stella told Lana she always told the truth. Scrupulously.

"I know, Ma. It's a core value."

Lana wanted to go into her bedroom and close the door, sit on the bed, and try to remember what it was that had happened during that peculiar, still moment by the stove. But there was no time for reflection. As soon as she hung up the phone, Kathryn had demanded her undivided attention, saying that if Dom decided to go to an attorney, one of the litigious superstars he lunched with at the City Club twice a month and with whom he owned joint shares in a Baja duck club and a Canadian fishing camp, Kathryn would almost certainly lose her daughters. This made her start to cry.

"Lana, all that stuff you threatened, the bad publicity, you can't really do that, can you?"

"That's not the point. This is all up to you now, Kay."

"What about Jacaranda?"

"And it's not about the horse. It's about you and the way you choose to live."

Lana had left her sister crying and gone to work. No sooner had she gotten to Urban Greenery and put her hands in the ground, than Grace Mamoulian's office called.

Lana leaned back in the driver's seat of the Toyota, closed her eyes, and again tried to remember that moment in the kitchen, but as if she were chasing a dream, it grew vaguer the faster she went after it. Until she knew, finally, that nothing had happened.

At that instant Micki emerged from Arcadia School at a run, her book-heavy pack slung over one shoulder and bouncing against her side. She used one hand to steady it, and with the other held high, she waved a square white envelope the size of a wedding invitation.

She climbed into the Toyota, tossed her heavy pack into the back seat, and tore open the Crane envelope on which her name had been printed in a labored Old English script. She and Lana sat in the car and looked at the enclosed printed card. *The Sisterhood of Fives is pleased to invite you to join them in a particular and private relationship.*

Lana laughed aloud. "I'm sorry, Micki. It's just so . . . pretentious."

"No kidding."

"So, what do you think?" *Particular and private*—good God. "If you want, I can go back in and tell Grace we've changed our mind. You can take the suspension and—"

Micki's eyes opened in astonishment. "Ma-a, get real. Why would I want to do that?"

"You don't want to be a Five?"

"Duh."

Which meant no.

Lana put her hands to her cheeks and laughed. "You are a rocket, girl. I can't keep up with you."

"They kiss ass, Ma. It was so not cool, after they heard about Eddie. The way they started dogging me with questions. And I didn't tell you this—it was so phony. Before school even started today, this senior girl who's never even spoken to me once in my whole life comes up and asks me—she's got this slow, lazy voice

like they all have—and she asked me to have lunch with them."
She laughed and shook her head. "Fives never eat with anyone but
Fives, Ma."

"Amazing," Lana said.

"That's why Tiff's been leeching onto me. She said they told her
she had to convince me to join even though they dinged me." She
waved the invitation. "I knew this was coming. And I already
knew I didn't want it."

Micki's good sense stunned Lana.

"So, fill me in here. Are you and Tiff still friends?"

Micki shrugged.

"Maybe if you're at Balboa and she's at Arcadia—"

"Whatever, Ma. I don't really care. Eddie says—" She stopped.

"You can tell me what he says, Micki. It's okay."

"Well, he says I've had some experiences that make me kind of
older than girls my age. He says it's not so strange Tiff seems like,
you know, silly now."

"You told him she's silly?" Before you told me?

"Yeah, I did."

"Well, he's right. Absolutely." And I should have told you so
myself.

Lana put the Toyota in gear and drove out of the school parking
lot and onto Washington Street, heading for home.

"What you did back there? With Mrs. Mamoulian? That was
hot, Ma."

"It's a stupid rule."

"Yeah, but I don't mean that. I mean how you stood up for me.
You could've backed down but you didn't."

Praise from a teenager, precious as strawberries in December.
Lana's cheeks tingled with pleasure.

"I love you, Mommy. I know, the other night, I said some
things—"

"I've forgotten them, honey."

"I wanted to make you feel bad."

"I know." Lana almost left it at that but there was something
Micki needed to know. "And you succeeded. You did make me feel
bad."

"I'm so sorry." Micki pressed her fists against her mouth. "Do
you forgive me?"

Lana signaled a sudden right turn and pulled into a red zone around the corner. She undid her seat belt and reached across the gearbox to wrap her arms around Micki.

"Of course I forgive you. I will always forgive you. And I will always love you. Nothing can change that." She held Micki's sweet face between her hands and kissed her cheeks. "Don't ever forget, even when we have fights and you hate me, you're still my darling daughter. Forever and ever."

Chapter Thirty-two

At the open air food court in Fashion Valley Mall, Beth snagged a round table and spread out her books and notebooks to discourage company. Not that she really had to worry about getting hit on. Damian was the only boy who had ever been interested in her, which was probably the most insulting thing she had ever thought about herself. The times she imagined her first serious boyfriend, she thought of someone with clean hair and good skin, handsome and probably an athlete, absolutely a good student and school leader, someone her father would have liked. Not Damian, the son of Satan.

When Beth told Kimmie this, she laughed in her high, squeaky way and said Beth was hopeless.

Kimmie and her opinions had seriously begun to irritate Beth. The girl was flat stupid. Half of what she thought came from *The National Enquirer,* the rest from conspiracy assholes like Strider who believed Neil Armstrong never walked on the moon. He said it was all a trick by the government to raise taxes. Plus she had no sense of the future. She talked about living every day like it was her last, but really she was just throwing her life away, smoking weed and cutting school and boosting cheap tee shirts and jewelry for excitement. Beth had been along on some of these sprees. To prove it, she had a crappy pink plastic puppy key chain in her dresser drawer. She only lifted it to show Kimmie she could.

Images of Kimmie alone in that dreary condo without any furniture came to her mind. Apart from Strider and Damian, Beth was her only friend, and she might as well be an orphan because weeks went by without her sister, Jules, making an appearance. And her mom was slow about sending money for food and other expenses. Beth was the only reliable person in her life. People left Kimmie, they abandoned her. Beth didn't want to be one of those.

She had been drawn to Kimmie because when she was with her she did not think about her father, but Beth saw now that she could not drop her father off at the bottom of the stairs and expect him to stay there like a duffel, waiting to be picked up on her way out. Over the last week or so a reasoning voice in her head had been gaining volume and she had come around to thinking that her father was inescapable. When she was slapping Damian's sweaty hands off her breasts, when she got drunk on peppermint schnapps, and when she smoked pot, his voice whispered that life was too precious to waste. Not in spite of how quickly it could end, but because of it.

She wished she could talk about this to her mom, or to Micki, but Micki was obsessed with her birth father. Beth wanted to slap her for being so disloyal.

The crowd in the food court was still mostly mommies and babies in huge strollers, stately as yachts. It had been another warm, dry day but the sun was only an inch above the roof of the mall and when it went down, the air would quickly chill. The mall would fill up with other teenagers then and civvie-dressed sailors identifiable by their bristle cuts and erect posture.

Beth had bought herself a Starbucks clown drink, sweet and foamy and no coffee at all, the kind of drink she could slurp down without taking her mouth off the straw even once. When it was gone she would want another, but all she had left from her allowance was a dollar and change. Even Kimmie usually had more money than Beth did. Maybe she would ask her mom if she could get a job. She could say she needed money for school activities, and she would automatically believe whatever she said because she trusted her. Kimmie was right. It was easy to lie when people trusted you.

These were the lies she had told today: she'd be late getting home because of a yearbook staff meeting; she told the basketball coach she couldn't play anymore because she'd hurt her ankle; she told the school nurse she had cramps so she could lie down during second period and miss the algebra test she had not studied for.

When he remembered, Kimmie's father sent her an allowance of two hundred and fifty dollars a month as part of the divorce agreement. Kimmie tried to act as if his generosity sprang from love, but Beth knew better. Her own father would never forget to send her money if he promised he would do it. He always kept his word.

Beth sucked up the sweet caramel-and-cream drink. The sun dropped below the mall and the heat lamps came on, spreading circles of warmth. The place had crowded up since she got there. Children and parents, groups of men and women headed for early movies, military guys. When they walked they bounced on their toes like they were grateful to be let out. At the table a few paces away from Beth a couple argued in Spanish. Something about money.

She opened the top of her drink and ran her index finger around the interior curve of the plastic cup to get the last of the cream. If she didn't exercise she was going to get fat, but so what. Damian wouldn't care; she might as well be invisible, for all he really saw or knew about her. Same for her mom. Beth could be a behemoth—great word—and her mom would never blink. If her father came back from the dead he wouldn't recognize her.

She wished she had enough money for a cinnamon roll. Sweets weren't as good as pot and booze for distracting her, but sleep was the best of all. She could barely get out of bed these winter mornings, even with the sun pouring through the balcony doors, creeping toward the bed. She used to like the warmth of sunlight on her face in the morning, and she remembered when she had jumped out of bed like a happy cricket and could not wait to get to Arcadia, to get her hands on a basketball. Now she hated the sound of her alarm and buried her head under the covers and prayed she'd get sick so she could stay home. Maybe she'd try to get suspended like Micki.

Beth had fallen asleep in Ms. Hoffman's class twice this week. After the second time, which was today, she had asked Beth to come in for a little lunchtime chat.

"You're in for it," Kimmie had said with glee. "I'll wait for you at the ninth-grade entrance."

Beth liked Ms. Hoffman's untidy office where the walls and shelves were crowded with mementos of past classes. On the wall behind her desk, half a dozen diplomas were arranged in two neatly squared off-lines. She was a graduate of Boston University and had a master's degree from Harvard; there was something up there about Oxford, too. So much work so she could end up teaching teenage girls, the sweat running down her sides.

On the corner of her desk in a crystal vase she had arranged a dozen daffodils.

"I spent a fortune for them," she had told Beth in a confidential tone that sounded half guilty, half amused. "They're worth it— they tell me spring is coming. Keep my spirits up."

Beth had never thought of Ms. Hoffman's spirits going down. She always seemed so enthusiastic, especially about lit'rature. At the same time there was a solidness about her, too—like a big oak tree.

"What time did you get to bed last night, Beth?"

"I'm sorry I fell asleep in class. I can't help it if I'm sleepy all the time."

Ms. Hoffman nodded agreeably. There was probably nothing Beth could say or do that would get a rise out of her. She had probably heard just about everything since she started teaching.

"Beth, do you know what a *syndrome* is?"

This was not a vocabulary word, but recently Beth had heard her mom on the phone telling Wendy that Aunt Kathryn suffered from *learned helplessness syndrome*. "I think it's like a whole bunch of things that mean something. When they're all together."

Ms. Hoffman smiled and nodded. Beth played with the pleats of her tartan skirt and wondered what next.

"Did you bring your lunch?" Ms. Hoffman asked. "You can spread it out on my desk if you'd like. I don't mind."

"I'm not hungry," Beth said. "Am I in trouble?"

"I don't think so. Should you be?"

"Micki is. She got suspended."

"And transferred out of school, I understand." Ms. Hoffman watched Beth as if she expected her to dance or scream or fall down dead. "Would you like to leave Arcadia?"

The direction of the conversation alarmed Beth. Maybe she was in trouble because of Kimmie. Were her grades that bad in just six weeks?

Ms. Hoffman cocked her head to one side like a big-headed bird. "You're not hungry, you're sleepy all the time, your grades have gone down, and there's a tone in your voice that I recognize . . . from other girls, and a look in your eyes—"

"What kind of look?"

"Distracted, Beth. Your mind is elsewhere, I think."

"I'm here—how can my mind be anywhere else?"

"Beth," Ms. Hoffman's tone was calm but cautionary, "I think you know what I mean."

Beth chewed her lip.

"I think you're depressed and—"

"There's nothing wrong with me."

"Not physically, no. But the last couple of years have been very hard for you and Micki. Anyone would be depressed."

"I told you, I'm fine." Beth stood up. "And anyway, it's none of your business. You're just my teacher." She sat down and waited for Ms. Hoffman's reaction.

Ms. Hoffman did not seem mad, but Beth could tell that she was figuring out what to say next.

"Can I go now?"

"No, Beth. Stay a little longer, if you wouldn't mind."

Beth did mind, but she said nothing. Kimmie was waiting for her but Beth did not really want to see her. All she talked about was her birthday party and how Beth didn't have to try crystal if she didn't want to, no one would force her. Beth sat back in the chair and fiddled with her hair, began to braid it.

"You're fourteen, Beth. I was twelve when I lost my father." Ms. Hoffman paused to look at her daffodils a moment. "My mother had no money, no way of earning much of a living, so we moved to Boston and lived with my grandmother who, as it happened, was just as glad to see my father go. She never liked him at all."

"How come?" Beth asked without thinking.

If the direct question fazed Ms. Hoffman, she gave no sign. "She was a practical, old-world type who did not have much time for more than basic education. She thought Papa was a ne'er-do-well because he preferred to read rather than work in a factory." Ms. Hoffman's yellow-green eyes sparkled. "Maybe he was, but he certainly instilled a love of lit'rature in me. No matter how she tried, my grandma could not drum it out. Sometimes, even now, when I take up a new book, I hear my father's voice in my head telling me I'm a good girl."

Beth stared at Ms. Hoffman for a second and then burst into tears, and though she wanted to stop them, she couldn't. Ms. Hoffman put a box of tissues on the edge of the desk.

"Just listen, Beth. If you listen for his voice you will hear it in your head. But you have to listen first."

In the food court she looked down at the blank sheet of paper before her. The assignment from Ms. Hoffman was to write an essay based on the title of the book the class had just finished reading, *The Things They Carried*. When Beth realized it was about Vietnam, she could not read it, didn't try. Her father had been in Vietnam.

Ms. Hoffman might know Beth hadn't done the reading, but if her essay was creative, she wouldn't make a fuss, although what she had said in her office about grades worried Beth. Her mom would freak if her grades weren't good. She had not gotten her most recent book report back yet, or the twenty-point Friday quiz, but she knew the report, written on the morning it was due, was sloppy and she had not studied for the punctuation test at all. Going in she had believed she knew all there was about commas and semicolons, but when she looked at the test sheet, her mind went blank and she couldn't stop yawning. She had better put some effort into this essay.

So: if Beth had to go somewhere, leave everything behind, what would she carry with her? Right now there was nothing in her life she valued, nothing she wanted to hold onto. It actually sounded like a good idea to walk off into the world with only the clothes on her back. How long would it take, she wondered, to forget everything, to go blank in the mind like a baby?

She decided to write about carrying nothing except the one thing she didn't want to forget. Her father. She decided to write about carrying her father's voice in her head.

She had been writing for a few minutes when the sound of Kimmie's squeaky voice interrupted her concentration. "I can't believe how much you study."

Beth stifled her impatience at the silly remark. She put down her pen and said, "Can I borrow a couple of dollars?"

Kimmie grinned. "You don't have to say it. You want a cinnamon roll, right? It is, like, so not-possible to hang here without eating one of those things."

Beth watched Kimmie walk across the court to the shop where they made thousands of sticky cinnamon buns every day between

noon and ten P.M. There was a line but Kimmie never minded waiting. She liked to be where boys and men could see her. Beth
watched the way she moved her body, sticking her butt out and
twisting from the waist, looking over her shoulder as if something
off to the right fascinated her. She kept clothes in her backpack and
changed after school in the bathroom at Bella Luna. She said she'd
rather walk through the mall stripped naked than wear her Arcadia
uniform. In her short, tight black sweater, a pair of shiny black
leather pants that rested on her hip bones, and high-heeled boots,
she thought she looked hot. Beth thought she looked like a wannabe
hooker. Not that she had ever seen one except on TV and in movies.

Kimmie came back with two rolls and sat down.

"What did the Gusher want?"

"She thinks I'm depressed."

"Listen, Beth, everyone's depressed in America. Being depressed
is a sign of intelligence."

"Micki isn't depressed. My mother isn't." At least Beth did not
think they were.

"Your mother is so scary."

"You always say that and it's just stupid. You don't even know
her."

"Hey, I didn't mean anything—"

Beth felt sorry for calling her stupid. That was the thing about
Kimmie. She acted tough but she had tender feelings.

"It's just that your house is like the Brady Bunch. I can't help it if
it creeps me out." Kimmie tore off a strip of cinnamon roll and
stuck it into her mouth. She licked her fingers. "Now listen, here's
the deal. Strider called me during fifth period. Saturday night's on
for sure. Can you fix it?"

"No way. I told you, Ma's in her Gestapo mode. You know that.
I can't breathe around that place without getting the evil eye."

"Make up a story."

"Like what?"

"Beth, you're the A-student—"

"Not anymore. That's one of the things Hoffman thinks proves
I'm depressed."

"Give me a break, will you? Do you want in on Saturday or not?
I mean, Damian will be really bummed out if you don't show." She
laughed. "Talk about depressed."

"I told you, I'm under total surveillance."

Kimmie stared at her, stricken. "I need you to come. You're my best friend. It's my birthday. You have to come."

Beth thought of Kimmie alone with Strider and Damian, someone named Tex, and all his friends from Tucson. She said it was her birthday and maybe it really was. Why would Kimmie lie about something like that?

"I'm telling you, she won't let me—"

"Forget it," Kimmie said. "I'll think of something."

Beth thought she could probably eat for a month and never get enough. At dinner that night she layered shredded lettuce, chili, salsa, sour cream, guacamole, and cheddar cheese on her baked potato. Since she and Micki were little, their mom had called this dinner Baked Potato Sundaes. Aunt Kathryn and the cousins were eating up at Grandma Stella's.

"I'm glad to see you've got your appetite back," her mother said.

"I'm glad you started cooking again."

Her mother laughed. "I have, haven't I!"

Beth and Kimmie had smoked a joint in the park less than an hour earlier, and between them they had come up with a way to get Beth out of the house on Saturday. As she ambled home afterward, listening to the hum of traffic and smelling the Santa Ana smell of dry earth and mentholy eucalyptus, rosemary and sage, and a whole hedge of mock orange with bees all over it, Beth thought that after Saturday night she was going to stop telling lies. She skipped through a chalked hopscotch grid drawn on the sidewalk in black chalk, stepped on a line, and went back and did it again. I will go to this party and then—she didn't know how she would cool it with Kimmie but she would definitely figure something out.

In the kitchen the phone rang.

"I'll get it," Beth said, and hopped up.

Micki looked at her.

"Hello." Beth counted to five and then handed the receiver to her mother. She felt her cheeks flush. "It's Mrs. Taylor."

"Do I know her?"

"Kimmie's mother."

Lana raised her eyebrows and took the phone. After a few moments, she said, "It does sound like a good time, but I wonder sometimes . . ." She turned her back. Beth could still hear her. "I'm not sure the girls are a good influence on each other." Another pause. "Well, I'm glad you've spoken to her. Beth and I had a conversation, too." Lana listened and laughed. "I'm glad we finally had a chance to speak. Yes, of course. Good-bye."

After she hung up, Lana stared at the receiver a moment. Beth watched her, pretending not to.

"You didn't tell me Kimmie's mother was English."

Beth put a forkful of food in her mouth and chewed like crazy.

"She seems nice." Her mother held her wineglass to the light. "Do you want to go, Beth?"

Beth nodded.

Micki was giving her the hawkeye.

"Do you know what church?"

"Kimmie wants you to go to church with her?"

"A teen dance," her mother told Micki.

Beth felt embarrassed for her mother, that she could be so easily fooled by Kimmie's sister and an English accent.

"And you do want to go?"

"I guess."

"Can I trust you? Do I have your word of honor?"

Beth felt Micki watching her. She swallowed. "Yes."

Micki said, "You don't even know how to dance."

"Shut up, punk." Beth kicked her sister under the table.

"What'll you wear?" Lana asked.

Beth thought of showing up at Kimmie's in a white satin prom gown and started to giggle, almost lost it. She took another mouthful.

"What's the matter, Bethie?" Micki snickered.

"Mrs. Taylor said she'd take you there and pick you up afterwards but be sure you take your cell with you." Her mom swirled her wine. "If there's any mixup you call me, okay?"

Beth finished her potato, skin and all. "Is there ice cream?"

"Help yourself."

"Did you buy more chocolate sauce?"

"In the pantry. Rinse your plates when you finish."

After dinner Micki walked into Beth's room without knocking. She closed the door and stood in the middle of the carpet with her knuckles on her hips.

"You're stoned. You practically inhaled that potato. Plus you lied to Ma."

"Mind your own business."

"You're not going to any church dance with Kimmie."

"What d'you mean? You heard Ma talking to Mrs. Taylor."

Micki scuffed the toe of her trainer into the carpet. "You're just going to hang at Kimmie's, right?"

Beth looked at the ceiling. "Yeah. After."

"That is such bullshit. You and Kimmie figured this out so you can stay over."

"What are you, my warden?"

Micki stared until Beth could not help but fidget.

"This is my bedroom. You didn't knock."

"I should tell Ma. About the grass, too."

"What's it to you, anyway? I don't mess around in your life."

"You got it from Kimmie, right?"

"What're you, a drug cop?"

Micki ignored the piled clothes and books on Beth's bed and lay down beside her. "She's a creep, Beth. She's a skag."

"You don't know that." Beth hit her in the shoulder.

"Jesus, why'd you do that?"

"You don't know anything about Kimmie."

"I've seen her boyfriend hanging around after school. That's enough for me."

"Strider's cool."

Micki crowed. "You are such a liar. I know you, Beth. You're my sister and my sister—"

"You're adopted, remember?" Beth was pleased to see Micki's expression freeze for a moment.

"We grew up together. We're the same as blood sisters."

"Except you have your very own private father."

"Is that why you're acting so hinky?" Micki sat up. "You're jealous?"

"You don't know what it's like to have your father die suddenly. It changes everything."

"He was my father, too."

"So what's Eddie, then?" Beth asked nastily.

Micki sighed. "I don't know. Exactly. Except he's not my father, not like Daddy was." Micki sat Indian style, resting her elbows on her knees, her chin in her hands. "I miss Daddy all the time. I even hear him talking in my head."

Beth sat up. "Me, too." She told Micki about her conversation with Ms. Hoffman and afterwards let out a heavy, relieved sigh. "Sometimes it makes me crazy."

"But we're both listening. That's good, huh? I wonder if Ma is."

"No way. She's too busy taking care of things." Beth held her palm up and pretended to check things off it. "Makin' lists and checkin' 'em twice."

"I wouldn't be too sure." Micki held a hank of magenta hair out from her head and stared through it at the ceiling light. "Stuff's going on with her. Tinera says she gave Uncle Dom hell when she was over there. And you should have heard her tell off Mamoulian— she was awesome."

Beth rose from the bed and went to sit on her desk chair. She did not want to be too near her sister for too long. Something—she had no idea what—would happen. "You've got your birth father, and after a while you won't think about Daddy so much."

"How can you be such a jerk-off?" Micki's glare burned her and she had to look away. "I mean, Beth, everyone gets it that Eddie French will never be my real father. He gets it, Ma gets it. How come you're the fucking holdout here? I think you're jealous."

So maybe she was—so what? Didn't she have a right to be?

"This is my room and you can't come in without permission. Daddy made that rule. *My daddy.*" Beth pointed across the room. "There's the door."

Micki stared at her, and then she rolled off the bed and walked to the door. "Know what, Beth? You may be smarter than me, but sometimes you're really really dumb."

Chapter Thirty-three

On Wednesday, Lana drove Micki to Balboa High School to make her public school enrollment official. Lana's reaction to the school was instantly negative, surrounded as it was with concrete walls and chain link fencing and every gate watched over by a dour security guard Lana suspected was carrying a concealed weapon. Televised images of school shootings and surreptitious drug exchanges in graffitied toilet stalls rose from Lana's subconscious and she almost lost heart.

There were other schools, private schools.

But as they walked across the inner quad on the way to obtaining a security pass, the sight of so many young people of so many races—Muslim girls in Levi's, their heads covered in scarves, boys in pants that hung perilously low on their butts, the sounds of all the young voices speaking a dozen languages—reminded Lana of something she had read a dozen years before about high school being a preparation for the real world. Surely this rich stream of humanity fit that description more than the sanitized waters of Arcadia School.

"What d'you think, honey?"

Micki grinned at her, grimaced, and grinned again, wider than before. She bounced on her toes with palpable eagerness to wade into this new life. Lana released a small, tight sigh. She had always known she would have to give her daughters to the world eventually, but she had not expected it to be this world, and not so soon.

Mrs. Gant, the director of the baccalaureate program, sat in a cubbyhole office without a window, bumf piled high around her. Immediately, Lana felt an affinity for her. She had a delicate-featured, round, dark face and each of her shiny cornrows ended in a bright blue bead and swung like tetherballs when she turned her head. She looked at Micki's transcript.

"Well, I guess we can agree you're not a math or science genius, huh? You must've been sleeping in biology." She looked at Micki over her half-frame glasses. "You qualify for special classes in English and history, though."

"Are the regular classes very large?" Lana asked.

Mrs. Gant looked at Lana. "Very. Close to forty in tenth-grade algebra." She was not trying to sell the program to Micki or Lana. It was obvious she did not care one way or another if Micki enrolled. The school was already overcrowded. Even the IB and AP classes were too large. And the amazing and wonderful and unique Micki Porter was no one special to Mrs. Gant.

Lana looked at Micki.

Micki grinned. "I don't care, Ma. I'm still gonna learn."

"There'll be a lot of distraction. . . ."

"Ma-a."

Lana lifted her hands and let them drop. "Okay, sign us up."

"You start on Monday." Mrs. Gant directed her comments to Micki, not Lana. She handed her a small stack of forms. "You can bring these back with you then." She stood and shook hands with Micki across the desk. "Welcome to Balboa High."

Thirty minutes later, Lana dropped Micki at home with orders to vacuum the entire house, clean the bathrooms, and go over every square inch of the backyard picking up dog poop. As if she were not being punished for smoking at school and had been asked instead to choose a new wardrobe, Micki frolicked from the car with a wave of her hand and leapt up the front porch steps with as much bounce as a new tennis ball. At the top she turned and waved again, grinning.

"Well, Jack," Lana said aloud as she drove back to work, "I hope I've done the right thing."

She stopped at a light on Lewis and waited for a pair of skateboarders in baggy pants to cross in front of the 4Runner. Sunlight struck the chrome bumper of a car across the intersection. The light flashed into Lana's iris, up her optical nerve, and into her brain—and she smiled suddenly. For no particular reason. A gust of warm air puffed through the car window. It lifted the hair that lay across her cheek, sending a shiver through her body. There was definitely something peculiar about summer weather in January, but she would not waste her energy worrying about it when there was nothing she could do. Enjoy it, she thought. A leaf of summer in the book of winter.

When she got home that evening just after six, there was a note on the oak table saying Micki had gone to Tiff's to tell her about Balboa. Beth had taken a bowl of cereal up to the playhouse, Tinera and the girls were with their father, and Kathryn was in the grownups' living room, clutching a pillow to her ribs, bawling.

Lana opened a couple of beers and went into the living room. She dropped onto the couch beside her sister and handed her one.

"Okay, what's he done this time?"

"I don't know. Nothing." Kathryn blotted her face with the bottom of her tee shirt and took a long swallow and hiccupped.

"What happened?"

The question brought on more tears, more hiccups.

"Hold your breath," Lana said. "You can't breathe no matter what I do."

Kathryn nodded and Lana began to tickle her. Kathryn held her breath as long as she could and then air exploded from her, taking her hiccups with it.

"Thanks," she said, and had another swig. "They were so glad to go with him. I felt so abandoned. Colette just danced when she saw him and waggled her arms in the air, wanting to be picked up like she's a baby and of course he did it. Swung her around . . ."

"I warned you," Lana said. "He seduces those girls—that's what he does."

"He loves them. You make it sound obscene."

"Whatever. When's he bringing them back?"

Kathryn looked down at her prim denim skirt and then at her feet in their neat little spectator heels. Her cheeks were blotched and so tear-stained that Lana wondered how long she had been sitting, crying by herself.

"I want to do the right thing."

Frowns and sulks had put a permanent downward twist at the corners of Kathryn's mouth. Between her wide blue eyes the worry lines dug as deeply as Grace Mamoulian's. As Lana blamed Dom for aging her sister prematurely, she reminded herself he had not taken a knife and etched those lines. Kathryn's passivity, her need to be adored, her martyrdom, had done it.

Lana sat forward, irritated suddenly. "Did you hear me?"

"What?"

"When's he bringing them back?"

Kathryn drank. "Tomorrow, I think."

"You think?"

"Please don't scold me, Lannie." She pulled her hand down her face. "I just couldn't keep them apart anymore. He loves them so."

"Even if they're not boys?"

"You have to understand. He and his brothers think having sons means they're strong, masculine."

"I thought that was demented the first time you told me and now that I've heard it fifty times, it's still demented."

"He's made more money than all of them combined but they still treat him like he's Baby Dominic." Kathryn looked at Lana from the corner of her eye. "He cries."

"You told me the other night he cries for effect—you said he turns on the waterworks."

Kathryn looked confused.

"Is that true, or isn't it?"

"You don't understand him—you never have."

"I understand him and I understand you." Lana drained her beer. "Tell him to grow up. We all have to, sooner or later."

Kathryn said reproachfully, "You mean me, I know you do."

"You. Him. All of us. It's the only way life works."

"He says he'll go to therapy if Jessie can find a man. She gave me a couple of names."

"When pigs fly."

"Well, what am I supposed to do? You tell me."

"I already did and you don't remember because you didn't want to hear it in the first place."

"What?"

"I'm not going to help you slide through life anymore. I've been protecting you since you were small and maybe it was the right thing to do back then, but I should have stopped a long time ago. I'm as bad as Ma, with all her doting and fawning over you. She hasn't done you any good and neither have I."

A stubborn warning muscle moved an inch below Kathryn's right ear.

"I'm talking about the real world. You're going to have to start learning how to live in it. I'm not going to help you anymore. You've got to learn how to take a risk."

"Oh, for goodness sake, I know about risk. What about Jacaranda?"

"Jacaranda's a horse. I'm talking about inside risks, not broken bones."

Kathryn looked fierce, as fierce as she could, given her marshmallow chin and cherubic eyes.

"Want another beer?"

Kathryn sat up straight. "No, I think I've had enough." She squared her shoulders and brushed her palms together like a baker dusting the flour from his hands. "I guess I'll just go home, back to business as usual. I *did* take a risk and look what it got me."

"Oh, shut up." Kathryn stood and Lana grabbed the waistband of her skirt and tugged her back down to the couch. "That martyr shit doesn't work with me."

"I thought you wanted me to make my own decisions. So I'm making one. I'm going home. The girls love their father and so do I and if he wants a son, I'll give him one. Anyway, it's the only thing I know how to do, get pregnant; and I do that every time the man looks at me." She paused, smiled sweetly at Lana, and added, "Unlike you, I'm really good at getting pregnant."

Kathryn meant to hurt Lana; instead, she just made her mad. "If I tell you to shut up and listen to me, is that enough? Or do I have to beat you up?"

Kathryn looked at her blandly, daring her to say anything worth listening to.

"You've put Dom on notice, Kay. For the first time he really believes you're not going to take any more of his stuff. This is your chance. You're afraid, I know, but don't let that make you do something foolish like give in and go home."

"I thought you were going to let me take care of myself."

Yes, but it was going to take some time to learn how.

Kathryn's mouth curled in a sneer. "You and Mars, you're both convinced that you're the smart ones and poor Kathryn, she's just plain dumb, beautiful but feeble in the brain, or she never would have fallen in love with—"

Lana grabbed her sister's wrist with two hands and twisted them in opposite directions. Kathryn shrieked.

"That's an Indian burn," she cried, rubbing her wrist. "Ma says you can't do that." She looked at Lana for a stunned second and then laughed. In another second she was crying.

Worn out, Lana sat back and let her sister go until she wound down and stopped. She said, "You have to take care of yourself. And the girls. Whatever that looks like to you, I don't know, but you can do it. You only think you can't."

Kathryn scrubbed the back of her hand across her wet and reddened eyes.

Shall I be honest, Lana thought, or kind? Or was honesty the ultimate kindness, the truest way to show her sister that she loved her? She paused over the question. "I've never thought you were dumb," she said, finally. "But you do more dumb things than most. And bigger. Plus, you don't think we all expect much from you and so you . . . live up to our expectations."

More tears. Lana watched, feeling distanced and cool-minded.

"You sound like a self-help book."

"I know you love Dom. I don't understand it, but I know it. Loving isn't enough, though. Unless you want more scenes like Monday night."

"I never would have hurt him—he knows that."

"If he knew that, he would have walked out of the closet and taken the gun away from you. But he didn't."

"So make your point."

"You have to be honest with him. If you are and if he really loves you, your marriage will be better."

"I suppose yours was so perfect."

"This isn't about me."

"You have the answers, you always have—"

"That's it." Lana stood up. "Do what you bloody well want."

That night Dom brought the girls back and Kathryn did not return with him to *Tres Palomas*, though Lana, standing in the kitchen, heard him beg her to. They had argued for a long time but rather than listen, Lana went upstairs and closed her door. Later Kathryn came into the bedroom where Lana was sorting laundry. She resisted the impulse to open her arms to her little sister and praise her determination.

"When's Eddie French coming?"

"Saturday."

"I'll be out of your hair by then."

"Stay as long as you need to. You and the girls are always welcome here." Kathryn turned away and Lana added, "By the way, I've decided to make Saturday a party. Like we used to do. Mars and you guys and Mom. It's time she meets him."

"Can Dom come?"

"Of course."

Kathryn nodded and walked back down the hall. Lana called after her, "And there will not be fireworks. In case you wondered."

"I guess that guarantees there will be, huh?"

Later, Lana lugged the laundry down to the porch and ran a load of wash. She stepped outside, put a rotary sprinkler in the center of the garden, and set the timer for thirty minutes. She let go a long breath and then inhaled, drawing down to her toes the fragrance of damp earth and star jasmine and wet stones.

Soon the girls will be gone. I'll be alone in this big house with my dogs and my plants. I'll run some days and read books. I'll be late for appointments and keep lists and even when I'm living alone, I'll still need a cleaning lady once a week to sort through my clutter. Alone, she thought with an acceptance that was neither stoical nor fatalistic, to which no adjective could be applied. In that moment, perversely, she felt Jack's warm touch, and without stopping to wonder, she reached up and patted her left shoulder.

Chapter Thirty-four

Micki prepared for Balboa High School by redyeing her magenta streak and applying henna tattoos up the outside of her right leg from ankle bone to knee. After school, Beth shot baskets in the driveway and at night she talked on the phone with her door closed. Kimmie seemed to have vanished.

Something about this bothered Lana but she brushed it aside, busy with other things.

On Saturday night Stella arrived early. She had done herself up for the occasion of meeting Eddie French, gotten a new tint for her pinkish blond hair, and coordinated her makeup: pastel pink lipstick, pastel blue eye shadow. Spike heels that must have killed her bunions showed beneath the hem of her long, rose-patterned silk caftan. She smelled of Shalimar.

Lana felt a pang of love for her stubbornly vain mother. "You look marvelous, Ma."

Stella peered into the corners of the kitchen as if she expected to see someone crouched there.

"He and Kathryn took the girls to the zoo. They'll be back in a little bit."

"You're gonna like this guy, Ma," Mars said from the sink where she was washing lettuce.

"You." She gave Mars a poke in the ribs. "You like anything in pants so long as he's young."

Lana and Mars looked at each other and laughed.

Stella sat on Lana's desk chair. "I don't know how you manage to do anything with this mess. You should get a rollaway desk so at least you could cover it up. The kitchen would look better and all your business wouldn't be right out here where anyone can look at it."

"So don't look, Ma," Lana said.

"I suppose you brought one of your boy toys, Marlene. Where is he? Playing Nintendo?"

"Just family tonight," Lana said cheerily.

"That's what you're calling him now, Lana? Family? What about Jack? I wonder how he'd feel about that?"

Mars put a hand on Lana's arm and looked down at the paring knife in her hand. "One quick jab to the heart—that's all it'd take."

A while later, Stella came upstairs where Lana was toweling herself after a shower. Stella sat on the bed and watched her dress as she had when Lana was a girl. And like a girl, Lana felt shy under her mother's scrutiny, aware of her naked body's imperfections. Stella judged and compared everything, even her daughter's middle-aged body.

Lana pulled on a pair of dark wool trousers, nicely tailored, and tugged a brass-studded belt through the loops.

"I like that Realtor friend of yours," Stella said. "We've been out a couple of times. And, of course, it's just as I suspected—there's not much out there even if I do get top dollar for the town house. Which this friend of yours says I will, since it's in excellent shape, well decorated and all."

If you like pink and blue with here and there some gold plate to catch the light, Lana mused.

"The places I like, right there at Bird Rock, I can't touch those. But she says next week we'll go over to the Shores. There's something there she thinks will suit me." Stella patted Gala and kissed her nose. "Of course, I don't want to go too small. I'm not interested in a cottage. I raised you and Marlene in a cottage and that was quite enough for me."

"And what did the loan officer say?" Lana asked as she applied a little makeup at the bathroom mirror.

"You need more blush, Lana. An older woman needs to put color in her face."

"Thanks, Ma." She brushed a little extra coral-colored powder along her cheekbones. Her mother was right. She did look better.

"The loan officer was most encouraging. And such a nice young man. I thought to myself, he'd suit Marlene, but he was married.

Showed me the picture of his two little boys. So cute. Anyway he told me to come back when I find a place I like."

"Have you thought about what I said?"

"You mean about taking Dominic's money?" Stella nodded. "I don't think you're right, that he would use it . . . to make sure I was on his side."

"Ma—"

"Just wait a minute, please. I'm not quite as dithery as you think I am, Lana. I keep my eyes open and I know he's not an easy man and your sister isn't as happy as I'd like her to be."

Lana was surprised. She stood in front of her mother, holding her sweater, listening.

"I just don't want to do anything that might make it more difficult for her."

"Ma, I'm proud of you."

"Well, I hope so." Stella walked to the dresser and examined her face in the mirror. "I think sometimes about all the packing up and signing the papers and I get a little tired. But yes, if I find the right place, I'll move. It will have to be perfect, though."

Lana pulled on the chocolate-colored turtleneck sweater that Jack had always said suited her. *You look like a Sees candy. I want to eat you up.*

"Are you listening to me?"

"Of course I am, Ma."

"And? I thought you'd at least have an opinion."

"I do and you've heard it—I won't go over it." Lana smiled. "I'm mending my ways. Saving my good advice for myself and my girls."

Stella raised her eyebrows. "What about you?"

"What about me?"

"You seem cheerful for a change."

Stella was right—Lana was cheerful and for the first time in many months she wasn't pretending.

"You've accepted this boy?"

"He's a man."

"Barely."

"And what I accept is that he's part of Micki's life and I can't do anything about it. I'm not sure I would change things even if I could."

"My, aren't we mature all of a sudden."

Forget *we*, Lana thought, and started down the stairs. Stella's next question stopped her.

"What about our Beth? How's she taking all this?"

"It's not easy, Ma."

"Why isn't she here? I thought this was a family party."

"I told you on the phone. She's at a dance."

"A dance!" Stella's face lit up. "How wonderful. What did she wear?"

Lana told her. Stella got upset and went on for several minutes about how the youth of America had been going downhill ever since the Sixties. And they went downstairs.

A dance. When Beth and Micki were little, Lana had day-dreamed ahead to their first dates and dances, but she had gotten it all wrong, imagining long dresses and corsages and handsome, tuxedoed boys at the door. Even her own teens had not included those, not for the kids who knew what was happening. Lana and her friends had boycotted their prom and gone to a midnight showing of *The Rocky Horror Picture Show*. Beth had gone off to Kimmie's clutching her overnight bag, wearing a black sweater, a tiny black skirt over black leggings, and black boots. She had skinned her hair back into a bun the size of a baby's fist.

So much black. What kind of church did Kimmie attend anyway?

"Have a wonderful time," Lana had said, and extended her hand. Beth jerked away. Tears filled Lana's eyes. She blinked them back but not before Beth had seen them and smiled and seemed to grow an inch as the world tilted beneath Lana's feet.

"I wish you'd stay home," she said. "It's going to be a wonderful dinner."

"Save me some *chiles rellenos*." She moved to the door. Her eagerness to be gone stirred the air around her.

"You remember your promise?"

"Ma-a."

"Just say you do."

"I do. Remember."

"And I don't want you to drink, either. No drugs, no alcohol. I mean it, Beth."

She was gone in a second, across the backyard and out through the back gate and down the alley. No sooner had she vanished than Lana knew it was a mistake to let her go, and she had been seized by a powerful intuition that she would never see her again. But then she knew she was being paranoid and probably overprotective. A few minutes later, Mars arrived with a triple order of *chiles rellenos* from Los Indios. Lana did not think of Beth again until the middle of dinner when she watched Eddie French take the last of the chiles and thought, oh, well.

Oh, well. Beth was at her first dance and wouldn't care about leftovers. Lana worried she would be a wallflower, though the old-fashioned word probably had no context at a modern dance. These days in movies and on television, girls dance with girls as well as boys. And why would Beth be anything but popular?

It was a wonderful family party. Lots of laughter and story-telling. Lana was having a great time—and then Dom appeared at the front door.

Hours before, Lana had asked Kathryn if she invited him and she said she had not. But there he was, expecting to be invited in, and Kathryn made a place for him. Lana resolved to be pleasant if it killed her. Tonight or tomorrow or next week, Kathryn and her daughters would return to *Tres Palomas*. Kathryn would not have her tubes tied and for a while longer she would try to bear sons, being miserable and telling herself she wasn't. She might actually have a son; if she kept trying, it was likely she would. And then Dom would want another. Tinera would bury her memory of the night her mother held a gun on her father and go back to adoring him. At dinner she was thrilled to have Dom sit beside her, and for the first several moments her arms could not be pried from around his neck. From time to time, through the remainder of the meal, Lana noticed Mars and Stella watching the pair of them, father and daughter, as she was.

After flan and fresh Ventura strawberries, the party split up. The younger ones went into the kids' living room to watch a video while the adults, along with Tinera and Micki, stayed in the kitchen drinking wine and beer and coffee and soda, cleaning up and get-ting in each other's way. Gala retreated to the porch, where she could watch the activities without getting stepped on. Buster dozed and kept his watch in the backyard.

How many such parties had she given in the house on Triesta Way? Lana could not begin to guess, and this one was too much like the others, too achingly familiar. No one noticed when she went outside.

Buster lay on the cement by the driveway gate, watching for villains through the slats of the fence. She saw his tail move when she crouched beside him, but he did not get up; as she stroked his hind quarters gently, she felt him wince beneath her touch.

"Not much longer, sweet boy."

There was a story Jack had told her, told to him by his grandfather. When people die, the old man said, they are met at the gates of heaven by all their old pets. Restored to health and vigor, the animals wait there, patient and congenial with one another, cats with dogs and horses and hamsters and birds and iguanas, and then they all parade into heaven together. But what of Buster, who had never been a pet?

"Will you wait for me?" She kissed his muzzle and caught the scent of illness and old age. "I'll look for you."

She walked into the kitchen just as Mars delivered the punch line to a joke and the room exploded with laughter. It must have been slightly risqué because, like a schoolgirl, Stella covered her smile with her hand. At the oak table, Tinera sat on Dom's lap. From the shadows of the porch, Lana watched him pat and smooth her hair, watched her kiss his cheek, the corner of his eye, fuss with his hair and the collar of his shirt. The sight of them together this way sickened her. Kathryn stood behind him, her hands resting on his shoulders.

Eddie leaned back against the counter, ankles crossed, his arms folded across his chest, watchfully sociable.

What does he make of us? Lana wondered. Are we a mystery to him as he is to us? And does he fear us as we fear him? Before that moment, she had not admitted that she feared him. She feared this boy for the space he would take in their lives if she let him. Thank goodness he was going away. Perhaps he would forget all about them.

Micki stood beside him, their shoulders almost but not quite touching. He certainly had that enticing glow of youthful masculinity Mars rhapsodized about. Looking at him, Lana could believe that sometime in the distant future she might actually desire a man again. Not him, of course. But she had to admit—how much wine had she drunk?—Eddie kindled something in her that, while not appropriate, was very interesting.

We're going to be all right, she thought. The worst is over. Except for Beth.

There it was, the truth, right where she had known it was all along. Lana shoved her hands in the pockets of her wool slacks. There was no dance. There was only Kimmie and whatever happened tonight. A draft rushed in under the back door, up her spine, and settled like an ice pack on her shoulder.

Mars stepped to her side. "What's the matter?"

"It's so cold suddenly."

"God, girl, it's a Santa Ana."

Dom said, "How old are you, Lana? Maybe you're having cold flashes."

The phone screamed across the kitchen.

"You're wearing that sweater," her mother said. "How can you be cold?"

Dom asked, "You going to let it ring?"

"I'll get it, Ma."

"Never mind." Lana reached for the cordless on the wall. "Pipe down, you guys. I can't hear."

Stella asked, "Who's calling at this hour?"

Beth said, "Ma? Is that you? Oh god, Ma, you gotta come help me."

Chapter Thirty-five

Earlier that evening, Beth had felt the caffeine perking through the Saturday night crowd at Bella Luna as she entered, her eyes scanning the noisy crowd for Kimmie. No sign of her and, luckily, no one else Beth recognized. She did not want to be seen dressed like a Goth-wannabe on a Saturday night. Walking to Bella Luna from home, she had decided if anyone asked she would say she was going to a costume party.

She bought a cup of tea and found a stool in the far corner of the coffee bar, a good spot for people watching. She would spot Kimmie as soon as she showed up. From a basket near the door she dug up an old copy of the *Union-Tribune* entertainment section and read an article on the music scene written by her mom's friend, Jilly Pepper. When she finished, she read the movie ads. Half an hour passed.

The arrangement was that Kimmie and Strider and Damian would meet her at Bella Luna at seven. Beth put her left hand on her lap and looked down at her watch. Casually. She did not want anyone to know that she was waiting and had maybe been stood up. She knew that no one was watching her or talking about her, but she still felt conspicuous. Nowadays everything about her felt wrong and that's what people noticed: the way she looked and talked, the things she was doing. For the first time she wished she were not so tall. She had begun to hunch her shoulders when she walked with Kimmie, who was so petite.

It was twenty minutes to eight. At home they were sitting down to eat.

She took her cell phone out of her bag and keyed in Kimmie's number.

"City of Love, Purity is Obscurity." Kimmie giggled.

"Where are you?" Beth demanded.

"What d'you mean? You were supposed to be here at seven."

Beth held the cell phone away from her for a beat.

"Beth?"

"Are you crazy? I can't walk to the Gaslamp. You guys were gonna pick me up at Bella Luna."

"You could—"

"I'm not taking the bus, Kimmie. I'd rather go home right now."

Kimmie squealed, "You can't go home, it's my party."

"Then you're going to have to figure out—"

"Wait a minute, wait a minute."

Beth heard the sounds of music and muffled conversation.

If she went home she would have a lot of explaining to do. She would have to lie. She could not just say the dance was called off. She thought of Micki and Eddie French doing their bonding thing and realized she did not want to be at home. The place she longed for did not exist anymore. She was like a refugee from her own life.

"Just stay where you are," Kimmie said. "Tex is going to come get you."

"Why not Strider? Or Damian?"

"They're not here yet."

"Who is?"

"I told you before, Tex and his friends from Tucson."

Beth's stomach sank. "Damian and Strider are coming, aren't they?"

Kimmie giggled and Beth could tell she had smoked a lot of grass already. "Right now, its just me and four guys so you better get here quick."

"I don't know, Kimmie. . . ."

The phone clicked off and Beth sat looking at it. If she went home, Micki would give her that smirky look and Grandma Stella would make a big deal. She thought of Kimmie in her grotty condo with a bunch of strange guys. Music, crummy food, drugs. No matter how irritating and boring she could be, Beth felt loyal to her. For a while it had seemed she led an enviable life without supervision or responsibilities, but the more Beth knew her, the more she felt Kimmie's desperation and her own powerlessness to do anything about it. Except stick with her. She could do that much.

She looked at her watch. Five minutes had passed—too soon to be on the lookout for this Tex guy. How was she supposed to identify him? She did not even know what kind of car he drove. Not a Jaguar convertible, she was sure of that.

She got up and asked for more hot water for her tea bag. The barrista gave Beth a look that said she was too cheap to live. When she went back to her stool, it had been taken over by a man with a laptop wearing a headset. Beth wondered why a man came out at night and shut himself off from the crowd with earphones.

Beth had never been lonely before she started hanging with Kimmie. Now she felt shut out of her own world. Madison and Linda hardly spoke to her anymore and she had not been invited to a sleepover since before Christmas. There were parties and secrets—a whole fourteen-year-old reality she knew nothing of now. Since New Year's she had gone from being at the center of things to dwelling on the fringes.

She leaned against a display of coffee paraphernalia, fancy pots, and espresso machines. Everyone in Bella Luna had a friend except Beth and the dude with the computer.

She walked out to the side patio and looked up and down the parking lot for someone who fit her image of Tex—tattooed, skinny, and pale as a tapeworm. The warm night air, the tiny sparkle lights festooning the pots of ficus on the patio, and the old-timey dance music from Ham Burger's across the parking lot reminded her of summer nights when her father hung out in the kitchen and sang dorky love songs to her mother. At Bella Luna, groups and couples occupied every table and a pair of old gays sat on a bench near her, holding hands with a little pug-faced dog squeezed between them. That little animal felt more a part of things than Beth did.

A horn honked in the parking lot. She looked up. A guy in a huge, black truck waved. Beth looked around her to make sure he was waving at her.

She walked toward the truck.

"You Beth?" He was good-looking, like a Ralph Lauren model.

"Get on in. You're missing the party."

"You're Tex?"

He laughed. "No, honey, I'm Santa Claus."

Beth remembered back to New Year's and all the fuss made

about Micki talking to the stranger in the Jaguar convertible. She remembered knowing that her sister would never be stupid enough to get in a car with a stranger.

"You are? Tex?" If she asked to see some ID, would he show it?

He looked irritated. "I am Tex and Kimmie sent me up here to get you. Satisfied?"

Beth walked around behind the truck to the other side. Tex reached across the cab and opened the door for her. Without looking at him, she stepped up and in and fastened her seat belt. The truck was perfectly clean inside and a little pine tree air freshener hung from the rearview mirror.

"You're a big girl," Tex said, as he maneuvered the car out onto University Avenue, the traffic heavy at this time of night on a Saturday. "Most girls have a hard time gettin' in this thing. How old are you?"

"Fifteen." In a few months.

Tex made a sound that was half a laugh and a bit of a groan and hit his palm up the side of his head.

"How old are you?" Beth asked.

"Old enough to know better."

Beth thought he was in his twenties but the light in the truck wasn't good. He was big and not skinny at all, more like a football player with broad shoulders and chest, and he wore his hair in a long, thick ponytail that shone in the light of passing cars. His face surprised her with its handsome, softly molded features. If she were older and brought him home to Triesta Way, her mother might like him as much as she did Eddie French. For the first time all night, she relaxed. He pressed a button on the dash and the truck filled with pulsing hip-hop. Beth was grateful the volume was up so high she did not need to talk.

Tex parked the truck in a lot two blocks away from the condo and as they walked through the crowded streets of the Gaslamp District, Beth imagined people thought she and Tex were on a date.

As soon as they walked into the condo, Kimmie dragged Beth into her bedroom and closed the door.

"Omigod, I am so glad you're here." She leaned her head against the door and closed her eyes.

"What?"

"Him. Tex. Isn't he awesome?" Kimmie wore a dark red tee shirt made of some slinky fabric that clung to her skinny torso.

"What about Strider?" Beth asked. "Where's he?"

"Oh, he's not coming." Kimmie sprawled on her unmade bed. "He got grounded or something. Who knows?"

"Damian, too?"

"Jesus, Beth, you know them, they're like, joined at the hip." She sat up, hugging a soiled pillow. "We're going to have a great time tonight. Better'n if they were here."

"Uh-huh." Beth opened her purse. "I brought you something." She held out a small gift wrapped in blue paper.

"What's this?"

"For your birthday."

"Oh. Thanks." Kimmie's face opened up and brightened with surprise. Maybe it wasn't really her birthday. Or maybe Beth's was her only gift.

"Aren't you going to open it?"

"Sure," Kimmie said, and tore away the shimmering blue paper. She grinned up at Beth. "Wow, a little cardboard box, thanks a lot."

"Open it, dummy."

She had bought Kimmie a mirror with glittering green and red and purple faux gems on the back. Kimmie looked up, her eyes sparkling.

"This is really beautiful."

Beth shrugged.

"No, I mean it. It's one of the nicest presents anybody ever gave me."

Beth hoped she exaggerated. It was nothing, a pretty nothing she had seen in the window of an Indian imports shop for two dollars. Kimmie's gratitude made Beth uncomfortable. She resisted the urge to tell her how cheap the gift was.

Kimmie bounced off the bed and hugged her. The smell of stewed chicken and sugary perfume, stale cigarette smoke and hair spray, was overpowering and Beth pulled away first.

She said, "So now you're fifteen."

"Yeah. But don't tell the guys, okay? I said I was eighteen."

Kimmie went into her bathroom and fiddled with her hair a moment. She applied another coat of eyeliner to her already darkened eyes, and then, grabbing Beth, she hugged her again.

"I can't believe you got me a present. You are the best friend I've ever had."

Something sank in Beth, and she felt leaden with a premonition that whatever happened that night, it would not be good. She followed Kimmie into the living room, feeling dull-witted.

In the light of the condo kitchen where he was mixing margaritas, Tex's skin was smooth and evenly tanned, almost as if he wore makeup. She wondered if he was a model. He held out a salt-crusted glass and grinned. "Chin-chin, little girl."

She thought of Eddie French, of her family at the dinner table telling stories and laughing, and she knew she had left them behind and could never go back. Get over it, she thought. She sipped the drink and it was good—a little oily, but sweet and sour and salty at the same time. It went down as easily as peppermint schnapps. She held her glass out for more. So what if she was a refugee—how bad could it be? Tex wasn't scary, just a little old. His friends looked okay and she had made Kimmie happy. There she was, showing off her mirror and proud as Diana on the day they made her princess.

A guy who said his name was William came into the kitchen smoking a joint the size of Beth's index finger. She took it from him and drew the smoke deep into her lungs, held it for a long time, and let it out slowly, admiring the way it curled up toward the kitchen light. If a genie appeared, what would she wish for? Something . . . Nothing important . . .

Later she was on the couch between two other boys nearer her age than Tex whose names she did not know. The boy on her right had dirt under his fingernails and the other had the worst breath Beth had ever smelled. What germs might be transmitted on a wet joint from a mouth that smelled like rotting teeth? The boy with dirty fingernails kept putting his hand on Beth's knee and she kept shoving it off until finally she just got too tired to bother anymore so she let him leave it there and wondered what would happen next. She pretended she was a tiny creature living in the corner of the ceiling. She imagined herself stretched out in a hammock-shaped cobweb and watching everything going on in the room.

"Do you ever wash your hands?" she asked the boy with his hand on her knee.

He looked at her and then at his hands. His lower lip shone with moisture.

"Your hands are filthy," she said.

"No problemo." He put his hands on his knees and stood up and walked slowly into the kitchen. Tex said something to him and he laughed. From the couch Beth watched him hold his hands under the water a long time. Tex gave him two margaritas. He brought them back and set them on a box they were using as a coffee table. He held out his hands and turned them over. They were still wet.

"Grease," he said. "I'm a mechanic." He put his hand back on her thigh, a little higher than before. She looked down at it and waited for the next thing to happen.

The next time she was aware of anything, she was sitting on the floor in the farthest corner of the living room with a blanket over her legs. She must have dragged it off Kimmie's bed, though she did not remember getting up from the couch. She looked around for her drink and saw she had a fresh one. She squinted at her watch. Almost eleven.

"You passed out," said the mechanic, standing over her. He held out his hand. His nails were dirty again, as if he were a magnet for grime. "Come back to the couch. We got something'll pep you right up."

"Oh, yeah," William sang out. "You can say that two times, two times."

The mechanic helped Beth to her feet. Her head hurt like the time she and another girl bashed into each other on the basketball court. She thought of home and standing in a hot shower until her skin turned lobster red, then going to sleep; in the morning she wanted to see her mother and sister in the kitchen, ordinary as pie, and Gala licking her hand and Buster wagging his hind end.

"I gotta go home," she said, and blinked.

"Not yet," Tex said from the couch. "We're just getting started here."

"I don't feel good."

Tex laughed. He was doing something Beth could not see with Kimmie and the guys crowded around the cardboard box. "Get on over here, li'l Beth. I'll fix you up."

Tex drawled his words now. She hadn't noticed that before. The mechanic guided her toward the couch and Tex slipped his arm around her and pulled her down between him and Kimmie. Up close, he smelled like smoke and wet leaves. She tried to pull away and he kissed her. His tongue slid between her lips and teeth, startling as a flash flood.

She pulled away, gasping. She told herself to stand up and leave but her legs wouldn't move. Kimmie draped her arm over her shoulder and said with sleepy urgency, "Will you be my best friend forever, Beth? We could get an apartment, or you could move in here. . . ." She rambled on, Beth did not listen.

Beth watched as Tex placed what looked like rock candy in a glass tube with a bulb at one end. No one spoke. Beth looked across at William and saw that he was as rapt as if he were witnessing a holy event.

"What is that?" she asked Kimmie. "Is that crystal?"

"Isn't she smart?" Kimmie sounded like she meant it.

"I'm not having any of that."

"It'll make you feel better," Tex said. "Put a little light in your eyes."

What was wrong with her eyes the way they were?

She stood up and Kimmie grabbed her hand and pulled her back down. "Nobody's gonna force you. Just don't run off, okay?"

"I don't want you to do it, either."

"One hit, Beth." The mechanic reached around Kimmie and laid his hand on her thigh again. "One hit never killed anybody."

She shoved him away.

Tex held a lighter flame under the bulb and the chamber bubbled and filled with smoke. He held his hand over the top of the cylinder and held it out to Kimmie.

"Kimmie, no."

"Shut up," the guy with bad breath said. "If you don't like it, go home."

"Stay, Bethie."

"I'll call my mom—she'll come and get us."

One of the boys mimicked her in a mealy voice: "I'll call my mom."

The smoke in the cylinder was thick and opaque as mushroom soup. Kimmie lowered her mouth over the opening. Beth reached out to knock it away.

The mechanic held her arms behind her back. She struggled but his hands were strong.

"Take it all, Kimmie," Tex was saying. "Yeah, yeah, atta girl, hold it as long as you can."

Beth stared at Kimmie, holding her breath with her until she exhaled with a groan. She looked stunned. As Beth watched she saw the color in her cheeks go from pale to pink to florid rose and then crimson. Her mouth went loose and her eyes widened and the pupils rolled into the back of her head. Her lids drooped and then she began to drag for breath.

"What's that shit?" William asked.

Beth grabbed Kimmie's arm and shook her. Her head wobbled like a big flower on a weak stem. Her throat made a sawing noise.

"Somebody do something," Beth cried. "She can't breathe."

The mechanic stood and began to move around the room, throwing things into a duffel bag. He bumped the CD player and the disc jumped. Rap, loud and raging, filled the room.

"Oh, Jesus," Tex muttered.

"What's happening to her?" Beth thought she could see the pulses at Kimmie's temples expand and contract.

The mechanic tossed the duffel to Tex and he shoved things into it—the pipe, a baggie, his lighter.

"Do something!" Everyone was standing now except Kimmie and Beth, who was screaming. "I think she's having a heart attack."

"Shit, my keys . . ."

William tossed them to Tex from across the room.

Beth felt her own heart ticking so hard she thought it might go off.

"Wait ten minutes," Tex said from the door. "Then call 911."

Chapter Thirty-six

Lana hung up the phone and stood where she was, frozen. "What is it?" Mars asked from across the room. "What's up?"

Lana turned and looked at Micki. "That was your sister. Did you know about this?"

"Not exactly." Micki squirmed. "I told her she was stupid."

"You purposely withheld information—" She heard herself, the voice of the Inspector General, and stopped.

"What's happened, Lana?" Eddie asked.

"Is she okay, Ma?"

"What's going on?" Tinera tugged on Dom's arm.

Dom said, "Go watch television with your sisters, Tinera." He gave Kathryn a nudge. "You go with her."

"I'm leaving." Lana moved toward the hook beside the back door where her car keys hung.

"Going where?" Dom said.

"Micki?"

"The Gaslamp, Ma. Kimmie's. But I don't know—"

"I do."

"You can't go alone," Dom said. "Kathryn, get my coat."

"No," Lana said.

"Do you want me to go?" Eddie asked.

Dom lurched forward, shoving Eddie French out of his way. "This is family business, Lana."

Lana knew she couldn't get in the car with Dom Firenzi.

"Ma, can I come?"

"You go watch the television," Dom said. "Kathryn—you, too."

Lana glared at him. "Stop telling people what to do. I'm going alone."

"You can't—"

"Shut up, Dom. Just shut up."

"Will someone please tell me what's happened?" Stella cried. "No one ever tells—"

"You shut up, too, Ma," Mars said.

As Lana passed through the porch on her way to the car, she heard Dom say, "Kathryn, get the girls. I'm taking you all home."

She did not pause to wonder how her sister responded.

Lana hoped she would recognize Kimmie's building when she saw it, but as she cruised Sixth Avenue, the buildings looked nothing like they had in the daylight. Garish club and restaurant signs, streetlights in the shape of old-fashioned gas lamps, and the pale wash of light from the staring moon combined to cast disguising shadows across the faces of the buildings.

"There," she said aloud. It wasn't the building she recognized. It was the sight of a red-and-white paramedic van parked in front.

She stopped the car in a loading zone and left the caution lights blinking. A noisy crowd of partyers came toward her with arms draped over each other's shoulders, taking up the width of the sidewalk. She felt herself shoved to the side against the iron rail of an outdoor restaurant. The crowd passed and she hurried forward. The noise of voices and music and traffic, the smells of food and drink and exhaust from cars, made the air thick enough to drink.

In the foyer of the condo building, Lana looked at the elevator buttons and realized she didn't know which floor was Kimmie's. She punched all the keys and watched the display. The elevator seemed stuck on three.

"Lady," said a man's voice behind her, "you can't just leave your car—"

She saw a lighted exit sign across the lobby and opened the door. She tilted her head and looked up at cement stairs rising several floors.

"You're gonna get your car towed, lady."

Racing upstairs, the noise of her footsteps echoed in the stairwell. At the third floor the door stuck. She lunged against it with her shoulder, feeling as it burst open like some kind of maternal super hero. At the end of the hall, Lana saw the paramedics loading a gurney into the elevator.

"Beth," she screamed and ran, stumbling, throwing her arm out against the wall to keep from falling, dimly aware of the building's residents in their doorways observing the drama. "Beth," she cried again, and in the next second her daughter flew from the apartment and into her arms.

Lana clutched her, grabbed her shoulders and hands and looked at her face, looking and feeling for injuries. "Thank God—I thought, I was afraid for you—"

A police officer with a round, flushed redhead's face stepped out of the apartment into the hall. "You this girl's mother?"

"Yes, I am," Lana said. She began to be aware of what was going on around her. The paramedics could not fit the gurney into the elevator.

"We're gonna have to take the stairs," one said.

"Jesus, I thought these places were supposed to be up to code," his partner said.

The body on the gurney was Kimmie. Thank God, though her eyes were shut and she was not moving, the paramedics had not covered her face with a sheet.

"I told you I called her," Beth said to the police officer as if she had been trying to convince him of this for some time. To Lana she said, "I told him I wouldn't say anything until you were here."

"The kid watches too much television." The policeman mopped his hand across his brow and down over his eyes. "So now we're all present and accounted for, let's go sit down."

Another police officer, a woman who could have used a uniform one size larger, squatted in front of the couch, examining the carpet.

"Do you know what's been going on here?" the red-haired policeman asked Lana.

"How would I? I just got here."

"Your daughter goes out at night and you don't know—"

Lana's eyes burned and she had to cover her mouth with her hands to keep from shouting that she had tried to do the right thing. That she was one woman on her own and she was doing the fucking best she could.

"Is Kimmie going to be all right?" Beth asked.

"Can't say," the officer said.

"She was fine and then—"

"What happened to her?" Lana asked.

"Seizure. Heart attack." The officer shrugged as if he had seen too many of these things to be concerned with details. "It happens."

"Heart attack?" Lana sat on the arm of a ratty couch, stunned. "She's only fourteen."

"Fifteen, Ma. I think today was her birthday."

The female cop said, "Nice way to celebrate. Crystal, from the looks of the mess on the carpet here."

Lana tasted *chiles rellenos* in the back of her throat.

The redhead asked, "Who all was with you here?"

Beth looked confused.

The female officer sat back on her haunches. "Just take your time, honey."

"But I don't know their names. Well, this guy Tex was one. And William. Kimmie said they came from Tucson. But they all left," Beth said. "As soon as she started acting funny, they left." Her eyes were round and disbelieving. "They said I had to wait ten minutes to call. . . . But I didn't. I didn't know if she was really sick or—"

"You called 911—that was the right thing."

"But I called you first, Ma." Beth began to cry. "If Kimmie dies it'll be because of me. I shouldn't have let her do it."

"Do what?" Lana asked.

"I think I'm gonna ask the questions here," the policeman said, and opened his notepad. "Your name's Beth. Beth who?"

Lana let her daughter answer. "Porter."

He looked at Lana. "And you're Mrs. Porter? Or is that too much to hope for?"

"Lana Porter."

"Okay, you all stay put and I'm gonna find out what went down here tonight."

"They had crystal," Beth said.

"You did crystal?" Lana could barely breathe. "Why, Beth? You know—"

"Just let me ask the questions." The policeman sounded tired. "Did you, Beth?"

"No, Ma. Honest."

Lana hugged her hard, then asked the policeman, "Where are they taking Kimmie?"

"Harbor View Emergency." The cop flipped his notebook cover open and shut and open again. "You all can worry about her later. Right now you got your own problems."

"What problems? Beth hasn't done anything wrong. She just said she didn't use any crystal."

"Yeah, that's what she said."

Lana took her cell phone out of her purse, "I have to make a call."

"Oh, Jesus," said the red-haired cop. "Here we go with the lawyer."

It was like a police drama, only frightening and less organized. While they waited for Michael to get there, the officers looked around the apartment and paced and clicked their retractable pens. Lana kept thinking: I knew she wasn't going to a dance. I knew but I let myself be fooled because I didn't want to see. This is my fault. All my fault.

After Beth had answered the officers' questions, Michael conferred with them for several minutes out of earshot while Lana sat on the couch with her arms around Beth.

"You're sure you're okay, honey? There's nothing you're not telling us?" Margaritas and marijuana and crystal meth weren't enough?

Beth shook her head and began to cry. "I let her down, Ma. I'm the only friend Kimmie's got and I couldn't stop her doing it."

"You did what you could."

"But what if she dies? Is she going to die, Ma?"

Lana wanted to say that fifteen-year-old girls never died from strokes or seizures or heart attacks but that wasn't true. Wasn't everyone who died someone's friend, someone's baby grown up? She had watched the murder-and-mayhem TV and never thought of what it would really be like to be involved. She did not want to think about it now.

"We don't know what's going to happen. We have to wait."

Michael came over to the couch and crouched before them. "This cop's a nice guy. He says you and Beth need to go down to the station tomorrow morning and give a formal statement. I'll pick you up—we can go together. I'll make sure everything goes the way it should. Beth's a good girl, never been in any jams—I don't expect there'll be any trouble." He gave each of them a hand to help them off the couch, then held out his arms and hugged them.

"It's going to be fine, everything's going to work out."

Lana had a parking ticket but she did not notice it flapping under her windshield wiper until she had driven up Sixth and across Broadway.

"Can we go see how Kimmie's doing?" Beth asked.

Much as Lana wanted to get her girl home and safe, she knew this was the right thing to do. She parked the car in the almost-empty hospital lot, grabbed the parking ticket and shoved it to the bottom of her purse, and they went in through the emergency entrance, down a long gray-and-white corridor and into a waiting room lined with plastic chairs. Like the bus depot, Lana thought. The admitting nurse told Lana that Kimmie had been taken in immediately. Lana spoke to the doctor in charge, who wanted to know if she was the girl's parent.

"I'm sorry," Lana said. "No one knows where her mother lives."

"Somewhere in L.A.," Beth said. "She has a sister named Jules but. . . ." She shrugged. "I don't know where she lives, either."

"Someone's gotta pay the bills," the doctor said and the wrinkles in his forehead moved like rubber bands. "We can't just let her out on the street."

"What happened to her?" Beth asked.

"She had a pretty big seizure." He yawned, treating Lana to a view of his molars. "Sorry. We're gonna do an EKG, take a look at her heart."

"Will she be okay?"

"She's a lucky girl," the doctor said and yawned again, turning his head away.

"I think I might know how to find the father," Lana said. "Let me make a couple of calls."

She walked outside. The wind from the desert had come up again. On the news the weather announcer had said Southern California was in the midst of the longest sustained Santa Ana condition on record. Lana believed it. But the oboe sound of the wind, the grit in the air, even the physical discomfort of burning eyes, dry, caked nose, and a sore throat were nothing compared to the eeriness of summer in January, February now. If Lana could not count on the seasons to stay put, what was there in the world she could trust?

She used her cell phone to call home. Mars picked up immediately.

"Finally! Is Beth okay?"

"Yeah, she's okay. Pretty upset, though. I'm sorry I took so long to call. I've got so much to tell you but we need to be sitting down. It's been crazy. How's Mom?"

"In your bed."

"Kathryn?"

"Gone."

Lana sighed.

"Dom's your friend for life."

"Yeah," Lana said. "I bet."

"Just tell me—"

"Later. When I get home. For now, I need you to get me Grace Mamoulian's home number. It's in the blue address book. Somewhere on my desk."

"You expect me to find it? Jesus, Lana, how do you—"

"It's there. Keep looking."

Grace did not answer on the first ring-through. Lana got her message machine. "Grace, it's Lana Porter. Emergency. Call me on my cell." She left her number and hung up, counted to ten, and called again. It was the middle of the night and Grace was probably in bed trying to pretend that the phone wasn't ringing. Lana left more or less the same message the second time. Hung up and called again. This time Grace answered.

"Who is this?"

"Lana Porter."

"Lana? What in the name of—"

"It's Kimmie Taylor."

"Who?"

"Kimmie. Taylor. Your student. She's in the emergency room at Harbor View."

"Christ, Lana, why're you calling me? What about her mother? It's almost—"

"I'm calling you because for the last six weeks Kimmie has been living alone in a condo in the Gaslamp."

"That's impossible. I spoke to her mother just a couple of weeks—"

"Her sister does an excellent imitation. I'm told she's a drama major at State."

"I don't understand."

"Tonight Kimmie's in emergency. She was doing crystal and had a seizure. She's lucky to be alive."

"But I can't understand . . ."

"Don't bother understanding. Just call her father—you have his Irvine number, don't you?"

"I suppose it's on the computer."

"Can you access from home?"

"Of course."

"Then call him and tell him to get down here. Now."

Derek Taylor was a short, slender man, nattily dressed even at half past four in the morning. He had a tanned and wind-bitten seafarer's face with deep, vertical lines scoring the cheeks. He probably sails every weekend, Lana thought, when she saw him walk into the waiting room wearing topsiders. And he's probably never invited Kimmie to go along.

"Where's my daughter?"

"They've taken her upstairs for observation," Lana said. "She'll have to be here a couple of days."

He moved toward the admitting window.

Beth said, "Can I speak to you, please?"

"Who're you?" He squinted at her. "Were you part of this?"

Beth looked at Lana and then nodded. "I'm her friend."

"And?"

Lana said, "I'd listen to her if I were you."

"But I'm not you, whoever you are."

"Lana Porter. This is Beth, my daughter."

He did not acknowledge the introduction. "I got woke up in the middle of the night, phone woke my wife and my son and he's probably still screaming, and I've driven two hours from Laguna Niguel—"

"Why don't you love Kimmie anymore?"

Derek Taylor looked stunned and then angry. "What's going on here? Where's my wife? My ex-wife?"

"No one knows," Lana said. "Kimmie's been living alone since Christmas."

"Christ!" He sat down on one of the plastic waiting room chairs.

"That bitch." He tapped his fist against his mouth and muttered to himself.

From what Beth had told Lana, this man had ignored his responsibilities as a father and virtually abandoned Kimmie. Lana had expected to despise him, but now she saw that he was probably not the demon father he had been painted. There were things he knew and things he didn't, truths he avoided seeing like all the rest of them. Problems everywhere and nothing simple. Being a father or a mother in Y2K: there was hardly a job more difficult. And yet everyone wanted to do it—from this man with his Mussolini-faced baby to Jack with Dom and Kathryn, herself, and Eddie lined up between.

She leaned forward and rested her head on her arms folded across her knees, too exhausted to speak.

"Tell me what you know," Derek Taylor said to Beth. "Don't bother covering up or lying—"

"She doesn't lie, Mr. Taylor."

"Yeah, right. Just tell me."

Lana listened as Beth told Kimmie's father what she had told Lana, Michael, and the police. But at the end she added, "I'm her only friend, Mr. Taylor, and she tells me things."

"What kind of things."

"She loves you." She told him the stories Kimmie made up about tickets to rock concerts, midnight phone calls, and a vacation in Tahiti.

"Well," he said, "she gets that lying from her mother."

"But, see, she wants—"

"Come on, Beth." Lana looked at her watch. She was so tired her vision blurred. "It's almost morning, time to go home."

Derek Taylor avoided her eyes when he spoke in his abrupt and irritated way. "I want to thank you, for taking care of my daughter." Lana supposed he meant it but there was no telling from either his voice or demeanor.

"Can she go and live with you?" Beth asked. "In Laguna Niguel? She could help your wife with the baby—I bet she could use help."

He looked at her as if she were speaking a language he did not understand.

"Come on, Beth," Lana said, and put her arm around Beth's shoulder. "Time to go home."

2002

Chapter Thirty-seven

When Lana talked about the first several weeks of the year 2000, she said that she and her daughters had gone a little crazy. Her friends, Mars, and her therapist denied this, but it was only by using words like *mad* and *crazy* and *totally wacko* that Lana could understand how close she had come to losing her daughters. Eventually, the puzzle pieces began to draw together and Lana thought she understood. Even so, her missteps—stumbling through fear and inattention—did not lose their sickening power. They all went zany for a while.

Two days after the scene at the condo, Wendy had called Jessie and given her an outline of what had happened. Jessie then insisted that Lana and the girls had to go into therapy. "You should have done it a year ago," she said. When Lana continued to hold out for reasons she could never explain adequately to anyone, including herself, the whole run-and-read club ganged up on her. Jessie recommended a woman in La Jolla, just up the road from Urban Greenery, a seasoned family therapist; worn down, Lana made the first appointment and felt such relief afterward that she told Mars it was as if every pore in her body opened wide and screamed thank you.

During their first session, a one-on-one, the therapist, a large, relaxed woman named Frances, helped Lana see that while she had been searching for the secret weapon that would make her a good mother, she had overlooked the strengths she had, her willingness and diligence, the love she had for her daughters.

In Frances's comfortably decorated corner office with large, sunny windows overlooking a busy La Jolla street, it was as if muscles held taut for months finally let go. Lana did not sit down in Frances's office, she sank into the embrace of the cushions and heaved a great sigh of relief.

After she had told Frances what was happening, she said, "When Jack was alive, we all got along so well."

"Is that what you mean about a family that works? It gets along?"

"Well, yes."

"Are you saying that before Jack died, you never had fights?" Frances looked skeptical.

"Oh, yeah, of course we did. And the kids weren't always good. But it all worked, like a machine that was oiled, and when he died he took the oil."

Sometimes Lana left Frances's office thinking they were going in circles and positive that therapy was a waste of money.

Beth and Micki went along with Lana to see Frances, and from their first family session, it was as if a window had been opened in a tightly closed room baking under a hot sun. Back on Triesta Way they breathed more easily, the house seemed less claustrophobic and, ultimately, less haunted.

Micki thrived at Balboa High School. No one called her "reject" or "trash-can kid." Her grades were good enough to satisfy Lana and by the time she was seventeen she was looking ahead to entering the University of California at Santa Cruz. She thought she would like to study horticulture, maybe go to the ends of the earth searching for substances in bushes and trees that would save the world from disease. But she was also attracted to theater and wanted to go on the stage, be a New Yorker. Beth said she belonged to the Career of the Month Club. Lana said she could do anything she wanted but secretly hoped she would decide on a more prosaic career. Maybe a doctor or lawyer or teacher.

The girls had graduated from family therapy after three months. Now it was Lana and Frances, one-on-one, once a week.

"I'm afraid for Micki." As she had always been. Frances helped her understand that her fear had been based less on Micki herself than on Lana's own interpretation of what it meant to be adopted.

"Why don't you tell her you're afraid for her?"

Lana shook her head.

"Why not?"

"I don't want her to know."

"And why is that?"

Lana thought about quitting therapy but kept going back every week. Afterwards she would sometimes visit her mother or drop in on Mars at the university but nothing she did could fully erase Frances's questions. She pondered them all week long but rarely felt like she learned anything from the effort.

However, she did tell Micki she was afraid for her and made her laugh and spread her arms wide.

"Look at me, Ma. I'm a survivor."

And so was Beth. Why hadn't Lana seen this before?

She decided she wasn't very good at therapy.

During the two years since he had entered their lives, Eddie French had been absent more than present. But he called Micki two or three times a month from European capitals, India, Japan, and South Korea. There was never a word from Barbara, and Lana no longer worried there would be. Lana accepted the fact that she was not a forever-inferior substitute for the woman who had given birth to her. And with this had come permission to like Eddie French.

"Which doesn't mean I want him living with us," she told Frances. "Not that he wants to. He and Micki are friends, but Jack's her father."

"He doesn't need protecting, then?"

"I guess he never did."

Jack was with Lana all the time. She was as much an agnostic as she'd ever been and did not believe his spirit actually kept her company. But she felt his presence through her memories, sometimes so powerfully she imagined that if she turned around she would see him standing behind her, his warm hand on her shoulder. The girls liked to talk about him and said they heard his voice in their heads, advising and directing and applauding. She went to Frances's office and said she was angry with them all the time.

"Why is that?"

"I envy them. I want to hear his voice. Why do they get it?"

"Have you told them that?"

"Should I?"

"What do you think?"

"I don't know if it would do any good for them to know I was jealous."

"Would it hurt them?"

"I'm their mother."

Frances had a soft laugh and a pretty smile; she was one of the warmest and most reassuring people Lana had ever met. But she often made Lana as mad as her girls did. I must be wacko, she thought. Once a week she paid one hundred and twenty dollars an hour so this woman could ask her irritating questions.

Beth had tried to contact Kimmie through her father, who said his daughter lived in West Hollywood with his ex. He gave her a number but when she called, a recorded message told her the phone had been disconnected. A few months later, just about the time Beth had stopped wondering aloud what had become of her friend, she got a postcard without a return address, announcing that Kimmie and her mother had moved to New York where her mother had a fabulous new job doing makeup for the top fashion models. Kimmie was going to be a model and had already signed a contract. Beth gave Lana the card to read; the bravado and false cheer, the lies, reached into Lana and twisted her heart.

It was not long before Beth was hanging out with her old friends and the basketball coach accepted her back with both hands extended. Her marks improved, she ate better, but still she was different. Changed.

"In what way?" Frances asked.

Lana had been in therapy for more than a year and she was used to the questions, the questions that never stopped, that had no purpose but to confuse and drive her around the bend and into the nut house. As far as Lana knew, Frances did not have opinions or a life outside the four walls of her office on Herschel Avenue. Lana's best guess was that she slept on the couch, kept her clothes in the closet, and spent her nonworking hours making up lists of impossible-to-answer questions for Lana Porter.

Most of the time, Lana sat in a chair facing her therapist, but sometimes she was overtaken by restless energy and had to get up and move around. She stood now, looking out the window at the people in shorts and tank tops, the woman walking a standard poodle.

Frances asked, "How is she different?"

It was hard to speak the answer. If she didn't say it, she could pretend it was not true. "There's something sad in her now. It's like she went somewhere and saw something and it changed her." Her voice cracked. "She's not innocent anymore."

"Is loss of innocence a bad thing?"

"It wasn't the guys and the drugs. I mean, they were bad but it was the way they all just walked away from Kimmie. That was evil, that was a touch of something really dark and nasty, and it's left a mark on her. She told me this guy named Tex French-kissed her. She said it was disgusting but if he'd done it again, she wouldn't have minded too much."

Frances sighed. "The gate has to open, Lana. Eventually. There would have been no story if Adam and Eve hadn't lost their place in the garden."

What the hell was that supposed to mean?

She asked, "Am I ever going to get this?"

"I think you've already got it, Lana."

For the first time since Lana had known her, Frances stepped out from behind her desk and came to stand beside her at the window. She rested her arm on Lana's back and patted gently.

"Your girls are doing well. Beth's going to get a basketball scholarship to wherever she wants to go. Micki's heading off to UC–Santa Cruz, full of ambition."

"But we fight—"

"Of course you do. And then you make up."

True.

"Not all mothers and daughters do, you know. In some families the resentments simmer along for years. But not in yours. Why do you think that is?"

It was not the first time Lana had wondered about this. She thought it was because, when they stood away from whatever they were arguing about—field trips or clothes or Micki's smoking— they knew the truth. That they loved each other. Though their world had changed, that fact had not.

"Lana, I don't think I've ever met a parent who did not claim to love his or her children. Look at Kimmie's father. But the rage and resentment goes on. Why doesn't that happen at the Porter house?"

Lana started to say she did not know. Frances stopped her with a cautionary finger.

"You always say you don't know. But you do. You do."

Down on the street, the woman was feeding her poodle an ice cream cone and a woman and small child had stopped to watch.

"I think we really know each other." But they had not always. Lana said, more to herself than to Frances, "So maybe what happened wasn't the worst. It made us stop pretending."

"Exactly," Frances said, and returned to her desk. "You're not going to stop having troubles with your girls. Believe me, Lana, if Jack had lived even he would not have been able to stop them. Kids and their parents, and especially girls and their mothers, always disagree; there is always the pull of one generation against the other. You know that from your own experience. You wanted your mother to keep the Hollywood Cafe, but she wanted to sell it so she could put that part of her life behind her forever. Well, she sold it but she's still the same old Stella, as you have said so often. Nothing has really changed except she has fewer manicures."

"But Jack took something with him—"

"He took himself, Lana, his physical presence, and when he did, you three got confused for a time and forgot how to be honest with each other."

Lana wasn't sure she understood. It could not be so simple.

Frances laughed. "This is graduation day, Lana. You don't need me anymore."

Chapter Thirty-eight

Buster surprised everyone by living until January 2002. And then, one mild morning, Lana went down to the kitchen before first light and when she rattled the dog dishes Gala came running, but Buster did not stick his face through the pet door and look around as if to ask if she was serious about this food business. With a sinking heart Lana fed Gala, and then went into her garden and walked the paths until she found him curled in the morning's first sunlight at the foot of an olive tree. Lana knelt beside him and ran her hands down the curve of his cold back. She imagined that he had not felt good the night before and planned ahead—she was convinced some animals could do this. He knew he wanted to feel the sun on his body first thing so he settled down in the bed of mint that grew at the base of the olive and fell asleep.

It had been as easy as that. She kissed his bony old forehead and felt a mixture of sorrow and relief.

He had grown light with age, easy to lift and carry to the wheelbarrow in the shade house. She laid him down gently and went indoors. In the guest room she rummaged in a wicker chest for a blanket she had been saving for this purpose, an old blue wool blanket she had when she was a child. Worn smooth and almost silky by time, when she pressed it against her nose she still caught a faint scent of whatever it was she had loved when she was little and carried it around with her and would not sleep without it. In the shade house she wrapped Buster in the blanket and then carried his body to the 4Runner and laid it on the back seat.

The girls came down for breakfast at a few minutes before seven and she told them. Beth put her face in her hands and wept. Micki got up and sat beside Gala and cried into her coat. Lana sat at the table and cried, too. No one pretended this small death was not a big thing, that her heart was not breaking a little and again.

"What're we going to do with him?" Micki asked.

"Linda's folks gave their dog to the pound."

"No way," Micki cried. "We can't do that!"

Lana had given this event a lot of thought and had even talked it over with Frances.

"I'd like to have him cremated." She paused, looking at her daughters. "I want us to take him up to Garnet Peak and scatter his ashes. Together."

The girls were noisily enthusiastic about the idea. She hushed them.

"I know what I did was wrong," she said when they could listen to her. "I've never forgiven myself and I spent hours—*hours*—in therapy trying to figure why I was so crazy. . . ."

Beth pulled her chair closer and laid her head down on Lana's knees. Micki stood behind, her arms draped over Lana's shoulders, her chin resting on the top of her head.

"I loved your father and in the end I didn't want to share him, not even the pain I felt about him. Partly I couldn't stand to see you two suffer but mostly it was just a selfish thing I did and I guess in my whole life it's maybe the only thing I truly regret. I know that scattering Buster's ashes together isn't the same but—"

Beth looked up at her. "It's okay, Ma. We get it. It'll be like a symbolic reenactment."

"A what?" Micki asked.

God bless Rachel Hoffman, thought Lana.

They chose a clear, still day when the ranger's office in Cleveland National Forest said there was little wind. At Micki's insistence, they dressed for the occasion in long skirts and brought flowers from the garden. Beth had chosen Buster's urn, a fancy ceramic cookie jar from the French Garden Shop. Lana flinched when she read the price tag but said nothing.

The Laguna Mountains lie forty-five minutes east of San Diego and are the southernmost extension of the Sierra Nevada, rising in places to almost six thousand feet. They divide the arid coastal plain from the vast desert to the east and are themselves dry through most of the year. It had been another winter of scant rainfall and there was no snow on the ground, although in previous years Jack and Michael had often gone cross-country skiing in the Lagunas, once encountering a mountain lion sitting in the trail with his back to them. Without the allure of snow and in the middle of the week, Lana and her girls did not encounter another car as they drove along the winding Sunrise Highway off I-8, passing campgrounds and lodges and occasional vacation homes with their blinds drawn. In the meadows the wild grass was the color of ripe wheat and woven through the forest like a rusty yellow thread, appearing and reappearing in groups and alone. Lana saw the damage done to the pines by drought and beetles.

At the Pioneer Trail exit Lana turned off and parked in the lot.

They were entirely alone.

Beth and Micki had figured out the details and Lana had only to nod and be agreeable. She remembered the last time she had parked in this place. There had been half a dozen cars in the lot belonging, she later supposed, to hang gliders. Still, she had felt utterly isolated.

They walked single file along the rutted dirt trail, Beth leading with the cookie jar full of Buster's ashes, followed by Lana and Micki carrying the flowers. They passed shrines Lana had never noticed before, cairns of stones with plaques and signs honoring men whose names she had never heard. Hang gliders, she thought. Or maybe just ordinary earthbound men, husbands and fathers.

Under a brilliantly blue and cloudless sky, the path to the peak led through a dun-and-green landscape of scrub oak, manzanita, and varieties of pungent shrubs Lana could not name. In sheltered crevasses, minute pink and white flowers bloomed. The rocky escarpment rose to the left, colored gold and deep maroon with streaks of green in the face of the rock. Beth led the parade to the east side of a rock formation and stopped. At their feet the path was only inches wide.

Lana bit back an automatic caution.

Micki said, "Watch your step, Ma."

"I want to say some words," Beth told Lana.

"Of course. Whatever you like."

On the day she scattered Jack's ashes, she had no voice. If she had opened her mouth she would have screamed.

Beth said, "Daddy, these are Buster's ashes. He's never belonged to anybody before us and we don't want him to be afraid. So we're giving you his ashes and asking you to take care of him."

Micki said, "And Daddy, we want you to know that we will always love you and always miss you forever." She looked at Lana. "Now you, Ma."

"I don't—"

"You have to say something."

"Just say what you're thinking," Micki told her.

The wave of emotion that tumbled over Lana was a cousin to that which had rocked her to the core three and a half years earlier in this same place. She resented her daughters' demand that she speak up and say what was in her heart, as if to do such a thing were easy or even possible. But then, a second wave of feeling passed through her and obliterated the first. This second wave was warm where the other had been cold, cool where the other had scalded her. She felt only gratitude. For Jack and their years together, for her daughters and for Buster. The tears in her eyes came from a pain that had joy in it. She reached into the cookie jar and withdrew a handful of ashes. She swung her arm out and opened her hand. The wind lifted the ashes and carried them away.